Marilyn was a regular feature and fiction writer for national magazines when her children were small. She set up her first business, selling toys, books and party goods from home before opening first one shop then another. When she sold the shops she moved into the world of travel, focusing on accommodation in New England, USA. Her advisory, planning and booking service flourished and she concurrently launched a publishing company, producing an annual, full-colour guide.

In 2007 she set up a copywriting consultancy, *Create Communication* to help businesses shape their messages to optimum effect at the same time as debunking marketing myths and mistakes that can prove devastatingly expensive to companies of any size. She's the author of the *Little Black Business Book* series – common sense stuff, she says, written because the crock at the end of the rainbow isn't always packed with gold. She divides her time now between writing website texts; press releases; speeches; advising on business strategies and working (she calls it busy-knickering) on book publishing projects, both fact and fiction.

She's been married to her very patient husband for more years than he deserves and they have two children, five grandchildren and, somewhat to their surprise, several grand-dogs.

RELATIVELY STRANGE

MARILYN MESSIK

Matador
9 Priory Business Park
Kibworth Beauchamp
Leicestershire LE8 0RX, UK
Tel: (+44) 116 279 2299
Email: books@troubador.co.uk
Web: www.troubador.co.uk/matador

ISBN 978 1783061 914

British Library Cataloguing in Publication Data.
A catalogue record for this book is available from the British Library.

Typeset by Troubador Publishing Ltd
Printed and bound in the UK by TJ International, Padstow, Cornwall

Matador is an imprint of Troubador Publishing Ltd

To Richard for yesterday, today and tomorrow

CHAPTER ONE

I was five when I flew for the first time, sixteen when I killed a man. Both events were unsettling in their own way.

It took five years to stumble across my gravity defying attributes, less than five minutes to gather it wasn't at all the sort of thing people expected. My other abilities revealed themselves gradually, often disconcertingly, over a period of years although by then I was slightly more savvy and anxious not to, if I could help it, traumatise any more family and friends than I had already.

I was, I think, an ordinary enough baby girl, greeted on arrival in the early 1950s by the usual anxious parental totting up of fingers and toes. Photos show me with a sparsity of dark hair brushed to a quiff, squinting into the camera like a slightly startled Mohican. Nothing odd showed then apparently.

We lived in Hendon. Nearby lived a Grandma; several Great-aunts; one really great aunt and various other relatives of assorted size, style and age. Grandma, my mother's mother, used to visit with greasily wrapped, cloyingly sweet and sticky *halvah* from Mr Grarber the delicatessen down the road. She also held a reassuringly large stock of chocolate bars in her bottomless, brown leather handbag. Matured alongside a tube or two of Polos and some wine gums the chocolate had a distinctive taste, smell and mottled appearance which, only when I grew up, did I come to recognise as stale. I'm still a sucker for a chunk of Cadbury's well past its sell-by.

Grandma suffered a stroke when I was small and although she recovered well, it left her with a tremor which made her head wobble fractionally but fascinatingly on her neck whenever she spoke. She was also, thereafter never very steady on her feet and fell over a lot, albeit extremely cheerfully.

"Silly bugger aren't I?" she'd mutter, unfazed, as we hauled her up yet again, dusted her off, retrieved the handbag and straightened her hat.

Widowed, she lived with two sisters, similarly bereft, in a flat in a mansion block – Georgian Court – just along the road from us. True, if transplanted, East-Enders, although only a generation or so away from their mittel-European forbears and a lot nearer than that in attitude, they enjoyed endless games of gin rummy and kalooki played with a ruthlessness, skill and lip-chewing intensity rarely seen outside a high-stake casino.

Aunts Kitty, Yetta and Grandma, iron-willed women all, lived in a state of armed neutrality, each having married and brought up a family before circumstance brought them full circle, to shared domesticity at the end of their lives as at the beginning. If two women in a kitchen is bad news, three is a recipe for disaster but, to their credit clashes over *knishes*, fierce though they were, died down a darn sight quicker than did the cut-throat threats and long held vendettas over the playing-cards. Yiddish curses are all the more potent hissed through clenched teeth and there were enough stand-offs to make the knees of strong men knock. Mafia shmafia, when it came to tough, the girls as they euphemistically termed themselves, in card-playing mode were merciless, their memories long, their fervour frightening. I don't think any of them ever met a grudge they couldn't bear.

On the stove in the kitchen at the Georgian Court flat there was to be found, at all hours, a simmering and apparently bottomless pot of thick, rich chicken soup into which, with much muttering and bickering went any number of essential ingredients along the lines of giblets, saffron and elderly chicken. If ever a Jewish take on Macbeth was required, we could have supplied the three witches, no problem and what came out of the cauldron was so steamingly, aromatically the very chickenest of chicken soups, we'd have had the cast catering angle covered too.

Big bosomed, with a stately if latterly uncertain gait, Grandma had a number of paranoid theories. These included a deep-seated conviction the government was out to get you and therefore you could never be too careful what you said, where you said it and to whom. As it transpired, she wasn't a million miles out.

"People always like to know your business." she'd mutter darkly and consequently much of her conversation was conspiratorially whispered, causing no end of irritated confusion as the sisters grew older and deafer.

Such sotto voce utterings of course made everything she said mysteriously exciting.

"Who're you talking about, tell me, tell me?" I'd demand, pulling on her arm.

"Mooley and Ashey." she'd say. This was satisfactory until it gradually dawned on me that either there was an inordinate amount going on with this peculiarly named couple or I was being given the runaround.

As if constant undercover surveillance wasn't enough for any woman to deal with, Grandma also suffered frequent, incapacitating migraine headaches. Naturally, she didn't trust pharmacists overmuch either, "Who's to know what's what in a pill?" She did however swear by vinegar and brown paper, overlaid with fresh potato peelings. I can see her now, stoutly ensconced on the sofa, paper and peelings on her forehead, arms and ankles firmly crossed. On a school trip to the British Museum, when I walked into the Egyptian room there was immediate kinship with any number of sarcophagi.

Physically, the sisters couldn't have been more different. Auntie Kitty narrow shouldered; thin-faced; beak-nosed; quick-witted; brim-full of nervous energy topped with thwarted ambition and intelligence. She'd worked all her life and continued, one of the original Typewriters, travelling daily, deep into the bowels of Threadneedle Street until late into her eighties. As each subsequent boss had come and gone she'd ratcheted her age ever downward. By the time she eventually retired she was ostensibly only a well-worn 60, with the powers-that-be too polite or more likely gimlet-glare intimidated to raise so much as a sceptical eyebrow.

Kitty was the most volatile of the three, too quick – *sehr geschwind* Grandma used to grumble – in everything she did. A woman of sharply defined intelligence, impatient with anyone less so, she was an inveterate hoarder and could never, though I don't think she ever tried, resist the lure of a shop sale. She'd snap up anything if it was reduced, although her particular vice was linen – table or bed, she wasn't proud.

"A bargain's a bargain" she used to state firmly, "On the day you need a good tablecloth, you'll thank me." For years she waded through bargain basements and bore home with marauder's delight any manner of items for which no one in the family had any use whatsoever. Cupboard-opening at Grandma's was always an exercise hazardous in the extreme because you never knew how many of Aunt Kitty's purchases were stockpiled therein, poised to make a swift, cellophaned descent onto the heads of the unwary.

My Auntie Yetta was a bigger woman altogether, broad at hip and shoulder with tightly permed grey curls lurking uneasily if immovably. She was more domestically inclined than the others, struggling always to balance the housekeeping which suffered terminally from Auntie Kitty's bargains and Grandma's tendency, after her stroke, to pay for things and walk off without waiting for change. Auntie Yetta dedicated herself to evening the odds and on the principle of every little helps, used to snatch the OK Sauce bottle mid-dollop with a brisk, "Enough already!" She also had a tendency to come and yell at you through the toilet door "Don't use so much paper, you think it grows on trees?" Disconcerting for us kids, even more inhibiting I imagine, for visiting adults.

Convinced financial disaster and penury leered and lurked round every corner Yetta, whilst watching the pennies, wasn't going to take her eye off the pounds and expended endless energy trying to counter the spendthrift tendencies of her two sisters. Who could forget the row when it came out she'd been conducting a flourishing cut-price linen business, flogging Aunt Kitty's purchases to the neighbours and putting the proceeds away for a rainy day. Kitty was incandescent with rage, Yetta stolidly unrepentant and Grandma so exasperated with both that she opened the window – they were third floor -and started hurling out even more of Kitty's stock. None of the sisters spoke to each other for weeks but communicated via fiercely underscored notes on a pad.

There's no doubt my mother's family veered towards the matriarchal. The views of the mothers being not so much handed down, as thrust firmly into the psyche of the daughters. It didn't do, they maintained, to wash your dirty linen in public, what happened in the family stayed in the family and what people didn't know couldn't ever hurt you. This of course was taken to the nth degree by Grandma, who wouldn't tell her left hand what her right was up to, even in an emergency. But, as a general rule and certainly when it came to my own little idiosyncrasies, perhaps they weren't so far wrong.

Auntie Edna was my mother's sister, older by five years. My Uncle Monty was warm and generous; argumentative yes; eccentric certainly; unpredictable – invariably. His party trick was bending his leg so his foot reached his mouth, a fascinating but ultimately not hugely useful achievement. Like Grandma, Auntie Edna wasn't one for wearing her heart on her sleeve and was, also like Grandma not over comfortable with physical demonstration of affection, "Oh get off." she'd say, only half joking, "Enough with all the kissing – making my face all wet." Individually, Auntie Edna and Uncle Monty were wonderful – combined, a somewhat uneasy alliance.

When I was about four, my mother was hospitalised with a bad back and I stayed at Auntie Edna's, awed to be in the company of my two, eight and ten year older cousins. Whilst for me, this sojourn was a time of unalloyed bliss, Auntie Edna never quite got over the experience, although I don't think I was a particularly wayward child. In fact, she never knew quite how wayward I could have been if I'd set my mind to it – fortunately at that stage neither did I.

Life at their house was a far more formal and structured affair than at ours. Auntie Edna was a great one for routine. Every morning in her pink, quilted satin dressing gown which zipped up at the front, she'd cook soft boiled eggs for us, precise consistency guaranteed by the trickling sand in an hour-glass held by a little wooden Dutch boy with grin, clogs and a room thermometer in his other hand. He was set on the shelf next to the gas stove and I wasn't allowed to take him down. I soon discovered however that I could make the little red line of the thermometer zoom up and down in a very satisfying way, so no need to take him down at all.

The very first morning of my stay the toaster exploded. It was all really rather noisy and spectacular. Wires, trailing bits of melted plastic and slices of blackened bread shooting every which way, accompanied by shrieks of fright from my aunt and cousins. I don't remember being particularly perturbed, the self-same thing had happened to my mother's iron, just a few weeks before.

Whilst their whole house was full of delights, the pinnacle of pleasure was the downstairs toilet with its swinging, liquid-soap dispenser, a glass-spouted silver globe supported by two metal arms. It was suspended over the sink, below the mirror. Inverted, it deposited a respectable dollop of soap onto expectant hands. A sharp little flick however, administered at just the right point and it spun several times, with a rewarding amount of soap flying in all directions, highly entertaining. As indeed was the very smart wooden, flower-painted, toilet-paper holder which played *Edelweiss* every time you pulled off a sheet – Uncle Monty always said thank goodness it didn't play the National Anthem! The gospel, according to Aunt Edna was that I once locked myself in that toilet for two hours and refused to come out. I really don't think it was anywhere near as long as that, but I would add that no toilet I've been in since has given me half such a good time as that one.

CHAPTER TWO

Family, back then, seemed to encompass many more people than it does today. It was also assumed and accepted that at every opportunity we'd want nothing more than to be together. On Saturdays we'd foregather at Grandma and the Aunts' converging about 3.00 o'clock to be lubricated by strong dark tea for the grown-ups, Nesquik or cordial for us and for all, sticky, nutty cake called, for unfathomable reasons, Stuffed Monkey.

In the midst of all this conviviality, at around 6.00 o'clock, there'd be a lot of inter-sister muttering and bustling and all at once the huge table in the living room, around which we were crowded, was groaning with what Grandma and the Aunts called deprecatingly, 'A little something' as in, "Stay, have a little something – just what we had in the fridge". And they'd dismiss with a modest wave of the hand, a week's worth of choosing, shopping, chopping and cooking. Why on earth such store should be set by not seeming to have gone to any trouble, was just another of life's little mysteries.

At these gatherings were always honorary family additions, fixtures by tradition if not blood. People like Auntie Esther, she of the certain aim, of which more later, and Aunties Hannah and Ginnie spinstered by the '14 - '18 War, sweet-faced and patient. Morrie Schwartz was another. In a shinily shabby grey suit, infused with the scent of the eye-wateringly strong peppermints he'd manoeuvre ruminatively from one cheek to the other he'd sit, still and vacant in the armchair by the window, watching traffic pass on the road below. He was treated gently, with kindness and spoken to loudly and slowly. We were told we must always smile at but not bother him. He was, Grandma mystifyingly told us sixpence short of a shilling.

His entire close family mother, father, twin brothers and a much older sister had been lost to a V2 one bloody night in the East End. He'd received a severe head injury but survived. His mind wasn't like other people's. It was divided by a rigid barrier. In front of this wafted random thoughts – might another piece of cake spoil supper? Was that the third or could it be the fourth Morris Minor to drive past? I once, with curiosity probed beyond the barrier and in a few shocking seconds understood why it was there. Fire rained, gobbled and spat. A miasma of brick dust and ashes coated and clogged throat and lungs and overall and over and again someone was screaming. I was unspeakably shaken and for a good while afterwards, fearful of going anywhere near him.

On the opposite landing to Grandma and the Aunts and therefore included much of the time in family gatherings were Mr and Mrs Kalter. Kind, accented, short and plump, Mrs Kalter was always *Baruch Hasheming* (tanking Gott) for everything from a portion of Stuffed Monkey to their timely pre-war flight and their continued health in the face of so much adversity, "So, I hev a little pain in the choints, what's to complain about?" and she would mime spitting into the wind three times, "Peh, peh, peh." to ward off the evil eye – it never did to sound smug and tempt fate. Of all the many benefits of their adopted country for which she was so grateful the Royal Family, "Gott bless und keep", ranked pretty high on the list. To them she had formed a fanatically loyal attachment and throughout the Kalter abode, newspaper and magazine shots of H.R.H. and family sat in egalitarian chumminess, side by side with equally carefully framed and cherished Kalter clan wedding and bar mitzvah shots.

"This mein brother Aaron, *oveh sholem,* at our wedding, this Elizabeth, Gott bless, learning to fix an engine, don't she look lovely in that uniform?" Mrs Kalter's main occupation when not dusting the royals was frying fish and at any hour she could be found, wrapped in a voluminous red and white check overall, hair hygienically scarfed, manically frying enough *gefülte* fish balls to sink a battleship.

"Feh. What is she doing in there?" Grandma would complain, "How many fish balls can two people eat already?" The smell of frying fish often permeated the entire block not to mention the Kalters and their miniature poodle Willum.

Mrs Kalter died quietly of a sudden heart attack when I was about nine and after that, Grandma and the aunts made sure Mr Kalter came into them for a hot meal at least a couple of times a week. The first time he came over they fried fish for him. He thanked them and explained that he'd loved his wife dearly, she was his angel and soul mate but if he never smelt, saw or ate another fish ball as long as Gott saw fit to leave him on this earth, he'd die a happy man. Devotion sometimes takes strange forms.

My father's family were considered a bit odd – or so my mother held, although if that wasn't a pot and kettle issue, I don't know what would be. My paternal grandmother died young and my grandfather remarried but not until he was well over sixty. His bride, Bertha, hailed from somewhere called 'Up North'. She was, at the time of the marriage in her early forties and, I once overheard my mother say, 'Properly on the shelf', although I really couldn't imagine where might exist a shelf sturdy enough to accommodate such an impressive girth. She brought to the marriage a funny way of talking; a humour by-pass; several budgerigars; a propensity for pickling red cabbage and within nine months and to the surprise of all, a baby.

Grandpa and Bertha lived in Shepherds Bush, in a tall, narrow, middle of terrace house maintained in a permanent state of twilight because Bertha held that 'Sun never did carpet any favours'. Our visits to Aunt Bertha and Grandpa were usually usefully combined with a trip to Uncle Doddy, the dentist who'd been treating all members of the family for years. It has to be said, although I didn't realise till many years later, Uncle Doddy was no stranger to a bottle of Scotch. Despite this he was marvellously light-fingered and light-hearted, albeit light-headed to boot. Mind you, his habit of firmly and unabashedly pinching any female bottom young or old which came within hands-reach would, nowadays without doubt have resulted in him being struck off one register and put on another!

"Killing two birds with one stone." Was how my mother once tactlessly summed up the dual dental and familial visiting arrangement, as we arrived at Grandpa's house and were engulfed in a cacophony of agitated budgerigars. Bertha, who wouldn't have recognised a metaphor if she tripped over it, paled visibly and had to be hastily reassured. She paled even more later that afternoon when, bored with grown up conversation and multiple helpings of red cabbage, I lifted the baby out of her crib and gently swung her round and round. She was fine, loved it and I certainly wouldn't have dropped her on the floor if Bertha, catching sight, hadn't let out an eldritch and totally unnecessary screech which gave me the fright of my life.

Sobbing, and pressing the now screaming infant to her bosom, Bertha swore blind she'd seen her fly through the air. Mark her words, she said, there was something more than a bit odd about me. Well, naturally, my mother leapt instantly to my defence. The conversation became a trifle heated and recriminations and a few home truths were exchanged that perhaps would have best been kept under individual hats. My mother, in her fiercely partisan re-telling of the incident was not slow to intimate that Bertha was prone to imagine all sorts of things and indeed, what could you expect, falling for a baby at her time of life and goodness only knows what the shock of that did to you. But thereafter relations were always a little strained and Bertha spent years watching me uneasily out of the corner of her eye.

CHAPTER THREE

It wasn't until I was five that I became consciously aware all was not as might have been expected. But thinking back, there were probably earlier indications. Dimly recalled, is a trip to a small sea-side zoo with my father. The reptile house was distinctly stinky and in a murky pool lurked a solitary crocodile. It took one look at me and opened its jaws wide. It was probably just yawning, there didn't seem much there to occupy a crocodile, but it scared me rigid and I think I might have instinctively reacted and done something from inside my head. The crocodile froze for a second or two before with alacrity, turning tail and scampering to the farthest corner as fast as his stumpy little legs could carry him. I used my own stumpy little legs to similar effect, in the opposite direction. I'd got quite a distance by the time my father caught up with me.

Waiting for the day of my fifth birthday party was an agony of anticipation. All year I'd been going to other people's parties – pleasant enough, but when someone else is getting the presents it's always tough to summon up the right degree of enthusiasm isn't it? Naturally, the family turned out in force for the occasion, seated at one end of the garden and looking on whilst shrieks of delight and outrage issued from a game of Blind Man's Buff at the other. Auntie Esther was there with Prince, a lion-faced chow with halitosis, morose expression and unpredictable disposition. A description, come to think, which applied equally well to his owner. These two would have had less than nothing to contribute to a fifth birthday party but, fixtures at all family do's, could not have been left out of this one.

Events were running pretty much par for the course, until our cat let valour overtake discretion and chose a quiet moment in the conversation to stroll, with studied insolence across Prince's field of vision, upon which all hell broke loose. Prince, who'd been surveying the party with habitual malevolence, struggled wheezily to his feet, barking wildly. Smudge arched his back and hissed, secure in the knowledge that the dog thing was restrained by a lead which, knotted round a chair-leg, was threatening to choke him as he lunged impotently. And thus the incident might well have passed, were it not for the intervention of Auntie Esther who, with astonishing accuracy lobbed a vicious, over-arm, smoked salmon bagel. It struck the unfortunate feline fair and square on the nose. He retired, hurt and at great speed, to the upper branches of the nearest apple tree.

Drawn by the commotion, I took in the situation and quite frankly found my sympathies fully with the cat. A fully loaded bagel's no laughing matter. By now, Smudge was playing to the gallery. He could, of course, have descended as easily and swiftly as he'd gone up, but that really wasn't the point. It was his house, he was our cat. So as a gesture of solidarity, I flew up and got him. It wasn't that high, it only took a moment and seemed the right thing to do, I didn't think twice.

Pet in arms, I drifted gently back down – to silence. Not something you encounter often at a Jewish gathering. As far as I recall, it was the first time I'd actually flown more than an inch or two off the ground. But you know what it's like at five, you're always finding you can do things this week, you couldn't do last, and I could already see any number of ways in which it might come in handy. It began to dawn however, from the frozen expressions and unnatural silence, counter-pointed by shrieks from the children still playing at the other end of the garden, that the family weren't half as tickled as I.

I put Smudge carefully down and he stalked off, tail and nose held high and honour satisfied. Then everyone began talking at once and I learnt something that's stood me in good stead ever since – when people can't believe their eyes, they usually don't. A sort of instant, judicious rationalisation takes place. A chorus of disapproval did, however smote the air.

"... trees? How comes climbing trees?"

"... fall, and they'll end up feeding you through a tube."

"Remember Renee's boy ... on his head, not been right since."

"... and in such a lovely new dress."

Grandma declared she had one of her heads coming on and sank back in her chair with her eyes closed. Auntie Esther, hand buried in the area between what would have been her neck if she'd had one and her waist – though that hadn't been seen in a while either – said her heart was doing what Dr Dannheiser said it mustn't and someone better run quick for her pills. Auntie Edna told my mother sharply this was what came of not being firm enough with the child, thanked God I hadn't been killed before their very eyes, touched briefly on the toilet incident and said she supposed it was down to her to go in and refill the pot.

My mother didn't say much at all and when she did it was in an odd and artificially cheerful tone, "Pass The Parcel next I think." she said, accompanying this with a brisker than necessary hand on my back, pushing me in the direction of the other children. Inside her head though, all sorts of thoughts were tangled up in each other.

My mother was a small, neatly made woman. Intelligent, articulate and invariably courteous. As physically demonstrative as her mother and sister were not, she was let down only, but severely, by an inappropriate sense of humour. This was never tickled so much, as by somebody falling over.

I remember once, proceeding at a suitably stately pace to catch the 113 bus for tea at Auntie Edna's. Grandma, despite me on one side and my mother on the other, lost her balance at the foot of the subway stairs. She was a solidly built woman – we weren't. For a ludicrous few moments the three of us, interlinked, lurched from one side of the passageway to the other like an ill assorted trio of drunks. Then gravity prevailed and we collapsed in an ungraceful, undignified heap. It was all just too much for my mother who was rendered hysterical and helpless, tears streaming, breath whooping. Grandma, hat rakishly askew, legs akimbo, berating her with several well-chosen if unladylike epithets only made matters worse.

My mother and Auntie Edna shared what my father used to wryly call 'An eye for a bargain'. They adored the Sales and having planned their strategy, would descend on Oxford Street with the military precision and implacability of a crack commando unit. If there was one thing, up with which they would not put, it was creasing in any garment, let alone one they were thinking of purchasing. To establish whether required standards were being met, material was seized, squeezed and reviewed with an über-critical eye. The underarm area of a garment was also subject to two expert noses to ascertain it hadn't previously been tried on by a person not as attuned to the benefits of Odor-Oh-No underarm deodorant as they should have been. It was always possible to track their rapid and decisive progress across a sales floor, by the tell-tale trail of crumpled rejects swinging sadly on hangers. My father, on the occasions he was forced to venture out with both of them, would lurk mortified nearby and adopt a contemplative expression. So successful at this was he, that people often mistook him for a floor manager and were apt to call upon him for directions. Too polite to disillusion, over the years, many a lost shopper had cause to be grateful for his concise and correct instruction.

My mother's unquenchable optimism was neatly counterpointed by my father's boundless pessimism so between them, they maintained a fairly even keel. He was a talented musician, touring during his teens and early twenties, playing theatres all over the country. Faded, dog-eared photos show him smiling at the piano, unbelievably young and as yet unscarred by the conflict to come, although he always said he had an easy war. Once they discovered he could play a variety of instruments, he was seconded to ENSA. But that wasn't the whole truth. There was a period about which he'd never talk, working as a medical orderly on the wards. It gave him memories which I think coloured him thereafter. When he was demobbed and with marriage on the horizon my father began working at the café owned by my grandfather, a temporary arrangement which imperceptibly slipped into permanence, although he continued his music, supplementing our income by playing the piano at an unending succession of weddings, bar mitzvahs and ladies nights.

Throughout my childhood, my mother contributed to our household budget as one of a team who answered problem page letters for Woman magazine under the name of agony aunt Evelyn Home. Her portable Olympia typewriter was kept on the kitchen table, fully loaded with paper and carbons so she could write between household chores and the staccato tap rap tap was a comforting and consistent background to family life. Our postman daily delivered fat, brown parcels forwarded from the magazine and crammed full of anxiety. Many of the letters were easily dealt with, others she agonised terribly over. She had a rule-book, which laid down strict guidelines on what was allowed to be written and what was *verboten*. My mother believed in calling a spade a spade and allaying misplaced anxiety wherever she could but waged a constant war of attrition with the magazine editor who was inclined to red-pen anything she considered 'Too biological!'.

CHAPTER FOUR

It took me a long and puzzling while to understand what other people could and could not do. Children learn by influence and example but that rather presupposes we're all marching to roughly the same tune. And whilst it was simple enough to grasp picking your nose in public didn't come under the heading of good manners, other issues often proved more elusive. After the distinctly negative reactions to my virgin flight at the party, I instigated cautious investigation amongst peers.

"Do you fly?" I'd ask friends. Most were gung ho to go but if the spirit was willing, the flesh proved disappointingly earthbound and I'd watch in bewilderment as they ran around, flapping their arms wildly. It pretty soon dawned on me it wasn't so much they didn't *want* to fly, they genuinely didn't know how.

Looking back, I know my parents, not unnaturally, were more than a little put out by the incident at my party but dealt with it in their individual ways. My mother worked on the principle that she hadn't really seen what she thought she had. Even if she had, she reasoned, it was almost certainly something that was just a very odd one-off. My father's, bleaker view, was that it might not be.

I know they conducted casually cautious inquiry amongst other family members seeking possibly a family history of the 'unusual'. Perhaps stories of a related crazy Sadie, flying from *stetl* to *stetl* in years gone by would have made them feel better, but there didn't seem to be any such precedents lurking. So, for their different reasons, they adopted what could have been viewed as a somewhat ostrich approach to the issue. And, of course, they made it as crystal clear as they could, without actually nailing my feet to the floor, that flying was out – not to be done – under no circumstances, never. Ever!

We were though, did they know it, only at the beginning of what was to be a long and somewhat eggshell-treading path for us all. Because, of course, it wasn't just the flying.

I started school when I was five. Mrs Groom, whose cross in life it was to take the baby class, was a vague, lavender-scented lady with untidily dusty brown hair, plaited and pinned into large coils over her ears. Her mind matched her hair, full of odd strands of information causing her to pause often in the middle of a sentence, as completely unrelated ideas drifted past. Not that we minded, not being overly concerned at five with how much syllabus is being covered and to be honest, school was even better than promised, overflowing with the delights of sand and water tables, plasticene, a Wendy House and creamily lukewarm milk at playtime.

For a long while it never entered my mind that everyone couldn't hear and see as I did. Why would it? It was certainly muddling though, sifting through what people thought, what they said and what they actually meant – often and puzzlingly, those three being startlingly different.

"No trouble at all," someone might murmur, meaning exactly the opposite. Or, "Lovely to see you." when nothing could have been further from the truth. It was indeed confusing, especially with all the other stuff going on. Tunes or phrases repeatedly circling, interwoven with sub-texts – hot/cold/tired/hungry/thirsty, headache? aspirin? umbrella or hat? All of this backgrounded by different emotions. Just one person is noisily discordant. Several create a dreadful din and the output from a crowd is a mind-aching mix. Opening up to that unprepared can make you physically sick as I found, embarrassingly, more than once.

Obviously, I learned early to automatically tune out and barrier-building keeps volume down but in the early puzzling days when I had no idea I was different, things were tricky. Startled by something I'd heard, I couldn't fathom why nobody else jumped or even looked round to locate the source. I compensated as best I could, mimicking other people's behaviour as I worked my way through situations. Unending input though made it hard to sort out what I *should* be hearing and understanding as opposed to what I *shouldn't* and seeking much-needed guidance often thrust me even further into trouble. It turned out there were some questions which were perfectly normal to ask and to which I received satisfactory answers. There were others which generated the uncomfortable reaction which, I came to recognise, meant I'd crossed an invisible and constantly moving line. It was really all very puzzling and I hit a fair old bit of turbulence along the way.

At school, for example, my reaction to Alan Sdimes caused problems, although I really couldn't see quite why. He once took a handful of sand, called my name to ensure my attention and threw it in my eyes. It hurt, I cried, he laughed. So I shoved him. His feet promptly shot from under and he landed with a very satisfying thwack on a nearby pile of wooden bricks which made him howl as loudly as me.

"Didn't touch him!" I was able to protest with complete honesty if not total innocence. And that was the truth, I hadn't laid a finger on him.

After that incident I reasoned if I could move Alan with no hands, I could probably move other things too. I experimented and found that indeed I could push things around easily – cups, plates, spoons. After a while, I was also able to lift and deposit them some distance away with no real effort, although experience had taught me the shifting of bigger objects (such as Alan) was apt to bring on an unpleasant headache and sickness. I also, even at that age, had the wit to realise practising on classmates might possibly not be the best route to winning friends. What I could do didn't strike me as particularly odd, just part of so much else you discover at that age. All new and exciting and whilst I did my best to steer clear of anything I'd learned might cause consternation, events sometimes just overtook me.

We used to have P.E. in the school hall, nothing so sophisticated as a separate gym, just bars around the wall for us to climb up and then down again – a pretty pointless exercise as far as I could see, but then so was the hurling to one another of a bag filled with beans. We were divided into teams, designated by different, faded-colour, fraying fabric bands worn diagonally across our chests. The team achieving most points gained a gold star at the end of each session. At close of term, the team with most stars won a silver cup. I couldn't get very excited about it – I'm not big on sports and this lack of competitive spirit displayed itself early.

I was Red-team, lined up to do a somersault on the thick rubber mats, redolent of plimsolls, socks and sweaty children. Greens were doing skipping and Blues were climbing the wall bars. I was heading into my forward roll – "Chins into necks." – when Margaret Claryn, snub of nose, loud of mouth, good at games and invariably first to clamber to the top of the wooden wall bars, for some reason lost her grip.

She was pretty high up, the bars extended to just below the ceiling of the vaulted hall. In seeming slow motion, mouth agape in a scream as yet unuttered, the upper part of her body began to peel outwards from the wall. Mrs Groom, shiny silver whistle clamped between her teeth and emitting small panicky toots as she ran, started from the opposite side of the hall to try and prevent the inevitable. She wasn't moving fast enough.

There wasn't time to think. I nipped back off the mat and skimmed it across the floor to where it was needed, at the same time trying to slow Margaret down as she fell. This was in an entirely different league from anything I'd ever done before so I really don't know how successful I was. She landed awkwardly twisted and with a sickening thud but on the mat, not the parquet floor. An agonising, red-hot pain shot through her arm and my head and I promptly threw up.

An ambulance was called for Margaret – wide-eyed and shaking, with her arm strapped across her chest. Mr. Jones, the caretaker, arrived with mop and bucket, Mrs Groom herded my team-mates away and I was taken upstairs to the headmistress's study while they phoned my mother to come and collect me. Everyone was shaken by the accident, puzzled too. They thought I'd shown lightening reflexes in flinging the mat across the room. Miss Macpharlane, the headmistress, told my mother on the phone that I'd acted amazingly promptly and, were it not for my action, Margaret would probably have hurt herself far more.

What puzzled them though was that the mats were so heavy, they were normally only hauled around by Mr Jones. While we waited for my mother to come and collect me, I was given a cup of hot sweet tea and a staff-room biscuit. Miss Macpharlane even switched on one bar of her electric fire because my teeth were chattering. I felt dizzy and sore and my head was thumping deeply and unpleasantly.

Miss Macpharlane was a canny Scottish lady. Tall and stooping, with glasses chained round her neck, she never put her arms in her cardigans but wore them draped over her thin shoulders from whence they were constantly slipping. She had a gentle, elongated face like an amiable horse, with large nostrils that flared fascinatingly as she spoke and a genuine love and understanding of her small charges. She was just a little Strange herself, but I don't think she knew it. She simply trusted her instincts a lot and extended, to staff and children alike, an empathy that permeated the entire school producing excellent atmosphere and results.

However, she was a very long way from daft, and sheer logic dictated I could scarcely have lifted the heavy mat, let alone flung it all the way across the width of the hall. Yet there was no doubt it had happened nor that I was involved. She wanted to question me further but I didn't think this was a good idea. I didn't know quite how I'd done it either and I hated that it had made me feel so poorly. I just wanted my mother to come and take me home. Miss M watched me thoughtfully as I sipped my tea, eyes downcast and teeth chattering chummily on the china cup which I was clasping with two hands, trying to warm up a little.

"Bit better?" she asked, I nodded silently and she turned away and busied herself with papers on her desk. There was something going on here she didn't understand and instinct told her, very strongly, to keep an eye on me in the future. My instinct, equally forcefully, suggested I make like Brer Rabbit – laying low and saying nothing!

Not long after I started school, a sister arrived. My parents had done the usual preparatory groundwork, explaining how and where the baby was growing and getting me to place my hand on my mother's tummy, so I could feel when it kicked. All of which I found only moderately interesting, although of course I wasn't so impolite as to say.

We didn't own a car ourselves but for occasions when one was needed, called on John, an amiable French-Canadian who ran a local taxi service. He was recruited to take my father and I to collect my mother and the new baby from hospital. He always talked a storm, which was fine, except his accent was so strong, none of us ever understood more than the occasional word. It was clear he was aware of this because he elucidated his conversation with elaborate hand gestures, turning round in the driving seat and fixing his polite but petrified passengers with his one good eye – he'd lost the other in an accident. All in all, he possibly wasn't the finest choice for Jewish travellers who are nervous at the best of times.

On our way back from the hospital, they gave me the warm,

surprisingly heavy bundle to hold on my lap. It was disconcerting, to say the least and what's more it moved and had a powerful, though not unpleasant, sweetly powdery, different-to-anything-else smell. Still, I felt on balance, it would be far better for all concerned if I were to hand it back immediately. This was confirmed when it suddenly woke up, and I was instantly engulfed by unbearably urgent need. She was hungry, she wanted to be fed and she wanted it NOW, NOW, NOW. Aside from the hugely desperate wanting, there didn't seem to be too much else going on in the baby's head. Certainly not the usual cacophony of interwoven theme and thought, which even animals give off. Instead, she was full of light and dark, warmth and hunger and absolutely no patience whatsoever. She opened her small mouth, screwed up her red face and vented all the way home, which made an already nerve-wracking journey, more so.

I'd assumed, because she was my sister, she'd be able to fly too, sadly this proved not to be the case. A great disappointment to both of us although I imagine a profound relief to our beleaguered and apprehensive parents. I learned in later years just how long and hard they'd agonised about having another child, weighing the disadvantages of a single offspring against the risks of producing an even stranger sibling.

When she first arrived, I used to lift her out of her cot and, holding her over my bed in case she fell – I was nothing if not thoughtful – wait for her to take off. She didn't and I wondered whether it was simply a question of stimulating her survival instincts. Apparently, throwing a new-born into the water makes it swim, but I had enough sense to appreciate there was probably an element of risk in chucking her out the window to test a similar theory.

However, for a long time I didn't give up hope. Flying of course is not an effort in fact it's exactly the opposite, it's a relaxing and letting go of what holds you down. It honestly couldn't have been simpler. But I suppose, like anything, once you break it down to step by step instruction for someone else, it takes on a complexity all its own and if interaction of brain, muscle and balance aren't working in the right way, you're not going anywhere. As she got bigger, I used to wake her at night and make her climb on to the blue-painted, wooden bedside table in our shared bedroom, an excellent take-off point. I explained how, over and over, but she never could get the hang of it and sulked a lot until I let her go back to bed.

CHAPTER FIVE

Lots of children have an imaginary friend. Beady was mine and I suppose it was inevitable she should prove more problematic than most.

Afternoon get-togethers with Auntie Cynthia, so her daughter Stephanie and I could play together, were never something I particularly looked forward to. An ex work-colleague of my mother's, Cynthia had acquired in rapid succession a husband in Ladies Underwear, a substantial house in Temple Fortune, a Poggenpohl kitchen and an inflated idea of her own importance.

On that particular afternoon, when we seated ourselves for tea at the massive, ornate dining room table with its surfeit of carved cherubs in unlikely and uncomfortable places, I noticed, next to Auntie Cynthia's plate, a small bronze hand bell. She utilised this almost before we'd started on the sandwiches. A moment or two brought the new daily help, Irene, to the dining room door, wiping water-reddened hands on her apron,

"Wot?" she demanded, obviously not as skilled in the fine art of service as Aunt C might have wished.

"Ah, Irene," Aunt Cynthia had apparently forgotten her background was Kingsbury not Kensington, "A little extra hot water please, and some more milk for the girls." Eyes raised ceiling-ward, an audible sniff and a grudging stomp across the room to collect the empty milk jug, gave an indication of Irene's take on the situation.

"I'm in the middle of the potatoes," she grumbled "If you want that stew on I can't keep running up and down the flaming 'all."

"Casserole Irene, casserole." murmured Aunt Cynthia, dabbing her lips with a monogrammed napkin and a weary air. "And just the milk and the water will be fine thank you, then we'll look after ourselves." My mother had by this time turned an interesting shade of pink, I could see she was struggling manfully not to laugh. She busied herself giving Stephanie and me another sandwich apiece.

Stephanie, was a stodgy-minded child – the inside of her head seemingly jammed as full of fat, soft Shirley Temple ringlets as the outside. A couple of months younger than me, she wasn't exactly a riot as playmates go. Her mother was fond of telling mine that Steph had never given them one moment's aggravation from the time she was born. My mother loved me dearly, but even she had to admit I didn't measure up too well in any non-aggravation-giving stakes. I always appreciated though, how adroitly she could move to another subject when a comparison arose, which might prove odious.

For a short while, we sat and munched our crustless sandwiches in ladylike silence, but clearly it was going to be the usual boring afternoon unless a livelier note was introduced. Luckily, I knew just the person.

"I brought Beady to see you today," I announced cheerfully "We can play fairies and witches if you like." My mother paled.

"Who's Beady then?" asked Stephanie without much interest.

"My invisible friend, haven't you got one?" Stephanie chewed for a moment or two while she thought.

"No." she said finally. And there the subject might well have safely languished and died, had it not been for Aunt Cynthia, sticking her oar in. With a light laugh she pointed out that Steph had so many real friends she'd never felt need to make one up. Well, I'm sorry, but I took umbrage, so would you, so certainly, did Beady.

The little bronze bell next to Auntie Cynthia's plate suddenly jerked up and swung irritably from side to side. Long and loud it rang – once, twice and then, just as it was sinking slowly down, a third time, for good measure.

"That'll be Beady." I said helpfully. Two pairs of horrified eyes fastened on the bell, a third pair, equally horrified, on me. Two mouths fell unattractively open on half-chewed egg and cress, another pursed into an unmistakeable and familiar wait-till-I-get-you-home shape.

And into the following, heavily pregnant pause, strode an irate Irene. A satisfyingly swift response, I felt. Flushed-faced, breathing hard and divesting herself fiercely of her apron, she was not best pleased and proceeded to put forward a couple of startlingly frank and interesting suggestions as to exactly where Auntie Cynthia could stick her bleeding bell. She went on to suggest that room might also be made there for her frigging airs and graces, her shitty wages, her stinking stew and last but certainly not least, her sodding silver candlesticks, the polishing of which apparently fell into Irene's regular sphere of activities. Having thus made her feelings abundantly clear and giving a good trample to the abandoned apron for final emphasis, Irene swung neatly on her heel and exited, slamming the dining room door behind her. On an adjacent shelf, one of Aunt Cyn's precious Capo di Monte pieces teetered. We all watched. I could, of course, have stopped it falling. I chose not to.

"No," my mother muttered tersely as we made our way briskly home, "An imaginary friend wasn't a *bad* thing as such. However, it was precisely because she was *imaginary* that people such as Auntie Cynthia," last seen pouring herself a recuperative glass of sherry with a shaking hand, "Were entitled to be somewhat startled if she suddenly started *doing* things."

"But," I protested, trotting to keep up with her agitated stride and grasping at last with relief exactly wherein lay the problem, "It wasn't really Beady, it was *me*."

"Oh sweetheart, I know." she said. And she sighed heavily and then, unexpectedly she gave a little snort.

"It's not funny at all." she said, "And I'm certainly not laughing young lady." but inside her head, she kept seeing the gob-smacked faces on Aunt C and Steph and her mouth twitched all the way home whenever she thought I wasn't looking. I don't remember going round there for tea again.

As I recall, it was shortly after Beady was given her marching orders that I was taken for a sixth birthday treat, to a variety show at the London Palladium. It was a wonderful, unforgettable evening – supper at the Corner House and good seats in the stalls. Although a long-planned and looked-forward to outing, possibly my parents hadn't really thought things through enough. Certainly I suspect they might have been assailed by a first tremor of apprehension when I leaned forward in sheer wonder as the star turn, Mr. Magica made his spectacular entrance. He was flying. Effortlessly and gracefully, soaring and swooping high above the stage, acknowledging the delighted applause of the rapturous audience and my heart soared with him.

"Oh," I breathed, "Like me!"

The bouquet of blooms produced from empty air; the miracle of multi-coloured scarves all coming out of his mouth; the sawing in two of his assistant so both bits of her waved from opposite sides of the stage – it was almost more excitement than I could bear. Entranced, I applauded each new triumph longer and louder than anyone else. And, had he not asked for a volunteer from the audience to fly with him, the evening might well have remained one of wonder, revelation, undiluted magic and the happy conclusion that I wasn't quite as odd as I was beginning to think. But he said he needed a lovely young lady from the audience and faster than you could shriek abracadabra, or in my parents' case, "No!", I was out of my seat and trotting busily down the centre aisle, hotly pursued by my panic-stricken mother whose restraining hand had grabbed a tad too tardily.

Eyes closed, finger to forehead, the better to 'Perceive vibrations with his inner eye', the great man was slowly making his way along a catwalk extending into the auditorium. He was, he intoned, getting warmer and could see clearly a beautiful blonde destined to take to the air tonight. With a triumphant cry he swung round, pointing a dramatic forefinger at a giggling, jiggling, glamorous effort in low-cut top and tight slacks. She was just rising to her feet, reaching for his outstretched hand when I arrived, breathless but determined, at the foot of the catwalk and tugged urgently at his trouser leg.

I was of course, blissfully unaware that the comfortably-upholstered young lady was a well-rehearsed and integral part of the act. However, presented with an eager, best party-frocked, curly haired moppet in front of some 2000 people chorusing "Aaahhh", what was the poor chap to do? Piqued, but professional to his beautifully manicured fingertips, he released the blonde abruptly and leaning down, swung me up beside him, to a round of applause all my own.

Of course, as soon as he touched me I knew and disappointment hit me like a punch to the stomach. He knelt to equal our heights. He wanted to know my name, my age – and this brought the house down – was this my first flight? And throughout the easy and effortlessly warm and amusing ad libs, he was furiously computing the risks of going ahead, against the damage if he didn't. Close up, he didn't look so good either, trickles of slowly sliding sweat were forcing shallow runnels in thick make-up and there was a strong, decidedly un-magical aroma of body odour. I could have cried and it was probably the sight of my trembling lower lip that spurred him into action. He rose and signalled to the conductor who was anxiously watching and wondering from the orchestra pit. The drummer started a roll, and the backdrop behind us rose, to reveal a shimmering expanse of blue-tinted silver curtain.

As he led me, his newly acquired and somewhat truculent partner to centre stage, a distinctly worried-looking assistant appeared and draped each of us in *Magic Flying Cloaks*. The cloaks smelt even mustier than he did and as she'd arranged billowing folds, I'd seen very clearly the fine wire harness he was wearing – what a phoney. The drum roll intensified and as he stooped to lift me, I really don't know which of the two of us was more peeved. He gathered me up, one arm under my knees, the other round my waist and told me tersely to hold round his neck and hang on for Christ's sake. And then we were jerkily airborne, to a gasp of delight from the multitude of upturned, expectant faces. His assistant passed a large wooden hoop over and round us, with almost imperceptible sleight of hand to demonstrate no wires and as we rose higher, my new friend adopted a suitable, flying-through-the-air position, one leg bent, the other stretched elegantly behind.

"Don't wriggle kid and you won't fall," he hissed spittily in my ear. His thought, amplified by stress was, "If the little cow stays still, I might just do it. Shit, she weighs a ton." Well, I may have been a bit of a solid six year old, but that's not the sort of thing a girl of any age needs to hear. I didn't like this man. I didn't like him one little bit. Not only was he a rotten smelly fake, but he was now clutching me so tightly, his nails were digging uncomfortably into the flesh of my leg.

I gently began to unclasp my hands from the instructed position behind his neck which had become unpleasantly moist. We were now suspended high above the stage and looking up, I could see a chap sitting on a wooden platform. Hidden from the audience, by the top drapes of the curtain, he was busy operating the winching equipment that was hauling us upwards. As I'd now taken my hands away from his neck, Mr. Magica was bearing all my weight and I suspect his fine wire harness was pinching painfully, in places best not pinched. It certainly wiped the smile off his face, or perhaps he just thought we were too high for it to matter. Eyes on his, I grinned, relaxing completely in his now quivering arms.

"What the f...???" he started. Now that really wasn't polite. So I left.

As I rolled outwards and away, there was a gasp of excited shock from the audience although naturally this was as nothing compared to that from my companion and his mate up top – after all they knew the routine and this wasn't it. For a few dramatic seconds I allowed myself to plummet, terror on my face, arms thrown out, flailing in a desperate bid to save myself. I think I may have even thrown in a "Help me, oh help me." Every upturned face was frozen, including those of the orchestra, who were petrified in mid-play, making for a pleasingly dramatic silence.

With the stage hurtling rapidly towards me, I let out a blood curdling scream then, with inches to spare, I changed direction and looped up smoothly again, blowing kisses to the crowd who were now raising the rafters with relief. Arriving back at the side of the riveted Mr. M. I stopped and hovered courteously, waiting for the next move. Unfortunately, he appeared to have temporarily lost the plot and was repetitively muttering,

"Ohmygod ohmygod ohmygod." As professional patter it left a lot to be desired. Well, someone had to do something, we couldn't hang around indefinitely. I took his arm and smiled encouragingly up at the man above, whose mouth was hanging open, I hoped he wasn't going to dribble. I gave a little downward flap of the hand, indicating now might be a good time to begin descent. And swinging gently, we began to head down, although halfway, I couldn't and didn't resist a small impromptu swoop round my rigid co-star, I was really getting into this performance lark, although you can always be let down by your fellow artistes. Indeed, by this time, he'd completely dropped his one leg bent thing and was just letting both dangle in a very sloppy manner. He'd also turned a rather alarming and unflattering pasty colour which, hopefully, was only visible up close and personal.

When our feet touched terra firma and we'd bowed several times, he managed to pull himself together enough to gallantly kiss my hand and lead me to the catwalk. His hands were shaking terribly badly and he was cherishing thoughts of kicking me headfirst and hard into the orchestra pit. At the same time, he was trying to work out how it had been done. He'd been had, that much he knew and he had in mind a rival or two who'd probably engineered it. It had been a bloody good trick, no denying, but he wasn't laughing. The effing shock, he was thinking, could have put him six bleeding feet under. The audience loved us, no doubt about that. Mind you the thunderous applause was as nothing compared with the thunderous expression on the face of my waiting parents. They and Mr. Magica exchanged a long, pained look. We didn't stay to see the end of the show, but left immediately and in some disarray through a side door.

I think my parents had, up until that point, chosen to deal with odd and worrying but hopefully passing aberrations as just that – passing! But that evening, round the kitchen table, fortified by strong tea and Bourbons they, as well as I, began the process of comprehending the depth and degree of my differentness.

They'd known, of course about the flying. They were also unhappily aware of my knack of moving objects without touching. Was there, they asked, with trepidation, anything else I'd like to share? In this new spirit of openness, I was determined to be helpful. Could everyone, I inquired, hear what people were thinking or was that also just me?

I think they handled things remarkably well, under the circumstances. Although I do remember my father, who was teetotal, going to the sideboard in our hall to extract a dusty bottle of brandy for a medicinal tot. They did, after all, have a fine line to walk – making me feel that what I had was very special and a not a Bad Thing, at the same time impressing upon me the virtue of discretion, because other people, Mr. Magica for one or indeed Aunt Cynthia for another, might not have quite the same appreciation of my talents.

My parents telling me not to use what I had – and they must have known it – was virtually impossible, like saying keep your right hand tucked away and make do with the left. I did try, but sometimes events overtook me and I simply reacted. Always in my favour though was people's consistent and instinctive need to rationalise, to make what they saw or heard fit within parameters they understood. Time after time, that let me off any hook I might have inadvertently got myself stuck on.

I do know however because, naturally, not much was secret in our house that my poor father and mother spent a huge amount of time thinking and discussing what, if anything, they could or should do about me. But most of these anxious confabs went round in circles and hit the same brick wall – who, if anyone, would be the correct expert to go to for advice? What, if anything would they actually want done? And in the long run – shades of Grandma here – might this not be a situation best kept under our hats?

CHAPTER SIX

There is in every school career, alas, one teacher who terrifies above and beyond all others. Mine was Mrs Treason. Square-built, solid-legged with year-round biliously beige knitted stockings and fat-soled brogues, she was an immovable object. Her shock of white hair, cut mercilessly short, bristled with malign energy and she was possessed of and never slow to use, a parade-ground boom that made the insides of your ears ache. Thursdays were Mrs Treason's dinner duty stints. Alternate Thursdays were tapioca pudding days – an ominous confluence.

Technically we were not allowed to get up from the long dinner tables that possessed the school hall from 12.30 – 2.00 until we'd cleared our plate. Loosely adhered to by most teachers, this was a rule governed in the final reckoning by their own desire to salvage a portion of the lunch-hour for themselves. Not so Mrs Treason who was made of sterner stuff and took her duties all too seriously.

It always seemed an absurd situation that, if you knew full well you hated something, you weren't permitted to say no thank you and go on your way, dessertless but happy. Sadly, the system didn't work that way, two courses were provided for us and two courses we had to consume. But, coming face to face with an off-white, gelatinous spawn, topped with a dollop of strawberry jam was an ordeal that even now, sends a surge of unease from stomach to throat. By the time, on that particular Thursday that Mrs Treason was standing over me, I was the sole occupant of the hall and desperation had me in its tearful grip. The tapioca, unappetising enough when hot was indescribable, stone cold and as I hung my head in defeat, the odd tear falling into the mess wasn't helping. Mrs Treason said if I cried like a baby I'd have to be fed like a baby, but finish my portion I would, if she had to wait all night.

As the noxious substance slid greasily down my throat, I sought frantically for a way out and lit on a solution to the problem that was so blinding in its simplicity, I almost sobbed with relief. Obviously I wasn't in any position to properly explain the depths of despair to which she was taking me. But if Mrs Treason were to be made fully aware, for just one moment, of exactly what I was going through, how truly awful the stuff tasted, she'd surely view the matter in a whole new and sympathetic light. I promptly opened my mind and did a little sharing.

Results were swift if not entirely expected. Mrs Treason began to turn an interesting shade of very pale green and suddenly seemed to lose all interest in me and my pudding. For a moment or two she gazed somewhere off into the middle distance, concentrating intently, it appeared, on some inner turmoil then,

"Back in a minute." she muttered thickly, "Don't ..." She didn't finish, but swung smartly on one sensible heel and headed for the door at a brisk pace which in anyone else might have been called a trot, I think she may have had a hand clasped to her mouth. I waited for ages, but she didn't come back. A kindly dinner-lady eventually taking pity removed my plate and said run along now, because they had to clear up. Mrs Treason didn't come back at all that afternoon, someone else took her classes, nor do I ever remember any other show-downs over the tapioca. Empathy's a great thing.

My closest friend in school from the earliest days was Elizabeth Mostroff, the younger daughter of parents who'd arrived in England from Russia in somewhat mysterious circumstances. They were apparently involved in something equally secretive once they were here – either that or they suffered from a similar strain of paranoia to my grandmother. Any inquiry about where they worked and what precisely they did was answered with a finger to the lips, a small smile and an admonitory shake of the head, causing much speculation on the part of Elizabeth's friends' parents.

The whole Mostroff family were frighteningly clever, with both parents fluent in over ten languages, although if they were as hard to understand in those, as they were in English, I'm not sure what good it did them. Their older daughter, Dora, played the cello; Elizabeth, the violin and piano; Mr. Mostroff the flute and Mrs Mostroff any instrument not currently occupied by any other member of the family. They didn't have a television or radio because, they said, they preferred to provide their own entertainment.

Tall and angular with short curly brown hair, the slightly foreign intonation of her parents and an infectious giggle, Elizabeth invariably came top in exams because she was exceptionally bright. I also did well, because she was exceptionally bright. She was one of those rare people able to concentrate on the subject in hand to the total exclusion of any distraction. Consequently, whenever I got stuck and had to stop and think, there was Elizabeth, blazing loud and clear, not to mention correctly. I didn't feel it could be considered cheating, since it was unavoidable. But on more than one occasion, our answers were so similar, suspicion was aroused and we were separated to either end of the classroom, to our mutual indignation. Such separation, of course, made no difference whatsoever, other than teaching me a little caution, but it was indeed a severe blow to my academic career, when in junior school we were put into different classes.

CHAPTER SEVEN

I was in the top class of the infant's school when I was voted May Queen – an honour indeed, May Day being a shining highlight of the school calendar. Nigel Lawrence was to be my Crown Bearer, along with ten attendants, a boy and girl from each year, to carry my train – a slightly stained, blue satin effort, kept in the school dressing-up box and handed down to successive monarchs. My mother laboured long and hard and between stints on the typewriter, produced a full-length, blue-bow bedecked, white dress, worn over a hooped petticoat that swayed gratifyingly with each step.

It was a thrill almost beyond description, to emerge from the doorway of the school in all my glory and our slow and stately procession across the playground to pass beneath a flower-decorated arch, was one of those moments of pure delight that should be tissue-paper wrapped and preserved. My throne was Miss Macpharlane's study chair, elevated to grandeur by a swathe of red velvet and set in front of the flower garlanded climbing frame. I was crowned, with due ceremony by Mrs Ford, an elderly ex-head of the school, roped in as visiting dignitary. My parents and sister had front row seats and as I graciously raised my sceptre – bejewelled with glued-on coloured winegums – the afternoon's activities swung into action.

Each of the classes had prepared a song, short play or acrobatics and the traditional grand finale was maypole dancing. This involved a complicated in and out routine, resulting in an elegantly plaited pole or a hopeless tangle, depending on whether people undered when they should, and didn't over when they shouldn't.

At the end of the afternoon, the maypole duly emerged for its annual airing in the arms of burly Mr. Jones followed by a scarlet-faced lad, staggering under the joint weight of the solid iron base and the responsibility of placing it correctly on the marked spot. With shuffling, nudging and self-important giggling, the children took their ribbons and positions. Mrs Gordon, on the piano and also in charge of a motley crew of tambourine, drum and triangle players nodded, hit the keys and the maypole dancers were off, teachers mouthing instructions and smiling relief as gradually the coloured ribbons wound a discernible pattern.

They established later the trouble was at the base of the heavy wooden pole, where it slid into its iron support. It had been around for years and where time and damp had done their work, the wood had gradually deteriorated to the point of disaster. Now, the uneven but determined pull on the ribbons of twenty or so children, was a final straw. The pole began to sway unnaturally far, first one way then back the other, its seven foot height and weight putting a disproportionate strain on the twelve inches of weakened material held within the unyielding base. Parents and teachers one by one, seeing the danger were already starting forward. But, occupied in the complications of remembering who went where and when, the children were blissfully oblivious.

From my throne vantage point I could see, all too clearly what was happening and my head filled with a keening, increasingly searing note of panic as awareness swept the rest of the audience. If that pole snapped and crashed, injuries would be inevitable but the warning shouts of the running adults couldn't be heard above the cacophony of a band now well into its discordant stride. I concentrated, reaching out, but the thick smoothly dark wood was as slippery to grasp mentally as it would have been physically; I closed my eyes, envisaging myself, feet spread wide for balance, arms wrapped tightly around it and held on.

I held it as long as I could and then when I could hold it no longer the slippery pole, ribbons now forlornly hanging, crashed with a gravel-raising thwump, to the asphalt. But by that time, all the children had been herded out of danger. I had a right royal headache under my crown and could feel the familiar surge of sickness. Only vanity saved me. I really didn't want to go down in school history, as the only May Queen who'd thrown up on the throne.

It was then that Nigel Lawrence, next to me, started making a very peculiar noise. I thought at first he was laughing but the rusty sound he was making didn't sound happy. As I turned, reaching out with automatic curiosity, I realised he wasn't laughing and why. There was no air where air should have been and my eyes must have mirrored the panic in his as my throat too, sought to stay open. This had happened to him before, though not as badly. He knew it was an assmattack. His mother, full of fear, nevertheless always told him it was nothing to worry about, just a nuisance and uncomfortable, breathe slow and regular and it would pass. Nigel was doing his level best to follow instruction, but it wasn't passing.

I'd gone in with curiosity and had simply been unable to find the way out. I wondered afterwards what we must have looked like, the two of us, seated still on our ceremonial chairs, gasping and clawing. It can't have been for very long though. I was briefly aware he'd fallen off the chair and into a dark black place and then I was hurtling down there too.

I don't remember anything else, until I woke up in Edgware General Hospital with some kind of a mask over my nose and mouth. When I tried to take it off, a nurse firmly slapped my hand, tucked it back under the taut covers and made a finger to lip, shushing. My parents must have been waiting outside because the next moment they were there, bright-eyed with anxiety, while a doctor listened to my chest with a stethoscope and made me blow, hard as I could into a tube. He made some notes and shook his head, as the nurse moved to replace the mask,

"It's OK, she doesn't need that anymore." And then to my parents. "Clear as a bell now, no trace of wheeziness. Odd. She wasn't good when she came in. My guess?" And he turned his back to me, dropping his voice, "Bit of a panic, when her friend went down, seen it once or twice before. Mind you, never quite as serious as this." He turned back to me with a louder, jollier tone, "Better now young lady? Gave mum and dad, bit of a scare. Remember what happened?"

"Nigel was making a funny noise and he was so scared, I thought …" I trailed off as I caught my mother's eye.

"Well, you got yourself in a proper pickle, didn't you?" He turned to my parents. "I'd like to keep her in overnight, she really was very poorly, they both were and her young friend'll be with us for a good few days, but I can't see too much wrong with this one now."

My parents were, as ever, on a sticky wicket. Clearly, this time I'd saved school mates from injury, but sticking my nose into Nigel's affairs had obviously been extremely dangerous and was something I must never ever repeat. Once again, they were treading that fine line, condoning one thing whilst concurrently discouraging others.

I did try to abide by the rules but when it came to flying perhaps, deep down, I was aware the knack wouldn't always be with me, that as I got older it would change and the release from gravity's hold would not be so easily achieved. I knew full well however that when I did do it, it was dangerous, both of itself and because of the risk of being spotted. But I ask you, in all honesty, how could I not?

I opted for brief night-time excursions, not often, just every few weeks, and tried always to stay more or less over the back garden. I wrapped up warmly, I knew my mother would be livid if she caught me flying but to catch me flying without a coat wasn't going to pour oil over anybody's troubled waters.

How to describe it? Rising, incongruously if sensibly kitted out in quilted, fur-collared anorak and pink knitted scarf; nevertheless, suddenly graceful, hair blown down against my head, eyes narrowed against the wind-rush. Moving through the air as smooth and sure as a dolphin slicing the water, and at a certain height the wind catching and holding me. Gliding, swooping, soaring, no clumsiness but a complex fluidity of movement, unimaginable when grounded and unbelievable, even as it was experienced. I would yell aloud in exultation and then, filling my lungs to bursting with clean, clear, sharply cold air, shout again. Too high to be heard, certainly too high to care. And at those times, I couldn't help but be consumed by an overwhelming delight in the fluke of nature that was me.

But it goes without saying, because life's like that, it wasn't always wonderful. I remember one winter's outing, circling slowly, rising and falling, allowing the wind to move me where it would, when it started to rain. Great ovoid drops bombarding me – a real euphoria buster which swiftly wiped the smile off my face. Soaked through almost immediately and no, I hadn't brought an umbrella – who was I, Mary Poppins? I headed back brought down to earth long before I reached it. Unfortunately, preoccupied with all that swooping, soaring stuff and in the cold rain I rather lost my bearings. Icy cold and shivering in wind that had suddenly turned spiteful, I spent an uncomfortable few minutes, hovering at second floor level, peering into windows trying to find ours. I counted myself lucky I was able to locate the right house and no one happened to be looking out of the wrong ones at the time I was peering in.

CHAPTER EIGHT

My childhood on the whole was surprisingly ordinary and not just a series of one extracurricular activity after another. And as we all adjusted, and I learnt a certain amount of caution, things settled down far more. My parents, whilst cherishing the hope I might simply 'grow out of it', were obviously not able to conceal their periodic and extremely natural angst. They nevertheless put a huge amount of effort into ensuring that angst didn't damage me. It was clear I was different, but I was brought up to believe it was only that. Not better, not worse, just not exactly the same. And over the years, peculiarities were adjusted to and accepted – after all you can't go on being amazed indefinitely. Some kids are musical, some maths prodigies, my talents just lay in an odder direction.

The way I handled things, evolved naturally, like all skills and I found a myriad of ways to shield myself from the constant cacophony of other people's thoughts. Most of the time, I only listened when I wanted to, although strong emotion usually managed to blast through. I'd also learned an early lesson via Nigel and his asthma and certainly wasn't going to go down that route again. I lived comfortably by a code of natural caution when I was out, but at home, things were naturally more relaxed. Bidden to pass the salt I'd do so whilst still wielding my knife and fork and no-one batted an eyelid. It was just something that was a part of our lives. My sister, Dawn, of course, had it drummed into her from babyhood that she wasn't, under any circumstances, allowed to mention my oddities. Truth to tell, I think much of the time, the whole thing just slipped our minds and I'm very certain, there were families with darker secrets than ours.

But from time to time some fresh incident would again bring up the question as to whether or not I should 'see' someone. But if so, who and to what end? After all, I wasn't physically ill. Psychiatrist then? But I wasn't imagining things, neither were they and there was the genuine fear and risk that officialdom might want to take me in somewhere and find out exactly what was what. And, as it transpired, whether governed by logic or coloured by conspiracy theories, the decision to keep things to ourselves was certainly the right one. It was just a shame it couldn't have been kept that way.

The passing seasons of my growing up, continued to be marked by large family gatherings on the various holidays, Jewish and otherwise. Spring, when we celebrated Passover, meant the whole kit and caboodle would troop over to Auntie Edna and Uncle Monty. Here, the *Pesach* service was traditionally conducted, with a certain degree of belligerence, by an uncle, Little Jack. I believe he was known as such, as much to annoy him, as to distinguish him from his father-in-law of the same name. On these special evenings, a riotous crowd of about twenty-five would settle themselves noisily round a table, extended to its fullest length for the event with the judicious addition at either end of two card-tables. Men were seated at the top end with piety diminishing the further down the table you were. We children would be placed amidships whilst the women were at the far end. This enabled them to make necessary forays kitchenward, from whence a continuous buzz of conversation emerged which stern shushes from the business-end of the table failed consistently to quell.

The security of extended family life was reflected and encapsulated in unchanging routine, the reading of the *Pesach* service in incomprehensibly rapid sing-song Hebrew. The annual familiarity of story and ritual, the same jokes, small witticisms provoking more laughter than they deserved in the unacknowledged relief that someone was still there to say it and we were still there to hear. A family miraculously un-decimated, though not untouched, by the horrors of the Holocaust, there was not a one of us unmoved, however briefly, around that table on successive *Seders* by the thought that all over the world, Jewish families were following the same ritual.

At a certain point in the service, a child would be despatched to the front door to 'let in' the angel Elijah. Tradition held he had to sip from the silver goblet of sweet kosher wine set out for him on the table by every family, with the annually aired mock concerns as to his sobriety at this stage of the evening.

"Nissed as a pewt." Auntie Yetta had once unforgettably and carefully enunciated, having had her own wine glass sneakily refilled once too often, by an errant grandson, while she wasn't looking.

My mother, at this stage in the evening always managed to find her way to my side to keep a firm, albeit unobtrusive grip on my arm, ready to squeeze sharply if I transgressed. One year I'd thought it would be helpful to add a little drama to the event. Still a bit shaky in those early days, I'd lifted the silver goblet a good couple of inches off the table to universal gasps, before losing my mental grip and upending it. Afterwards, everybody had a different but equally firm take on what had happened, that good old judicious rationalisation – someone kicked the table leg; there was a ruck in the tablecloth; the goblet had been over-filled. The family talked about it every year and I always felt it added an extra frisson to the evening's events. My parents thought otherwise.

Alcohol is always bad news for me. Even a tiny amount has consequences which can best be described as unfortunate. At the age of ten I was one of six bridesmaids at the wedding of my cousin Susan, Auntie Edna's older daughter. I think we were chosen as much for height regimentation as familial fondness. I know for a fact, Auntie Edna had her doubts about my participation; she never could quite get the soap incident out of her mind. Kitting us out, involved several trips to a redoubtable lady called Sonia Lyman in Swiss Cottage. She ran, with a rod of iron and a row of dressmakers pins clamped between her lips, a children's clothes shop from whence it would seem, all bridesmaids' dresses this side of the Thames originated.

It was thus, in pink, full-length, befrilled, beflowered and belaced numbers, over petticoats so starched they stood on their own, that we followed Susan stiffly down the aisle carefully balancing atop our bouffanted hair, densely flowered coronets skewered firmly in place with a multitude of fiercely administered hair grips. The bride needn't have worried about us fidgeting on duty, we were so firmly pinned, tied and lacquered that even walking at a stately pace was an effort.

Sitting down for dinner later was tough too. As soon as your bottom got anywhere near the chair, the rigid front of the petticoat became correspondingly elevated. Having once managed to get seated, the only way to get food within striking distance of its destination was with a sideways approach around the petticoat. Going to the loo – complicated at the best of times by the inflexible toilet-paper-on-the-seat rule which, as all well brought up North London girls know, requires certain deftness – bridesmaid garbed, became well-nigh impossible. As you hoisted the skirt, such was the rigidity of the structure that it pushed shoulders to ear lobes. Simply reaching your underwear was an achievement in itself, let alone doing anything constructive with it.

There was wine on the table at the wedding dinner and despite the problems of the dress, I must have knocked back nearly a whole glass. It was at this point that the band hurled itself into the traditional *Hora*. Guests flowed into the familiar enthusiastic circles, moving faster and faster to the beat. Hands sweatily linked, feet stamping, bodies – old, young, fat, thin, chiffoned, beaded, black-tied – turning left, right, dipping and stamping to the rhythm of the dance. It was around this time the alcohol started to hit home. I loved dancing and standing up, the dress wasn't so much of a hindrance, more a support really.

I'd let down my usual mental barriers a little, and was warmly and pleasantly engulfed in everyone else's enjoyment. I felt light and floaty and discovered, with mild astonishment that in fact I *was* light and floaty. About six inches off the floor to be exact. Fortunately, in the general melee my enhanced status seemed to go unremarked. Unfortunately, the exact mechanics of getting down again, temporarily eluded me. Whilst I'd never encountered this problem before, in the overall haze, it didn't seem to matter all that much. Way above me, decorating the ceiling of the hall, were multitudes of multi-coloured balloons. I was lazily contemplating drifting up to bring some down, when an urgent hand grabbed mine.

"What are you *doing*?" hissed my mother, tugging downwards, beaded bosom heaving in consternation.

"Just hanging around." Well, laugh? I doubled up. My mother, evening bag clamped firmly under one arm, my hand tightly under the other, steered me rapidly off the dance floor and reinforcements in the agitated shape of my father arrived. Not before time either. My mother wasn't a heavy woman and to my astonishment and delight, was rising now to join me.

"Hello," I said, pleased.

"Put me down."

"'Snot me," I murmured virtuously, "'Syou." My father meanwhile, from my other side, was exerting firm pressure on his errant air-borne first born, but I couldn't imagine why. It had simply never occurred to me I could take passengers and the idea held immense charm and endless possibilities. I think I might have started to try and explain this, but all of a sudden, I didn't feel quite right. Somewhere, under all that pink lace, something ominously uncomfortable was stirring.

"Uh oh, storm brewing skipper." I muttered and came, very abruptly, down to earth. My mother, touching thankfully down with me, took one look at my face and with a quick grasp of the situation and an impressive turn of speed, bundled me towards the Ladies just in time to avoid undue unpleasantness. I don't recall much else about that particular wedding.

CHAPTER NINE

Miss Peacock came into and went out of my life very briefly, around 10.00 o'clock on a bitterly cold, late November evening. I was ten, just turning eleven and perhaps only with the chill wind of her passing, came my first inkling of just how thin was the curtain that separated my almost too comfortable daily existence, from a completely different and far more dangerous arena.

I was returning from a friend's house, a journey permitted only because the 113 bus stopped outside her front door and deposited me practically in front of mine. Downstairs – where the conductor can keep an eye, was the rule, but climbing the stairs and installing myself in that nice little bit at the back, was what I usually did. On this particular occasion, there were just two other passengers up there, a woman about halfway down, middle-aged I thought, thin, even in a thick camel-coloured winter coat. Narrow shoulders, iron grey hair chopped uncompromisingly short and wispily showing below the type of unflattering, knitted, chocolate-brown pull-on hat, equally at home on teapot or toilet roll. She was knitting, not another hat I hoped. A few rows nearer the front and on the opposite side sat a bowler hatted florid-faced man, nose buried in an Evening Standard.

At the next stop, a group of youths boarded; eighteen or nineteen years old, creating the racket that boys in a crowd find obligatory. There were only half a dozen of them but they stormed the stairs like an army, laughing, shouting, swearing and filling the hitherto quiet space with noise and something else. Skin-tight jeans, creaking leather jackets, aggressively side-burned and fancying themselves something rotten. I wasn't nervous, despite all my mother's fears I was more than capable of looking after myself, but this lot had been drinking, the smell was tangible and that made me uneasy.

Most of them were simply silly and noisy. Moving in a pack, staking out territory, harmless enough. But there was one, plump belly overhanging a studded belt, tow-haired, pale and pock-marked who was wrong. Simmering sullenly beneath the surface, he was brim-full of anger and resentment. He was I'd have been prepared to bet, always angry. It's a natural state for some people but with it goes the frustration of being unable to express it adequately in daily life. He'd had several more drinks than was good for him and he had a lot to prove, his need to impress his peers incidental, to reassure himself, overpowering. He it was who led the group, swaggering, towards the front of the bus where they spread over the seats like mould and lit cigarettes, holding them in identical fashion, twixt thumb and forefinger, to indicate just how non-conformist they were. I turned back to my Georgette Heyer, until an abrupt change in the atmosphere made me look up again a few minutes later.

Pock-face had moved to sprawl across the seat directly in front of Evening Standard man and was making play of scanning the football results on the back page of the paper. Huge amusement amongst the troops, but if he was looking for a reaction from the reader, he didn't get it. This didn't suit; successful clowning needs a straight man so, with a wink, he inhaled deeply and blew a deliberately insulting lung-full of smoke into the face of the older man. A curt,

"Cut it out laddie," and the man continued reading. He honestly wasn't concerned, certainly not in any way intimidated. He was, in truth, bone weary. He'd had a hard, unpleasant day, indeed a rough few months altogether at the office. Passed over for a desired and, in his opinion, well deserved promotion he was reading, but not absorbing the newsprint. His head was full of redundancy fears, bank managers and mortgages. He certainly wasn't nervous or worried about the boys, they were just unpleasant, overgrown kids showing off, strutting their stuff, he didn't feel threatened. Indeed at that point, he wasn't wrong, but Pock-face was fast heading past unpleasant and teetering on the edge of something else altogether. Even then it might have been all right if one of the other youths, weasel-faced, duck-arsed hair, hadn't laughed out loud. Now it was no longer the man who was the butt of the joke, control had to be taken back.

"'Ere," said he of the pitted skin to weasel-face, "Wot you laughing at?" and in those few seconds the situation turned, fuelled by a volatile mix of testosterone, bravado, alcohol and adrenaline. Pock-face drew himself to his feet, turned and suddenly, ridiculously out of place on the 113 to Hendon Central, the overhead lights were glinting on a flick-knife blade, a vicious shine.

Weasel, as if attached to the other end of a tautened thread rose as swiftly, still smiling but with his lip curling back from his teeth and a hand moving to his own pocket – I didn't think he was reaching for a comb. The group, leather creaking, shifted and in an instant there were two clear sides. It was beginning to look like something out of West Side Story lacking only Chita Rivera wading in with a song. Pock-face was still angry but also now frightened at the situation he'd so quickly provoked, thus making him far more dangerous. I really was going to have to do something, I could hardly stand by and watch gang warfare break out round me.

"Young man." A clear, irritable voice. "Put that away immediately and both of you sit down and be quiet." The woman passenger several rows in front of me had looked up briefly as she spoke but now, matter settled, she continued knitting, I don't think she'd even dropped a stitch. Newspaper man having sized up the new situation and not finding it to his liking, utilised the gawp-filled pause that followed to move swiftly out of his seat and down the stairs, leaving just the woman in the centre of the bus and me, sitting unobtrusively at the back. Weasel and Pock, shocked at being spoken to like that – did no-one have any manners nowadays, were instantly united and gleefully in their element against this common and comfortingly unthreatening enemy.

"Oy", said Weasel, "You, droopy drawers," guffaws egged him on, this was easy meat.

"Nobody," he said, jaw thrusting, "Talks to me and my mate like that." This time she didn't even bother looking up, although he'd risen from his seat and, following the pocked one was advancing down the aisle towards her.

"Then it's high time somebody did." she said. Well, that's it, I thought. I knew all about keeping my head down but I couldn't just sit there and see this daft old bat insulted, assaulted or worse. She could have absolutely no idea what was going on in Pock-face's head but I did and it wasn't healthy. He'd gone way too far to retreat without losing face but more importantly, he really didn't want to, he wanted to hurt someone, he wanted it so badly he could already taste it.

He was still holding the knife, so it seemed best to deal with that first. I began to heat up the handle; he was too high on aggression to notice immediately so I turned things up a few degrees. That concentrated his mind. With a howl of pain and shock he flung down the offending object, now red hot and glowing from base to tip. I was just wondering if perhaps I hadn't overdone it a wee bit, when a funny thing happened. His feet flew backwards from under him with great force, exactly as if he'd walked into a concealed trip wire or rather, as if it had walked into him. He landed heavily in the aisle, flat on his face. Then, startling all of us, himself I think most of all, he bounded smartly upright again as if jerked by an unseen string – you can't keep a good yob down. His face was a comic mix of amazement and fear. His nose was oozing blood and he didn't seem to know whether it was that or the painfully burnt hand which should be receiving priority attention. And then he began to march down the centre of the bus with a peculiarly odd lurching gait, for all the world as if someone had one firm hand on his collar and another grip on the seat of his grubby jeans. He appeared to be extremely preoccupied with the unexpected turn events had taken.

Weasel and the others watched the jerky but rapid progress of their companion-in-arms with silent astonishment. I've never seen such a communal jaw-drop. They'd been a pretty gormless lot to start with but now even the ghost of gorm was gone. Still doing his jerky Bill and Ben imitation, Pock-face had now reached the top of the stairs where one arm was floppily raised to press the bell before proceeding hippety-hoppity, lippety-loppety down the stairs and out of sight. Of one thing I was certain, his exit was no doing of mine.

"And the rest of you." said the brown hatted lady.

"This ain't our stop." Someone piped up.

"It is now." she said, quietly pleasant and she looked up. They were stupid these boys but not that stupid. Something must have looked out at them then which made any argument pointless. A glance out the window as we pulled away, showed a less than vociferous gathering at the bus-shelter. Sheepishly subdued I think would describe it best, with the exception of Pock-marked who was waving his burnt hand around and doing a bit of pain-induced hopping.

I moved forward, drawn implacably and sat on the edge of the seat across the aisle from her. My heart was thumping so hard in my ears I thought if she spoke I wouldn't hear her. I knew exactly what I'd witnessed, but still doubted. She didn't so much as acknowledge me and I couldn't read her at all, her mind was totally silent, a smooth-surfaced, impenetrable grey against and around which, I slid helplessly. I don't know why but I reached out my hand to her, she moved away fractionally, avoiding the touch – I felt like a kicked puppy.

"Can we talk?" I ventured.

"No." No dithering there then, indeed she'd speared her wool decisively with her needles, stowed the knitting in a capacious, battered suede bag and was rising to leave the bus.

"What's your name?" I said. Of all the hundreds of questions jostling that was, without doubt, the silliest and least vital. She looked at me, heavy lidded eyes muddied by the artificial lighting of the bus. A thin, narrow lipped, arrogantly high cheekboned face. She rose.

"Peacock." she said, "Miss."

"I'm ..."

"I know." And I felt her sweep briefly and thoroughly through my mind. She was pepperminty cool, sharp-green and fresh and she moved through my carefully nurtured defences as though they were non-existent. She nodded once, more to herself than me in acknowledgement of something, God knows what, she certainly wasn't giving anything away. And then she was moving swiftly and surprisingly gracefully down the stairs. I watched her from the window as she walked briskly away, her camel coat orangey in the street-light, head bent against the November evening chill. She didn't look back.

When I got home and recounted the tale, slightly modified to ameliorate parental alarm, they said they were positive I was mistaken. There was no doubt, my father said, filling his pipe, that those yobs came on strong but my Miss Peacock was probably a teacher or something similar and well used to dealing with troublemakers. A firm reprimand and somebody standing up to them was probably all they'd needed and I shouldn't let my imagination run away with me. And, my mother added sharply, perhaps today's unpleasant experience would bring home the sense of the sitting near the conductor rule. Unsatisfied, I reluctantly put the incident to the back of my mind and pretty soon there were other matters to claim my attention, but I knew what I'd seen and sensed.

CHAPTER TEN

A two-page letter in a brown windowed envelope franked Department of Education was the first intimation we had of The Survey. The DoE letter was accompanied by another from Miss Macpharlane, pointing out that whilst involvement was purely voluntary, only a relatively small number of pupils from the top year of our junior school had been selected. Indeed only a few schools had been chosen to submit candidates in the first place, and it could be nothing but beneficial were some of our children to participate in this ambitious project.

It seemed that a range of high academic achievers from all over the British Isles were being screened for selection and those chosen would become part of an ongoing educational and sociological study, the like and scale of which had never been attempted before. Taken from different economic, ethnic and social backgrounds and having recently passed the Eleven Plus exams, progress would be charted every four years from now on, throughout secondary school and into further education or jobs. Miss Macpharlane was at pains to emphasise that whilst participation did require an ongoing commitment, once selected, involvement was predicted to be just a day or two every few years.

My mother and father were not happy, not happy at all. As far as they were concerned, the less surveying anybody did of me, the better. On the other hand, they didn't have a worthy excuse for my non-participation. With misgivings they reluctantly signed the consent form, reassuring me and each other that of the several thousand children involved, chances of my being picked as one of the ongoing group, were extremely remote and all the more so if I kept a low profile!

Several weeks later, packed lunch bag in hand and last minute exhortations hissed in my ear, I climbed the steps of the coach for the trip to the test centre in Oxford. There were, in addition to Elizabeth and myself, only five others from our school and whilst she and I stuck together, we soon lost sight of the others as children scrambled for seats in each of the three coaches assembled for the journey. I imagine there must have been around a couple of hundred of us all told, from schools all over London and on that blue-skied, cloud-studded day tagged on the end of a squally April, an outing atmosphere prevailed even amongst the half dozen or so accompanying teaching staff – after all a day off school is a day off school.

The journey from the terminal in Swiss Cottage took about an hour and a half, enlivened by a sing-song and some regrettably early investigation of lunch boxes. Just around the time we were starting to get bored, our coaches which had managed to travel in convoy the whole way turned through some open, impressively high, wrought iron gates. They trundled and bounced down a longish, winding drive bordered by high hedges through which we glimpsed lawns and flowerbeds and then jerked to a stop like well-trained circus elephants, one behind the other where the drive widened into a circular, gravelled area with a fountain in the centre that disappointingly wasn't working. We'd stopped in front of an imposing, red-brick, multi-windowed building which even to my untrained eye had a pleasing symmetry only marred by a large, contemporary, glass and concrete extension which seemed to have attached itself to the left hand side and back of the building with no rhyme or reason. To the other side of the front doors and also looking as if they so didn't belong, was a row of three, extremely large, grey-walled portakabins, each with half a dozen steps leading up to a closed door.

We descended with relief, from the now stuffy coaches in a rowdy crowd and there was a fair bit of disorganised milling while abandoned blazers, coats or lunchboxes were reunited with careless owners. Then we were chivvied into a two by two crocodile and led through the high, oak double-fronted doors. Whilst the building had that unmistakeable institutional smell, rubber shoes, floor wax and elderly cooked cabbage, it still trailed traces of former glory. To our right an impressively sweeping, elaborately-bannistered staircase soared to a balconied landing whilst to the left, off the entrance hall area was a series of highly polished wooden doors gleaming in brightness shed from a stained-glass sky-light high above us. At the back of the hall there was a counter-style reception desk manned by two women. It all seemed to be very well organised, each teacher being issued with safety pins and paper labels to distribute to their charges. These, bearing our names and schools, were to be pinned to our uniforms and not, repeat not, removed until we were back on our coaches at the end of the day.

As we waited for tardy badge-pinners, my eye was caught by a movement on the landing above. Looking down on the controlled chaos was a slim young woman with milk-chocolate coloured skin. She looked startlingly exotic in those surroundings in a flame-coloured, full-length silky dress, shiftingly spotlighted by the coloured shards of light from the skylight. Her black hair was braided thick and high on her head and a hoop of gold earring swung against an elegantly defined cheekbone in an oval face.

She stood motionless, face impassive, leaning gently against the waist high balustrade, eyes moving slowly over us. In our regulation uniforms of greys, blacks and browns we must have looked a pretty dull bunch. For a moment I thought her gaze fastened on me as I gazed up and I smiled awkwardly, embarrassed to have been caught staring, but there was no acknowledgement so perhaps I was mistaken. My attention was momentarily distracted as the chattering died down and we were shepherded towards one of the doors off the entrance hall. Filing in, I glanced back, she was making her way gracefully down the stairs, hand lightly on the banister, back very straight. As she reached the bottom I saw the slim white stick extended in her other hand, tapping the ground before her.

CHAPTER ELEVEN

It's always illuminating to look back on any experience with hindsight. The Survey, even viewed retrospectively was comprehensive, clever, well devised and should have been extremely successful and ultimately productive. That it wasn't was directly due to some unscheduled interference, the existence and extent of which was never fully appreciated by the powers that be, nor by the gentleman responsible for creating and implementing the whole shebang. Given his somewhat alarming propensities, this was probably all to the good.

Dr Karl W. Dreck had a curtly clipped South African accent, flat oily black hair and a smile which aimed but failed to project an easy charm, probably because it never reached grey-washed, sandy-lashed eyes. His face in repose lacked expression making the smile all the more disconcerting when it appeared, as if an unseen hand was working an on/off button. His larger than life image, whirringly projected on a screen at the front of the large room with blind-shrouded windows where we'd been seated in cross-legged rows, didn't do a great deal to put anyone at their ease.

In a short jerky film, his voice booming from a loudspeaker, he welcomed us to what we learned was called Newcombe Hall and told us how fortunate we were to have this opportunity of participating in one of the most ambitious social studies ever undertaken in Britain. However, he went on, whilst some of us would be picked to continue, many would be eliminated for one reason or another although, (pause, smile,) this was in no way a personal rejection, merely an endeavour to obtain as complete a cross section of the population as possible. He said that he and his staff – shot of a group of people in white coats, also smiling – wanted us to truly enjoy all the various tests and games they had lined up for us today.

Accomplished though he undoubtedly was in his field, Dreck was never what you might call a people person and his appearance, albeit onscreen, was more than enough to put a dampener on our previously rather noisy high spirits – a bit like finding Boris Karloff was going to be your party entertainer. Quieter now and with the promise of a refreshment break to follow, we were divided into alphabetically defined groups, mixing pupils from different schools so before I realised what was happening I was separated from Elizabeth and lost sight of her completely. The degree of efficiency with which this was achieved by staff members who had taken over from our accompanying teachers, spoke of long practice. I wondered how many children had already passed through the high oak front doors to earn a place in or be eliminated from The Survey.

Individual groups, each headed by a white-coated member of staff were being led at a swift pace from the entrance hall towards the back of the building, and mine was taken up a flight of stairs to a corridor of numbered rooms, amongst which we were distributed. The room I entered with about six other children was itself sub-divided by blue curtained screens to form a couple of semi-private cubicles. On the opposite wall was a row of chairs on which it was indicated we should sit although, even as we settled ourselves, a couple of names were called and those summoned were shepherded to each of the cubicles from whence soon came a rising and falling hum of questions and answers.

I didn't have long to wait before my name came up, a relief, because I was next to a boy whose personal habits left something to be desired in the flatulence department. Seated inside one of the curtained cubicles was a plump, cheerfully brisk, white-coated, frizzily blond lady,

"Call me Mo, dear," pen poised over clipboard. She ran through a list of illnesses I might or might not have had, questioned me about vaccinations, weighed me on T bar scales and took my blood pressure. An unpleasant thought suddenly occurred as she enthusiastically pumped the little black bulb.

"We don't have to have a blood test do we?"

"No dear," said Mo, moving her fingers to my wrist and timing my pulse, "Probably not."

That rattled me, needles and I didn't mix. Never did, never will – I'm not even any good at sewing. The reason for this was of course pretty straightforward with a mother who hit the ground running at the mere mention of an injection. She'd always put on a brave face when it came to my childhood jabs, but as I could hear her frantically reciting the twelve times table in her head, I remained uncomforted. It was an ordeal for both of us, not to mention for the unfortunate clinic nurse who simply couldn't understand why every time she came near me, all feeling in her right hand disappeared. She dropped four hypos and her Florence Nightingale manner before my mother insisted on taking me outside for a little talk.

And so, nerve-wracked as I was by the possibility of a blood test it was with attention at half-mast that I started answering Call Me Mo's questions and it was only a change in her tone that pulled me back to the matter in hand. She was looking even more cheerful than when we'd started, like someone who's lost sixpence and found half-a-crown,

"Jolly good," she said. "Well done you. How about another few sections?" We'd been doing what she called a word association test. She, giving me a category and me supplying the first word that came into my head. Mo was now looking down at her clipboard and then expectantly up at me,

"Flower," she repeated, pen quivering. She was looking at a small sketched rose next to the word and it dawned, belatedly that it might not be the brightest move in the world for me to get these all correct, which is what I'd obviously, absent-mindedly been doing. This actually might not come under the low profile my parents had advocated.

"Daisy."

"Nursery rhyme." She was looking at a black sheep.

"Jack and Jill."

"Item of clothing."

"Trousers." I said, rising above the socks.

She had my full attention now as I was uncomfortably aware I had hers. We ran through some twenty or so more items and I made sure that not one of them did I get right. There was silence for a moment or two while she looked back over the form, before downing her pen and giving me a puzzled look. Could I, she asked, sit tight for a tick or two, she'd be right back. Within a few moments she popped her head back round the blue curtain, beckoning me to follow. We exchanged our cubicle and classroom for another, further down the corridor where with a little nod of her head she handed me and my forms over to another white-coated, altogether more intimidating individual called Iris.

Iris, beetle-browed and unsmiling had obviously been issued with instructions to be friendly and not frighten the children but was having a struggle. More questions, this time on circles, squares and triangles – if this was an example of the fun time promised by Dr. Dreck, we'd been short-changed I reflected. I think Iris was getting paid by the question because she moved at a pretty nifty pace. I found the easiest way to answer was to opt each time for the symbol to the left of the one she was looking at on the page and once I'd established this rather cunning m.o. we bounded through the questions like things possessed, stopping breathlessly at the end of some thirty or so.

Iris looked up at me and I belatedly realised maybe I hadn't been quite so clever after all. In that same instant someone spoke inside my head,

"Idiot!" they said and it suddenly felt as if my head had been swaddled in a thick, black, blanket. I suppose I'd never realised quite how much my extra senses supplied until suddenly they weren't supplying any more. Sound instantly became flatter with no resonance of thought beyond, sight was only surface, where normally there was depth. I searched Iris's frowning, increasingly confused face, her expression probably mirroring mine, and could sense – nothing. She was talking, but in the grip of a rising tide of panic, she might as well have been speaking in tongues. My hands and feet were freezing, my heart was thumping and something strange had happened to my breathing, I hoped I wasn't going to have another of Nigel's asmatacks. I broke out in chilly sweat. I didn't think it could get any worse. I was wrong. The voice in my head was back.

"Idiot," it repeated irritably, "Calm down." Calm down, *calm down*? I was as far from calm as it was possible to be. My surroundings were acquiring a deeply unpleasant black outline and I could feel blood draining from my head in a sickly rush. Iris jumped up from her chair, grabbed the back of my neck in a firm hand and forced my head down on to my lap. This wasn't, I felt, an improvement. I struggled weakly and from a million miles away Iris asked someone to fetch a glass of water quickly.

"Bit over-dramatic?" inquired the voice in my head conversationally. I jerked convulsively, Iris jumped correspondingly and the glass of water someone had handed her soaked both of us.

"Oh get a grip." The snapped, inside-my-head command, started to bring me back to what few senses I had left and clambering down from panic stricken heights to just plain shocked, I realised I, of all people, surely should be open to the unusual. It was just that I'd always listened when I chose, been the one in control, now here was someone invading my space. Iris, a towel in hand, reappeared and started mopping up, I could see she wasn't having a good morning either.

"Sorry." I muttered.

"Not to worry." She said, obviously not meaning it. "What on earth made you jump like that?"

"Nothing."

"Nothing?" I nodded, I was determined not to so much as twitch at any further internal comment, after all it was hearing voices that landed Joan of Arc in the soup. It was so strange though, not to be feeling anything extra, and I suddenly realized that this must be what everyone else felt all the time. This was Normal. How disconcerting. How extraordinarily quiet. Iris nudged me,

"I said, how do you feel now?"

"Sorry, yes, better thank you. It must have been the coach journey – I get travel sick, but better now, honest."

"Best get you checked out anyway, be on the safe side." Checked out? Things definitely didn't seem to be staying low-profile, I quaked at what my parents would say. We left the relative security of the blue curtain and I followed Iris's broad beamed stride and damply discoloured Hush Puppies as she led the way downstairs again. Trotting a little to keep up with her, I felt clumsy and uncoordinated, bumping into the wall a couple of times and finding it oddly difficult to keep my balance.

Iris took me to an open, airy, glass-roofed extension at the back of the building where she opened the door on a brightly painted waiting room already containing several anxious looking parents with children in assorted sizes who were being kept amused with coloured building bricks and picture books. At our entrance, everyone looked up expectantly and a cheerful receptionist, working through a pile of forms and seemingly oblivious of the surrounding noise, nodded at Iris and smiled at me,

"Hello there. For the Doctor? Won't keep you a tick. Have a seat."

Iris continued to pat her damp skirt and shoes while we waited. I could see I'd made a firm friend there. A dough-faced baby stared at me from the safety of its mother's lap, I smiled, but it looked away expressionlessly. A door at the end of the room opened on a thin, red-eyed woman, carrying a child, seemingly far too big and heavy for the support her arms could provide. Dr. Drek, instantly recognisable from the earlier film, came out with her, patted her encouragingly on the shoulder and stroked the child's head briefly. In his spotless white coat, he cut a thinly elongated figure with disproportionately large hands and head. I instinctively liked him even less in person than on screen. To the couple who'd started to gather bags and child at his appearance, he smiled and gave a small apologetic bow,

"Yes indeed, you are next but may I possibly keep you just one moment longer?" Then to Iris, "Thank you. I'll see she gets back to the others." And to me, "This way, young lady."

There was a mahogany desk in the middle of his consulting room and on the walls an uneasy combination of nursery rhyme illustration interspersed with diagrammatic illustrations of the brain. In one corner of the room a high, brown leather examination couch was next to a movable screen on wheels which partially concealed a couple of instrument trolleys and a small sink. Closing the door behind him, Dr Dreck leaned back against it and looked at me for just a moment longer than was comfortable.

"So." he said, "Stella?"

"'Sright."

"Iris tells me, there was a dizzy spell?" clipped accent and rising intonation at the end of each sentence made question out of statement. He indicated the couch, "Please."

Perched high on the slippery leather surface, legs dangling. I felt totally at a loss. I was unable to read the situation in any way other than with inadequate eyes and ears but even so, I could sense there was more going on here than there should have been and my stomach clenched with unease. The door re-opened and a woman smoothed into the room. She was tall, nearly as tall as him and he must have been well over six foot. Thin also and tight-featured with high-bunned ash-blond hair and a white blouse, starched to stiffness and buttoned tight under her chin. He introduced her without looking round,

"My assistant, Miss Merry." She gave no response to my polite smile which didn't really surprise me – hers wasn't a mouth made for warmth.

With Miss Merry gliding between couch and instrument table – I never worked out how she moved like that, she certainly had feet like everyone else, they just seemed to operate differently – Dr Dreck took my blood pressure again, my pulse, checked my eyes and ears then had a go at my knees and elbows with a small hammer. From my vantage point high on the couch, I had an unattractive view as he bent, of thinning black hair overlaying pink scalp and caught the faintest whiff of strong aftershave.

He kept darting glances at me, searching my face for some kind of reaction other than the one he was getting and our gazes kept clashing in mutual bafflement. Finally, he straightened, tapping the small hammer sharply in the palm of his hand.

"Well, no obvious problems to account for the dizziness. How do you feel now?"

"Very well, thank you." I said politely. "It was probably just the coach journey." He nodded, not really listening and moved over to his desk with Miss Merry. I couldn't quite see what they were looking at but I thought they were the forms Iris had been completing earlier. I could have kicked myself. Something in my stupidly glib responses to the tests had set alarm bells ringing, although that in no way accounted for the black-out still going on in my head. They talked for a while longer in undertones, of which I only caught the occasional word before he turned back to me.

"Do you think," he asked "You could tackle just a few more of our tests?" I nodded, I didn't think I had much choice and it would be a relief to leave his unsettling presence.

"Right you are," he lifted me down, "Off you go now." I obediently followed the smooth-moving, inscrutable Miss Merry.

CHAPTER TWELVE

Miss Merry wasted no time on small talk, a relief as I needed all my breath to keep up with her. It felt, one way and another that in the course of that morning I'd done a great deal of walking from one place to another. I followed her down a flight of narrow stairs which led steeply from the older part of the building. There were no windows down here and we moved down a short artificially lit corridor, at the end of which she hauled open a heavy door which swished silently closed behind us. Through a second similar door and then we were in an enormous space, one side of which was taken up with about six small glass isolation booths, the sort Hughie Green put people in to Double Their Money. On the other side of the room one whole wall had been glassed over, floor to ceiling to create a separate area in which I could see three, seated, head-phoned people talking into microphones in front of them.

Several of the booths were occupied by children, also with head-phones, facing the back wall of their booth. There must have been a lot of soundproofing because other than a low level sibilant hiss which I took to be some sort of air conditioning, you could have heard a pin – or in my case, a heart – drop. The worm of unease in my stomach, coiled and uncoiled. I really didn't like this set up which seemed infinitely more scientific than the cosily curtained cubicles in which I'd started my day. These elimination tests were proving more uncomfortable by the minute.

Miss Merry ushered me towards a vacant booth and told me what they wanted me to do. In the oddly artificial atmosphere her voice took on a metallic quality. The door to the booth was thick and heavy, like a phone box. Sliding onto the plastic coated bench, in front of me was a shelf holding head-phones and inbuilt was a console with three rounded buttons – red, green and black. Apparently I simply had to press whichever colour I chose, every time I heard a bleeped signal. Facing the grey featureless back panel, nose stinging from the disinfectant saturated cloth with which she'd wiped the headphones before handing them to me, I could see and hear nothing until low static told me the headphones were now live.

Obediently then, in response to irregular beeps I began to press the coloured buttons. My choices were truly completely random and because I was still totally extra-senseless, I had no glimpse or grasp of what was going on. What I did know was it was hot and airlessly uncomfortable in the booth and the irregularity of the beeps was surprisingly unsettling.

Nerves were cramping my stomach, I could feel my palms becoming sweaty and the headphones pressed uncomfortably tight on either side of my head so blood thumped loudly in my ears, counter-pointing the beeps. Panic was heading back in. What if I lost control? What would happen if I suddenly found myself floating off my seat in the booth? True there wasn't room to swing a cat, but a demented Strange person like myself could just keep going up and down, up and down …

"Enough! Calm down. Don't talk. Concentrate on what you're supposed to be doing and get a grip."

"But … "

"I *said* don't talk, you can be seen. Top right hand corner, a camera, *don't look*." I ripped my gaze away. "When they get you out, ask for the toilet." And the voice was gone again, leaving just beeps and disinfectant. I don't know how long I was pressing buttons. It felt like hours. I was cramped and sweaty when Miss Merry finally opened the door and let in some blessedly fresher air and it wasn't only because I was following instructions that I asked for the toilet. Miss Merry, receiving my request with the disdain of a being not troubled by such considerations gave directions. As I hauled open the first of the heavy doors, I glanced back. She was conferring with others in the glassed in section.

I was thankful, once in the toilet that the visiting voice had the social sensitivity to lay low until I felt able to chat.

"Right," it announced, while I was washing my hands, making me jump in spite of myself.

"Time's short. You need to know what's going on. You make your own choices then. Clear?" As mud. I hoped she – I was pretty sure she was a she – was going to elaborate.

"Close your eyes."

"Why?"

"Because I say so – need to concentrate, otherwise I see what you're seeing." I obligingly closed my eyes, wet hands still suspended over the sink. I probably looked as if I'd opted for a nap, mid-wash, still that was as good a story as any, certainly more believable than what was really going on.

"O.K. This whole set-up is government funded. Stated aim to select and chart progress of high achieving children over a period of years. Assessing and evaluating external influences – cultural, political, financial etc.

"I know all that." I interjected out loud.

"Shut up."

"Right."

"What they're really looking for is psi factor."

"Psi factor?"

"Like you and me." I knew it! I knew there were more. I was facing the mirror and could see my face flush with excitement.

"Eyes – shut. And if you must talk aloud, keep it down."

"Are there a lot?"

"Didn't think you were unique, did you?"

"No, but ..."

"Lots of people have latent ability but every now and then, genes, chance, whatever, sparks something off and you get oddities like us."

"How did you know – about me I mean?"

"Just listen can't you. No questions." she may have been big on psi but not on patience. "When you started to panic earlier, you blasted the place down, could hardly miss you. You, and others like you are what this project is really all about."

"I don't understand." although of course, in that instant, I did, perfectly.

"Exactly." She said. I didn't like that, didn't like her reading my mind, the exchange of ideas before they were fully formed, uncomfortably intimate. For a brief moment I sensed her amusement before she blacked me out again.

"Taste of your own medicine? Anyway, your choice. Get involved, don't get involved, I can only give you facts."

"Facts?"

"Good God Almighty child, must you repeat every word I say? Listen – Russia and China are way, way ahead on this, been at it for years, huge sums gone into research. The West has a lot of catching up to do, although America's got its act together now, they've set up something in Washington DC. You're a valuable commodity and there's a lot at stake. If they confirm what they suspect – you really messed up those tests – they can't afford to leave you alone. You're good, stronger than many I've come across. They'll want you, want you to work with them, want to find out what makes you what you are."

"They can't force me." I said. She carried on as if I hadn't interrupted but irritation filtered through, "Maybe, maybe not. Look, in the eighteen months or so this's been going, they've only found a couple of adepts, they've lost several others."

"Lost?"

"I got to them before he did." a cruelly accurate caricature of the unctuous Dr Dreck oozed briefly through my head,

"Is he ... ?"

"No and pretty sour about it, give his right arm for what you've got. Don't underestimate him, he's clever, persuaded the government here to fund him for at least five years, despite the fact he had to leave South Africa in a hurry – some experiments went very wrong."

"Experiments?" We were fast advancing into areas I wanted nothing to do with and momentarily I wondered hopefully if maybe I'd eaten something that disagreed with me and was hallucinating this whole episode.

"Forget it, you're not Alice in Wonderland and this is no fairytale." There, she was doing it again, the woman had no manners.

"Pay attention, not much time. He thinks – and he's convinced others, people who hold the purse strings for these sorts of project – that the capability of individuals with even mild psi ability can be boosted with drugs. Sometimes it can."

"Sometimes?"

"Sometimes it can't. Meet Peter." A hospital bed, a boy, my age I thought, hooked up to an array of monitors, drips, tubes. Eyelids half-open, dead-flesh white face, mouth drooping on one side, bubble of spittle inflating, deflating with each machine-forced breath.

"And this is Peter's mind." she said and showed me – nothing, a slate wiped clean.

"What happened?"

"A drug they used – didn't have quite the desired effect."

"Will he be … ?"

"Anybody's guess. There's more. Got to be quick." Indeed she was getting fainter, fading like a radio tuner going off station. Suddenly I didn't want her to go.

"Marina Daskanyeva, seven, Moscow." She hauled my attention back. Not quite in focus, but clear enough. I knew what I was seeing was a memory, something she'd herself seen in the past. A pretty, round-faced, blond-plaited child, concentrating intently, upper teeth pinioning lower lip, eyes narrowed. She was watching something scampering around a wire cage – a rat I thought it might be. I could feel the intensity of the child's concentration folding in and around itself. Then the rat blew apart. Literally. Bloodily raw bits, spreading in slow motion, seemingly filling the cage before they began to settle in grisly piles. I gagged, opened my eyes quickly, but the taste of the picture wouldn't go.

"Powerful stuff, huh?" soft now in my head. "It's not all like that you know – constructive, destructive, depends how it's used."

"I don't want to be involved." I said miserably, shaken to the core and beyond. I knew, with instinctive certainty that what I'd seen done, I could also do – it wasn't a pleasant thought.

"Who are you anyway?" I demanded, fear generating belligerence. "Why should I trust you?"

"I'm not asking you to. Make your own decisions. Your life – do what you want. Use what you've got, don't use it, entirely up to you. I've told you what you need to know, tried to stop you giving yourself away, although frankly, you've made a real pig's ear of things so far – they know something doesn't add up, but maybe we've muddied the waters enough to put them off. Remember, if you want to lie low – random, always random answers. They can't catch you unless you let them, but they will try to trip you up. And try not to blast out so, you're giving me a splitting head – and trust? Don't. Not anybody. Good luck." and then she simply wasn't present any more, just a faint echo taste like lemon-sherbet fizz although that too disappeared, so quickly, I couldn't be sure I hadn't imagined it. Trust no-one – great, I'd just met a psychic version of Grandma.

CHAPTER THIRTEEN

I was frustrated – and angry. I had questions by the truckload. There was so much I didn't understand and what I did was enough to scare me rigid. With her going, my world had snapped into focus and back to normal. I was also feeling – probably for the first time in my comfortably secure existence – vulnerable, scared and way out of my depth. I was still standing with my hands over the sink, when the door opened.

"You took your time young lady." If Miss Merry was aiming for jocular, she missed by a mile, "Going to be all day?"

"Sorry," I mumbled, "Tummy upset." and dried my hands. As I did, I tried to read her but I was too nervous to concentrate. Was she, I wondered, the warning voice, she was certainly snappy enough but I didn't think so, she had an acrid, dry taste, very different from Irritable's. She was looking at me intently and I adopted what I hoped was a suitable, *Psychic? Not-me!* face as I again followed her rigid white coated back.

She led the way back along the corridor but turned off to take us up a different staircase. I could feel an odd, fine trembling in my arms and legs and was acutely aware I hadn't the faintest idea how to keep my mind under wraps. My concerns had always been to shield myself from others, vice versa had never arisen. Miss Merry was talking over her shoulder.

"Sorry?" I hadn't heard a word,

"The others," she repeated, "Are just finishing a session, so you'll stay with me until it's time for lunch. Have you found your day interesting?" Interesting wasn't quite how I'd put it and a one on one session with Miss Congeniality was way down my list of wants but I mumbled politely as I followed her into a small office. Scrupulously tidy and sharply redolent of the same disinfectant she'd used on the headphones. She waved me to a chair on one side of the desk and produced a few comics which she said I might like, while she moved to the other side, opening a drawer to extract a blue, elastic-bound folder. I felt twitchy and alert on any number of levels, trying to catch, make sense of and steer clear of whatever was going on. My choice, Irritable had said, well, there was certainly no way I wanted to follow the route trodden by Peter and the Russian girl. Did I doubt what I'd been shown? No, actually not for one single second. She'd said trust no-one but she'd been in my head and I'd sensed enough to know, whatever she'd shown me, she believed implicitly to be the truth.

Miss Merry had her head bent over her file and I, to all intents and purposes was engrossed in a Bunty comic, when there was a subtle change in the room. I kept my eyes down. She'd turned a page within the folder and was looking at a series of photographs, six of them reproduced on the page in stark black and white. She was concentrating unnaturally hard and even in my confusion I realised they must be from some medical textbook, they were like nothing I'd ever seen before, certainly nothing I ever wanted to see again. For just a few seconds, before I shielded, I shared, a partially dissected baby on a slab and another unforgiving shot of an infant with a grossly malformed skull – *Anencephalic* – the label beside the picture was as sharp as the image and both etched themselves irretrievably into my brain. Merry was looking across at me now, assessing my reaction and the sun opaqued the lenses of her wire-framed glasses, turning her gaze dead and blank. For the second time that day I felt blood draining but if the stakes were as high as I'd been told, I must not react. I glanced up from my comic, as if surprised to catch her eye and smiled, polite and expectant.

"Is it lunchtime?" There was a pause before she snapped her folder closed on its unforgettable content and rose abruptly, looking at her watch, her face expressionless. "I'll take you down now."

Children and teachers were spreading noisily out across the grass of the gardens and as Merry and I emerged from the building, I took in gulps of the fresh air wanting to rid my nose of the disinfectant, my mind of what I'd seen. The green ran the whole length of the back of the building, circled and split by a stone-paved path bordered by well-trimmed hedges. The spring sunshine was warm, the crowd noisy and the outing spirit had resurfaced with the promise of food. It seemed to me I was the only one stiff and stale with sweat and fright.

I spotted Elizabeth and some others from our school and went slowly to join them. Of the group, it appeared I was the only who'd been singled out for the boothed room. Maybe, they said, with envy I was going to be picked for the survey and even Elizabeth, used to effortlessly scoring highest marks in any test, was intrigued and slightly put out both by my selection and my monosyllabic responses to her questions.

Merry was now nowhere to be seen and I retrieved my lunch bag from the diminished pile and paid lip service to the contents before scrunching it up and handing it to one of the teachers, who had a large plastic bag for the purpose. We had about an hour's grace before the white-coated staff reclaimed us to muttered groans. The general consensus seemed to be this wasn't turning out to be half as much fun as had been promised. We were again split into groups, some people shepherded back into the main building, others, including Elizabeth and myself, directed to the Portakabins at the front of the building. As we all went our different ways. I spotted my old friend 'Call me Mo', who found time to give me a friendly wave and my other friend Iris, who didn't.

Surprisingly more spacious than it looked from the outside, within the cabin were half a dozen rectangular tables set well apart, with chairs either side. Three boys and three girls were allocated to each table, in the midst of which sat an outsize dice. Merry, clipboard in hand was, I noted with apprehension, taking our group, accompanied by an assistant, someone I hadn't seen before. Gliding smoothly to the front of the room, she took up position in front of the blackboard and such was her chilly presence that chatter, laughter and chair scraping promptly died.

"I expect you're tired after this morning's efforts," she smiled tightly. "So, we're starting this afternoon with a game." She paused, if she was waiting for a hurrah, it was unforthcoming. "Each team, girls against boys, is going to try and get the dice off the table. But, no hands – you have to blow." She puckered lips and blew an example in case we were in any doubt. "First team to get their dice off the opposite side of the table and onto the floor gets the prize. Now," she paused and looked around, "Everyone, hands behind backs."

The dice were heavier than they looked. With the best will in the world and enough co-ordinated huffing and puffing to blow the house down, it was well-nigh impossible to move them. It was obvious to me, full of recently acquired knowledge, what it was they were hoping some of us would do to compensate. Flushed faces around me bore testimony to effort if not results and there were howls of accusation when one set of boys, using their initiative and not their hands, tilted the table with their knees. I couldn't always see Merry as she moved around the room, but sensing her fish-eye on me more than I liked, decided it couldn't do any harm and might take the heat off to introduce the odd red herring.

Continuing to puff energetically and non-productively, I turned my attention to the dice on the table next but one to ours, giving it a hefty nudge or two and sending it toppling over the edge of the table. As it hit the floor, three triumphant girls shot to their feet in excitement. Then an uneasy thought occurred. Might that not have been such a cunning plan after all? Might one of those girls right now be attracting rather more of the Merry interest than would be comfortable? I couldn't risk that. So, working to a somewhat muddled theory based on needles in haystacks, I did a swift round of the room. In no time at all, three other tables were diceless too.

The room descended into noisy chaos and excitement with Merry having to raise her voice to make herself heard and get everyone re-seated. Tight-lipped, clipboard rammed to chest, she surveyed us for a moment in silence. Someone, she suspected, was making a monkey out of her and although I kept my eyes studiously down, I thought she looked at me a little longer than the rest and, for a moment, I picked up her confusion and the strength of her cold anger. Merry with the laughing eyes was a scientifically-minded individual and for her, there always had to be pattern, consistency, logic and reason even within the field in which she was working. Today wasn't panning out that way and anything that didn't fit her parameters disturbed the order of things, provoking a violent frustration, the force of which I sensed, alarmed even her. As she moved her head, I could see where sharp, starched white shirt collar had scored an angry red mark below her chin. I hoped it was sore.

"Well," she unclenched her jaw, "I don't think we've ever had quite so much success on that one before. Thank you everybody. Now, Mrs Metcalfe," she nodded and her assistant turned to gather up an armful of boxes from a pile in the corner of the room, "Is going to give each table a Snakes and Ladders game board. We'll do girls against boys again as you're already sitting that way. Yes," she snapped in answer to a raised arm, "Of course you can use your hands this time."

Now, here was another fine dilemma I'd got myself into, what exactly were they looking for this time? Would it be a good idea to lie low and do nothing or should I rig some scores across the room? All action seemed fraught with possibly un-visualised traps. By this time I'd acquired a solid headache, the uneven rhythm of discomfort that was the familiar follow-on from too much activity on the cerebral front. As I dithered, Miss Merry glided to the door in response to a knock, it was the young woman I'd seen earlier on the stairs – longer ago it seemed, than the few hours it really was. Miss M put a hand on her arm as she entered and they stood conversing quietly for a moment.

It was hard to tell her age, anywhere between eighteen to late twenties and she was smaller than I'd thought, shorter by a head than the older woman. Slim, finely boned, holding herself as if to balance the mass and weight of the hair dressed high on her head. The material of her dress, close up, was richly gold and orange, the colours changing where they reflected the light as she moved. Cut away at the shoulder it left narrow arms bare except for several thin gold bangles that jangled musically as she moved.

Her face in profile was as expressionless as Merry's, together, these two must be the life and soul of any staff do. When she turned slightly I thought she looked – carved – is the best way I can describe it, with the fine line of her forehead moulding, seamlessly arrogant into nose and mouth. I wondered why she wasn't wearing dark glasses like other sightless people I'd seen. In fact her eyes, depth-filled and dark seemed focused not on the woman now earnestly speaking to her but on a far-beyond point. Merry finished what she had to say and the younger woman nodded, murmured something and turning, swept her sightless (were they sightless?) eyes over the room.

Everyone of course had stopped what they were doing, it was impossible not to stare she just seemed so oddly out of place in the pedestrian grey setting of the Portakabin. Holding the white stick before her, she began now to move slowly round the perimeter of the room. It was quite clear to me why she was there and who she was looking for. I knew now that what I was, was more than just a socially embarrassing problem for my parents.

People had turned back to the Snakes and Ladders but the whole pace of things had slowed, all surreptitiously watching the young woman slowly circling. Every now and then she would pause by a child, her head slightly tilted while the object of her attention sat wide-eyed and very still, and then she'd move on. I didn't know whether to try and scan, but the very act of doing so might draw the attention of the 'diviner' for I had no doubts at all that's what she was. In the next instant I realised I was being a fool, of course I could be heard, even if I wasn't doing anything, how else had Irritable found me? Desperately I tried to haul everything inside my head and blank my mind. For a moment I thought I'd succeeded – a cat smugly hiding under the curtain, with tail twitching in full view. The woman paused by our table, turning her face to me across the heads of the three boys sitting opposite. She couldn't see me, but she flooded my head.

"Hallo," she said aloud, a low voice, surprising from such a small frame, "We bumped into each other earlier didn't we?" I sat mute, sweaty and gawping.

"You were waiting your turn at some tests." she reminded me politely and, with fizzy lemon-sherbet recognition, came a familiar irritable snap in my head.

"Answer me – *aloud. Now!*"

"Ah yes," I said, nodding my head up and down. Turning to Merry with a slight smile, she answered the unasked question,

"Soap," she said, "This young lady uses my favourite, Morny, Lily of the Valley, I'd recognise it anywhere. Right?" She raised an eyebrow in my direction, I continued to nod, then realised belatedly she couldn't see.

"Yes, yes, that's right. My mum always buys it." I had not the faintest idea what soap we used, but if she said it was Morny, then Morny was fine with me.

"You had a bit of a funny turn – feeling OK now?" she asked,

"Yes, thank you." like a nodding toy dog in the back of a car on a bumpy road I was having a terrible problem with my head.

"Good," she said and made to move on. Miss Merry, grasped her arm and asked a soft question, her eyes on me and I saw the woman shake her head and shrug. Miss Merry said something else, sharply and from where I was sitting I could see white indentations where her nails were digging into the flesh she held. For a moment the younger woman was still, then gently but firmly she lifted the spitefully restraining hand from her arm,

"No, I'm sorry." She said, "Nothing." And she moved on.

Baffled, but emboldened and, as fright receded, dangerously nosy, I reached out tentatively and was slapped down hard, a sharp mental cuff round the ear.

"Scat."

"One question?"

"Quickly."

"Who are you?"

"My name's Glory Isaacs."

"No, I meant …"

"I know what you meant."

"You work with them? I thought … I don't understand. Why?"

"Go home, forget about today."

"But …"

"I said shut it."

"Right."

Shadowed by Merry, Glory continued her deliberate circumnavigation of the room, once or twice she stopped and spoke to people but I didn't think it was politic to stare. When I looked up again she was at the door. I saw her shake her head firmly in answer to more questions and then she turned to go. She couldn't see the expression on the face of the lovely Miss M. – but maybe she knew anyway. They say the eyes are the windows of the soul, for a moment as Merry turned back to the room those eyes met mine and I felt an atavistic shiver run all the way up my spine and lodge jarringly in the back of my head. This was one lady not to be on the wrong side of and unless I was mistaken, that's exactly where I was and I certainly didn't need any special powers to tell me that in the Merry popularity stakes, Glory wasn't lagging far behind.

After the drama of preceding events, the rest of that day was anti-climactic, even though about twenty of us were kept behind after two of the coaches and the majority of children had left. We were required to do a further hour-long session of what they called Rorschach Tests, which involved looking at splodges and saying what they looked like. I studiously followed the earlier-given advice, kept my answers random and ignored the images being broadcast by the members of staff with whom we were working. Despite this, I didn't relax, even a little, until we late-stayers were finally given the go ahead to clamber wearily on to the last coach and head back to London. We would be informed by letter which of us, if any, had been picked to continue.

CHAPTER FOURTEEN

There returned from Newcombe an infinitely wiser, more cautiously subdued person. Everything had suddenly moved on to a different and altogether more serious level. Grandma's pronouncements suddenly didn't seem quite so paranoid and my parents saw all their vague fears coalesce into clearly identifiable threat.

"Work harder at pretending, sweetheart." my mother demanded again and again, "Keep telling yourself you can't do … things and after a while, perhaps you won't be able to."

And I did try. After all, I wasn't stupid. At home there was a radical change of regime and foibles, tolerated over the years, were now banned completely. The phrase 'Hands, darling, hands.' became part and parcel of our lives and I woke on several occasions, sweaty from nightmare scenarios featuring slick-soled Merry, the unctuous Doctor and small animals blasted bloodily apart. Two weeks after my return, to our relief, a letter arrived informing my parents that regrettably I was not one of the pupils selected to continue on to the next stage and we blessed Glory, whoever she was, whatever her motivation.

Fright engendered by the Newcombe experience lingered, reinforcing the value of tight control. But raging hormones and the ups and downs of early teenage angst don't lend themselves to restraint. As I reached adolescence, all hell seemed to break loose. Looking back, I'm filled anew with admiration and wonder at the way my family coped, unperturbed by temper tantrums but, as always, concerned about how much might be revealed.

When I'd just turned thirteen, Dawn was seven with, it seemed, the sole aim in life of making mine a misery. One day a bicker grew into a row which escalated into a fight. My mother hot-footing into the room to haul us apart, as usual, blamed me – I was older, more responsible. Hot, bothered, scarlet faced, chest aching where my sister had punched me – I turned away in high dudgeon. It wasn't fair, she'd started it. I could feel the rise of frustration and anger. Beyond my control? Probably not at that exact point but heading there fast without any argument from me. Two books flew off my bedside table, and thwunked heavily against the far wall.

"Stop that, right now." ordered my mother. A china ornament, one of my favourites – a little bit of martyrdom creeping in maybe, rose and smashed oh so satisfyingly against the opposite wall.

"Stella." a rising note of alarm, "Enough now, you've made your point." The light in the centre of the ceiling began to sway, at first gently then faster, my mother and sister looked apprehensively upwards.

I started to cry. Not sad, simply constipated with crossness and frustration and all the feelings that come with being thirteen and sorely misunderstood. Events suddenly took off of their own accord and I temporarily, and not unwillingly, mislaid the off-button. My bedside table heaved ponderously sideways sliding alarm clock, lamp and glass of water in leisurely fashion to the floor, while a large framed poster of Sean Connery ripped sharply away from the wall to swamp the cat just emerging from a favoured position beneath my bed. Dawn, shrieking with fear-fed outrage rushed to the rescue. Connery was shaken but not stirred, unlike the cat who was patently both. Things were well and truly out of control now and what was coming out was unstoppably on its way. Around and above all three of us, crouched now in the middle of the room, swirled ever-faster, pictures, books, clothes, pillows and finally and ignominiously the cat.

I honestly didn't think I *could* stop until I saw the sharp end of the broken china Dresden lady slam sharply into Dawn's forehead. With the welling of blood and the expressions of horror on the faces of my mother and sister, I remembered the Russian girl I'd seen and what she could do. I was suddenly appalled beyond words. I'd never for one moment in all the years imagined this thing could move beyond my ability to control, become almost a separate entity. The indisputable fact that it could, was a salutary lesson that maybe I had to learn the hard way.

I made myself an Angry Box which had, in an earlier incarnation held Quality Street but now became the repository of so much more. I worked desperately hard at analysing and focusing. I had no real terms of reference but knew I had to recognise and haul back those high-voltage surges I could haul back, and channel safely to a specific point, those I couldn't. The box lies today, dented and scarred with frustrations and failures, at the back of my wardrobe, an ever-lasting reminder of and testimony to the values of self-discipline.

CHAPTER FIFTEEN

I'd passed my eleven-plus exam with flying colours, a rewarding combination in differing ratios of my ability and Elizabeth's brains and had moved on to St. Margaret's County Grammar School for Girls. In the smaller, safe environment of Junior School I'd had an assured place in the hierarchy. In this new establishment I was a somewhat nervous small fish in stiffly unyielding, brand new winter uniform, clambering daily on to the bus and heading to a vastly larger pond. In my form there was no one from my previous school and I was, frankly, unsure whether there was best friend material there at all – certainly not another Elizabeth.

For a while, things looked bleak. Everything was big and intimidating; miles of beige linoleumed corridors which confusingly all looked the same; new routines; more regulations than you could shake a fist at and a constant balance to be maintained on the horns of my own personal dilemma. I certainly knew by then the rules I had to abide by. On the other hand, I was what I was and it was no more possible for me to switch off some things than it was for others to emulate them. There were times though when I was so much more than thankful for my talents.

Once a week we had Art which stretched, God help us, over three, forty-minute periods. The two art mistresses Mrs Burrell and Miss Rawn had fiery tempers, fearsome reputations for artistic eccentricity and were spoken of in the hushed tones usually reserved for triple axe-murderers. First weekers, lined up outside the art studio for our inaugural session with Mrs Burrell, beneath regulation green overalls, several sizes too large to allow for future growth, stomachs were a-churning and knees were a-knocking.

For full ten minutes after the 9.30 bell had tolled and no need to ask for whom, we waited in quivering anticipation. At 9.40 the studio door was flung wide with enough force to hit the wall, where missing plaster chunks testified to previous impacts. In a once-upon-a-time-white now grey and paint-splattered smock, towered Mrs Burrell. Her head was haloed by bright, upstanding hennaed hair and two pairs of glasses, suspended by knotted shoelaces, bounced uneasily on the mobile shelf of her unfettered bosom.

"Well?" she barked. We all jumped, as one.

"What in hell's teeth are you playing at eh? eh?" Twenty eight pairs of eyes widened. No one spoke, no one shuffled and I suspect several of us tried to stop breathing for a while.

"You sad, sorry lot, just how bloody long were you going to stand there like cows waiting for milking? *You,*" A nicotine-stained finger shot under the nose of Helen Schlieman, whose misfortune it was to be at the front of the queue. "Was there a little something you might have done?" Even from where I stood, halfway down the petrified line, it was obvious that all logical thought, let alone power of speech had temporarily deserted poor Helen. She opened and shut her mouth a couple of times but nothing was ready, or willing, to come out.

"My sainted Aunt Fanny!" Mrs B. smote herself dramatically on the forehead, raked her hair to even more upstandingness, stalked further down the line and fixed another hapless victim with a basilisk stare.

"*Well?*" she yelled, "Have you not got the wit God gave you. *What should you have done?*"

"N-N-N-knock?" ventured one bright and brave soul.

"No, no, no, no. You don't knock. YOU. COME. IN! It's on your timetable isn't it? It's your lesson isn't it? Now for what little time we've got left – *move!!*" Miserably, trampling each other's heels in our haste, we crowded into the enormous sky-lighted room and stood, huddled together for protection.

"Well, don't just stand there stargazing. Find yourselves a donkey." A donkey? We stared desperately at each other, mutual incomprehension merging with blind panic. The woman was totally mad, certifiable, no doubt about it.

"*A donkey, a donkey.*" shrieked the lunatic Burrell, stamping first one sturdily shod foot then the other. "You." with one demonic bound, she was before me, I nearly wet myself before I realised she was addressing my neighbour – still, too close for comfort.

"You girl, blondie, what's a donkey?" In desperation, if ever a bit of extra help was needed it was now, I scanned and knew. Alongside me Sylvia Witters was making a despairing start.

"Well it's got four legs and …" I nudged her sharply and she followed my glance to the paint-splattered, wooden combined seats and easels around the perimeter of the room.

"One of those?" she said pointing doubtfully.

"Well, thank you, Thank you *very* much. Now everyone go and sit on one. No, not you." She'd reached out and secured my arm in a vice-like grip, "Since you're such a clever puss you can be our model today."

In her welcoming speech our new Headmistress, Miss Frearsome, a lady, making up with undeniable and unbendable authority what she lacked in inches – the only time I ever saw her disconcerted was when a camel spat in her eye once on a zoo outing – had informed us our schooldays would be the best of our lives. Sitting for an hour and a half, too terrified to so much as twitch and draped in dusty velvet with a laurel wreath on my head, wax grapes in one hand and anchoring a jug, achingly on my shoulder with the other, I was inclined to think differently.

Like anyone, I craved popularity at school, and of course it wasn't hard for me to say the right things. I gained a reputation for being sensitive and intuitive and friends always said I gave good advice, although this was usually because I knew what it was they wanted to hear. In any institution however, there are always those whose main source of entertainment is making someone else's life a misery. There was a group of four third formers, tall, cruelly supercilious and universally feared by anyone younger and smaller and not a few older and larger. And within the school and its surroundings, there were plenty of unobserved areas, in which head honcho Tina Braun and her coterie could be found on most days, giving someone grief.

Peripherally aware of them and their activities I happened to be passing the games store one day and heard the unmistakeable, shrill tone of Tina B, amidst much laughter. I knew if Tina and Co were having fun, odds were, somebody else wasn't. I won't pretend I leapt in there ready to defend the weak and vanquish the wicked but as I walked past, my mind already on other things, I caught a mental whiff that made me acutely uncomfortable. A musky excitement; feral pleasure multiplied by the several minds concentrating – very unsavoury. Almost against my will, after all it wasn't my fight, I pushed open the door. In the gloomy, sweat and rubber-scented interior of the large hut used to store rounders and tennis equipment, the gang were in full swing and were delighted to see me. Someone come to stick her nose in – what could be more fun than that?

The wretched girl they'd cornered, pale face blotched and tearful was in my form. Linda, a nervous person with a habit of rubbing her thumbs frenziedly together when called upon to speak in lessons, as if hoping to produce a spark, physically if not mentally. She was struggling to recover the contents of her school bag which had been strewn around the floor of the shed. Her relief washed over me as I stood there, she saw another victim too, but at least someone to divert some of the attention. I moved forward to pick up one of the exercise books from the floor. Tina moved at the same instant, placed her foot on the open page and ground down triumphantly.

"Oooh, seems to be ever so stuck." she announced. Hysteria rocked the ranks – that Tina was a wit all right, no doubt about it. I ignored her, stooped for another book. Quick as you like the foot descended again. This time she also caught the tip of my finger, it hurt. I straightened up, annoyed, this was silly.

"Haven't you got anything better to do?" I asked.

Tina and cronies could hardly believe their ears, or their luck – first-formers didn't talk back, they did as they were told, made it snappy and were scared. This was way too good to be true.

Phillipa, another jewel in the crown of the school, sauntered over and turning sideways used her not insubstantial hip to give me a hefty shove that made me stagger. Linda, who'd been unobtrusively backing towards the door, found her exit blocked by a blonde bombshell called Shona. Linda started to cry again and I got fed up. I visualised an ants' nest we'd had outside the back door last Summer. I remembered clearly how it looked when they swarmed one day in July, a heaving, scuttling black mass, silvered by newly grown wings. It took just a second or two to assemble the picture fully in my mind and then I opened up to Tina. The effect was gratifyingly instantaneous, unexpectedly contagious and truly educational. Tina shrieked loudly and commenced a strange little jig, brushing and slapping desperately at herself. I'd supplied the visuals, it seemed Tina's imagination and fear was supplying the rest.

Whilst the other three had no idea what could possibly be causing Tina such sudden grief, the general consensus seemed to be if she was that scared, she knew something they didn't and they also started shrieking and hopping, it was all rather lively. I helped a baffled, still snivelling Linda retrieve the rest of her books, no interference now – everyone seemed to be otherwise occupied and we left. I felt more than a bit pious and I'd like to say that such a salutary experience reformed my chums in the third form. Sadly that wasn't the case and although they never troubled me again, poor Linda became the focus of their ire for almost an entire term and short of attaching myself to her permanently, there was little I could do to help. I wondered, guiltily and often whether, without my interference they'd have simply teased, bullied and then moved on.

CHAPTER SIXTEEN

When I was sixteen I killed a man. I didn't mean to do it, but on the other hand it wasn't quite an accident either.

In our second year at the school we were re-streamed according to which subjects we were taking for 'O' level and in my new form I became close friends with Faith Brackman. The physical antithesis to me, she was a tall, slim, quietly spoken, graceful girl – refined, my mother stated approvingly. She had short-cut, fine fair hair and was blue-eyed, with a soft dreamy expression belying a quick and astute mind and a formidable rapport with a netball. Together with Rochelle Lind and Elaine Henner we became a close-knit group. We were at an age then when we were being allowed further afield on our own and weekends were taken up with outings to the cinema and wonderfully long, warm, lazy summer days, swanning around in Hyde Park. We'd consume vast picnic lunches; formulate grandiose plans for the future; launch hysterical rowing sessions on the Serpentine and on the way home cram into tiny photographic booths in Woolworths to create wacky and witty strips of photos.

Rochelle and Elaine were both very open, thoughts and emotions bubbling continually on the surface. Faith was the opposite, introverted and with a curiously rigid, compartmentalised mind, the like of which I'd never come across before. Whilst with most people the head-jumble is simply horrendous, Faith's was neat, tidy and orderly, almost filed and labelled. She was extremely restful to be with although, for my own protection, as much as anyone else's privacy, I did try to keep myself to myself and made it a point of honour not to go paddling about in friends' heads.

Rochelle's parents were acrimoniously divorced, a rift from which fallout was still descending on Rochelle and Tom her seven year old, bespectacled and front-toothless brother. She was a comfortably built girl with shiny, curly long brown hair and glasses forever sliding in unscheduled descent down her short nose. Asthmatic, with a slightly breathless way of talking, whenever she told a story our breath hitched unconsciously in sympathy. We were always hunting for her inhaler which was never where she thought she'd put it. She was also endlessly weary from reassuring whichever parent she was with, how infinitely superior in every way they were to the other.

"Honestly," she told us, "It's like having three children in the family, with Tom the most sensible." It was sad to see how, as time went on, matters only seemed to sour, worsen and grow more complicated. Each of her parents found then broke with subsequent partners and Rochelle, a nurturer born and bred, took on an astonishing variety of equally angst-ridden ex's, including two new sets of siblings with completely fresh sets of problems.

Elaine's parents were much older than mine, She'd arrived to an astonished mother who, happily putting a spreading waistline and missed monthlies down to an early Change, never really got over the shock of finding she was seven months pregnant with her only child. I don't think her father, early fifties then, mid-sixties when I knew him, ever fully adjusted either. He'd answer the door when we walked Elaine home after school and there'd be just a second or two of polite but puzzled inquiry as he peered from the entrance hall, as if trying to place her.

Elaine's mum, Mrs Henner was a sturdily bosomed, eminently sensible looking lady who seemed likely to be a pillar of the local WRVS. In fact she was the most dithery, butterfly-minded person I'd ever met, the inside of her head was like a feather duster. The simplest of decisions threw her into paroxysms of concern and confusion and it remained a total mystery to all, her included, how she'd not only produced uncomplicated Elaine but raised her, unscathed to this stage. Elaine, managed both parents with easy and tolerant affection and got her way in all things. Her bedroom was like a small extension of Selfridges, with fully stocked book, toy and fashion departments, the contents of which she was unstintingly generous with. She was a refreshingly warm, uncomplicated person, welcoming each day afresh for what it was, without worrying unduly about what tomorrow might bring. Whilst Rochelle found it a near impossibility to relax and enjoy the moment, Elaine was incapable of doing anything else and so was always caught short with injured feelings by school tests or exams, which conspired to hit her out of the blue.

Faith's father was in the police, a Detective Chief Inspector and they lived in a forces-owned development not far from the Police College in Hendon.

"Bet burglars steer well clear of your street." my father commented when introduced to Faith's parents one school sports day – thus confirming, if confirmation was needed that parents inevitably make exactly the excruciating remarks you expect them to.

On that particular occasion Faith's dad had come straight on from some kind of presentation at the College and was in uniform, not how we were used to seeing him, in plainclothes. His was an impressive presence. Not as tall as you'd expect, probably at the low end of the height requirement, but broadly built. He had a sharp, blue-eyed stare below bushy, prematurely grey eyebrows and a habit of raising himself on his toes that was so stereotypical, you were never quite sure whether or not he was taking the mickey. The first time I met him I thought I'd hate to feel his hand on my collar and until he spoke, there was indeed about him a slight air of menace. But in fact he was charming, the life and soul of any gathering – although presumably that only applied to the non-criminal fraternity. He had an unending stock of jokes, a silent laugh which shook his not insubstantial stomach and a nice way of bending forward, inclining an ear from his greater height to catch what you said and make you feel important. Faith and her two years younger sister Shirley, adored him, and whenever he was around would stand as close to him as they could get. He laughed at them for that, called them his shadows, said one of these days he'd trip over and they'd all break their necks, but I noticed if either of them moved far, he was the one to reach out and draw them back. Her mother was an older version of Faith, quietly spoken with the same slim figure and fine hair but despite, or perhaps because of their similarities they didn't get on very well.

My mother always said she'd love to take Mrs B 'in hand' – put some lipstick on her, bit of eyeshadow and she'd look like a new woman. But Mrs Brackman never wore make-up, not even for Parents' Evening and always dressed in light pastel colours which did her naturally pale skin no favours. She was the sort of woman who blends, so effectively chameleon-like, into any background you could never quite recall afterwards whether you'd actually seen her there or not. Mind you, when she was accompanied by the large, reassuringly noisy presence of the DCI, she seemed to borrow confidence and colour, cheeks pinked and eyes brighter.

Her one vanity was her hands with their long slim fingers and beautifully kept almond shaped nails which she regularly manicured and re-varnished in the very palest of pinks. She'd in her younger day, been a hand model for Cutex nail-varnish in ads that were still to be seen occasionally in Woman's Mirror and Woman's Realm. She was a stickler for a clean house, although never undertook a task unless fully Marigolded. At the Brackman's, surfaces shone ferociously and the smell of Ajax bit the back of your throat as soon as you walked in the front door. Eating there though was far from relaxing as Mrs Brackman would appear at unexpected moments to damp-cloth an orange juice glass mark and swoop hawk-like on crumbs as they fell, muttering,

"Not to worry, no harm done." I know Faith found it pretty stressful when we all went there for tea and after a while, unspoken consensus ensured we didn't go often as a group.

We were made to feel welcome at Elaine's house although Mr Henner was always there, having retired from doing something in the city. Despite his insisting it did him good to have young life around, there were two small pained furrows that often appeared between his eyes when we played loud music or clattered up and down the stairs. Mrs Henner, on the other hand was always preoccupied when we went there, she couldn't decide whether to give us orange juice or chocolate milk, marmite or peanut butter or indeed whether we'd be better off sitting round the kitchen table or in the dining room and if so, should she put a cloth on?

Rochelle, although technically better off, with two homes, wasn't comfortable in either. And, after a couple of experiences, once when her mother insisted on joining us in Rochelle's bedroom to 'giggle and gossip' and another time when her father felt compelled to share with us some of the many things that had caused their marriage break-up, we found ourselves agreeing with her.

Mrs Brackman was the only one of our mothers who worked. She was a part-time receptionist at the local doctor's surgery, a good thing, according to Faith. She was always injuring herself in the pursuit of cleanliness and what better place to work if you insisted on falling off ladders a lot. She'd badly dislocated her shoulder that particular time and on another occasion had to have stitches in a nasty gash on her knee when she fell on and broke a glass lampshade she was taking through to the kitchen to wash. There was another incident involving the stairs and a heavy Hoover – she was in plaster for six weeks after that – during which time, Faith's life, she reported back to us, was a pure misery of polishing and dusting.

Occasionally Mrs Brackman would give us all a lift home from school after collecting Shirley and, once or twice, treated us all to chocolate milk shakes at the Wimpy Bar in Hendon Central. She was a far more relaxed person there, presumably because anything spilled wasn't on her floor. Over a period of time we discovered that if you could catch Mrs Brackman without her rubber gloves, she had an astonishing, quietly dry and extremely irreverent sense of humour which seemed to surprise her when it surfaced as much as it did us, although Faith, I noticed, didn't join in the laughter that much. Perhaps she felt that knowing she and her mum didn't get on, we three others were being disloyal in having such a good time.

For all the above reasons, it was at my house we spent most of our time and my mother, for whom making people welcome was a mission, gathered my friends in willingly. They, for their part, appreciated different aspects of what was on offer. Faith loved the fact that my mother, whilst believing a clean floor is a happy floor, wasn't obsessive about it. Rochelle relished my mother fussing over her and her inhaler without requiring Rochelle to listen to any problems in return and Elaine was delighted that swift and decisive rulings were made on any number of things with little or no fuss and certainly no consultation.

CHAPTER SEVENTEEN

Within our little group of four, we fell into natural divisions, Faith and I, Elaine and Rochelle. So, whilst it would have caused a terrible rift if I'd gone off somewhere with Elaine, it was perfectly acceptable and no feelings were hurt when Faith and I slipped into the habit of doing our homework together at one of our houses every Tuesday – late school nights for both of us, she attending netball practice, whilst I was at drama club.

Although I preferred the times we were at mine rather than hers, Mrs Brackman could it seemed, cope well enough with just one guest for tea. Additionally, because she was usually at the Surgery on Tuesdays and then picked Shirley up from a friend on the way home, we often only saw each other in passing. This was something of a relief, I liked her a lot – her unexpected, arrow-barbed comments made me laugh but the tension between her and Faith was sometimes palpable and uncomfortable to be around.

The day my world turned, wasn't a Tuesday. Various happenings including a concert and a prize-giving meant a postponement of normal after-school activities to the following day. We'd spent time at my house the week before and so on that afternoon, made our way back to Faith's. On a Wednesday Mrs B was home earlier and was there to greet us, at the same time ensuring we left our shoes neatly in the under-stairs cupboard and hung our coats, right side out, on the coat-stand in the closed-in front lobby.

"Good day?" She asked us. Now, I'd had my feathers severely ruffled that afternoon by Mrs Pearson, head of Games, who'd called me to task for claiming severe period pains as reason for being excused rounders. She'd pointed out acidly that as this was the third time I'd had a similar problem in five weeks, a visit to the doctor might be in order and I was cross with my own carelessness. One should always bear in mind an excuse used on previous occasions, especially as relations with the PE mistresses were already, sadly, a little strained. There'd been an unfortunate incident the previous term when I'd been so incapacitated around the time our gym session started, by a pain located in my right side and inspired by a recent episode of Dr Finlay's Casebook, that things had gone a little further than the hot cup of tea and lie-down in matron's room I'd had in mind. I'd ended up in an ambulance, siren blaring, heading for Edgware General.

I'd bent Faith's ear all the way home with my Mrs Pearson grievances and I was ready and willing to unburden to Mrs Brackman too, but no sooner had I launched into my tale of woe, than Faith insisted we get some homework done. I reluctantly followed her upstairs, force of habit keeping my hand hovering just above, but not touching, the newly polished and gleaming banister rail and Mrs B disappeared back into the kitchen, promising tea and sympathy shortly.

When we heard the key in the front door about fifteen minutes later, Faith's face lit up.

"Dad – said he might be early." He often worked late, so I knew this was a treat, I was pleased too. Of all the friends' fathers, Chief Inspector Brackman was the most interesting. In our house, all homework would have been dropped in favour of a lunge downstairs and lots of hugging and kissing but this was the Brackman's, where restraint was a virtue and so we worked through to the conclusion of the maths we'd been set. Or rather, Faith worked through and I absent-mindedly wrote down answers that were, coincidentally, pretty much the same. Whilst we put our books away – Faith maintained separate areas in her school case for exercise and text books, whereas I worked on an all-in-together basis – we argued about which film we should see at the weekend. Then, after a quick visit to the bathroom that looked as if it had never seen a really dirty person, we trotted downstairs in search of something to eat and some entertaining stories from Faith's dad.

Their house, duplicated exactly by the hundred or so others in the development, was long and narrow, stretching back deceptively farther than was apparent from the front. The stairs took you down to just by the front door and you had to do a sharp left turn into the hall and then right into their lounge. Once you were there it was a nice long room. They had a small dining table at the end, although most of the time they used a fold-down in the kitchen, which ran along the back of the house and could be accessed either through the door at the end of the hall or via the dining room. As we rounded the bottom of the stairs we could see down the corridor into the kitchen, where Mr and Mrs Brackman were looking closely at something on the kitchen counter.

"What is it?" I heard him ask, puzzled.

"Bit of butter, must've slipped off the knife when I was making the sandwiches." she said. He chuckled,

"Silly girl, I really don't know how you manage to make such a mess." And raising his arm across his body he hit Mrs Brackman full on the side of the face with the back of his hand. Her head snapped with the force of the blow and she staggered up against the worktop, on which was laid out a plate of sandwiches, egg mayonnaise I think, and a half sliced Madeira sponge.

I suppose I must have made a sound then, I know it was me and not Faith and he turned and caught sight of us.

"Allo, allo, allo," he said, doing the hands behind the back and the bent knees policeman thing which always made me laugh. "I didn't know we had a visitor and how're you my lovely?" Behind him, Mrs Brackman had straightened and was smiling too. There was a tiny trickle of blood from her nose and, suddenly aware of it she utilised the back of her hand quickly so it became just a small brown, Charlie Chaplinesque smudge over her upper lip. Close to me, Faith was standing perfectly still and in her head was running over and over one of the maths problems we'd just done.

"If it takes six people three hours to paint the outside of a house and they get through four cans of paint, how many hours …?" The strength of her calculations were loud and overriding. Chief Inspector Brackman was still smiling jovially at us,

"Not your usual day?" he was asking. I'd been brought up too well not to answer an adult's question politely.

"No, it's usually Tuesdays."

"Thought so, thought so. Getting on a bit, not senile yet though, eh?" I reached out, past his twinkling bright blue friendly gaze and into his head. Nothing different there, just the usual bluff, brisk, gruff jumble I'd always been aware of and below that a curious blankness.

"Tea, girls, come and get it." Sang out Mrs Brackman, clattering plates out of the cupboard.

"Get your skates on then, or Shirley'll be down before you get a look-in." DCI Brackman strode down the corridor towards us, giving us both a gentle push, kitchen-wards as he passed and then leaning around the banister, holding on to the post for balance yelled, "Shirley, love-bug, tea's up." Shirley bounded down the stairs and he gave her a piggy back to join us and we all sat round the kitchen table and had tea and laughed – quite a bit more than usual actually.

I was, as we used to say, more at sea than the Titanic. I tackled Faith about it the next time we were alone together.

"He hit her?"

"It's her fault, she drives him mad."

"How?"

"He works so hard," she was defensive. "Some of the things he has to do and see, you've no idea ... traffic accidents, people all mushed up and other things – horrible. He always says he needs the house, the place where he lives, to be different, clean you know and smelling nice and no filth anywhere." I digested this.

"Does he hit you?"

"No." she looked genuinely shocked, "Why would he?"

"Will they get divorced?"

"Course not, stupid, every family has rows, yours does too, I bet." Well, certainly we did, and with much yelling and pounding of the table (my father), shouting back (my mother) and things flying around the room (me), but other than the time I'd accidentally cut Dawn's head, I couldn't recall anyone ever getting hurt.

"My dad doesn't hit my mum." I said.

"Yeah, well, I bet she isn't a lazy bitch." I turned and stared at her, aghast. Gentle Faith, gentler times then and I'd never heard her utter anything remotely like that. I was shocked.

"It's what Dad says and Mum too, sometimes she doesn't do the things she should. It's her own fault." Faith's mouth was tight, bitter-pursed. "If she wasn't like that, he wouldn't get so upset." Inside her head, bleeding out from one of the compartments, kept as neatly as her school case and normally locked tight, was a shockingly fierce anger at her mother, the sole cause of so much upset and unpleasantness. Suddenly there clicked into place a rather dreadful realisation,

"All those other times, when you said she fell ...?"

"No! Are you crazy? He only ever gives her a little slap, doesn't ever hurt her." Before Faith swiftly caught and cauterised the trickle in her head, I shared with her for one moment the almost rock solid belief in what she said, along with the tiny, smothered-to-death doubt. We didn't talk about it again for a good year, nearly two.

CHAPTER EIGHTEEN

GCE 'O' levels loomed large in our lives for at least a year before we took them although for some, they loomed larger than others. Elaine was peripherally aware she needed to get down to some hard studying but, convinced there was no point, until it felt right, was confidently waiting for that time to arrive. Rochelle, whose mother was in the midst of launching a third matrimonial offensive, found her input was required on everything from finger-foods to honeymoon outfits and was torn nightly between filial affection and revision. I struggled for a mind-shut mode and tried to study, but have to confess, didn't worry unduly. Shamefully, I knew, in maths or science where I truly didn't stand a chance, I could do a quick poll of those around me and pick up what I needed. Cheating? Well perhaps, but twinges of guilt were, I always equivocated, more easily dealt with than fail marks.

Of the four of us, Faith was the most academic. She was a scrupulous student and although very bright, worked hard to keep her marks as high as they consistently were. Her exercise books were, as might have been expected, meticulously covered in brown paper, mitred at the corners and labelled neatly at precisely the regulation two inches down from the top on the front cover. She was a shining example to the rest of us, particularly to me, who hadn't then, come to think of it haven't to this day, mastered the art of mitreing a corner. Faith took revision as seriously as she did everything and devised her own strict timetable to which she stuck rigidly, refusing like the rest of us to be seduced by the live-now-revise-later philosophy and restricting herself to just an hour's outing on a weekend. As the months slid away though, it was impossible not to notice that, thin already, Faith was losing more weight and her normally pale skin had acquired an unhealthy pasty look, with under-eye, mauve markings. My mother, when she saw her after a few weeks gap was horrified and didn't mince words,

"Faith, sweetheart, you don't look good, far too thin. Are you sleeping? You're working too hard, let me see you eat this cake right up." Faith good-naturedly did as she was told, eyeing then eating the glistening, crumbling apple strudel together with a hot sweet cup of tea and just a little of the tension went out of her, but she wouldn't stay too long – she had to pick up some shopping for her Mum.

A few weeks earlier her mother had, it seemed, tripped over an uneven paving stone and not only badly broken a wrist but also cracked a couple of ribs. Faith was taking over many of the day to day chores of which, in that house, there were many. Elaine and Rochelle had been with us when Faith came into school the day after the accident. She didn't look at me when she talked about it and for a couple of weeks had made it her business for us not to be alone. Not that I was going to say anything, what could I say? Once she realised this, she relaxed a bit. But what I saw in her frightened me. The walls of Faith's compartments were crumbling. There were things she knew, couldn't help but know and the careful barriers and beliefs she'd been handed by her parents were gradually and painfully, breaking down.

I'd never said anything to my parents about the incident I'd witnessed a year or so earlier. I was embarrassed, even once removed as I was, but it began to play increasingly on my mind.

"Faith's father hits her mother." I said suddenly one evening over supper, after a day in which Faith had drifted into school more strained and wraithlike than ever.

"Nonsense," said my mother, "Who on earth told you that?"

"I saw." My parents exchanged glances.

"When?"

"A year or so ago."

"Why didn't you say anything?"

"What for? What could you have done?"

"Well, what do you think we can do now?" my father pointed out reasonably.

"Nothing, forget it, forget I said anything." I snapped. My mother cut a few more slices of roast chicken, absent-mindedly put a piece on everyone's plate and slapped Dawn's hand away as she reached for a potato with her fingers.

"Fork! I think you must have made a mistake darling, they're a very happy couple from what I've seen, and sometimes … "

"Sometimes what?"

"Well, sometimes," her eye met my father's again but he telegraphed – it's all yours – to her.

"Well sometimes married couples can be … how would you put it dear?" blank from my father, so she struggled manfully on,

" … Playful, you know, they muck around together and can be a bit silly, like teenagers and I expect that's what you saw. I bet they weren't even having an argument were they?"

"No, but …"

"Well, there you are then and were they upset when they saw you'd seen them?"

"No, but…"

"Well exactly." And she triumphantly dished up the few left-over potatoes, apportioned some stray sprouts where she thought they were most needed and rose to get dessert.

"It does happen, in some families, nasty stuff and all that, but not in this case sweetie, not with a Chief Inspector." And she bent to kiss my cheek as she passed, "I wish you'd told us before and then you needn't have worried about it all this time. How many times do I have to say, never keep things to yourself."

Faith was getting into trouble at school. It was trouble reluctantly dealt out. The staff knew there must be something wrong and didn't exactly come down on her like a ton of bricks, but they couldn't let some things continue to pass uncommented upon. Late homework, blotted, unfinished and – totally un-Faithlike – incorrect.

Our form teacher, Miss Headlam, who took geography and had quite a formidable topography of her own in the shape of a bottom, bosom and stomach that dipped, swelled and swayed as she progressed in stately fashion along the corridors, called Faith in for a chat one morning break. According to Faith, this took place in one of the little side rooms off the staff room and involved a cup of tea, ginger biscuits, a lot of questions and no conclusions. I knew she wouldn't have been moved to confide in Miss Headlam, but there was no doubt that Faith's life was slowly unravelling and my heart ached for her.

Although I did still go to her house, by unspoken agreement she came more often to mine and whilst things were very nearly normal when Elaine and Rochelle were with us – slightly more strained when we were on our own – I think there was a certain amount of relief for her in the fact that, unlike the rest of the world, I had some inkling as to what was going on.

One unseasonably bright day in February we had an unexpected half-day study period. Elaine and Rochelle had been hauled into an extra German session by a determined Frau Kempfer who seemed to feel Teutonic pride was on the line and they needed to deal with a few basics which until now had utterly escaped them. So Faith and I were on our own. It was a Tuesday, Mrs Brackman's late working day, so I felt happy enough to agree to Faith's suggestion that we go to hers.

CHAPTER NINETEEN

When we arrived at Faith's we discovered that in fact Mrs Brackman was there. We didn't see her at first, not until Faith opened the kitchen door and found she couldn't. There was something in the way. We took the other route through the dining room. We thought perhaps the towel had fallen off its hook and somehow wedged itself under the door, preventing it from opening.

It wasn't the towel though, it was Faith's mother, lying curled up with her knees to her chest, arms covering her head. She was shivering spasmodically, deep shuddering judders that shook her whole thin frame. We moved forward slowly. Faith's face had turned bone white, her mouth open as if she couldn't pull in quite enough air. I wished we'd had Rochelle's inhaler with us.

"We have to call an ambulance." I said.

"No." Mrs Brackman wasn't unconscious as I'd thought, but she wasn't fully compos either. In a movement that seemed to take forever, she turned her face up to us.

"No ambulance." One of her eyes was swollen closed, the flesh tinged livid red and blue. Her lip was cut and puffy on one side. She started to speak again. We both automatically leant in closer to hear her. She had something in her mouth which, after a second or two's work, she expelled feebly with her tongue. It fell on the floor and rolled a little along the lino – small, white, hard, a tooth.

"Shirley, upstairs." she breathed. Faith and I looked at each other.

"I'll go." I ran upstairs. Couldn't hear anything. Heart in mouth I opened Shirley's door slowly and peered round. She was sitting on her bed, cross-legged with an open book on her knees. She had her head down, eyes on the page, didn't look up.

"Shirley?" I said "Shirl, you all right?"

"Fine."

"Look, your mum's had a bit of a fall."

"I know." She glanced up then and smiled brightly at me. "I'm reading my book. I'll carry on reading till Mum feels better, then I'll come down for tea." She turned back and I saw she was holding the book upside down.

"You'll be all right up here for a bit then?"

"Oh yes, I'm happy as Larry, Daddy always says I'm happy as Larry." And she handed me another of those terrifyingly blank smiles. I closed her door quietly.

In the kitchen, Faith was trying to help her mother sit up, they were both sobbing quietly.

"I don't think we should move her." I said, "She may have broken something, she needs a doctor."

"No. No doctor. Fine in a minute. Shirley?" There was more than a swollen lip and broken tooth stopping Mrs Brackman from speaking properly, she couldn't seem to catch her breath. What with Faith and her mum, there was a fair old bit of panting going on. I quickly grabbed and soaked a dishcloth in cold water and knelt to place it gingerly and gently against her lip which was oozing blood. She raised her hand to help me and I saw that two of her fingers, her long slim fingers of which she was so proud, were bruised and swollen and one of them, the little finger on her right hand was completely twisted to one side and oddly limp. I had to make a couple of attempts to get my voice working properly, it came out though nearly as croaky as hers.

"Shirley's fine, Mrs Brackman, she's just upstairs, reading." She was trying to talk again,

"Time? What's time?" I looked at my watch. My own hand was shaking rather badly and I had to hold it with the other to keep it still enough.

"Ten to four." She moaned and grabbed my arm fiercely, trying to pull herself up but the movement must have hurt something inside because she lost whatever vestige of colour she had and slumped back against Faith, who moaned in sympathy. Her mother took a shallow breath, held it, then got out on a gasp, words distorted by her swollen mouth,

"Donal. Polsh. Coming back." I didn't understand what she meant, I scanned her, God, she was in such a lot of pain, I didn't know how to stop it, didn't want to feel it, I withdrew quickly but I knew what she was trying to say. He'd gone to the local shops. He'd gone to buy polish because he wasn't happy with the shine on the dining room table. No, he wasn't happy at all, that was what he'd been making clear to Mrs Brackman before he left.

"Faith," I hissed, "Your Dad's coming back, he's only gone down to the shops." She didn't question how I knew, she was still holding her mother.

"Why mum, why, why, why d'you do it? Why get him all upset?"

"I'm sorry, so sorry."

"Faith," I interrupted desperately, crouching, reaching out and gripping her chin, forcing her to look at me. "Listen to me, your Dad'll be back any minute, do you understand? Is there a neighbour, anyone, someone we can call? She's got to have a doctor, she's badly hurt." I was shouting now, Mrs Brackman flinched, Faith gaped at me. I stood up, my mother would know what to do, the phone was on the window-sill. As I grabbed the receiver, we heard the key in the front door. Mrs Brackman moaned into the wet cloth,

"Faith, upshtairs, go 'way quickly, go to Shirley."

"Don't be silly," I said more staunchly than I felt, "We're not leaving you, not going anywhere." In my haste, my finger had slipped sweatily on the phone dial, I had to start again.

"Allo, 'allo, 'allo what's a goin' on 'ere then?" Chief Inspector Brackman had on his smart, blue uniform he wore for official dos. He cut an imposing figure. Mock-accent in place, smile as wide as a barn door, he'd come in through the dining room and was eyeing us all warmly.

"Wasn't expecting you home yet girls, but nicest surprises are the one's we're not expecting, eh?" We all stared at him. He looked back cheerfully and held up the carrier bag of shopping,

"Faith, your Mum's got a wee bit of polishing to do. You and Stella run upstairs and we'll call you when it's tea-time. Helen, here's the duster and the other stuff you needed." He stepped carefully over Mrs Brackman and Faith on the floor and took the kettle to the sink where he filled it, placed it on the gas hob and used the Ever-Ready Igniter to light the gas.

"And while you're at it Hells, hows about a bit of the cup that cheers?" he looked down inquiringly at Mrs Brackman.

"Come on love, ups-a-lazy-daisy, won't get much done down there." Mrs B was indeed struggling obediently, trying to shake off Faith's arms and get up. His eyes, blue and clear, lighted on me, frozen with the phone receiver in my hand.

"And who's that you're phoning, Stella pet?" he inquired mildly.

"My mother."

"Not now, call her later love, more convenient later. Put the phone down." I did, his was a voice used to giving orders. My hot hand had left a damp imprint on the black bakelite.

He grinned companionably at me over the matching fair heads of Faith and her mother. Inside his own head, beyond the everyday jumble – station shifts, road-safety talk at local infant school, tyre that needed replacing – there was a terrifying and complex blankness, a deep nothingness I'd never encountered before. The kettle began to bubble softly, such a familiar domestic sound. He moved a few steps away from the cooker and stood over his wife and daughter, loosening his tie,

"Come on old girl, that table's not going to polish itself now is it?" And he drew back his foot with its impeccably polished black shoe and kicked her in the side, just below her ribs, I didn't know whether it was the same side she'd been hurt earlier. The force of the blow went through her and into Faith, still with both arms round her mother, so that Faith's head jarred dully against the kitchen door. Mrs Brackman didn't seem to have a moan left in her, she retched once and her breath hitched even more in her chest, an ugly, uneven sound.

Faith very carefully and gently withdrew her arms from her mother, trying not to cause any more pain, lowered her to the ground and rose stiffly to her feet. She was a tall girl and nearly on a level with her father. Ice blue eye met ice blue eye. Within her head all those carefully constructed walls were coming down and from behind them was first seeping then trickling then pouring knowledge, known but denied for so long.

"Don't touch her." She said. I could see her teeth were chattering and she had to clench her jaw against that to talk. "Not. Ever. Again. Do you hear me." He smiled, cocking his head to one side, humorously quizzical as he'd been, to our amusement, so many times before.

"Faith, sweet pea, don't interfere in things you don't understand. Helen?" he appealed mock-plaintively to his wife who had crawled a little way, reached up to the oven door handle and was trying and failing to haul herself up.

"Tell her Helen. Tell her I'm not a difficult man. Now am I? Tell her I sometimes spot things you've missed, tell her I help you out with that." He moved forward again. I didn't know whether he had in mind to hit her or help her, because he didn't know either, but whichever, he didn't get a chance. Faith moved swiftly in front of her and blocked him. He frowned.

"Now, Faith, if you really want to help your old dad, run upstairs, get my slippers, there's a good girl." Faith looked past him at me.

"Call an ambulance." She said. I picked up the receiver again. He slapped her hard round the face and she rocked back on her heels.

"Ah now, look what you made me do." He was genuinely sorrowful and I mean genuinely, there was no doubting what I read. She didn't move one muscle, stood her ground his finger marks livid and reddening on her chalk white face. Mrs Brackman reached out with one hand and caught hold of his trousers.

"Don, no, please." It came out 'pleashe'. He swung on his heel, moving swiftly across the kitchen as I was dialling the second 9 and knocking the phone clean out of my hand. As it hit the floor, he wrenched the brown plaited cord out of the socket on the wall and I thought he was going to hit me too, but no, he seemed to want to keep it in the family.

He moved back to his wife on the floor and their daughter. He stood face to face with Faith again, shook his head, more in sorrow than anger drew back his arm, fist clenched tight this time.

"Noooo." I screamed. "Don't." He turned his body slightly to ensure maximum impact and I went into his head. I didn't know what I was looking for yet I found it immediately and acted. Nothing very dramatic, just a small pull, a minor twist. The result was instantaneous and terrible.

He toppled where he stood, falling backwards in strangely slow motion, not crumpling but going down full length like a felled tree. He hit the tiled floor with a solid thwunk and his cheerful blue gaze, glazing over already, contemplated the ceiling without much interest.

I think we stayed in silent tableau for a good few moments, Faith, Mrs Brackman, me and of course the DCI, before movement returned to three of us. Mrs Brackman let out a high-pitched howl that seemed to last forever. Faith's legs gave way and she sank to the floor beside her mother putting her arms round her again, to receive as much as give comfort. I moved around the Chief Inspector cautiously on stiff limbs. It wasn't a big kitchen and there were a lot of people on the floor.

"I'll get help." I said. But there was no doubt in the minds of any of us that he was dead. A tidy home, or lack of it, had ceased to be of any further interest to D.C.I. Brackman.

I walked steadily down the garden path and up the adjacent one, to their next-door neighbour, no-one I'd ever met before. A nice lady who came to her door wiping floury hands on a flower-patterned apron and smiling inquiringly. If she was shocked to find a teenager she didn't know, on her doorstep with a story of accident and emergency, she didn't let it show. She didn't panic and she didn't ask unnecessary questions. She phoned for an ambulance whilst divesting herself of the apron, gave the address and the minimum details I'd passed on, yelled through to whoever was watching television in the living room that she was popping next door for a tick and, pausing only to gather up some sort of picnic rug from an under-stairs cupboard, followed me at a brisk trot back next door.

She sucked in a deep breath at the scene that greeted her but wasted no time – the sort of woman who copes for England. She utilised the picnic rug to drape gently over the ex Chief Inspector, covering his rapt gaze and despatching me upstairs quickly to bring down eiderdowns from the bedrooms. I dragged one off Faith's bed and then tiptoed into the room that I knew was Mr and Mrs Brackman's and pulled another off the bed there, dragging them past Shirley's closed door. I didn't go in. She was probably better where she was for the moment. Neighbour Joan wrapped the eiderdowns swiftly round Faith and her mother, tucking them both in, tutting and there thereing all the while. She handed me the damp cloth, to rinse out so it could be re-applied to Mrs Brackman's now purple, still-swelling lip.

"Ah, Helen, Helen," she kept murmuring, "There, there, my dear, there, there, you'll be all right, we'll get you to hospital, you'll be all right." She knew, had known what had been going on for a long time, had helped Helen before when she'd had 'accidents', tried and failed to get her to seek help. She glanced up at my ashen face and ordered me to make tea, strong, hot and sweet, mind. Actually, she didn't think we'd have time to drink it, but she knew shock when she saw it and in her book, action was always by far and away the best course. I dutifully utilised the water, boiled, was it only a few moments ago, by the late, not yet lamented Chief Inspector and in no time at all there was the sound of sirens.

The police arrived at the same time as the ambulance, a couple of very shocked constables from the local station who, of course, knew the family and were on first name terms with neighbour Joan. Mrs Brackman was lifted swiftly and efficiently on to a stretcher by the ambulancemen. She was, even in the midst of all the pain, grief and humiliation, still polite and thanked them over and over. She made them stop for a moment as they carried her out, pulled her arm from under the blanket and took my hand briefly,

"So sorry, you were here pet, so sorry." Faith was led out too, still eiderdown wrapped,

"Shock, poor kid." One of the nice ambulancemen had his arm around her and she rested against him heavily, she seemed to have forgotten I was there.

Neighbour Joan had leaned over the stretchered Mrs Brackman and said not to worry dear she'd see to Shirley and me and would lock up the house right and tight after the lads and all had done the necessary. We both went upstairs to get Shirley. She greeted us brightly, accepting without question Joan's brisk explanation about her mother's fall and Faith going with her to the hospital to keep her company. We went back next door, accompanied by one of the constables. Shirley hadn't seen the shape lying under the picnic rug and I think the rest of us were only too delighted not to see it any more. I finally got my cup of hot tea. Neighbour Joan phoned my mother and a policewoman turned up and sat down on the sofa with me, put a kindly arm round my shoulder and said she just needed to ask a few quick questions and, if I felt up to it, could I say what happened?

I could of course, say exactly what happened but decided it might be best not to. I could read clearly that D.C.I. Brackman had been a hugely popular member of the local team, respected enormously, liked by colleagues and public alike. Always the bloke to step forward for an extra shift without a moan, first to put his hand in his pocket at the pub and invariably ready with a word of advice and help with the paperwork, for many an out-of-depth raw recruit. I didn't know exactly what Faith and Mrs Brackman were going to say but I did know how very important to them was all of the above. I didn't lie.

I said it was all muddled in my head because it happened so fast. I said, truthfully, that I couldn't say exactly how Mrs Brackman had come to fall and I didn't fib when I confirmed Chief Inspector Brackman was in a very cheerful mood and not at all unwell when he arrived home. When the policewoman said was there anything I thought I might have left out, I sobbed quite a bit and she said, now, now, I'd done very well and had known to go for help and to try and put it all out of my mind now.

At one point I looked up and caught the knowing and saddened eye of neighbour Joan and she smiled and nodded at me encouragingly. She was thinking what a blessing it was it had all gone right over my head and shortly after that, my mother arrived in a state, in a taxi to take me home.

93

She and neighbour Joan, complete strangers, nevertheless came into the room with arms around each other's waists, the way women do in a crisis and I could see from my mother's appalled expression that she remembered our conversation a while back.

"Was it you?" asked my parents with terrible apprehension, that evening when I was finally home and in bed.

"No." I said. And because they couldn't live with thinking otherwise, they chose to believe me.

Faith didn't come back to school for a week and when she returned people did their best, which wasn't brilliant. They either tackled things head on, went up and said how really sorry they were or else pretended not to notice her as she came into class, developing an urgent interest in the contents of their case until the teacher entered and talking was prohibited anyway. She deeply loathed both approaches, any approach actually.

They said it was an aneurysm, a blood vessel that burst in his head, a time-bomb they said, which he'd probably been walking around with for years. It could have gone anytime.

I didn't go to the funeral but, with my parents, attended the impressive memorial service. Mrs Brackman had only stayed in hospital for a couple of nights, insisting she needed to be with the girls. At the service we learned how and why her husband had earned such a string of commendations during the course of his career. Several high-ups, sombrely blue-uniformed and silver-buttoned spoke movingly and told us that not only the family but the Force had lost a true one-off. When at the end Mrs B, flanked by Faith and Shirley stood to bid farewell to the attendees, her normally pale face, despite red-rimmed eyes, was flushed, with pride alongside the grief. The swelling round her eye and lip had gone down but she still moved stiffly, grimaced at certain angles. She thanked my parents for coming, accepted their condolences but reserved a special hard hug for me which I returned, as fiercely as I thought her bruised ribs would allow.

When Faith and I were alone there was a certain amount of constraint between us, inevitable I suppose if you've just killed somebody's father, although of course she didn't know that and we certainly never talked about what she knew I knew. There was never one single breath of scandal, the story was Mrs Brackman – and wasn't accident her middle name? – had yet again come to grief, falling off something unspecified in the kitchen. Faith and I, arriving home from school had found her and Chief Inspector Brackman had arrived shortly after that. It was entirely probable that the shock of seeing her like that, combined with trying to lift her had just been enough to fracture that traitorously unsuspected, weak vessel, deep in his brain.

We were with Faith a lot, Elaine, Rochelle and I, celebrity status conferred as best friends of the bereaved and with each recounting, the lines of memory and knowledge blurred and shifted, obscured by repetition and I almost bought into the fantasy, wanted to so much, but couldn't.

I felt completely frozen inside, unable to think about what had happened, unable to stop thinking about it. I was sleeping poorly. Mrs Brackman and Faith wailed through my dreams, Shirley turned and smiled blankly at me and I woke to find the Chief Inspector rising on his toes beside my bed, cheerfully inquisitorial. I often couldn't move, muscles locked in place by what my father said was sleep paralysis. Quite common, you think you're awake but you're not really, a fraction of time when the brain thinks it sees something but doesn't let the body respond to disprove it. Lots of people have it apparently, although of course not a lot of them shared what lay on my conscience.

I knew, beyond a shadow of a doubt, that Chief Inspector Brackman at the point I'd stopped him, had crossed some sort of a line. What was in his head was the conviction that unless he sorted out his misguided wife and daughter, they didn't stand a chance in this life and the fact that he might have had to beat them to death to do it, wasn't going to stand in his way. One small part of me and it shamed me then and appals me still, was unmoved by what I'd done. It was common sense, one life against two – four, if you factored Shirley and me into the equation. Because I'd had no doubt that once that line had been crossed, there would have been no going back – only forward!

CHAPTER TWENTY

Over the weeks and months that followed, Faith began very slowly to heal but despite all my rationalisation I didn't. As well as not sleeping, I lost my appetite and my mother fussed over me, cooking my favourite meals and buying me special little treats. But I was feeling continuously haunted and guilty and at the same time, desperately ashamed of not feeling guilty enough.

Mock exams came and went and I did my stuff in a daze. Faith's mother who was coping, everyone said, wonderfully well, under the circumstances, decided to take them to the seaside for the Easter holidays. I was pleased that she and Faith seemed, in the turmoil of the last few weeks to have rediscovered their relationship. There was laugher coming back to that house and if it was a little less feverish than before, then that was a good thing too.

Other changes were also happening round me. Within the extended family, seismic shifts altered the landscape of our lives, as marriages took place, babies arrived, new in-laws were integrated and people you thought would be there forever, suddenly weren't. Auntie Yetta moved to the big Kalooki club in the sky. She was followed, quietly, a few months later by Morrie Schwartz who breathed his last so unspectacularly, in his normal armchair, that it was a good hour amidst the noise and kerfuffle of a Saturday Tea, before anyone spotted he'd gone. And then, just as things were settling down again, Grandma suffered another, much more severe stroke and my parents' attention shifted away from me and my issues, to a new regime of hospital visits and a different anxiety.

I cried off from those visits as much as I possibly could. Truth to tell, I found the hospital unbearably painful, as if I was wearing my nerves on the wrong side of my skin. Accumulated vibrations of hope, fear, pain, humiliation and acceptance were densely there even before we entered the building, overpowering once we were inside and I seemed, somehow to have misplaced the knack of keeping things out as well as I should. Equally painful was the fact my mother swore Grandma was reassured we were there and could hear us, whilst I knew for certain she wasn't and couldn't, but lacked the courage to say so.

When our doorbell rang one Saturday afternoon, my parents were at the hospital and I was deep in *Jamaica Inn*, with a Beatles LP providing anachronistic background. I ignored the bell. We weren't expecting anyone and I had the rest of the book and a Walnut Whip to get through. It rang again, longer and harder. The impatient finger obviously wasn't going to take no for an answer. Peeved, I padded out in slippered feet, it was probably an over-enthusiastic Jehovah's Witness.

It wasn't, it was a slim coffee-skinned woman and close behind her, the largest, squarest person I'd ever seen, he looked like a fridge on steroids – shoulders bulging and moving independently under a tweed jacket which seemed ready to split under the strain. He wasn't old, mid to late twenties I thought, with a disproportionately small and slightly misshapen head, a pale, expressionless face and a nose that looked as if it had been in several fights, with or without him. I took a rapid and astonished step back into our hall.

"You could at least," said Glory Isaacs, as tartly lemon sherbet as I remembered, "Say good afternoon." She put out a hand and the big man moved smoothly forward so she could rest it on his arm. Bending his head slightly to clear the doorway, he led her inside. I gawped after them and as an afterthought, shut the door. The big man looked at me and I indicated the open door to his right and he nodded and walked her in to our through-lounge.

"Tea might be nice?" she seated herself on the sofa, back straight, the same elegant posture I remembered. She slipped off her long, belted mac, folding and placing it neatly next to her. Revealed, was a purple and gold emblazoned, kaftan top over wide black trousers. Where full sleeve dropped away from narrow-boned wrist, several thin, dull-gold bangles slid against each other and in her ears, cascading gold links looked too heavy for the lobes from which they swung.

"Whenever you're ready?" She'd not lost the sarcastic edge in the years since I'd seen her. "Ed," she added, "Sit, you must be making the place look untidy." The large man and I looked around dubiously. My mother favoured contemporary furniture, armchairs with splayed black-painted wooden legs and multi-coloured cushions. Ed opted, sensibly, I thought for one of the upright dining room chairs which were a tad sturdier than the rest.

"Tea." she reminded me. As I left the room I scanned and wasn't really surprised to hit a couple of blank walls, although I could have sworn I could hear faint music, Andy Williams and Moon River?

Tea and biscuits and a surreal gathering. Glory and I, either end of the sofa and Ed on his chair nursing one of my mother's delicate, good-china cups.

"How did you find me?" I asked. I had ghastly visions of my Brackman-inspired guilt, broadcasting far and wide. She ignored my question and followed her own agenda,

"We need your help."

"Help, how?"

"You owe me a favour."

"A favour?"

"Dear Lord," she tutted in exasperation and carefully but accurately centred her cup in its saucer on the coffee table in front of her, "Why is it not possible to have a conversation, without you repeating every single damn thing I say?"

"Sorry."

"We have ..." She paused, "... A bit of a situation."

"Situation?" I couldn't seem to help it.

"I'd like you to come and meet a couple of people – easier for them to explain than me. You know," she continued without pausing, "You really shouldn't feel quite so dreadful, you had very little choice." For one moment, with the lemon sherbert flooding, I was thrown completely. But of course she'd know about my fatal brush with the law, it was, after all, always at the forefront of my mind. I didn't say anything, I thought it wisest, but an icy lump I'd been carrying around in my chest since it happened, now seemed to be rising unpleasantly. It lodged, uncomfortable and thick in my throat.

"There was something wrong with him wasn't there?" she asked. I thought of what I'd seen in his head, opened my mouth to try and explain but didn't have the words, so flashed what I'd sensed. She nodded briefly in acknowledgement.

"Like I said, no real choice, not at that moment. You come across people like him sometimes, not often, thank God – there's just a gap inside them, a blank where there shouldn't be. After a while that blank fills up with obsession and lots of other rubbish and sometimes, not always, but sometimes, a lot of violence too."

The icy lump had reached my head and was, to my mortification starting to come out. Large, fat, sour-tasting tears seeped from my eyes and down my nose and throat, it felt like there were a lot more on the way. A large, spotlessly clean, white handkerchief found it's way into my clenched fists and the chair creaked as Ed re-settled himself. I cried and they waited quietly.

"You know," Glory said reflectively, after a bit, "Some people are born wicked. No conscience, get a huge kick out of wrongdoing. They do know, nevertheless, the difference – between right and wrong I mean. Others, don't seem to recognise the difference at all. I don't know which category your policeman fell into but he had totally come off the normality track." She sighed, "Anyway, what the hell, end result's the same, they all muck up the world dreadfully, not to mention other people's lives." She turned her face towards me, met my eyes with hers, sightless yet seeing. "You made a snap decision, you thought lives were at risk, they probably were. You did the best you could at the time. You probably learnt more in those few seconds about how vital control is for someone like you, than you have in the previous sixteen years. What's done is done. Move on."

I blew my nose, I felt lighter than I had for weeks. I put this new feeling away to analyse later and was just re-filling Ed's cup when my parents arrived home from the hospital. If they were surprised to find an exceptionally large man and a blind lady taking tea and biscuits in their living room, they were too well-mannered to show it other than the slight start neither of them could hide as they came through the door. Ed immediately stood up, silent but polite and they watched him unfold to his full six foot five or so with more than a little apprehension for my mother's crystal chandelier. I made the introductions, although I knew my mother had already instantly and correctly identified Glory.

Glory got straight down to business.

"We'd like your daughter to meet a couple of friends of ours."

"Couple of friends?" said my mother tightly. Glory suppressed a sigh – the echo thing again. I noted with surprise that my mother had always thought this would happen, that 'they' would come. She wasn't sure who 'they' were or what they'd want but she'd anticipated something like this moment. She sat down now heavily on the sofa,

"You're the one she … ?"

"We met in Oxford, yes." Glory put out her hand, my mother reached automatically to take it and Glory drew her nearer, my mother staring intently, as if in her inability to read the woman's mind, she could make sense of that lovely impassive face instead.

"I'm here because we need her help." Glory said.

"Why?"

"She's strong. There aren't many like that and we need someone young."

"To do?"

"Whatever's necessary."

"That's no answer."

"It's all I can give you." I scanned her and for a moment there was just the smooth-surfaced wall then, realising perhaps she wasn't going to get what she wanted unless she gave me more, she opened up.

There was a child, dark, sweat-curled hair. Young, five or six I thought. We were looking through the eyes of someone taking a blood sample from his arm. He was deeply asleep, didn't stir as the needle slipped in, sucked, slipped out. There were wires terminating in electrodes attached to his head, snaking out from various bits of machinery. A monitor by the bedside, green electronic peaking lines pulsing across a black screen. As our angle of vision changed, I saw leather straps round thin wrists, could even see the angrily red chafe marks where they'd shifted, moved and abraded the flesh. The straps were at the end of short metal chains attached to the frame of the bed. A hospital room? Not like one I'd ever seen. An iron framework barred the window and the door had a large, circular, wheel-like handle set halfway down. There was someone else there, other than the blood-taker, male or female I couldn't tell, because they were dressed in protective clothing, a sort of all-in-one silvery grey outfit with a white mask obscuring mouth and nose.

"Who is he?"

"Sam. He's six. He's in isolation, in a room with reinforced steel walls and a door similar to those used in bank vaults. He's being kept heavily sedated."

"Why?"

"I expect you can guess."

"He's like us?" she nodded.

"They're scared of him?"

"Extremely."

"With cause?"

"Absolutely."

"Hang on a minute." my parents had followed this exchange, aware they'd missed a lot and hugely uncomfortable I think watching Glory and I interact. I told them what I'd seen and turned impatiently back to the blind woman. My mother had withdrawn her hand but was still staring at her, white-faced, tight-lipped and hostile.

"What's he to do with me?" I said

"We want … need, your help to get him out."

"From?" but I knew – The Newcombe Foundation. "Why me?"

"He's beyond frightened already, if we send you in we think he'll be less scared. You look even younger than your age, surprise at seeing you might just reassure him, earn us a precious few minutes. Look," Glory's insubstantial stock of patience was running out, "Could you just stop asking questions and take my word. There's a lot to tell you but there are others who can tell it better. We think you can do this. Actually, we think, at this precise moment, you're probably the only one who can. Will you trust me? Come and hear us out before you make up your mind?"

"No." said my parents in unison.

"Yes." I said and turned to them, "I think I have to, I want … " I paused, what was it I wanted?

"To find out more?" suggested my father heavily.

"Is this risky?" my mother turned back to Glory.

"Yes." At least she was honest.

"Don't go." said my mother.

"Go carefully." said my father.

CHAPTER TWENTY-ONE

My parents watched as I left with Glory and the still silent Ed. I didn't look back. Selfishly, I didn't even want to know what they were thinking. Glory had covered her rather vivid ensemble with the neutral coloured mac again, although I couldn't help thinking, if she was aiming for unobtrusive, she'd have done better to have stuck with the colourful outfit and dropped Ed.

Parked in the road, at the front of our house was a white Morris Marina. Ed courteously opened the front door for Glory, the back for me and managed, by some miracle of manoeuvring, to wedge himself into the limited space behind the wheel. Glory had closed her mind to visitors and there was what sounded like a Dean Martin medley running relaxingly through Ed's. I sat back in my seat with a certain feeling of unreality. Generally, I feel it's good to plan ahead, to have a strategy in mind. Sometimes however, and this seemed to be such an instance, you're catapulted into a situation so bizarrely beyond your ken, so surreally out of keeping with a quiet Saturday afternoon in Hendon Central, that anything other than acceptance of the moment is an impossibility.

We drove for around half an hour, although I couldn't be sure – one of the things I'd forgotten in the general exodus was my watch. It was a silent drive. I tried a couple of conversational openers but Ed wasn't having any and Glory seemed to be dozing. When we drew to a halt, it was in a quiet residential street of detached, well-kept white-stuccoed, black-shuttered houses. Ed, Glory's hand on his arm, matching his pace to hers, led us up a flight of half a dozen white-washed stone steps, bordered by luxuriantly flowering planted pots. We paused in front of a glossy black, gilt-knockered door which he opened with a key.

Inside, Glory walked wordlessly down the narrow hall towards a door at the far end. I followed her, not without some apprehension. When I looked back for Ed, he'd vanished – I wasn't sure when or where to but for someone built on such a large scale he moved surprisingly soundlessly. Glory opened the white panelled door at the end of the hall, locating the door-knob without hesitation and the dark corridor flooded instantly with warmth and light from the brightness beyond. It was a lovely room that I followed her into, stretching out onto a sweeping lawn, bordered by riotously lush rose bushes. It looked as if the original living area had been doubled by the glass walled and ceilinged, conservatory-style extension which ran along the whole width of the back of the house bringing light, lawn and flowers into the room. There was a large modern-looking kitchen to my right with a wooden table and lots of stainless steel. The living room was given up to two squashily over-stuffed sofas and another couple of armchairs on which the weekend newspapers were liberally strewn. There was a low coffee table serving both sofas, the surface of which was almost totally obscured by a teetering pile of books and publications. More books crowded floor to ceiling shelves along the opposite wall. Gaudily coloured children's classics rubbing spines with chunky, darkly bound academic-looking tomes. An additional slightly unstable tower of homeless volumes was stacked nearby on the floor.

Something was bubbling quietly on the hob, it smelt chicken soupy to me and my mouth watered. Plants were everywhere – someone had a green thumb – several chained pots hung from ceiling hooks by the window swinging slightly in the breeze and arranged along the sills were cut flowers in vases and jugs. Their scent mingled comfortably with whatever was cooking.

I was, I suppose, rather surprised – don't know what I'd expected, maybe something out of the Adams Family, certainly nothing as domesticated as this. I was just relaxing a little when there was some very heavy breathing behind me and something shoved me hard in the bottom. Caught completely off balance, I lurched forward into Glory who was still just in front of me. She in turn clutched desperately at me to avoid falling. I shrieked as something wet hit my face and grabbed Glory tighter. She slapped my hand hard.

"Stop that, you stupid child, stop it. He won't hurt you. Sit Hamlet." Hamlet sat, which actually didn't make him look any less tall, even sitting his head came nearly up to my shoulder. Glory detached herself impatiently from my clinging fingers.

"He's just always pleased to see anyone, won't hurt you. He's a dyed in the wool coward, more scared of you than the other way round, we use him a lot with the children."

"Children?" I echoed weakly, she snorted and didn't deign to answer.

"Make yourself comfortable." she indicated the sofas with a sweep of her hand. "You're OK with dogs aren't you?" And before I could answer she'd left through the door we'd come in by.

Hamlet and I contemplated each other thoughtfully. He was an enormous animal, he looked like a bit of great dane and a lot of something else, no idea what. I thought he might be going to head over for further investigation, but he settled where he was, lowering himself carefully to the ground with a ridiculously human sigh and resting his head on both paws so he could keep an eye – I'd have to take Glory's word it was friendly – on me. I gingerly moved a pile of magazines on which I was partially sitting, Hamlet twitched an ear but otherwise took no notice. I was extremely apprehensive of meeting the people I'd been brought here to meet but that rather paled into insignificance compared with continuing my tête a tête with Hamlet. He yawned massively, revealing an impressive array of teeth. I put my hands in my lap where he could see them and sat very still indeed.

CHAPTER TWENTY-TWO

I knew who she was, moments before she entered the room, no mistaking that sharp, cool peppermint and somehow, in the general unreality of that whole afternoon, the fact that she and Glory Isaacs should be connected, seemed no odder than everything else. Miss Peacock strode in briskly, Hamlet rose in welcome but she pointed to the floor and he sank down again. I rose too, but she pointed to the sofa and I obeyed as instantly and unquestioningly.

"Hello again." she said. I hadn't thought about her in a long time but her voice was unmistakable, sharp, authoritative and now I heard it again, faintly accented. Someone accustomed to giving orders and having them obeyed. She was as thin as I remembered, although seeing her now, face to face I realized she was younger than I'd thought, early forties maybe. Her knee-length pleated grey skirt was topped with a crisply white blouse, a slightly chipped black and white cameo on the revere. A lighter grey cardigan, slung over narrow shoulders matched grey hair, cut in no particular style to just below her ears and brushed back from a widow-peaked, pale-skinned finely lined high forehead.

Behind tortoiseshell-framed glasses, on an aquiline nose her eyes were the only other colour in that angular face, a bright, deep hazel. Anger wasn't what I'd expected, but it surfaced immediately I saw her. I remembered all too clearly our encounter on the bus nearly five years before, my bewilderment and sense of loss when she snubbed me so firmly. The first person I'd ever met who could have answered some of my questions – and wouldn't.

She swept through my defences, swiftly peppermint and impatient, as naturally and as easily as before, a knife through butter. That made me even angrier. My carefully nurtured blocks obviously counted for nothing and she made no attempt to hide the fact, although at the same time I wanted fiercely for her to know exactly how I felt.

"Control." she remarked coolly "Is something you need to cultivate."

"I'll bear that in mind."

"You need to sort your shielding."

"I manage."

"Not very well."

"Shame then you didn't have any tips, when we last met." Fury was rising.

"Careful." she said softly and into my head shot Chief Inspector Brackman's dead blue gaze. "Never forget how easy that was to do." She moved to the coffee table and decisively halved the pile of books that was threatening to topple.

"Point taken. But you haven't answered my question." I was deliberately insolent.

"You surprised me – on the bus. It was unexpected."

"All the more reason to have stopped and listened?" At my raised voice Hamlet lifted his head.

"I'm not good with surprises." She said, "Or post-mortems!"

"Ah Rachael, on a charm offensive as usual, I see."

Another woman had come in quietly and was pausing now to scratch Hamlet under the chin. Miss Peacock inclined her head,

"My sister Ruth." 'My sister Ruth' was a couple of years younger, several inches shorter and a great deal rounder than her sibling. She was wearing bright red stirrup trousers and a psychedelically colourful jumper that appeared made for a taller person altogether, stretching as it did down to her knees and overlapping plump be-ringed hands almost down to pearlised pink nails. Brown hair was liberally silver stranded and untidy, held away from her face by a pink velvet alice band. While I was still taking her in, she was moving toward me, smiling, both hands outstretched, I rose automatically to take them.

"My dear, welcome. Take no notice whatsoever of my sister, she didn't handle things well when she met you – oh yes we heard all about it – and that makes her snappy and rude, well snappier than usual! I'm delighted though to finally make your acquaintance. Now, can I get you a cup of tea? Are you hungry? Supper won't be too long, we eat early here."

"Ruth, we don't need tea now." Miss P the first, was impatient and her sister subsided, much as had Hamlet and I, landing on the sofa next to me with a resigned thump that shook its frame and shot fine dust motes into the air. Her eyes, I saw, confirmed the relationship the rest of their

106

physical appearance denied, they were the same bright hazel, sharp with intelligence and much more.

I was by that time so mixed up, I didn't even particularly warm to Ruth although she was certainly an improvement on her tersely rude sister. It didn't help that whilst I couldn't read a thing from either of them, Miss Peacock could obviously stroll in and out of my head as she chose. As could Ruth also I assumed. Her mind was as smooth-walled and impenetrable as her sister's and Glory's. Whilst I was reflecting on this Glory came back in followed by Ed who didn't return my tentative smile. She elegantly settled herself on the second sofa, the other side of the coffee table from Ruth and I – she obviously knew the room well because she made her way through with no faltering. Ed brought up a solid wood-framed chair to sit beside her and everybody looked at me.

There was an energy vibrating in the room, the like of which I'd never come across before but at the same time, none of the normal background babble which was as much part of my daily existence as breathing. I thought I could hear faint Frank Sinatra – Ed, I presumed – but other than that, nothing. Despite my mixed emotions, it was, I had to confess, a uniquely blissful quiet and one I'd have been mad not to savour.

"So?" Miss Peacock had perched on the arm of Glory's sofa.

"I've told her a bit, shown her. Had to otherwise she wouldn't have come."

"She's not got much shielding." Miss Peacock complained.

"We can sort that."

"Quickly enough?"

"Absolutely."

"Hey," I interrupted sharply, "I am here you know, talk to me not about me."

"Take no offence dear," Ruth placed on a hand on my arm for an instant, "My sister gets carried away, leaves her manners behind completely."

"Sorry." Miss Peacock smiled briefly at her. It was a quite astonishing smile which lit up her sallow features with unexpected depths of warmth and humour. However, I was in no mood to be charmed, neither by Ruth's ostensible concern nor by one unexpected smile. Miss Peacock turned back to me.

"We asked you here because we need your help."

"I'll want to know a lot more than I do already."

"She's got a lot of questions." Glory confirmed. Ruth snorted,

"She's entitled."

"I'm not arguing." Miss Peacock pointed out. "Ask away." I hesitated, it was like being handed a big box of chocolates, way too many choices – and I couldn't be certain I was going to like everything I picked.

"Can we start with this child, I've forgotten his name. I'll ask other questions as we go along."

"Agreed and it's Sam." Miss Peacock moved off the arm of the sofa and slipped down next to Glory who eased over to make room. "He's six years old, we think he may be autistic he's certainly very withdrawn, although that's hardly surprising. He's very frightened and he's very dangerous."

"How do you know?"

"He's killed." I digested this.

"Who?"

"A nurse."

"How?"

"Very easily."

"I didn't mean that. Did he mean to?"

"Who knows? I told you, he's terrified. She was clumsy with a needle, kept trying over and over to take blood, she hurt him. He hurt her back." There was silence for a moment. Poor little boy was my first thought and then a shocked second later, poor nurse too of course. I glanced up, appalled, but there was no judgement on their faces. Maybe I'd have preferred it if there had been. I cleared my throat,

"What about his parents?" Ruth shook her head,

"No parents. Foster-care from a baby. Father unknown. His mother abandoned him at a few weeks, probably frightened of him, it's a familiar pattern."

"Familiar?"

"Of course. Those of us who are different ..." she paused, "I don't know how you term it?"

"Strange," I said, "I ... we, my family I mean, we've always just called it Strange." She chuckled,

"I like that – Strange, yes, a good word, and you're comfortable with it. Not just the word, your family have much to be proud of my dear, they've done a sterling job with you. Now where was I?"

"Ruth, for goodness sake." Miss Peacock obviously felt any niceties were a waste of everyone's time, her sister ignored her.

"Those who are – Strange are just born like that, but sometimes it doesn't surface until around five or six years of age – sometimes not until puberty. Occasionally an ability remains latent for nearly a whole lifetime and is only brought to the fore by some overwhelming injury or deep psychological trauma. But in children like Sam, the abilities are there from the start and that's an alarming and dangerous combination." She paused, "With me so far?" I nodded, I was way ahead. I could clearly remember the strength of emotions in my baby sister.

Miss Peacock opened her mouth to take over again but I interrupted,

"Why's he at the Foundation?" Ruth slipped in,

"In addition to supervising the research project there, which, as you may recall, is not all above board as regards its aims, Dr. Karl W. Dreck," she rolled the syllables around her mouth and spat them out as if they'd gone off, "Has developed a high-profile practice, dealing with severely disturbed and disabled children. Sam was referred there because his foster parents were having so many inexplicable problems. When Dreck suggested he hospitalise the boy for observation and treatment the foster parents and Social Services were only too pleased to hand over responsibility." Her mouth tightened, "If there's one thing they can't abide, it's children who make their case-books look untidy. The clinic is run on the same premises and under the auspices of the Foundation, it's earned itself a considerable reputation for successful treatment."

"But don't people know?"

"What?"

"What goes on there?" She arched an eyebrow,

"Research. What could be wrong with that?"

"But they can't keep him sedated forever." I said, "What then?" Miss Peacock and her sister exchanged the briefest of glances and Miss Peacock took over,

"You need to be quite clear. Dreck is a man obsessed. He knows there

109

are people out there with different abilities. In years of searching, he's only been able to identify one or two who're this naturally talented. Sam's his Holy Grail, he can't and won't miss the opportunity of taking him to pieces bit by bit to find what makes him tick. There are no parents to interfere and the social workers are being fed a steadily deteriorating case progress. If a death were to occur, there would be no undue investigation." What should have sounded melodramatic somehow, in her evenly neutral tone, merely sounded factually accurate.

"What can you do?"

"Get him out."

"How?"

"We need to move swiftly. As you point out, they can't keep him sedated forever, his system won't take it. But they're scared to death of what he'll do if they bring him out of it – you've seen the protective clothing." She snorted, "Goodness knows what good they think that's going to do. The point is, someone has to go in there and get him." There was a pause, they all looked at me, I looked back.

"Surely, you can find someone better than me?" For just a second I felt the lash of her restrained fierce irritation, before she masked it.

"Unfortunately not. You look younger than you are, we hope he'll see you as another child, far less threatening."

"There must be someone else, surely?"

"You're our best chance. He's learnt, the hard way, not to put his trust in any adult he's ever met."

I'd inched forward during this exchange so I was sitting on the very edge of the sofa. Now I pushed myself back into its comfortable depths and shut my eyes for a moment. They waited while I mulled over what I'd been told. I opened them again.

"Why should I trust you, believe what you're saying?"

"Don't be obtuse girl, how d'you think? If we were lying you'd know."

"I can't read you."

"Doesn't matter, you know full well you wouldn't have come with Glory if you hadn't believed she was telling the truth." She was right of course. I'd seen the boy, I knew in the deepest core of me what I'd been shown was genuine but I wanted more.

"I don't understand this whole set-up. Who are you anyway? What's

110

it all got to do with you? And – oh yes, last time I saw Glory, she was actually working with Dreck and that ghastly assistant."

Miss Peacock tutted briskly,

"We haven't time to go into everything." This time it was Glory who intervened.

"Rachael, she's right, I'd want to know more."

"We'll be talking till the cows come home."

"She needs some background." Glory argued, "Or she won't co-operate, you see how obstinate she is." I shifted crossly, polite, obviously wasn't something this lot did.

"I don't know." Miss Peacock was dubious. Glory was firm.

"No choice. Ruth?"

"Agreed." Ruth said quietly

Swivelling my head from one to the other, I felt like an enthusiastic spectator at Wimbledon. Miss Peacock raised an eyebrow at Ruth who nodded,

"I'll do it now." she said. Miss Peacock turned back to me.

"Right. If you know more, it might make up your mind but because time is short it will be intense, do you understand?" I nodded. I didn't at all, but presumed I would shortly. Ruth moved a little closer to me,

"Give me your hands dear, that's right. If you've had enough at any time, just pull away from me. Don't look so apprehensive, I'm only going to share some memories with you. I'll try and keep things brief and in order but remember, these are my recollections – from my heart as well as my head – not edited like a film or a book. Close your eyes." Her plump little hands encircling mine were warm and dry and held me very firmly.

CHAPTER TWENTY-THREE

They were two sisters, Ruth younger, Rachael eighteen months older. Father was as tall as the ceiling. Waist-coated; fob-watched; balding; distinguished; a doctor; heart specialist; highly respected. People from all over, in fear and need came to him to be cured or comforted. With colleagues and patients he was cool, calm, reassuring, with his wife and beloved daughters he played the clown and they sometimes laughed until they cried. He'd bend, sweet-cologne smelling and gather both girls in his arms, rising with them to his full height and it felt to them as if they were going to touch the sky and catch the clouds, but they knew, in his arms they were safer than safe.

Mother was soft, rose-petal cheeks, warm, soap-smelling neck with long brown braided hair which she wore coiled and pinned up, held in place with tortoiseshell pins which she took out at night and laid on the dressing table ready for the morning. Sometimes she let the girls brush her hair with the silver-backed brush, gift from her own mother. She was a cushiony bosom and baking and bedtime stories, a warm lap when they were cold after the long brisk walk home through snowy streets from school, a cool hand on a fevered head when they were sick and sweating.

There were two Grandpapas one strict, stern, generous with pocket money but needing a perfectly recited times-table first. Another, *Zaider*, soft like butter who let them do whatever they wanted, from plaiting his beard to riding on his back. No grandmas sadly but variegated uncles and aunts and cousins some in the city, lots in the country for weekend visits – late nights, full stomachs, falling asleep lulled by the rhythm of the adults talking downstairs. Happy days, swinging on a tyre suspended from a tree, a bloodied knee bringing pain but also a pleasant shower of attention. Ruth and Rachael watched their mother light candles on a Friday night and yearly they sat with the family around a *Seder* table. Life was good. They spoke another language, but I understood everything because these were Ruth's memories.

What the two girls knew they could do was shared simply between themselves, taken for granted, nothing out of the ordinary. They were very close, in age and affection and it seemed entirely logical that they shared each other's thoughts, along with everything else. They assumed this was the way it was with sisters. Because they didn't know they were different, there was never any reason to talk about it. By the time oddly unsettling incidents started to emerge, objects accidentally smashed in transit, fires inexplicably ignited, their parents were preoccupied with altogether different concerns.

Ruth and Rachael were, naturally, aware far earlier than their contemporaries of what was taking place, reading if not quite understanding what their parents sought to keep from them. At first their father was not unduly perturbed. Of course he didn't like what was happening in Germany, despaired of the direction in which things were headed although, as he reassured his increasingly anxious wife, nobody at his level, in his profession, was likely to be affected in any way. But he was wrong, he couldn't have been more wrong.

Unbelievably swiftly the whole structure and fabric of their lives began to unravel in unimaginable ways. I saw yellow stars sewn onto sleeves of coats by women too fear-filled to cry. Listened in on visits from anguished relatives who thought they'd lost everything, but were not yet aware of how much more they were to lose. Familiar streets became foreign territory, changed and corrupted by shattering glass, crackling fire, shouts of hoarse hatred. Father – and surely it was only their own growth, Ruth and Rachael's that made him look shorter, diminished in size – no longer went to the hospital, no longer clowned. He was allowed to see a few patients at home but gradually even the neediest of patients deemed it better for their health to seek treatment elsewhere. Once, more frightening than anything, they thought they heard him crying, rusty, gut-wrenching noises more like retches than sobs. Over the months, Mother's plump cheeks sagged and paled, her hands shook now.

Rachael and Ruth, with their parents were taken in 1939, they were amongst the first. They became separated from Mother and Father when they were herded into different carriages of a train with no windows. I was Ruth, clinging to her sister, the two of them inundated into near unconsciousness by, not only the smells and sounds of fear and despair, but the sensory overload of what was going on in the minds of the three thousand desperate men, women and children who travelled with them.

113

I jerked my hands away convulsively, tears streaming still, mine or hers I couldn't tell.

"My dear, I'm sorry, I'm so sorry. I just needed you to understand who we are so you would know us, I forget, stupid woman me, how intense it can be." Ruth's arms were around me as I shook. Her own face was pale and strained, chin quivering, her stress doubled by mine. The others weren't in the room any more, how much time had elapsed I couldn't tell. I tried to tell her she shouldn't apologise, I wasn't crying for me. But of course she knew that. She pressed a tissue into my hand, watched while I blew and wiped.

"It's important Stella, my dear, for where we go from here, that you know as much of us as I can convey in the short time we have. Look, let me just talk you through the next bit." She reached for my hands again, I couldn't help but flinch. She shook her head, "No, not sharing, just telling, all right?"

"We were ten and twelve when we entered the camp, sixteen and eighteen when we were liberated. We survived because of what we were, though we knew enough by then to make sure nobody else guessed. If there'd ever been even the slightest suspicion, we'd have been taken for experimentation immediately. There were things, my dear, we had to do that I will not talk about, but we did them to survive and survive we did. We developed our abilities beyond anything we had thought possible and we learnt more about human nature than we would wish anybody else to ever know. We learnt, as you have done, how very easy it is to kill and how powerful is this thing we have, although it wasn't powerful enough to get us out of that place." She paused for a moment, eyes closed lost in thought and I waited hands quiescent in hers.

"We tried," she said softly, "Never to forget that for every man or woman who sinks to untold levels of wickedness, depravity and sheer inhumanity there are others who rise equally in the opposite direction." She opened her eyes to look at me, "That's something very important to know, to remember, to hold in your heart whatever happens, do you understand?"

"Your parents?" I asked the question although I knew the answer.

"We never saw them again."

"The rest of your family?" she shook her head.

"All of them?"

"All of them. When we were liberated we didn't want to stay in Germany, couldn't bear to. It was arranged we would come to England, we were very lucky." I snorted, couldn't help it,

"Lucky?"

"Yes," for a moment her sister's impatience was echoed. "You'll find, my dear, I don't use words lightly. We considered ourselves lucky to be alive and lucky that a family who'd come over years earlier took us in, looked after us, that we became fond of them and they of us. We studied, we learned the language quickly, we took exams," she smiled sideways at me, softening the previous rebuke, "We did well, naturally, and in due course we both trained as teachers."

"And that's what you do now?" I could visualise no insurrection in the classes of Miss P the elder. Ruth smiled catching the thought,

"Both of us deal with tutoring special needs children, children who have physical, mental or learning difficulties. Some are damaged at birth, some come from broken or abusive homes and have suffered physically and hence emotionally all their lives, others have differing degrees of autism. Sometimes we're a last resort, when all other avenues have been exhausted. There are those whose difficulties we can solve very easily, others who require much more from us, but there are few we cannot help, even if only a little. We're actually rather successful at what we do, sometimes people say it's as if we can see into the minds of these sad children." She laughed, deliberately breaking the sombre mood and I smiled with her. Hamlet who I'd almost forgotten was there, raised his head briefly to look at us, whumpfed gently and lowered it again.

"And sometimes, my dear, the children who need our help, need it desperately because they are like us in one way or another. You'll do it, won't you, help us get Sam out?" It wasn't really a change of direction but where she'd been heading all along and far more statement than question. I was to learn about Ruth that she was master of emotional blackmail, with a knack for playing people in a way that, had her motives ever been less than pure, would have been downright immoral. Glory called them, she told me once, the Stick and the Carrot, both sisters achieving their ends equally effectively, albeit by differing methods.

115

There was much more, so much more I wanted to ask but after our brief, shockingly intimate and painful walk down her personal memory lane, I felt I knew Ruth more than a little. There was no doubt in my mind she was totally genuine and if she was, so were the others. As for Sam – well, I didn't really think I had a choice. In the strange situation I found myself, all the time-consuming rituals of social intercourse and interaction were stripped away and openness was all that was left, no room for prevarication, compromise or empty courtesies. My earlier irritation had subsided to let in, if I'm honest, a gradually mounting sense of anticipatory excitement, albeit mixed with apprehension. This was an unsought and unthought of opportunity to find answers to questions that had been with me all my life.

If I imagined though that things on that strangest of Saturdays couldn't get much stranger, I was wrong. First, though there were practical arrangements. I phoned my parents who answered so swiftly they must have been sitting on it at their end. Launching cautiously into a carefully reasoned argument as to why I should be allowed to spend a few days with my new acquaintances, I was amazed when my mother said yes. I was even more astonished to find they'd already spent some time talking on the phone with Miss Peacock. I don't know exactly what she'd said to them or they to her but once they'd received my assurance that I was fine and did want to stay, they acquiesced without further discussion, the only proviso being that I phone every day.

"Now," my mother said, "I've packed for a week and …"

"Sorry?"

"He came back."

"Who did?"

"The tall gentleman."

"Ed?"

"Yes Ed, lovely manners, he came back and picked up your bag." I turned away from the phone,

"Ruth, your sister sent Ed back to my house to get my things?" She nodded comfortably,

"We thought you'd say yes dear." I turned back to the phone. A person likes to at least maintain the fiction they're in control of their own destiny; my mother in the meantime was listing things I should and shouldn't do. She was concerned also that I'd arrived empty handed – no flowers, no chocolates, no joke! She'd remedied this with a big box of

Black Magic in the top of my case but was that enough? Although she was putting a brave front on things, her acute anxiety was thrumming through the wires and my head and when she abruptly said goodbye and handed the phone to my father, I knew she hadn't really just remembered she'd left something on the gas. My father was brusque, equally concerned and equally unskilled at hiding it but perhaps, like me, aware that in this strangely unfolding situation might lie answers to questions we'd never before been able to put to anyone.

Glory showed me up to the room I'd be occupying for my stay, finding her way unerringly without use of the stick, just lightly touching the bannister as we went up the stairs. She indicated a bathroom to the left in the upstairs hallway then opened the door of a small sunny room with brightly patterned, heavily lined, floral curtains in cream and pink, looped back from a window netted in white and slightly open to let in fresh air. The bed was piled high with pillows and what I learned was a continental down duvet. A thickly luxurious cream rug was on the floor and, incongruously familiar in these new surroundings, one of our large, metal cornered, rigid black and battered suitcases from home.

One wall here too was book-lined and a vase of yellow tulips brightened the dressing table and scented the air, there was even a small radio – everything ready for a guest, including a still-cellophaned toothbrush and toothpaste at the side of the sink. Glory must have caught the thought, because she nodded.

"We often have unexpected guests, we're always prepared. I'll let you unpack but first …" She surged into my head, briskly took the defences of which I was so proud, altered them a bit and then let me explore what she'd done. The change was subtle. Like looking at an optical illusion, a vase becoming, with only a subtle shift in perception, two witch's faces. I immediately grasped what she'd done and its resultant strength.

She withdrew and tried to get back in again. I successfully kept her out for a while but she was too strong. I grimaced, she laughed,

"Practise'll make perfect. Come down when you're ready, we eat about seven."

CHAPTER TWENTY-FOUR

I re-entered the living room cautiously, I didn't care how friendly Hamlet was held to be, he was still a question mark in my mind. Ed, incongruously clad in a floral plastic apron – sadly inadequate for the substantial area it had to cover – was to my surprise, busy in the kitchen. He looked round as I came in but when I smiled across at him, merely nodded his head and returned to stirring something. He wasn't the friendliest of souls, but at least supper seemed in the offing and smelt good, it'd had been a long afternoon and I was pretty peckish.

Ruth was working on a pile of papers spread over the kitchen table and raised a hand in greeting but didn't look up. Glory and Miss Peacock, who was knitting – I wondered if she was responsible for Ruth's jumper and if so she needed suing – were seated one on each of the facing sofas. A paperback book suddenly hurtled through the air and thwacked me hard on the forehead. I staggered backwards.

"Ow!" I clapped a hand to the injured area. Miss Peacock tutted,

"Slow." Rubbing my head, I was indignant,

"I wasn't expecting it."

"It's the unexpected you'll have to deal with. Catch." This time I was ready and caught the cushion that shot towards me. But it fought and bucked in my hands like an animal and was covering my face, even as I struggled to get it off.

"Break her hold." Ruth had glanced up, but at first I didn't understand the calmly issued instruction. As fast as I backed away, the cushion followed, blocking my mouth and nose, extruding sharp feathered ends that scratched my cheek.

In my confusion and rising discomfort I felt Glory in my head – so much for my newly reinforced shielding. Again she showed me something from a slightly different angle, how to visualise where the control of the cushion was and how to snap it. With the thought came the result and the offending object, inanimate now, dropped to the floor. I was breathless and there were a couple of feathers in my mouth which I spat out resentfully.

"Again." I snapped and another cushion slammed into me. I felt outwards, focusing on the strength that was powering it and I snapped the control, sending it triumphantly and harmlessly to the floor.

"To me." Miss Peacock ordered. I swiftly bent and picked up the cushion, years of conditioning hadn't fallen on deaf ears – hands, always use the hands!

"No," she lashed, I dropped the cushion, picked it up with my mind, shot it forward and felt as she snapped my control before it got anywhere near her. It plummeted, knocking off balance a large silver jug of fatly pink peonies which teetered for a second or two on the table before over-ending. Flowers and water shot over the head of the nearby sleeping dog who leapt up, barking wildly in fright and in the general melee I thought – if I'm quick – grabbed a particularly plump bloom and sent it to Miss Peacock, lodging it fetchingly and incongruously behind her right ear.

"Enough now," Ruth bustled over, righting the jug, mopping the water with a cloth and consoling the quivering mass that was Hamlet.

"You shouldn't be doing this in here Rachael, that's why we have downstairs."

"Sorry," Miss Peacock removed the flower and nodded at me,

"Sit," I went over to take the place next to Glory.

"Shield." reminded Glory. I did and could feel as they both began to probe. I held on as long as I could but they were strong and broke through easily. I clenched my jaw and tried again. This time I held out longer.

"Better. Now, light that." Miss Peacock pointed at a pile of logs and kindling arranged in the stone surround fireplace in the corner.

I looked at the wood with trepidation, this was strictly forbidden, a taboo ground deep into my psyche from the time we'd attended a firework party given by two-doors-away neighbours – intriguingly already lightly brushed with scandal – the word was she'd been an au pair, he the father of her charge and they'd run off together. When we pitched up at their house, 'Dun Roamin' I remember my mother wondering whether that was a statement from him or an instruction from her.

I hadn't wanted to go to the party, mood unimproved by their obnoxious son, ten going on five who kept poking me painfully in the back with an unlit sparkler and running away. I only meant to light the wretched firework and give him a fright but it turned out to be a case of over-egging the pudding. I lit not only his sparkler, which he flung away with a satisfactory yelp of shock, but also unfortunately a further selection of sparklers. It wasn't, and I maintain that to this day, my fault that the sparklers happened to be at the bottom of all the other fireworks. Alarmed at what I'd started and panicked into a bit of muddled thinking, I tried to take the heat out of the situation by re-directing it elsewhere and inadvertently ignited the bonfire. Chaos reigned as the fire, meticulously prepared with just the right quantities of dry wood and a well-dressed guy on the top, whooshed cheerfully into action and crackled, spat and burned in the centre of the lawn, while a couple of hundred pounds worth of fireworks went off in the space of three minutes. It was, you might say, a party that went with a bang.

What they lacked in telepathic skills, my parents always more than made up for with instinctively accurate guess-work and there was no doubt in their minds who was to blame for the Great Firework Fiasco. The next day my father hauled me down to the local library. I don't know how he found the book he showed me, but it featured fire disasters through the years and by the time we'd worked our way through that – sepia photographs of contorted-faced factory girls screaming on window sills, sooted firemen and unconscious, unrecognisable stretchered victims – he'd made his point and I ring-fenced that particular part of my ability so tightly I rarely remembered it was there. Now, I was being asked to use it again. I shook my head firmly,

"I won't do that." Ruth, stacking her papers now and capping her pen, looked at me over half-moon reading glasses,

"You should you know, learn to control it. Never let it control you. That's the coward's way of dealing." I glared at her. I really hated the way they strolled in and out of my head like there was a set of swing doors with a welcome notice.

"Shield better and we won't." Glory was smug. I gritted my teeth and flung the frustration at the fire. Miss Peacock nodded judiciously as the wood started to smoke then smoulder.

"Not bad. Ed, have we time before we eat?" Ed, expressionless as always, cutting vegetables briskly, said over his shoulder,

"Five minutes all right?" His voice was light, not at all the sound you'd expect from that frame and I realised they were the first words I'd heard him utter. A stainless steel colander swung through the air towards him. He reached for it, tipped in the carrots, rinsed them under the tap, turned them smoothly into a waiting saucepan and moved over to check the soup. Ruth meanwhile, left the table and came over, bouncing herself down on the sofa next to her sister with a little sigh of pleasure, removing her glasses and rubbing forefinger and thumb on the bridge of her nose.

"Damn glasses pinch."

"Take them back, they need adjusting. Do you understand what I mean by a *gestalt*?" I realised Miss Peacock had addressed her second sentence to me. I shook my head,

"Sounds like something my Grandmother might cook." Miss P gave this small sally the respect it deserved and ignored it,

"Easier to show you. Here." she reached over the coffee table and took Glory's hand, Glory in turn extended her's in my direction. I hesitated for just a second before taking it, small and cool in mine then felt Ruth, her touch familiar now, grasp my other one. Connection to the three older women was an experience that even today, even after it's happened many times since in one form or another and in a variety of circumstances, not all of them good, is still almost impossible to describe.

I could sense and taste them individually. Peppermint Miss Peacock, Glory's lemon-sherbert fizz and a rich purple-deep lavender that was Ruth. I could feel the falling away of their smooth, rigid-walled screening and, my recent encounter with Ruth still raw in my mind, for an instant tried to pull away but they didn't let go physically or mentally and the strength of what was happening kept me locked in place. I could see now how carefully and meticulously they protected and preserved their privacy, how multi-layered and carefully constructed were their defences and even in this most intimate of moments, there were areas I was unable to reach. But rising from the combination of their minds was something greater and more powerful than I could have imagined. And, unhesitating now, I joined with them and gasped at the increase, the surge in the power as I did. And I felt, through their hands and their minds their acknowledgement of me and my contribution as an equal.

How long we sat joined I'm not sure, probably only a matter of minutes before the contact was broken gently, first on my left by Glory and then slowly by Ruth on my right. Loss and relief warred briefly and equally strongly.

"Powerful stuff eh?" Glory matter of factly, put both hands in the small of her back and stretched first to one side then the other.

"Understand now?" Miss Peacock had also risen and was setting out cutlery at the kitchen table. I nodded, still shaken. I couldn't believe she could move so swiftly from that soaring sharing to the prosaic task of laying the table. She continued,

"Of course, the stronger the component parts, the greater the effectiveness of the grouping, physical closeness is good but not essential, we can work from a distance too."

"Effectiveness?" I was intrigued, "What do you do with it?"

"Plenty." She was a real specialist in the oblique. "Shall we eat?"

Ed was carrying brimming soup bowls to the table, one in each hand, three floating along next to him. His face was expressionless as ever as he concentrated on no spillage. Someone had pulled full length, pale gold drapes together to cover the windows, so the large room behind us which earlier had been so light and bright and open to the garden was now lamp and fire-lit and cosily enclosed. The scent of good food and Hamlet's snoring blended companionably with the pop and crackle of flames as they worked their way through the logs I'd so frighteningly easily ignited.

The meal was delicious, Ed apparently a devoted Fanny Craddock fan. This was, Glory pointed out between mouthfuls, hugely important, because she and the Peacock sisters didn't have a domestic instinct between them. As it was, we sat down to rich home-made chicken soup which grandma wouldn't have been ashamed to call her own, followed by chicken and crisp potatoes with buttered carrots, comfortably finished off with chunky slices of apple pie and ice cream, Ed's own apparently!

Nobody spoke much at first but it was an easy silence. As we ate, I couldn't help but notice Glory was wielding her knife and fork as easily as the rest of us, cutting her food unhesitatingly and precisely although Ed, seated next to her, kept glancing over at her plate as if to make sure she was managing well. I'd no experience with blindness and the problems it created and wondered just how she did that. I intended to ask her later but there she was again, jumping in, answering the thought as it was formulated, I needed to work on that shielding.

"Ed's letting me see through his eyes. And yes you do, don't worry we'll practise."

As we finished, Ed accepted thanks with solemnity waving away my offer to help with clearing up and in an instant crockery and cutlery were leaving the table to land in neat piles in the sink. Nobody batted an eyelid. I was rather enchanted with this openness, a complete contrast to the keep-it-under-wraps conditioning I'd grown used to. I could feel the grin on my face as I caught Ed's eye, he nodded his head once in acknowledgement and it belatedly dawned on me – he wasn't expressionless from choice.

"Moebius Syndrome." Said Ruth behind me,

"Sorry?"

"Ed has something called Moebius Syndrome."

"I didn't mean to be rude." Ruth smiled,

"You weren't. We're so used to it, we tend to forget. It's a neurological disorder that affects his cranial nerves, means he can't move the muscles of his face. Life would have been tough enough for you as it was, eh Ed dear, without further complication?" She rubbed him affectionately on the back as she walked past to put the kettle on. She was short, only about my own five foot and she looked even more so as she passed him. He turned briefly from the sink to look down at her and expressionless though his face remained, there was no doubting the absolute devotion in his eyes. I wondered what his story was, immediately tried to suppress the thought and shield but not quick enough. I wasn't sure whether he could read me but Ruth certainly could,

"He came to us a very frightened little boy," she was spooning coffee into cups and raised an eyebrow to see if I wanted one, I shook my head, "Couldn't smile, couldn't cry but could do oh so much more to get the attention he desperately needed. He was, as he often says, a proper pickle!" I looked up at the proper pickle, more in astonishment at the thought of him stringing two words together than at what she'd told me.

"And he stayed?" I asked unnecessarily.

"He stayed all right." She looked across at him and laughed. "No matter how many more suitable places we found for him, he just kept turning up again and again like a good penny."

"It's a bad penny." A muttered aside from over at the sink. She laughed again,

"I think Ed, dear I know the difference!"

When I finally went upstairs, a couple of hours later, eyelids drooping, the amazing, soft duvet – what a difference from my normal sheet and blankets – pulled me instantly into a deep and dreamless sleep, perhaps too deep because I awoke with a start, a jolting sense of dislocation and no idea at first where I was. My watch when I switched on the bedside light, showed 4.30 and after a bit of fruitless, not to mention fretful, tossing and turning I gave up and decided there was nothing for it, but to head downstairs and see if I could forage a warm drink, I didn't think they'd mind.

Donning my quilted pink dressing gown, needless to say there was nothing my mother had omitted to pack, I made my way down quietly, stepping on the side rather than the centre of each stair, aiming for a creakless descent. Opening the living room door cautiously, I recalled too late, I'd no idea where friend Hamlet slept. I wasn't in suspense for long. As I shut the door quietly behind me, a solid body hit mine, knocking me back against the wood, whooshing the air right out of me. With a paw on each of my cringing shoulders he was attempting to lick my face off. My relief that he hadn't barked the place down almost overcame my nerves at such close canine contact and I guiltily banished from my mind my mother's horror at the hygiene aspect – a woman who made you wash your hands if you so much as looked at the cat.

With some effort I persuaded him back to all fours, although he was clearly so delighted with the company that he wasn't going to put any distance between us. With him padding at my somewhat apprehensive heels and occasionally batting into my side affectionately and almost overbalancing me, I made my way across the curtain-darkened room to the kitchen. I filled and put the kettle on to boil, unearthed the tea in a container helpfully marked and opened the fridge in search of milk.

"Top shelf." I jumped and turned, nearly falling headlong over the hound. She was sitting on the sofa, a fleece blanket over her lap for warmth. I hadn't noticed her because she was so still.

"Sorry," she said, "Thought you'd seen me." I made the tea, poured two cups and took them over placing hers on the table in front of her, she leaned forward feeling for it, the first time I'd seen any real sign of her disability and as I sat, I concentrated on maintaining my privacy of thought so she shouldn't know.

"Are you up late, or up early?" I asked.

"I don't sleep well, a few hours then I'm done. You?"

"Too much going on in my head." We sipped in silence, Hamlet having planted himself companionably on the floor between us. After a few moments I said,

"I wondered ..."

"I know," said Glory, cupping her hands round the cup's warmth, "I'll tell you."

CHAPTER TWENTY-FIVE

"I was abandoned when I was few days old. Someone – my mother presumably – left me on a convenient doorstep. The owners of the house found me when they went to take in the milk. Luckily it wasn't too cold a night – she hadn't bothered to wrap me particularly well – and equally luckily there wasn't a bombing raid. Still, when they found me I was suffering from hypothermia.

The nurses at the hospital called me Glory because that's all the woman who brought me in could say, over and over, she was so upset – 'Glory be, who on this earth'd leave a baby like that?' Isaacs was the name of the ward they put me in. My earliest memories are of the childrens' home, I suppose I'd be about four or five then, not sure. How far back can you remember?" she looked up at me.

"About the same I suppose." She nodded and continued. "Nobody knew I was blind for ages, I didn't either of course, had no idea I was different from anyone else in any way other than the name-calling my skin colour earned. They knew I was clumsy and fumbled and bumped into things, but they just assumed I was slightly backwards. As for me, well I simply managed my daily life by utilising whoever's eyes were nearest. The people in charge weren't unkind or uncaring, simply overwhelmed by numbers, responsibility and damaged kids – orphaned, injured, traumatised in the blitz, so many worse off than me.

They found, quite by accident I think, that if they put me to sleep in a room with some of the most disturbed children, it seemed to soothe them. Truth was, I couldn't bear the noise, the screaming and crying hurt my ears and their nightmares ripped my mind. I learnt, in order to protect myself, I had to create a sort of soft blanket around and inside their heads. It smothered very successfully what was going on in there, both for them and for me and we all got to sleep well." She paused to sip tea. "Eventually it got so I was spending all my nights and the majority of my days with the most seriously disturbed children, the ones most difficult to handle. Even though many of them were sedated a lot during the day, they were still much less restless when I was near and after a while I became as indispensable a part of the nursing team's armoury as any of the medication they had available."

"What about you though, what was it doing to you?"

"Well, obviously nothing too drastic because here I am today." She was matter of fact. "Of course it wasn't good for me, but they were so hard-pushed they had to use what they could and they had no idea what was really going on. Of course, neither did I really. From time to time I suffered shocking headaches, migraine attacks I suppose you'd call them. I'd be violently sick for hours on end and the pain in my head made me cry and scream as badly as some of the worst cases I was supposed to be helping. When I was really bad they'd sedate me too – the relief of being pushed down into unconsciousness was so wonderful, well worth the pain of the headache. The headaches were probably just a result of sensory overload. They don't happen very often now but in those days, even when I slept, a part of me had to stay alert to maintain that blanket cover for the other children – it was tiring."

She shifted slightly, made herself more comfortable on the sofa. Hamlet stirred too, whining gently and rolling heavily over on to his side. Her memories were all the more evocative for their un-dramatic recounting and the serenity of the woman sought no sympathy for the torment of the child – completely unaware she was gifted and disabled in equal measure.

"When I was about seven I had a particularly agonising attack which lasted longer than previous ones. There was a new doctor at the home then. When it was over, he insisted on giving me a more thorough examination than those previously carried out and he made the assumption that it was the latest ferocious attack that had damaged my eyesight. But he and colleagues he called in were completely baffled by the level of optic impairment. My eyes reacted like those of a completely blind person, yet when they tested me with picture cards I could describe them perfectly accurately.

Naturally, they were completely at sea, as was I. I'd learnt in my short life the benefits of fitting in, doing what everyone else did, reading what the people in charge wanted me to do and acting on it. But in their total bafflement they baffled me and I no longer knew how to react, how to please. I understood from them that I wasn't fitting normal parameters and was desperate to do so, but how could I when I so totally hadn't grasped what normal was?" Her voice rose a little, an echo of the puzzled and frightened small girl. "I'm really not sure what would have happened to me if Rachael Peacock hadn't turned up. She was still a trainee in those days and part of an assessment team that travelled to schools and institutions, working with children with special needs." She chuckled, "And there was no doubt my needs were pretty special, not to mention desperate at that point.

Because each answer to every question put to me by the medics seemed to make matters worse, I had by that time simply stopped answering any questions at all – it seemed safest. I was withdrawing more and more to where they couldn't reach me, wrapping myself in the blanket I used for the children but this time making sure it was just tight round me. By the time I was brought in to see the assessment team I wasn't talking at all, hadn't spoken for weeks and had become quite used to it, found it rather restful actually.

Mrs Mokovsky, a heavy-set lady with a drooping face – like a bloodhound with depression – was in charge. I remember she had a hectic dab of rouge on each cheek, perhaps to cheer herself up. Outside she wasn't at all reassuring but inside she was kindly, well intentioned, extremely knowledgeable and instinctively understanding of the disturbed children who trooped in and out of her examination rooms each day. Her colleague was an elderly man, Mr Smuss. He'd been brought out of retirement by the post war effort and was inclined to be a little sceptical of Mrs Mokovsky and some of her methods which he considered 'new-fangled and alarming.'

The third member of the team was a severe looking young woman in a black suit who didn't join the other two behind their table, but sat on a chair a little distance back as befitted her student status. Rachael Peacock." Glory paused to take another sip of tea and finding the cup empty, held it out in my direction, I organised refills.

"I really don't know," continued Glory reflectively "Which of the two of us was more electrified when I was brought in. She recognised me instantly for what I was and tried to calm me. I knew only that there was somebody in my head and I started to scream." I nodded wryly, I could well identify with that and I'd been quite a bit older when Glory had introduced herself.

"Everything went wild for a while. I tried to get out of the room,

Rachael and the assistant, Mandy who'd brought me in, struggled to grab my arms and legs, holding me still to stop me hurting myself or them. Mr Smuss said a good slap never did a hysterical child any harm and Mrs Mokovsky, bless her, sat there calmly waiting for the storm to pass. Wise woman, she knew it would. And sure enough, after a little while when I had no voice left with which to scream she suggested that Miss Peacock keep Mandy and me company while we went to get a glass of water, then perhaps we'd all talk some more.

The three of us went into the room next door and Rachael suggested to Mandy that perhaps rather than a glass of water, a hot cup of tea might do us all good. Mandy wasn't going to be gone for long. Rachael looked at me and I looked through her eyes too at a small, fearful, snotty-nosed, seven year old with sweat-matted hair and wide unseeing eyes, too shocked and scared now to even cry out again. I felt her sweep straight through me and she read and instantly assessed all that had gone on and with her comprehension came mine. In those few moments I learned the answers to so many of the questions that until then had baffled me completely. And she did the only thing she could in the time we had. She opened her arms to me and I went into them unhesitatingly."

I sniffed and she looked up sharply,

"Nothing to cry about for Pete's sake, it was the best thing that ever happened to me. By the time Mandy came back with the tea, we were sitting on chairs on either side of the table and nobody would have known that anything out of the ordinary had taken place."

"But wasn't it awful to finally realise you were blind?"

"God no. After the initial shock, it was like having a dislocated shoulder put back – everything suddenly clicked into place. I could make sense of it all, understand the way things were. And in truth I was no blinder than before."

"And then?"

"In due course Rachael took me back in to Mrs Mokovsky and Mr Smuss and they asked me all the questions they needed to ask and were delighted, not only that I answered, but that I spoke up coherently and intelligently and whenever I got stuck, she was there, in my head, helping me.

The report they put in concluded my emotional problems and withdrawal in recent months had been due to understandable distress and shock over the sudden loss of my sight. They recommended I be given practical help in dealing with my disability that a place be secured for me at a school for the blind. Other than that they found me to be normal and, considering the circumstances, reasonably well adjusted. And at the end of the day and after assessing about a dozen other children, they packed up and left."

"Left?"

"Well, they were never going to stay, this was just one of the many homes they dealt with."

"But what about Rachael? Weren't you scared you'd never see her again?"

"She told me I would."

"Was it awful when she left?"

"Awful? No. What had gone before had been awful, but afterwards … well, I wasn't alone any more was I?"

"So what happened?" I leaned forward, I could see her elegantly chiselled features more clearly now. It was getting light outside and the first bird call was joined soon by a chorus. Hamlet pricked his ears momentarily, decided it was nothing to do with him and carried on sleeping.

"Rachael had to complete a thesis to pass her final exams and get her qualifications. She chose me as her case study, gained approval from the authorities and came to visit me every week for a year. Ostensibly she was following and charting my progress, in reality she was shaping it. She showed me how to shield and protect myself and also, over the period of time, how to work more effectively with the damaged children. She taught me that sometimes, in some cases, although there are things you can do, the end result does more harm than good and wisdom lies in knowing when not to interfere. She made me appreciate the strength and weaknesses of what we are and become aware that it should never be underestimated nor misused." She paused thoughtfully then added, "Well, only under exceptional circumstances! As the year drew on, she was allowed to take me out of the home on outings and I came here and met Ruth." She smiled slightly and I saw how the two young women who'd come through the war and lost everyone but each other, and the child who'd never had anyone in the first place, had formed their own family.

"By the time Rachael had finished her case study and passed her exams she was such a regular visitor and everyone was so used to seeing her, she just kept on coming. Meanwhile, I'd not only learnt Braille, but more importantly, how to meet people's expectations of what a blind person can and can't do. And that's all for now." She rose abruptly, pushing off the blanket, stifling a yawn and stretching her elegant frame. "I'm going for a hot bath."

"You can't, I want to know the rest."

"Later." she said and left.

CHAPTER TWENTY-SIX

Tiredness caught up with me as she left and I suddenly felt like I'd run a marathon. I couldn't face heading upstairs so I curled up on the sofa pulling the blanket over me, still warm from Glory. I must have fallen asleep because when I woke, the curtains were drawn back, the room was filled with light and there were breakfast type noises going on. I was lovely and warm, someone had covered me with an extra heavy blanket, although as I moved it did too and I realised Hamlet, an opportunist if ever I met one, had made himself at home. My mother would have died a death!

Ed was setting out the breakfast things in his inimitable way.

"Morning." I said and if he was surprised to find me asleep under Hamlet, he naturally didn't show it. I headed for the door to wash and dress, out of the corner of my eye I noted a box of Cornflakes and jug of milk on their way to the table.

I was starving, so in the upstairs bathroom administered only what Grandma called a lick and a promise although, as the familiar phrase came into my mind, so too did the woman in the hospital bed who wasn't Grandma any more.

When I came down again it was to find the three women already at the table. Glory, in a hectically patterned canary-yellow silk top and matching trousers looked as exotic as usual and showed no sign of having been up half the night. Ruth, the half-moon glasses halfway down her nose was scanning a newspaper and smiled at me. She was in another oversized jumper, this one with a migraine-inducing wavy line theme. Miss Peacock herself, looked exactly the same, I was to learn she had a whole wardrobe of white shirts and grey skirts, maybe it was a reaction to the choice of the others. I helped myself to a bowl of cereal and poured a cup of tea.

"Eat quickly, lot to do." Briskly unprepared to waste greeting time, Miss P was working her way through the post, sorting it decisively into two piles.

"Glory said she'd tell me the rest of her story." I protested.

"I'll do some of the telling, she's eating." Ruth folded her paper and sat back, nursing a coffee. "Now where did she get to?" I opened my mouth but she was there before me, "Right, I'll carry on from there." I'd no doubt get used to this in time, but was obviously still leaving far too much hanging out for public consumption.

"By the time Glory was – sixteen?" she raised an eyebrow for confirmation and Glory nodded, "Just a little younger than you are now, my dear, she'd come to live with us full time. In the intervening nine years, Rachael and I had continued our teaching work, often obtaining surprising results and our reputations and practice had grown accordingly.

"Hang on." I said, "The children you help, are many like us?"

"It's not as simple as that." Miss Peacock stifled, not very well, a sigh. I hoped she had more patience with her patients. "There's an enormous spectrum of ability, no two people exactly the same, you must know that by now." I was stung,

"Why would I, you're the only ones I've met."

"Nonsense," she shook her head, irritably, "You haven't been looking properly – there'll be people you've known with particularly sharp intuition. People whose guesses are always a shade more accurate than they should be. They're at the other end of the scale from you, nevertheless they're on the same scale, even if they never know it." I thought – Miss Macpharlane.

"Precisely," said Miss Peacock, "Quite a number around like that, not so many like us."

"How many?"

"Heaven's sake girl, we can't be exact. We've personally seen over the years and with all the children who've been through our hands, probably only about four true adepts, another eight or so with varying milder degrees of ability."

"But there must be others, people you haven't come across personally."

"Obviously, but I can't dish out facts and figures. We believe these abilities are latent in almost everyone, although it's only a tiny minority who seem to have a switch thrown to activate them."

Ruth leaned forward a hand on my arm to call my attention,

"Understand dear, for many this is not a gift, but a curse. Voices in the head have driven people insane for centuries. Those who are unable to learn control, who don't know what they're hearing, end up sedated in mental homes, often misdiagnosed schizophrenics." She paused while I thought this through then went on, "An acceptance of what you are, is essential, your parents have done an excellent job with you. They can be very proud." I stored that to take home.

"But in the long run, each and every one of us has to choose our own path. Some opt to school themselves to as near normality as possible, teach themselves to completely shut away what they have, what they are. Others shape their ability, grab it with both hands and make it work for them." I opened my mouth on a host of questions, but Miss Peacock interrupted swiftly.

"Levitating, can you still do it?"

"Levitating?" She tutted,

"You think of it as flying, it's not really you know."

"Not like I used to," I was regretful both for the vanishing ability and the different slant on it, "It takes so much more effort now, makes me feel a bit sick, so I don't bother – no fun anymore." She nodded,

"Goes that way, never come across anyone who really enjoys it after a certain age. We think it's simply an increase in body weight." She looked at me critically and I automatically pulled in my stomach. "You can still do it though?"

"Don't know, haven't tried in ages."

"We can help, but we don't have a great deal of time. Ruth, finish what she needs to know. I promise I won't interrupt again." Ruth rolled her eyes at me in disbelief, took a sip of coffee and continued.

"The number of people working in our child-care field is small. When there's interesting news it spreads quickly and around the time Glory came to live with us, we started hearing about a doctor who'd come to this country from South Africa. He'd some interesting and innovative theories, was covering new territory with his work with disabled and disturbed children. Rachael and I went along one day to a lecture he was giving in London. He was younger than we'd expected, mid-forties probably then, and a thoroughly unpleasant piece of work." She made a small moue of distaste. "He was, it quickly became apparent, exceedingly clever, drivingly ambitious and hungry for a breakthrough discovery that would make his

134

name and fortune. He'd trained, qualified, risen through the ranks and been working for a number of years in various hospitals in South Africa. He'd opened his own highly successful private practice and, we later found out, left the country in something of a hurry, just ahead of a breaking scandal.

Apparently some of the work and his methods were a little less than orthodox – he was never much in favour of due diligence on some of the drug combinations he used. He'd also, it was rumoured, been involved in highly unsavoury stuff involving tests – experimentation? – on children from some of the most poverty stricken townships. There was no doubt, he'd produced some interesting results and, as sometimes happens, something about the work he was doing was of its time. It caught the imagination of professional colleagues over here and he became the blue-eyed boy for a while, with pieces in the paper, articles in the Lancet, comment in the BMJ and plenty of people happy to hop on his band-wagon.

His research was based on the fact that some physically or mentally disabled children can be gifted in often unlikely ways, musically, artistically or with precocious numbers skills. His ostensible aim was to establish a series of standardised tests to locate, identify and quantify these special talents. Theory was sound – once found and isolated, these talents could be nurtured. This would not only enormously enhance quality of life for the individual child but could be utilised to bring him or her on to develop everyday skills. Progress was gratifying.

He spoke of a severely brain damaged boy, unable to communicate verbally but with an uncanny ability to hear a complicated musical piece just once and then correctly reproduce it, even after a gap of several months, note for note on the piano. Another example was a five year old girl, blind, deaf and dumb from birth but given an object such as a carved statuette to handle for just a few moments, able to reproduce it completely accurately on paper." Ruth paused, only for breath, but long enough for her sister to nip in again.

"Ruth and I knew though, immediately what it really was Dreck was looking for and locating in these children and it wasn't just musical abilities! He was frustratingly difficult to read, occasionally you come across people like that, can't get anything from them unless they're in a highly emotional state. They're not shielding deliberately, they wouldn't know how, there's just a natural barrier that only lets things in or out in a strangely muted way, like listening to a radio underwater. Dreck's a prime example, although we could sense enough to know he was not good news.

At the end of the lecture he announced he'd received some serious Government funding and was establishing a base at Oxford where the project would develop, eventually offering hope to disabled children and their parents from all over the country. Similar centres in Europe and America, were already working on methods to establish new brain path patterns in such children, but he hoped, within a short time, he and Britain would be leading the field."

"Couldn't you have stopped him?"

"Stopped him?" Miss Peacock snapped, "We're not Batman and Robin!" Ruth grinned,

"She's right of course, my dear, think about it, what could we have done? For all we knew, the whole scheme could have come to nothing. We agreed we'd keep an eye on him, but other than that, there appeared to be little action we could take."

"Things went quiet for a while, but after a year or so," Glory had finished eating and now took over the telling, "Rachael and Ruth started to get odd whiffs of fishy goings-on at the Foundation now established in Oxford. Rumours flying around which, if you put up your hand and caught them weren't very substantial, a whisper here, a raised eyebrow there, nothing widespread or concrete. He was still the blue-eyed boy of this area of research and most professionals, working in glass houses as they do, are pretty cautious about casting the first stone. She paused and Miss Peacock slid in,

"There was a child, Ben, an eight year old I'd met at one of the respite centres. His mother asked if I'd see him privately as he seemed to respond well to me. He'd suffered hypoxia – oxygen deprivation – at birth and the resulting handicaps were pretty overwhelming. He was unable to communicate verbally, had no vision and very little motor control. His mother was a scrap of a thing, devoted to Ben, worn down with his care. I've no idea where she found the strength to haul him about the way she did. Her husband had left early on, couldn't cope and I'm not sure she was sorry, meant she could concentrate on Ben without distraction. She was wracked with guilt, poor woman, blamed herself for his condition.

She swore Ben had always been able to communicate and ask her for things. The doctors were kind but reiterated, it was just her excellent care of him that enabled her to guess his needs instinctively – I think they didn't want her to build pointless expectations. They told her he'd never develop beyond the mental age of a year to eighteen months and the best she could ever hope for was to keep him comfortable. She was right though, they were wrong, always trust a mother's instinct. Ben did have an ability to communicate his needs but because of the scrambled connections in his brain, only on the most basic level – too hot, too cold, hungry, thirsty, tired. He was also, up to a point able, with no frame of reference and retarded mental development, to comprehend what he was reading from his mother and others. A little boy lost and locked in his own body with the damaged part of his brain blocking the way to all the rest." She stopped and I caught just a fraction of the depth of pain she felt for this child and all the others. Ruth and Glory were silent. I plunged in, had to know,

"Couldn't you make him better?" She turned and looked at me,

"Better?"

"Yes, cure him, make him right, isn't that what you do?" Her hand shot out, I jumped at the unexpected contact, then she flooded my mind and I shared all too completely the terrible everyday dilemmas she and her sister faced.

Of course there were children they could help. A small blockage removed, repaired, can change a life for the better but so many others – like Ben. How far to go? How deeply to interfere? How to judge the potential damage? Even just seeing him that first time; alerting his mind by her very presence in it, to possibilities undreamt of, offering him mind to mind communication from an outside world full of communication. Unable to stop him reading in turn, how much lay beyond, out of reach. The fear, confirmed in Ben's case that the doctors were wrong, that behind the damage lay not the mere sentient needs of an infant, easily dealt with and satisfied, but the desperation of a growing mind with until now, no hope of being able to bypass terrible physical restraints. Miss Peacock removed her hand from my arm.

"I'm sorry," I was deeply ashamed,

"Indeed. There's a lot for you to learn and the first lesson is to not waste time with stupid questions. I saw Ben regularly over a period of a few months and found that although the brain damage was permanent, he was developing far beyond the gloomy prognostication of his doctors. His psi abilities were only moderate but through them, his communication skills were growing. Most importantly though, he improved immeasurably in his ability to send to his mother and was able to more easily let her know what he needed. One day when I saw him, after a gap in our sessions because I'd been away, I found he'd also discovered how to manipulate objects. Nothing too startling, but enough to enable him to bring a vase of flowers closer so he could smell them or re-angle a lampshade if there was glare in his eyes. He was, despite everything, a happy little soul and I was so delighted by his progress.

His mother of course wanted more. She saw the improvement, had no doubt he could be brought on further still. She phoned me one day, full of excitement, to say she'd managed to get an appointment to have him assessed at a clinic in Oxford that was doing ground-breaking work with brain damaged children. I tried to talk her out of it, but she didn't want to hear. All I could do was ask her to keep me informed.

Apparently at the first appointment they put Ben through a battery of tests to try and find his 'special talents'. She wasn't allowed to stay with him, they said he'd concentrate better without her, so she couldn't tell me exactly what went on. She was charmed however by Dr Dreck, who confirmed she had a very special little boy. So special, the Doctor felt he'd like to work with him further and thought it worthwhile admitting him to the clinic for a few days, to allow for further, more detailed tests. There was a newly-developed drug which the Doctor was convinced could prove invaluable to Ben's progress, but the dosage had to be carefully regulated and monitored to suit him.

She dithered a bit – she and Ben hadn't ever spent a night apart, but the Doctor was persuasive and of course the trump card was that everyone wanted the best for Ben, so she agreed. Ben was in the clinic for five days." Miss Peacock paused,

"And then?" I prompted,

"And then he died." The evenness of her tone belied the starkness of the statement. "I didn't find out until a couple of weeks after it happened. He'd been doing so well, his mother kept telling me, so very well but it was a heart attack, a weakness probably always there, just another of his many physical problems, but one tragically not identified until too late."

We were silent, reflecting on the brief life and swift death of a small boy.

Ruth had quietly got up and made a fresh pot of coffee, her sister thanked her with a glance, poured herself a cup and continued.

"There was no proof of anything untoward in the treatment Ben received, nor reason to suppose he came to harm through tests conducted – other than my gut feeling. But from what we were hearing, more and more children were being referred to Newcombe. If there was something going on, we reluctantly decided, we owed it to the children involved and to ourselves to find out more. We'd no choice but to send in a mole."

"Who?" but it was all starting to fall into place.

"And," said Glory, "Don't think I went willingly, they had to do a lot of talking to convince me. I knew it was the right thing to do, but that didn't make me any more thrilled."

"But, dear girl," protested Ruth, "It was only going to be for a couple of weeks."

"Turned out a lot longer didn't it?"

"But that," pronounced Miss Peacock, rising to her feet, pushing back her chair decisively and brushing non-existent crumbs from her neatly pleated skirt, "Is another instalment altogether. Don't worry," she forestalled my protest, "We'll fill in the gaps, but now we need to find out more about you and time's short." She headed briskly for a door I hadn't noticed before, at the other side of the kitchen and Ruth, pausing only to send the breakfast dishes to the sink, followed in her wake obediently, as did Glory and I. I was peripherally aware of Glory using me to see where she was going, but there was no sense of intrusion.

CHAPTER TWENTY-SEVEN

We made our way down a flight of softly lit, uncarpeted stairs which led into a sizeable, low ceilinged area which must have run under the entire ground floor of the house. Highly polished wooden parquet flooring reflected diffused overhead lights back onto mellow, glossy wood panelled walls, so the lack of natural light wasn't really a problem. At one end of the room, around a low table were grouped a few comfortable looking leather chairs and nearby were several upright wooden chairs around another higher table. The opposite end of the room however was a far more intimidating set-up. Facing each other were two thickly, frosted-glassed, telephone-box sized booths, uncomfortably reminiscent of the one I'd done time in at Oxford. Further along the same wall was another much larger glassed booth although I could see into this one. There was a large double spooled tape recorder fixed on the far wall, alongside a tv screen. There was no sound of traffic down here and I assumed the whole room was soundproofed, it must have cost a fortune to fit out. I knew teachers' salaries weren't high. Nobody else round here was backward in coming forward, so I turned and asked Glory, she grinned,

"Money's never a problem, Ruth dabbles on the Stock Exchange."

"Oh?"

"Takes herself out regularly for a nice lunch in one of the city restaurants popular with stockbrokers. Let's just say, she picks up more tips than the waiters."

I was still turning this over when Miss Peacock put a hand on my shoulder and steered me towards one of the smaller glass booths. I saw Ruth had already opened the door of the other one and entering, was reaching for a set of headphones. Miss P explained what they wanted me to do. I stared at her appalled. She tutted crisply and gave me a little shove in the direction she wanted me to go. The booth's glass door swung easily on its hinges, although it was surprisingly heavy, it must have been at least three inches thick. It swung shut again, just as silently, behind me. I settled uneasily in the high-backed, padded leather chair which was set facing the blank wall against which the booth was set. I swivelled the chair round and pushed the door open a bit to see what was going on. Glory and Miss P had seated themselves in the upright chairs at the other end of the room and the latter, catching my eye, cupped both hands over her ears impatiently. I looked around me, black leather headphones were on a hook on the wall. I put them on gingerly and at once her dulcet tones came through, tinnily amplified. I looked around again to see she was leaning forward to speak into a microphone placed on the table. She whirled her finger to indicate I should face the wall, the door swung shut again and she repeated in my ears what it was she wanted.

I was genuinely frightened to follow her instruction. In the not yet twenty four hours I'd spent at that house, I'd learnt more about myself and others like me than in the whole of my previous, often confused sixteen years. But knowledge acquired, showed me just how much more there was to learn. And now, now they wanted me to hurt Ruth. I didn't think I could do that. I'd already discovered, to Chief Inspector Brackman's cost, just how easy it was to do.

"Well?" Miss Peacock was impatient.

"I can't." I didn't know whether she could hear me but obviously there was a mic somewhere in the booth because she came back quick as a flash.

"You're not a lot of use to us unless you can."

"Fine. Find someone else."

"Do it."

"Sod you." If I was a little surprised to find one of Grandma's more vulgar expressions flowing so easily off the tongue, I was satisfied it seemed to fit the bill. Through the mic I heard Glory and Miss Peacock arguing, then it went dead. I was waiting for the next move but when it came, it was from an entirely unexpected direction. My head bounced painfully back against the headrest of the chair, my face stung as if it had been slapped – hard. It was Ruth, I recognised her taste instantly.

"Now," she commanded in my head, "Stop me." I hesitated and she slapped me again. This time as my head rocked backward I bit my tongue in surprise – it hurt and my mouth filled with that unpleasant metallic flavour blood brings. When she came at me again I was ready, I didn't know quite what I was doing, but I blocked most of the blow and felt it just as a minor shove. I shoved back.

141

"Again." she said, "I won't let you hurt me, but you have to try." I pushed back, harder this time, but immediately felt the force of my move slide harmlessly away down some sort of a mind chute she constructed. When she came for me again, I was ready. My chute was nowhere near as effective, but it did some of the trick and I didn't bang my head so hard. I made as if to strike her again but this time, changed direction at the last moment, she wasn't ready for that and I sensed her pain, surprise and beyond that, pleasure that I was thinking for myself. I turned to see if I could crane my neck and see into the neighbouring booth.

"Don't look round." Miss P was back, buzzing in my ear. Honestly, I thought, with Ruth in my head and her sister in the earphones, it was like Piccadilly blooming Circus. I was just grinning to myself at this amusing thought when the blank back wall of the booth to which I had obediently turned back, imploded in my face. Glass shot in towards me, followed by black roiling smoke and beyond that, fiercely licking flames propelling raw heat. I felt the small bones in my neck crack against each other as I ducked reflexively, desperately protecting my eyes and face from the cutting shards. I was scrambling frantically to get the headphones off and get out of the chair, out of the booth but I couldn't get the door open. Choking smoke sandpapered its way down my throat, I needed to take a breath, had to but as I gasped and sucked, the small space in which I was trapped, became an airless vacuum, all oxygen swallowed by the greediness of the flames. And then they were gone, not there any more. Glass wall intact.

"Bloody Norah!" Another favourite of Grandma and the Aunts, my language was deteriorating as fast as my nerves.

"That wasn't fair." I yelled, hoarse and indignant.

"Fair? Do you think people are always going to play fair?" In Miss Peacock's mimicry, whined my own offended tone.

"O.K." I thought, "O bloody Kay." and I shut my eyes and went into Ruth's booth and into her head and I started with an ominous darkening. And then the walls of her glass compartment became opaqued by millions of tiny fissures and when the thickened glass could hold out no longer, the water broke through. Initially it trickled through the cracks and then, as force built, it smashed and gushed, covering first her feet then rising swiftly to her knees, causing her to gasp deeply. It was icily salty and it rose swiftly and inexorably to her chest then her chin. I could feel her desperately trying to banish it, eject me, but I took it further. Her mouth then her nose filled not only with the water but with its rank odour. The power of what was rushing through me and out of me felt liberating. Her vision blurred as she held her breath despite herself and her eyes, wide now with fear, stung unbearably as the salt-filled waters flooded them. Then they engulfed her and she lost consciousness.

I tore off the headphones and wrenched open the door, reaching Ruth's booth at the same instant as Miss Peacock, Glory not far behind. She was slumped forward, her head turned to one side, lips slightly blued, mouth open in a last desperate gasp for air not water. I think, beyond doubt, that moment remains one of the most awful of my entire life and I include all those subsequent, as yet undreamt of occasions, when things got pretty dreadful. I'd killed her. Got carried away, showed off and killed her. Glory and Miss Peacock had both squeezed into the booth and obscured the stricken woman from sight. I stood, sick and frozen and waited.

"Not bad, not bad at all." her voice was weak, but as they helped her out of the booth, one on either side, she smiled at me. "Good girl." My knees gave way then and I sat heavily on the floor. My stomach debated throwing up, my throat muscles, spasmed tight with fear, said not a chance.

They helped Ruth into one of the armchairs and she beckoned me. I got up and staggered over on rubber legs,

"I'm so, so sorry." She grinned and I could see colour coming back into her cheeks,

"We needed to know whether you can take care of yourself. Those booths are designed to sort the men from the boys."

"She means," clarified Glory, "They're thick, bullet-proof glass. If you can read and send as easily as you did through those sort of barriers, you're pretty strong stuff. I thought you probably were, I just wasn't sure."

"You don't understand ..." I stopped, aware both of the absurdity of that statement and the depths of my self-disgust. I didn't want to be pretty strong stuff, not when the stuff involved was so unpleasantly vicious. I could feel my clothes sticking where I'd sweated effort, anxiety and exhilaration. Glory said softly.

"I told you once before – use it misuse it, up to you."

"Nothing wrong in enjoying something you're good at." Added Ruth.

143

"But …" I struggled to explain.

"What you felt," she interrupted, "Was the exhilaration of the power, not what you were doing with it. You were pushed hard, you reacted and some day you might have to do it for real."

"And," pointed out Miss Peacock, "You weren't out of control, some part of you knew exactly what you were doing, how far you could go. You didn't kill her did you?"

A sickly thumping headache had arrived, fully fledged above my right eye. A glass of water and two white pills floated gently over my left shoulder, followed by a clean white hanky. Ed had come in, was leaning on the wall, head nearly touching the ceiling.

"Like a gun," he said in the voice that seemed too small for the rest of him. "Enjoy target practice, you don't have to use that skill to kill." I reached for the glass, swallowed the aspirin, utilised the handkerchief and nodded. At the rate we were going, he and I were going to get through a lot of handkerchiefs. He nodded back expressionlessly then turned away. He went to stand in front of a television set I hadn't noticed, set in a far corner of the room, reached behind him for a chair sat and began to gaze at the screen which was completely blank. Odd, but then no odder than anything else that was going on.

The three women were talking earnestly, Ruth still in the chair, Glory perched on the arm. I felt too drained to bother listening and moved to an unoccupied chair, leaning my head back to let the aspirin do its stuff. After a moment, I became peripherally aware of Ed and the tv which was starting to disintegrate or rather to dismantle itself. At first slowly, then faster and faster. Screws, backing board, wires, tube, control knob, glass screen – each of the component parts flying swiftly through the air, coming to land gently in neatly assembled piles – a tidily set out assortment of innards, not to mention outers. He contemplated this pile with satisfaction then closed his eyes and put it all back again, re-building the set from the inside out in even less time than he'd taken to demolish it.

I closed my eyes too. I was, by that stage, pretty much beyond being surprised at anything. I must have dropped off, because when I came to, I was alone. My headache seemed to have cleared thanks to Ed and aspirin. I suspected it would take a lot longer to get rid of some of my other feelings. I climbed the stairs like a little old lady, arms and legs heavy and achey and shut the door to the basement firmly behind me. Kitchen and living room were deserted apart from Hamlet who, after what I'd experienced in the last hour or so was really the least of my worries. He obviously though, felt good manners called for some action and dragged himself politely to his feet to give me a hefty but companionable shove in the hip with his head. I tottered a little, I was glad Hamlet was my friend and not, as my father was wont to say with a wink, my enema. That brought to mind the fact I hadn't phoned home yet but to be honest wasn't quite sure how to give them a run down of events without causing them to send in the troops. I'd phone later.

There was something savoury on the stove and I was surprised to find, despite everything, eating didn't seem to be out of the question. As if summoned by the thought, the household re-congregated one by one, Ed's pilaff was served – Fanny would have been so proud – and Glory kept her promise to tell me more.

CHAPTER TWENTY-EIGHT

Preparation for Glory to get into The Newcombe Foundation hadn't taken long, she didn't need a cover story, her own being quite adequately dramatic. Miss Peacock called Dr Dreck direct as one professional to another. She'd heard, she explained, through the grapevine about the sterling work he was doing and indeed had been fortunate enough to attend one of his lectures a couple of years back, most impressive. She was calling to find out whether there would be any chance of him seeing her young ward. Although, at 18, Glory was possibly a little older than many of the patients he habitually dealt with, nevertheless she did suffer from a major handicap which appeared to be pulling her into a spiral of depression. There had also been some rather unsettling incidents recently, on which she would very much welcome Dr Dreck's professional opinion and input.

Further questioning allowed Miss Peacock to elaborate a little. As a teacher and therapist herself, dealing with young people with a variety of issues, she was naturally disinclined to believe everything she saw, and felt that perhaps the aforementioned 'incidents' were mere bids for attention. Nevertheless, they certainly came under the heading of 'worrying'. She was vague, almost embarrassed, preferring she said, not to discuss the matter fully on the phone but hinting darkly at objects flying through the air and other equally mysterious happenings. Dr Dreck swallowed the bait – hook line and blinkered and even managed, as a professional courtesy, to squeeze them in for an early appointment – within a week of the phone-call in fact. He suggested to Miss Peacock that she allow for a full day to be spent at the Foundation as he would want to run a series of tests.

Miss Peacock and Glory duly turned up at the appointed time. Miss Peacock fluttery and anxious, every twitchy inch the spinster teacher, way out of her depth with a young, unmanageable ward and Glory, sulky, impatient and completely, angrily and helplessly blind. The tests she took that day were not dissimilar to ones I was to take a year or so later, the difference being Glory knew exactly what she was doing. There was no mistaking what the tests were designed to show and, giving them full value for money, she made sure she scored well but not as well as she could easily have done – no sense, she thought, in over-gilding the lily. While Miss Peacock waited anxiously, fluttering from magazine to window and back again in the waiting room, Glory was given over, for the duration of the tests, to the tender mercies of the misnamed Miss Merry who, though younger than when I'd had the pleasure was, apparently not a jot more jolly.

Excitement generated by Glory's test results was to be expected, although it opened up a whole new can of worms. Until that point, the theory had been that psi ability was most likely to be found amongst those who'd suffered brain damage. Glory, although handicapped by blindness, was certainly in no way mentally impaired. The mind of Dr D. immediately began racing like a demented greyhound. And as a fevered subtext to his measured comments to Glory and her handkerchief-twisting guardian, he was already formulating a detailed proposal which he would submit to the relevant funding bodies, just as soon as he possibly could – a stream of normal children had suddenly become top of his wish list. His state of agitation rendered him suddenly and ominously readable to the Misses Peacock and Isaacs and they were less than thrilled at the direction in which he was planning to move. It seemed, that by their very action, they'd already set in motion an unpredicted and undesired chain of events. As is often the way!

Dr Dreck's suggestion to Miss Peacock, that Glory's tests were inconclusive and that she should spend a few days as an in-patient at the Newcombe Foundation's clinic for further investigation, was greeted with near hysteria and a great deal more fluttering and uncertainty. It took the combined charm of the Doctor and his assistant – and if they believed that, they'd believe anything – to persuade both women, one desperately anxious, the other sulking for England, that this was by far the best and wisest course of action. No, no reassured Dr D., patting the hand of the anxious Miss P who was, at this stage, inclined to the tearful, he really didn't think there was anything at all to worry about. However, there were obviously some major issues regarding her handicap that Glory had to be helped to come to terms with and where better than the Foundation, so used to dealing with disturbed youngsters.

So far, thought Miss Peacock to herself, as the train took her back to

London, so good. So far, thought Glory as she settled into the little side room off the main ward in the clinic, so good. Little did either of them know it was to be nearly two years before things would revert to anything near what they would consider normal.

Dr Dreck didn't let the grass grow. The first night Glory spent at the clinic she was given something to drink that she knew was going to be trouble. A bitterly pink mixture in a small, measure-marked medicinal beaker, 'A little something to help you sleep,' Miss Merry, gliding in silently in her oiled-wheeled way had handed her the beaker, folded her arms and raised an eyebrow expectantly. There was little Glory could do to avoid swallowing the lot, despite clearly reading she shouldn't. The whole of that next week, as far as she was concerned, was something of a sickening blur and she was certainly in no fit state to pursue so much as a coherent thought, let alone any undercover activities.

Miss Peacock, ringing as instructed the following day for news was told that unfortunately, Glory had come down with the nasty stomach flu that was doing the rounds. Over the following days, the illness ran its course but, Dr Dreck was sorry to report, Glory's depression was giving cause for concern, no doubt exacerbated by the effects of the severe viral infection. He pointed out it wouldn't be in her best interests to return home at this point. Indeed, such was her distress it might be best if Miss Peacock put off visiting for a week or so. For the Peacocks, as much as for Glory, those first couple of weeks weren't good news. Glory, because she was suffering continuous drug-induced vomiting and Ruth and Rachael because she was in no fit condition to let them know what was going on. It would appear that even with the best laid plans, things can go askew far quicker than you'd think.

CHAPTER TWENTY-NINE

The programming of Glory had begun even as the drug induced sickness subsided. It wasn't subtle, but as there was no reason to believe Glory was anything other than she seemed, it didn't need to be. First, Dr Dreck established just how firm was Glory's affection for her mentors, the Peacocks. He played heavily on the fact that it was sad, not to mention deeply damaging to the professional reputation of the two sisters, so well known in their field of expertise, that they'd abjectly failed to spot and deal with the advancing depression of their own ward. It didn't show them in a good light, did it? Not in a good light at all.

Glory, ostensibly sceptical at first, gradually allowed herself to be concerned and then deeply worried. What, she asked her brand new friend, would be the best way of dealing with the situation, the optimum method of getting her depression under control without compromising in any way the reputation of Ruth and Rachael to whom she owed so much?

Dr Dreck, after some consideration, suggested the best plan might be for her to stay on for a while at Newcombe. Already her tests, he pointed out, were showing some interesting results and it was just possible she may be in a position to help him a little with his research at the very same time he was helping her come to terms with her own situation. Agreement for this arrangement sought and obtained, Glory was now back on track and with greater freedom of movement than they could have hoped for, hovering in status, somewhere between patient and assistant researcher.

Miss Merry, under whose chilly authority, many of Glory's tests were conducted disliked her intensely. She was the most tightly buttoned individual Glory had ever come across and not easily readable, being as possessive of her thoughts as she was of her close working relationship with the Doctor. However, it was clear that Glory's propensity for wry one-liners, together with her exotically colourful attire disturbed and unsettled Miss Merry on some deep and complicated level, as indeed did Glory's bearing and her air of self-possession. Other than the strength of her feelings for her employer and her dislike of almost everyone else, Miss

Merry was pretty emotionless. There was not one of the children she dealt with who moved her in any way, she simply maintained a detached and keen interest in their reaction to various stimuli. She was, however, it has to be said, an excellent administrator who masterminded the running of the whole place like clockwork. At any given moment she had in her head, a complete duty roster and a total awareness of who should be doing what, where they should be doing it and when they should be finished.

The Doctor, predictably, was in a state of bemused delight that Glory's test results were showing such strong abilities. She was by far and away the most talented subject he'd come across in a long while and he was convinced that under his skilled tutelage she could develop significantly. He'd already seen progress – she was able now, to their mutual triumph, to move a wooden brick back and forth across the floor and roll a pen across the table without touching it. Oh yes indeed, she was coming along very nicely, one might almost say in leaps and bounds. Of course for Glory, who could without breaking sweat, have rolled not only the pen across the table but Dr Karl W. Dreck with it, there was a tremendous amount of energy expended on restraint. Meanwhile, they were feeding her a steady diet of anti-depressants which she obligingly received and carefully palmed, although she'd taken the precaution of establishing exactly what, if any, side effects she needed to simulate.

Regular blood samples were also being taken, lots of them, she reported with disgust to Ruth and Rachael. And electroencephalographs, which meant she spent a great deal of time with wires stuck to her head while printouts of her brain waves were intently studied. On one occasion she was taken by Miss Merry to the John Radcliffe for a full brain scan, which necessitated her being fed into a claustrophobic cylinder for what seemed like ages. Dreck had ostensibly referred her, she found, when she scanned the technician who was busy scanning her, because of symptoms that might indicate a brain tumour. Whilst Glory had no fear that any such thing was really suspected, she knew he was desperate to unearth physical evidence of her ability and also knew he'd have few qualms and no real limits when it came to taking her apart to find it.

There was no doubt the range of tests devised by Dreck to pinpoint what he was after, were productive and in many cases, lastingly beneficial for children who often, until that point had never been challenged or pushed beyond what was thought to be their limitations. Dreck was a clever man and despite his oily avuncular manner which Glory loathed, had a flourishing and ever-growing practice, with parents begging for appointments and paying highly for the privilege. Unctuousness itself with parents and patients, he was singularly lacking in charm when it came to the work force and although reasonably plump pay packets compensated in part, he was not well-liked by colleagues or staff. The exception to the rule was the divine Miss M, who would have unreservedly continued to adore him had he mown her down twice daily with his car then strolled over her with spiked running shoes.

Glory and her co-conspirators were fully aware they were on dangerous ground, dealing with a man who was at no point to be underestimated. They were also aware, his fascination with the power of the mind over the restrictions of the body was moving beyond ambition and heading fast into obsession. He was vain too. On the occasions Glory was able to go into his head, she tripped several times over the Nobel Prize for Medical Research and he was constantly consumed by concern that others would beat him to a breakthrough that should have his name written all over it.

Whilst aware when she took on her mole role that it wouldn't be a barrel of laughs, Glory was nevertheless working under considerable strain. She found the constant stream of children brought by anxious and in some cases near-desperate parents to be both heart-breaking and uplifting and to present enormous dilemmas. Amongst those who were treated, there were undoubtedly some with abilities beyond the norm, although in the early days she never met anyone particularly strong. She was loath to point these children out, but reasoning that the tests were designed to achieve the same ends was able, with complete accuracy to pre-inform the Doctor which children would score the highest. She was, to his growing delight, pretty infallible.

Probably due to Dr Dreck's excessive fear of being pipped to the post by a rival, areas of operation at Newcombe were divided into four clearly defined sections which functioned more or less autonomously and completely independently of each other with only Dreck and Merry overseeing all.

The Consulting Suite with its stream of daily patient appointments was manned by the efficient team of Mary Moffat and Mary Bevan who controlled phones, patients, appointments and refreshments with formidable efficiency and Joyce Grenfell-like forbearance. The in-patient clinic took up the whole of the building's second floor and was a ten-bedded facility, six bays in the main ward, four side-rooms and the nurses used different doors from the rest of the staff. In fact – other than the Matron the well-upholstered Mrs Millsop, all were temporary agency staff who changed on a regular basis.

In the older part of the building, in what used to be the basement, were the soundproofed, two-way mirrored, specially equipped rooms where the children were taken for their 'tests'. And finally there was a small but impressively cutting-edge laboratory, where a number of white-coated researchers kept themselves to themselves. In fact, probably the only members of Newcombe staff who came and went between all the sections were Sid and Reg, a lugubrious father and son team. They dealt with all general handyman tasks in the building, kept the gardens pristine and meticulously cared for the rats and mice kept in serried ranks of cages and used for testing different drug combinations. Glory said, she knew she ought to mind more about what went on in that laboratory, but because of a rampant fear of anything that scuttled, didn't even really want to think about it.

Because of this highly effective and impenetrable 'Chinese Wall' system within the organisation's management, it was only the Doctor himself, Miss Merry and now Glory who had a complete grip on the overall picture and two of the aforementioned had not the remotest idea of the amount of poking and prying being undertaken by the third.

Whilst there had indeed been a few brow-raising rumours within the profession about experimental work and drug development carried out at Newcombe, this had been balanced by the excellent results demonstrable in some of the children for whom there had previously been scant hope of improvement. It broke your heart, said Glory, to see the joy on the face of a parent when a child, previously totally non-responsive, reacted with a smile or a squeeze of the hand. There also now arose for her, the interference issue about which Ruth and Rachael had warned her. How very tempting to just go in and do a little tweak here, a little adjustment there – and how very dangerous.

Glory had been able to read the notes on Ben's short stay at the clinic because Miss Merry had by chance reviewed them whilst she was in the room. His records showed daily doses of a drug listed simply as L/23 which was summarised as a vitamin and mineral compound but Glory had her doubts. At the end of Ben's notes – a shortened lifetime sewn up in a few paragraphs – was the bleak information that death was unexpected and due to heart failure. Whether this would have happened anyway or whether the barrage of needles, wires, questions, expectations and the cryptically named L/23 made it happen sooner, was impossible to prove.

Glory may have gone in as a mole but there was no doubt she became a catalyst. Her ability it was which tipped the scales that gave Dr Dreck the idea and incentive to extend his search parameters into the general population. She was the reason I, and so many others, found ourselves heading in an Oxford direction over the next few years. Naturally, this turn of events presented Glory and the Peacock sisters with some even more contentious issues.

To date, children passing through the clinic with any demonstrable extra sensory abilities, had already been suffering from congenital brain damage or physical disabilities and very often the tests and the drugs Dreck used to establish how much they could do, did in fact help them. However, with the new direction – and within a very short time Government approval was received, funding provided and a wide-ranging social study story established – there was going to be a stream of completely healthy youngsters available to Dreck.

This put the whole thing on a completely different plane, practically, said Glory sourly, on a different bloody airline. How could she not stick around a bit longer to see if there was anybody she could help. These kids, should any of them prove to have the odd extra ability, were unlike the others, able to be warned, capable of making choices as to whether or not they wanted to be subjected to batteries of invasive tests and continued observation.

Ruth and Rachael, making their regular visit to take young Glory out to tea, argued with her long and hard that now was the time to get out.

They'd met up with Dr Dreck briefly in the reception area when they arrived. Time only for a quick handshake but that was enough to take in an overall and over-riding impression of feverish, obsessive excitement running out of control. He was lamentably short on ethics, medical or otherwise and quite determined to do whatever he had to, to whomever he had to, in order to fulfil ambition which was now all-consuming. Glory, whilst not disputing any of this, insisted she had no choice but to stay on a little longer.

Dreck had, meanwhile, introduced a new drug into Glory's daily cocktail which was still, unbeknownst to him, regularly finding its way down the toilet. Glory had been unsurprised to read from Miss Merry, who dished out the medication, that the extra white pill was L/24, presumably an evolved version of the drug given to little Ben. Things for Glory weren't getting any simpler and she was unsure which way to play it. Was it better for her to show the drug being spectacularly successful or disastrously ineffective? She decided that successful in a moderate and perhaps not immediately verifiable way, was the safest path and accordingly over the next couple of weeks allowed herself to progress in small steps.

At one of their sessions she made Dr D's jacket sleeve smoulder and any irritation he might have felt at the appearance of a black-rimmed hole in the herringbone, was outweighed by excitement that this was something she appeared only able to do after a week or so on 20 mg of L/24. Then there was the discovery that now, not only could she move small wooden bricks, several at a time across the floor but, with no problem, was able to make them fly through the air to land safely one by one a short distance away. Unfortunately the first time this happened, her control apparently wasn't all it could have been. All six bricks rained painfully down on the head of a note-taking and thereafter slightly dazed Miss Merry, and if there was any moral issue involved, it didn't trouble Glory unduly.

CHAPTER THIRTY

By the time Glory's few weeks at the Foundation had turned unbelievably, to just under a year, wheels set in motion were inexorably gathering their own alarming momentum. A team of builders had completed a two storey extension at the rear of the original Newcombe building, facilitating a doubling in size of the in-patient facility and allowing increasing numbers of children to be processed by a growing number of staff.

Glory – more staff member than patient now – had proved her worth, devising and participating in many of the proposed screening procedures. Her own abilities on the psi front, to Dreck's frustrated disappointment had not progressed nearly as fast as he'd anticipated. However, there was no doubt she was invaluable in pointing out those children most likely to be of interest to the testers. The fact that she muddied the waters, sometimes picking people who turned out not to be special at all, simply meant her scores weren't 100% perfect. 100% perfect would, she reckoned have been foolish.

The Doctor had devised a levels system by which to grade ability. A number of kids had what might be termed informed intuition, which meant only that they consistently scored higher than average on tests. Then there were those with a very mild but inconsistent ability which seemed to spike and fall at random, totally beyond the control of the child involved. The third and rarest level was the one the Doctor hungered after and it was those children Glory was there to try and help, although putting theory into practice proved no easier for her than it was for him.

Working on the principle of forewarned is forearmed, Glory nevertheless had to ensure that nobody knew who was doing the warning. Reaction from the individuals involved was mixed, some grateful some not. Peter Atkins was the most hostile. He was also the most powerful she'd come across in the whole time she'd been there and she felt that raw strength, even as his coach was drawing up outside the building.

He was twelve, a tall, skinny lad with dark hair, pale thick skin and an arrogant eye. There was, about him, a contained and calculating air of menace, which immediately raised all the hairs on the back of Glory's elegant neck. When she cautiously made contact, he assimilated her presence and intention with little or no surprise. Neither did he bother to hide the shaft of elation that shot through him at the knowledge that he was exactly what was being sought here. She didn't like him but quickly did her best to lay out the facts. She'd decided at the beginning, in concert with the Peacocks, the only action she could or would take was a warning, no more no less. Decisions had to be up to the individual, she couldn't and wouldn't play God.

Her foray into Peter's mind was brief and appalling. She hadn't come across anyone quite like him before and what she saw in there, along with his unpleasantly feral musky scent, lingered long. He was the product of a father with problems of his own and a mother who really didn't care what anyone's problems were, as long as she could indulge uninterrupted, her insatiable appetite for anything that money – lots of it – could buy.

Neither parent had a great deal of time for their only son and although the house was magnificent, the schooling private and the toys endless, so too was the stream of nannies then au pairs, most of whom never warmed, even slightly, to their small charge. His repertoire of amusing tricks grew as he did. The mildest involved worms at the bottom of a coffee cup, the direst a dead mouse and details you wouldn't want to go into. Peter, easily able to read what people were thinking was in no doubt what they thought of him. He also knew where he ranked in importance in his parents' life.

Just over a year earlier, arriving home from school and letting himself in to make his own tea, he'd heard a noise in his parents' room when both were supposed to be out. Quietly pushing the door ajar he was riveted by the sight of a complete stranger, tall and thickset, moving around the room. This person was fetchingly clad in pink and frilly baby-doll pyjamas, matching negligee and teeteringly-high, feathered mules. He didn't need the stranger to turn before recognition hit, and the shock on the lipsticked, rouged and mascarad face of his father must have been mirrored on his own, even as he struggled to rationalise and make sense of what he was seeing.

At that instant, Peter had the opportunity of reading the mix of emotion – shame, embarrassment perhaps a certain amount of relief in his father's head. Perhaps, at that point, Peter had the chance to see it was this shameful secret and not dislike of his son that lay at the root of the distance all these years. But Peter wasn't a great one for thoughtful introspection, perhaps no boy would have been under the circumstances. His lip curled, his resentment, fear and incomprehension blended and boiled over as he stared at his father – unloved in suit, tie and bowler, how much more despised, in pink lace.

Creativity Peter didn't know he had in him, took over with a will all its own and an opened tube of lipstick rose from the dressing table. It slashed deeply and wetly red all over his father's quivering cheeks and double chin, mixing with tears and stubble as he stumbled backward, covering his be-crimsoned face with both arms. Not a single word was exchanged and the boy stood by the door as the man was marched inexorably into the ensuite bathroom to clean off the make-up.

Nobody ever quite got to the bottom of what really happened. Certainly not Peter, who successfully and completely blotted any assistance he might have given his father from the surface of his mind, putting it somewhere only someone like Glory could have seen it. The assumption was suicide. Mr Atkins had climbed into the bath and slashed both wrists with his own razor. He was dressed, by then, in his own conservatively striped pyjamas and if the police and examining medical officer spotted traces of cosmetics on the jowly dead face, they looked the other way and saw no possible reason for mentioning it and bringing further distress to a hysterical widow and her silent son.

As far as Peter was concerned, his father's end justified any means and it genuinely didn't cause him undue angst. However, he was bright enough to know there were clearly defined patterns of behaviour to which it behoved him to conform. He was therefore silently deep in shock when people expected him to be and sobbed and screamed for his father when he read it was the correct time for him to break down and let it all out. And all the while, he was preoccupied with this wondrous and growing power he possessed. Tentatively at first, increasingly bolder as he explored its possibilities and limitations, to his pleasure he found that the former were far greater than the latter.

Being in the top percentile of his class where exam results, if not popularity, were concerned, Peter had naturally been included when his school was approached to participate in the social study at Newcombe and had set off on the coach, unconcerned at the lack of kids clamouring to sit next to him. Never much liked at school, his new-found talents certainly hadn't earned him any new friends and most of his peers instinctively gave him a wide berth. He'd amused himself on the journey by playing with the coach-driver's mind, causing his eyes to slide shut and his head to nod until the coach veered dangerously to the middle of the road, allowing the poor chap to jerk himself awake only at the last moment, appalled by his inexplicable and potentially lethal drowsiness.

Discretion, decided a severely shaken Glory, as she hastily withdrew from her initial contact with Peter, in this case was almost certainly going to be the better part of valour. Being what she was, through the years she'd been unable to avoid a thorough grounding in the vagaries and often more unsavoury aspects of human nature, but Peter was something else altogether and she'd been startled and repelled by his hungrily avaricious response to her approach. The sensation of his reaching out, seeking via the contact to climb up and into her mind, was not something she'd forget in a hurry. It seemed, that while Peter was on the scene, it would be sensible not to stick her head above the parapet. She therefore made sure that whilst she pointed him out to Miss Merry as being worthy of further attention and a potential high test-scorer, she added no further details and took good care to batten down her hatches.

The surging pleasure of Peter, at finding this wasn't really some sodding social study as he'd been led to believe, was equalled only by the Doctor's unmitigated delight at such a promising new subject. Having at this stage, already been through the testing of three or four hundred healthy children and found nobody who set bells ringing, the Doctor had been running short of patience. When Peter turned up he was greeted like manna from heaven and that, as Glory put it, was when the shit really hit the fan.

"And ...?" I'd been hanging on every word, only partially aware everyone had finished eating and the table had been cleared.

"Sufficient for now." Ruth gave me a friendly push in the direction of the stairs, "Go, pack your things so we can get off."

"Off?"

"To Oxford."

"I can't go just like that, I've got to call my parents."

"All dealt with, Rachael called already."

"She keeps doing that." I was indignant.

"Saves time." said Miss Peacock who was whisking the last of the lunch things away. I sensed Ed was torn between gratitude at her doing anything at all in the kitchen and exasperation at the way she was sending things into all the wrong cupboards.

"That," I said with dignity, "Is beside the point."

CHAPTER THIRTY-ONE

Outside the house, parked behind the Morris Marina in which I'd arrived with Ed and Glory, sat a grubby white van that had clearly seen better days – lots of them. Someone had written 'Clean me for Pete's sake!' on one side and 'Kilroy wouldn't even dream of it!' on the other. However, when Ed unlocked and slid back the side door, we climbed into an immaculately roomy interior with two rows of comfortable, high-backed, deep brown leather bench seating, ranged behind the bucket seats of the driver and front-seat passenger. It had that unmistakably delightful brand-new vehicle smell. Ruth was amused at my expression,

"Unobtrusive doesn't necessarily mean uncomfortable." She pointed out.

Ed having opened the back door and ushered Hamlet up inside – a somewhat hefty arrival which caused the van to rock alarmingly – took the driving seat. Miss Peacock settled herself next to him, Glory and I sat in the next row with Ruth behind us. We were a somewhat ill-assorted group. Big Ed, concentrating now on re-angling the driving mirror was resplendent in a flannel, blue and white checked shirt, sleeves rolled up over meatily massive, hairless forearms. Drifting back from him was a whiff of lemon-scented after-shave, not dissimilar from his own fresh, tangy, signature-smell. He caught my eye in the mirror, as if it were easier to hold a gaze reflected than a direct one. I hoped he hadn't caught my swiftly smothered thought that if looks were anything to go by, I'd have expected sweaty over citrus. I looked away hastily as he released the handbrake and moved the van smoothly away.

Miss Peacock was as usual, white and grey, skirted, shirted and cardiganned but as a concession to the dubious warmth of the April afternoon had discarded a black raincoat and folded it neatly over the back of her seat. Ruth, when I glanced back, appeared to have fallen promptly asleep. She'd, in honour of the outing, donned a bilious orange, sleeveless top which, unfortunately, had a jacket to match. It wasn't possible to look at her for too long without getting an after-image. Glory had dressed down, going with a long mauve shirt over black slacks, hair knotted at the nape of her neck. She'd restricted herself to a mere half inch or so of gold earring, nothing to speak of really and was, as always sitting carefully upright in the seat, no slouch our Glory. I couldn't see the dog, but every now and then a gentle snore rose from the van's nether regions, blending and harmonising with Ruth's exhalations and the sound of the engine.

We drove for a while in silence although I could, if I listened, hear Buddy Greco – with Ed there really was no call for a car radio. Glory seemed lost in thought but I couldn't wait all day and it wasn't going to be that long a journey, I leaned over and poked her firmly in the ribs with my finger. She jumped,

"What?"

"Peter?"

She heaved a sigh,

"Can't a person get any peace? Where'd we get to?"

The coming together of Peter and the Doctor was a match made in hell, a recipe for disaster. Adult ambition, ruthlessness and amorality meeting its match in a twelve year old boy. Peter had soared through the initial round of tests, nearly knocking the conducting member of staff off her chair with excitement at his scores. The Doctor and Miss Merry were notified and hastened to one of the two-way mirrored rooms to watch, while Peter obligingly completed more tests. His power was raw and uncontrolled but there was no doubting its strength. Glory, listening in cautiously from a distance, could feel it peaking and subsiding, reaching beyond the glass to the other room where the two adults were standing, and she could feel his amusement that they thought they could spy on him without him knowing.

Sidling in a few moments later, beaming with delight and tailed by Miss Merry who didn't really do beaming, the Doctor, at his oiliest oozed into a chair across the table from Peter. He would he said, like to invite him, with of course the permission of his parents to stay on at the clinic for a while longer to participate in further tests. Peter didn't let him get very far before he put him straight on several things including his awareness of what they were after, the naffness of these tests for someone of Peter's ability and the stupidity of hiding behind a two-way mirror. He suggested the Doctor and his happy clappy friend there, cut the crap and tell him what this was really all about. If Miss Merry didn't do beaming, Peter didn't do subtle.

He stated he was fully prepared to take part in whatever experiments were necessary, as long as they didn't hurt and on condition they'd help develop his talents to their fullest extent. There were also some other things he'd like which he'd get to later – Glory was amused, despite herself to see that in his mental list of priorities, a regular supply of Coca Cola came just after pots of money – he was, after all, only twelve. He was not, he stated baldly, thumping the table for emphasis, a gesture he'd seen and fancied on Z Cars, but never had the opportunity to practise before, under any circumstances prepared to be pissed about, but if the Doc played fair with him, he'd play fair back.

The Doctor, if a trifle taken aback at the ease with which the boy had assimilated the situation, not to mention his use of the vernacular, agreed and Miss Merry was despatched post haste to obtain Peter's mother's permission for him to enter the clinic for a few days and to ease any parental concerns. It transpired that Peter's mother, by this stage in fond and frenzied pursuit of husband number two, wasn't concerned in the slightest. In fact lately the boy had been giving her the creeps. He seemed to know what she was going to say before she did herself and certainly couldn't be counted on to give a good impression to her gentleman caller. Yes, yes, she agreed, anxious to get Miss Merry off the phone, she'd certainly inform the school and yes indeed, a call in a few days from the clinic to let her know how Peter was getting on, would be nice – if she wasn't in, perhaps they'd just leave a message with the au pair.

There were no school pals of whom Peter wanted to take a fond farewell and truth to tell no-one seemed to notice he didn't join them for lunch that day. If anything, his supervising teachers seemed mightily relieved to be told by Miss Merry of the new arrangement. Peter was escorted through to the clinic, where he was given into the hands of the capable Mrs Millsop with instruction to give him a full physical and, in the interests of not letting grass grow under anybody's feet, his first dose of L/24. Glory didn't try to make direct contact with Peter again. She'd told him what was what, choices he made subsequently were his. She was however aware of the need now to shield herself more than ever. She didn't think she'd given anything away – as far as Peter was concerned, the words of warning could have come from anyone, but better play safe than sorry.

Whether L/24 had a different effect on Peter than it would have had on someone else is a matter for conjecture. Everyone has different reactions to even fully standardised and tested medications and if there was anything to be said about what the Doctor was producing, un-standardised and un-tested about summed it up. Glory, whose toilet had in the last several months, carried more pills than Boots the Chemist, was vastly relieved she'd never taken it even once.

She had though, smuggled a sample of L/24 to the Peacocks for analysis. The report had been rushed through and delivered back personally by a research scientist associate of theirs. He didn't know, he said, nor did he want to, where they'd obtained the sample they'd given him but he couldn't even begin to conjecture what such a drug combination could have been developed to treat. Two of its components, a powerful hallucinogenic stimulant and a strong muscle relaxant would appear to act against each other and a third was currently banned from use, pending investigation into untoward side-effects. He would, he added, eat his hat with mustard on it if this ever came anywhere near being granted a licence by the authorities. The Peacocks thanked him, sent him home with one of Ed's fresh-from–the-oven strudels, and forebore to share that the drug in question had, in fact, been developed in a Government funded laboratory.

As was only to be expected, Glory was called in at an early stage to work with Peter but she was prepared and cautious. She'd now had an opportunity to study him a little and knew that although he had perhaps the strongest potential of any of the kids she'd come across, he actually wasn't that bright – which made him all the more dangerous. She was also delighted to read that although he did remember the brief contact when he first arrived, he put it down as another of the tests they were using, to see who registered anywhere on the psi scale.

When she was led into the room in which they were to do some supervised tests together, he automatically scanned her but unable to by-pass her shielding was not interested enough to try harder. He thought of her dismissively as the black, blind bint. He was told that, like him, she'd demonstrated psi abilities but as, during the tests they were called upon to do, her performance was consistently disappointing and low-scoring, she obviously wasn't in his league so he was unbothered. The Doctor, on the other hand, was very bothered as well as disappointed and frustrated by the lack of effect his pet pill was having on Glory. The conclusion could only be that her talents lay in one direction and one direction only – she was simply an excellent diviner of other people's abilities.

Within the first few days and with each successive drug dose, the effects on Peter became more evident. Whether this was genuine enhancement as a result of the pills or a question of barriers being broken and inhibitions released, Glory wasn't sure. She knew only that she could sense him from wherever she happened to be in the building and with every increment in Peter's power, her apprehension grew apace. She could see all too clearly what the Doctor, in a high old state of excitement now, clearly could not. The daily drug dose was increasing the power but not the ability, nor the intellect to govern it. It was putting a loaded gun into the hands of an emotionally unstable twelve year old and saying, there now, show us what you can do with this.

Some results were predictable, others not so much. Peter was having his lunch one day when Miss Merry entered the room. Quick as a flash, his plate with mashed potatoes – he'd asked for chips and they'd sent him bloody mash and green beans, how many times did he have to tell them he didn't do vegetables – flew swift as a bird through the air, turned a leisurely 90 degrees and landed on her hair, with remarkably little spillage. Twelve year old humour?

On another occasion, one of the psychology students drafted in as testers, twenty-two year old Polly, who'd once told Glory if she heard one more kettle joke she might commit murder, was doing Peter's daily update. As Polly gathered her notes and stood to leave, Peter, from the other side of the room where he was lounging, feet on table, blowing pinkly fat gum bubbles ripped her shirt from throat to waist and giggled. Polly was livid, less concerned that her white Playtex Cross Your Heart bra was on display than that she'd paid good money at M&S for the non-iron shirt only last week. Twelve year old lust?

Two weeks to the day that Peter began participation in the residential programme at Newcombe, all the lab rats were found dead. Exploded in their cages. Eighty or so of them. The mess was unspeakable, the devastation of Sid and Reg total. Twelve year old spite? And not slow to boast about it!

A small but urgent meeting was convened. The Doctor, Miss Merry – mash and beans gone but not forgotten or forgiven, Mrs Millsop – capped and formidable in blue and white starch and Glory. The meeting took place in one of the outside Portakabins coincidentally, although no-one mentioned it, on the opposite side of the building and at the farthest point from Peter's quarters. The agenda was Peter's progress, the hidden agenda far more complicated. Glory as usual was dealing with both.

The Doctor knew things were moving a little too fast, phrases like tiger by the tail, kept floating in and out of a mind made less opaque today by his agitation. But whilst the saner side of him argued caution and a slow approach, the side where the Nobel Prize was regularly buffed up was screaming go, go, go.

Miss Merry, given her way, would quite happily have strangled the little bastard. Her dignity and standing as second in command at the Foundation was hugely important to her and people turning away to hide their smiles as, mash-bedecked, she made her way down the corridor to clean herself up, lingered sourly in her memory.

Mrs Millsop, whose heart was in the right place, albeit not always immediately locatable under the starch, was uneasy. This was a cushy post, very cushy indeed. Money was good, she had her own nice little bed-sit with bath ensuite, furnished now just as she wanted it. She ruled the roost at the clinic which wasn't too taxing, never more than a couple of patients at a time and then not really ill, just check-ups and obs. She'd be nowhere near as well off back in the NHS and back into the NHS she'd have to go if this didn't work out. She'd never envisaged still having to work at this stage in her life and indeed wouldn't have had to, had Mr Millsop not buggered off two years previously with Peggy from the Phone Exchange. Before he upped and offed, he'd not only re-mortgaged their Ruislip semi – only another year to go on that there'd been – but also cleared out their building society account. He was now living it up on the Costa del Sol with her hard-earned savings and stinking Peggy who, to add insult to injury, was only three years younger than Mrs Millsop herself and no oil painting to boot.

All said and done though, Mrs Millsop didn't trust Dr Dreck any further than she could throw him. He'd not know a medical ethic if it came and bit him on the bum and as for that Miss Merry – Miss Moany more like – so stuck up it was a miracle she could sit down. Watching her with the children sometimes turned Mrs Millsop's not inconsiderable stomach, the woman was a cold fish and no mistake. No, there was definitely something going on that didn't feel quite right and if that L/24 pill was really a vitamin and mineral supplement she was Brigitte Bardot. Look at the effect it was having on that Peter, unpleasant little sod, another one she wouldn't turn her back on for a minute. Mind you, she'd give him bloody psi factor right up his backside if he tried any of his funny business with her.

Glory sat quietly, sifting text from sub-text while Mrs Millsop, in best professional mode, delivered an up to date report on Peter's physical condition which, she was pleased to say, remained 100%. Miss Merry discussed the exciting developments and improvement in his testable psi abilities, agreed, with a tight smile that he was indeed a feisty little chap and that brought them on to the recent drastic drop in the laboratory rat population. Mrs Millsop put forward the suggestion that perhaps Peter was coming on a bit too fast and the dosage of the supplement should be lowered and after some discussion, the Doctor reluctantly, Miss Merry far less so, agreed this might be the wisest course of action.

Wise course of action or not, there was no time to put it into practise. The phone on the wall of the portakabin shrilled, summoning them back to the clinic where all hell, apparently was breaking loose. Glory heard Peter screaming in her head as Mrs Millsop grabbed her hand and, following fast on the heels of the Doctor and Miss Merry, hauled her along with none of the normal compassionate, mind there's a step here dear.

Peter must have had more of a conscience than he'd thought, because now, back into his head, stimulated by the drugs he'd been given, had marched his father, pink baby-dolled and fully made up and he'd brought along a few friends – eighty to be exact. Small, furry, long-tailed and actually not really very friendly at all.

In one corner of Peter's room, Polly lay in an unconscious, ungraceful heap where she'd been flung and hit her head. Peter was wedged tightly into the opposite corner, knees to chest, heels of his rubber sneakers scrabbling and skidding against the floor as he attempted to push himself even further back. He was shivering so convulsively his head was banging an uneven syncopated rhythm on the wall behind and, blinder than Glory's had ever been, his eyes were starting whitely out of his head. A trickle of blood and spittle snaked leisurely down his chin from a chewed lip and mangled tongue. He was screaming inwardly and out, a high, unbearable, unlistenable-to, keening shriek of a scream that lacerated ear and mind.

Outside, at the front of the building, two coaches bringing lots of excited children for their testing session at the Foundation had just drawn up.

The power of Peter's projections as he tried to fling them from his mind broke through Glory's shielding in a sickeningly overwhelming rush and for a moment, she too was face to face with the heavily eye-shadowed, sorrowful gaze of the late Mr Atkins as he flounced past. At the same time her skin was brushed in a dozen places by soft fur, scaled tails, sharp claws and, as she shrank away and drew breath, she smelt theirs, foetid and alien.

She didn't know she was doing it but she too sank to the floor, an instinctive primitive move to protect herself – shut it out, curl up as small as possible. And in that instant, Peter became aware of her. Drowning in horror-fuelled panic, he desperately tried to scramble along that mental contact into her open mind, seeking sanctuary, looking for succour she didn't have to give and pulling her under with him, until she too began to drown and scream.

Of those observing but thankfully not blessed with the ability to share, Mrs Millsop was the one whose instinctive and prompt reaction saved Glory's sanity and probably her life. With a turn of speed, unexpected in one of her build and already separating the appropriate key from the bunch on the chain at her waist, she reached the locked drugs cabinet at the end of the corridor in record time and, with a steady hand, prepared a valium dose. Galloping back she leapt, like a chunky gazelle, over Glory writhing now on the floor and expertly plunged the needle deep into Peter's quivering thigh.

Peter's screaming subsided slowly, followed by Glory's, as he lapsed into unconsciousness in Mrs Millsop's arms and for a moment there was blessed silence, before everybody else belatedly remembered their professionalism and moved into action. Polly, coming round, shaken and bruised but otherwise apparently uninjured, was taken to be checked over. Glory was moved to another room where she lay, speechless and shivering despite the hot water bottles they packed round her. Then she felt the small cold bite of a needle in her arm and even as she was shaking her head to tell them that wasn't what she wanted, she slipped under. Peter was undressed and put to bed. He never woke up.

CHAPTER THIRTY-TWO

"He *died*?"

"No," said Glory, "He didn't die." I wet my lips with a dry tongue from an even dryer mouth. So evocative had been her re-telling, so strong her memories, I'd lived through them too. I could see the toll it had taken. Her normally even-coloured, milky-coffee skin was pale and blotchy, her lips tight. We'd pulled smoothly into a lay-by without my noticing, while Glory was talking. Ed and Hamlet had got out quietly to stretch their legs and Miss Peacock came round to the passenger door and slipped her grey cardigan gently over Glory's shoulders.

Ruth stirred with a grunt of surprise to find us stationary and thrust a virulently orange clad arm between us, to distribute polystyrene cups. Ed, it seemed, had thought of everything and although rendered tasteless by the thermos, what could have been either coffee or tea was sweet, hot and wonderfully welcome, as were the bars of chocolate produced from a capacious bag between Ruth's feet. I felt relieved to see Glory starting to look more normal, guilty because I desperately wanted to hear more.

It wasn't until we were all back in our seats and Ed had re-started the van that she continued.

"He was in a coma, what they call a persistent vegetative state."

"What's that mean?"

"Alive, but totally unresponsive to outside stimuli." I stared at her, aghast, "But that was ..."

"Five years ago. Yes." I was silent, recalling the image she'd shown me that day at the Foundation. The boy who I now knew was Peter, drips in his arms, tubes down his throat, more snaking from beneath the blankets, eyes open but as dreadfully blank as his mind.

"Was it the pill – the L/24?"

Glory shook her head slowly, "We never really knew." Miss Peacock twisted round in her seat,

"We think the drug stimulated then magnified hallucinations to such an extent, his brain couldn't take the strain – it blew. That sort of thing's been known to happen with LSD, but in Peter's case the damage was so catastrophic because of what he was."

"What about you? Were you OK?" I turned to Glory.

"She was not," Ruth leaned forward, "We wanted her out, right away, there and then, but couldn't get through to her for three days. Didn't know if she was alive or dead."

"We were," admitted Miss Peacock, "A little concerned."

"I was unconscious for a long time," Glory said, "Far longer than I should have been from the dose of tranquilliser they gave me, I suppose my head was just healing itself, then as soon as I did start to come round, I was nearly knocked out again by these two who were yammering away at me, long distance." She grimaced, "One way and another I didn't know whether I was Arthur, Martha or an iced tea cake. I had Mrs Millsop, who'd certainly saved my bacon, on one side of me slapping my face and pinching my hand to bring me out of it; bloody Doctor Doolittle on the other side shining a light in my eye, and pricking my arm with a pin; Miss Merry po-faced as ever writing up my chart and Ruth and Rachael like a couple of demented chipmunks in my mind – lucky I didn't have a complete relapse." She shook her head in disgust, drained her cup and followed it closely with a couple of squares of chocolate.

"And then," Ruth took over again, "Began the battle to get the wretched girl out."

"They wouldn't let you go?" I asked. Ruth snorted,

"She wouldn't come."

"If I had," Glory looked at me, "You mightn't be here now, think on." I was silent, of course she was right. Knowing what I did now, my own experience had taken on a very different and far more threatening dimension.

"There were things I had to do." She said.

"Who," humphed Miss Peacock, "Died and made you queen?" Glory laughed, this was obviously a well-chewed bone of contention.

Ed had, I realised turned off the main road now and we were, not altogether comfortably, bouncing down a narrow lane, hedges either side scraping the side of the van. He swung into an entrance almost totally obscured by a mature weeping willow, steered the van straight through the hanging fronds alongside a small stream and brought us to a halt in front of a cottage that looked as if it was auditioning for Hansel and Gretel.

"Only four rooms so you and Glory share." Miss Peacock crunched across the gravel to unlock a solid wood front door, while Ed unloaded the bags from the back of the van. The cottage inside was deceptively spacious – all the Peacock residences seemed to have a Tardis factor. It had an instantly homely feel, generously deep fireplaces in every room and a large helping of beams, if it didn't work for Hansel and Gretel, the Seven Dwarfs would snap it up.

Ruth started passing me provisions she'd brought with.

"We were spending so many weekends down here and a fortune in rent, so in the end we bought this," she winked, "A bit of luck with some of my shares. It belonged to the farm up the road, they still keep an eye when we're not here and leave milk and eggs when we are."

The front door opened straight into the almost circular living room, dominated by the lovely red-brick fireplace with a fire already laid. At right angles to the fireplace was a large well sat-upon sofa and several comfortable-looking chairs in various shapes and sizes. Above the fireplace was an imposing portrait of Queen Elizabeth I with, on adjoining walls, various other framed prints and a number of black and white etchings, I spotted Churchill, Shakespeare, Victoria and, more up to date, H.M. and Prince Philip with the family and some corgis.

"Very patriotic."

"They used to rent it out a lot to visiting Americans." Miss Peacock said "And every time we've been here, décor's been the last thing on our minds."

There were two doors leading from the living room, one to a not unsurprisingly well equipped kitchen where I stacked Ruth's provisions and the other to a narrow winding staircase with Nelson, Disraeli and Henry VIII all looking distinguished on the way up. The bedroom I was directed to was just big enough for both beds it held. A low, unpolished pine chest of drawers was set between them and a bay window overlooked a small but densely mature walled garden. There was a small window seat in the bay, cushioned in faded pink buttoned-velvet and ignoring Miss Peacock's dulcet tones as she issued instructions to everyone, I slipped the catch and the mullioned windows swung wide. It was wonderfully peaceful, birds singing fit to bust and not a traffic sound to be heard, the sort of silence that's a presence in itself. Kneeling on the window seat, hands on the low sill, I was inhaling the sweet heavy scent of a plump yellow climber rose and watching a bumble bee do his stuff when Miss Peacock came up behind me.

"Nice view." she said and pushed me out the window.

Because the window opened directly above the cushioned bench on which I'd been kneeling, my centre of balance wasn't anywhere useful and I shot outward like a startled bullet from a gun. I didn't even have time to draw breath and probably still wore a dopey, smelling-the-roses look. If I'd harboured doubts about the aerodynamic soundness of a well-fed bee, this now applied to me in spades and I couldn't, for the life of me, remember what was once so simple to do. I was also aware, time for rumination was running out.

"Sodding Ada." I muttered – honestly it was amazing how much I'd picked up from the salty east-end lexicon of Grandma and the Aunts over the years and how very handy these pithy little phrases were now proving. Not the time though for reminiscing. If I was coming in to land, head down probably wasn't ideal. I muscle-wrenched my body into a twist and grunting with effort, scarlet-faced with strain, hauled myself back up through air that in the good old days hadn't seemed half so resistant. She was still standing at the open window and reached out a hand to help me in.

"Not bad" she said, "Bit of practice wouldn't go amiss though."

CHAPTER THIRTY-THREE

Miss Peacock was coolly unrepentant.

"Had to find out if she could manage." We were back in the living room and my anger was adrenaline fuelled.

"You could have killed me." I sounded shrill and petulant which was precisely how I felt.

"Oh, I don't think so dear," Ruth was pragmatic, "She wouldn't have let you hit the ground."

"Well I didn't know that." I shrieked, certainly the old sang-froid had gone out the window around the same time I did.

"Shut up. Now." said Miss P "We have a small boy in danger of losing his life his sanity or both, have you finished sulking or must we wait?" I glared at her, bloody woman.

"Right. This," she settled back in her chair, "Is what we want you to do, should you agree to go in." Wonderful, I thought, Mission Impossible.

"Will you self-destruct, once you've given me the instructions?" I inquired, she ignored me, "Sam's in the clinic on the second floor, you're familiar with some areas from when you were there before, but you didn't go into the clinic, right?" I nodded. "Glory will go through it with you, so you know exactly what's where. All doors will be unlocked."

"Surely they lock up at night?"

"Ed'll deal with that."

"Ah." I subsided and glanced at Ed who was planted, massively immobile and expressionless on the sofa. I hated to be rude but it had to be said.

"Um, is Ed suited for undercover work? I mean he's not exactly built to slip in and out of anywhere unobtrusively." Miss P pursed her lips,

"He'll be working from a distance." She paused and added thoughtfully, "Unless it becomes necessary to go in. You just worry about your part, which is to make contact with Sam and get him out. Now there may be a small problem."

"Just the one?"

173

"We can't gauge Sam's reaction, but he's bound to be very frightened."

"He won't be the only one!"

"That's why you'll have Hamlet with you."

"Hamlet?" Hamlet raised his massive head at my squeak, unsure whether he was being called. He waited, decided it was a false alarm and settled down again. Blimey O'Reilly, I thought, hadn't the poor little sprat in the clinic gone through the mill enough, without waking up to find himself nose to nose with a bloody great beast – wasn't there a fairy tale? Was it Hans Christian or the Brothers Grimm? A dog with eyes the size of saucers?

"Now you're just rambling." Miss P brought me sharply back and I gritted my teeth, I was, I felt, entitled to the odd private thought.

"Well, shield better." She shot back.

"Now Rachael," Ruth, moved in to avert an outbreak of hostilities, "She's entitled to voice concerns."

"Only if they're valid." Miss P was unequivocal, but she gave a slight nod in my direction which I took to be her version of a fulsome apology. "You just have to trust us, Hamlet will prove an asset."

"But he's so damn big, how do I get him to do what I want, he doesn't really know me?" Miss Peacock looked at me over her glasses,

"Are you deliberately stupid? she inquired,

"Right, that's it, enough already," Ruth bounced up from her chair. "Rachael, you're impossible when you're in this sort of mood. Go. Put the kettle on or knit something useful. Glory and I will talk her through."

"I need to …"

"Shush." They glared at each other, identically shaped, obstinate jaws jutting, until Miss P the elder gave in and stalked off to the kitchen. Ruth swung diamond-patterned green tights back on to the foot-stool,

"Where were we? Ah, Hamlet. Now, how do you think you might get him to do what you want?" she raised a humorous eyebrow. I gawped,

"Naturally." she said "How else?" I was not happy about that. Over the years I'd listened once or twice to animals but didn't like it at all – they were so, well, so animally.

"Nonsense." Ruth had borrowed her sister's voice and I felt like someone who'd flung themselves gratefully out of the frying pan into an even hotter predicament.

"Go ahead," she ordered, "Try."

Hamlet's scent was hot, musty and doggy, a bit like a sweaty slipper. His mind was warm and full of smells, a world of odour, extending far out of the room we were in, each individual scent distinctive and meaningful. And hungry, Hamlet was hungry, although somehow I gathered Hamlet was almost always hungry, happy to eat at any time.

"Get him to do something." Ruth instructed. "No, no, no, it's no use giving it to him in words silly girl, *show* what you want, *show him*." I was at a loss, did she want me to get down on all fours and trot to the other side of the room? I looked at her, her face was impassive. Glory was still and silent as only she could be and Ed, who of course, did expressionless better than anyone was no help either. I looked helplessly at Hamlet who'd woken up. This was ridiculous. I shut my eyes and concentrated. Delighted I'd finally made some sort of sensible contact, Hamlet hauled himself up and ambled over to where I'd sent him. I suggested he pick up a cushion and bring it to me, he did. I got him to sit, to stand, to lie down, to collect a shoe from Ruth and give it to Glory and he did all I asked, until I could feel his attention beginning to wane.

"Good girl." Ruth was grinning, Glory was petting Hamlet's head, he had his tongue lolling out and his eyes closed in pleasure – I felt much the same.

"Right." Now Glory took over. "Shut your eyes. I'm going to walk you through the part of the building you've never been in before." And she did, so thoroughly I felt I could find my way blindfolded, which I suppose was more or less what Glory usually did.

"When are we going in?" I had a horrible feeling I knew.

"Tonight."

"But I haven't heard the rest of what happened, after the thing with Peter."

"Ah" said Glory,

"What does that mean – Ah?"

"We were hoping not to cover that till later." I waited, eyebrows raised, I didn't know whether she was looking through anybody's eyes at me, but she got the message. She and Ruth exchanged a thought faster than I could catch,

"Go, phone home." Ruth instructed "Then we'll bring you as up to date as we can before it's time to leave."

I dialled my mother from the phone which lived on the sideboard between a bust of Queen Victoria looking bored and a photograph of Glory and the Peacock girls. Ruth and Glory had their arms round each other and were laughing, Miss P had hers crossed and from the look on her face was telling the photographer to get a move on, I couldn't see her foot, but I guessed it would have been tapping. My mother was more than delighted to hear from me. She sounded strained, they'd been going back and forward to the hospital. No change though in Grandma's condition. She was also, needless to say, worried sick about me. How was I? Was I getting the answers to questions? What was it exactly they wanted me to do? When was I coming back?

I said I was fine and thought it best not to mention my hostess had just pushed me out of a first floor window. I said yes, I was finding out a great deal of stuff I'd always wanted to know and didn't add that the ghastly nightmares of the unfortunate Peter would disturb my sleep well into the future – certainly far more than they'd ever now disturb his. And as for proposed activities, well – I'd be going, under cover of darkness, to a Medical Research Centre run by a lunatic doctor. I'd be taking with me the biggest damn dog you've ever seen and I'd be breaking and entering with the intention of kidnapping a small boy, who, if push came to shove, could kill me with a single thought. I crossed my fingers and said nothing much was happening this evening and no I wasn't sure yet how long I'd be staying, but I really was learning a lot.

I replaced the receiver carefully with a clear conscience and a lump in my throat. I'd given them too many worries through the years to add more now and what they didn't know, couldn't drive them round the bend. What I'd learned, over the last couple of days, had shown me the reality of how wonderfully well they'd coped all my life, evidenced by the fact I was never made to feel anything other than just a bit Strange. I reckoned I owed them the odd little white lie.

We sat down to supper and it was a measure of how I was feeling that I can honestly say I have no idea what we ate. Then we went to change into warmer clothes.

"Dark stuff." Miss Peacock instructed. If, I couldn't help thinking, breaking and entering was on the agenda, it would have been a nice hostessy gesture to have mentioned it in the original invitation so one could have packed accordingly. But I needn't have worried, on my bed were soft trousers, a grey T-shirt, a thick black jumper and a long waterproof jacket.

When we re-congregated, Glory and Ruth were looking uncomfortably unlike themselves in items clearly allocated from the elder Peacock wardrobe. A long grey jumper swam on Glory's thin frame, a dark brown one looked as if it was feeling the strain on Ruth's. Glory had even left off the earrings.

"We still have a bit of time," Miss Peacock decreed as Ed, pottering in the kitchen, sent us four mugs of milky coffee and, each taking over smoothly from the other where relevant, the three women began to weave the rest of the story.

CHAPTER THIRTY-FOUR

After the unfortunate 'Atkins incident', as it came to be known, and as soon as Ruth and Rachael were able to reach Glory, they demanded she get out of there immediately. But it seemed, that for everyone, the stakes had changed.

Glory stated categorically she couldn't possibly leave however much she might want to, her conscience simply wouldn't let her. No amount of ranting and raving on the part of the Peacocks – mental, telephonic and, when they eventually got to see her, face to face across a small iron table covered with scones and jam in an Oxford tea-shoppe, would change her mind. You had to hand it to her, when it came to ranting and raving there can't have been many to rival the Peacock sisters in full and double flow.

Things had changed too for the Doctor. Hard on the heels of Peter's last stand, some Men from the Ministry had come hot-footing down from London. Glory, regaining consciousness only after a good forty-eight hours of Atkins-generated trauma, could vaguely remember them peering in at her in her room, 'Like a flipping fish in a tank', she said resentfully. Under the eagle eye of Mrs Millsop, she was being kept in for bed-rest and observation. One catatonic patient, Mrs Millsop paraphrased crisply, was sad, two could be considered careless.

Mrs Millsop, empowered by having snatched Glory from the jaws of Peter's fate, had in fact, become a rather unexpectedly solid tower of strength. When the Doctor wanted to start immediate tests, to ascertain whether Glory's ability had been affected, Mrs Millsop put her size nine, sensibly rubber-soled foot down firmly. For the next few days, she stated, any tests would have to be done over her dead body, and as this would have proved a substantial obstacle to even the most determined, the Doctor gave in petulantly and Glory was grateful for the breathing space.

It was never quite clear from precisely which Government Department the Foundation's funding flowed, although it was almost certainly MI something-or-other. In any event, Glory said, there'd been three visitors and looking through various eyes she saw identical dark suits, ties and sombre expressions. They were shown round by the Doctor who was all over them like an oil slick. It seemed though that it was this visit which moved things suddenly onto a different level altogether. Whilst they'd had enough faith in Dreck's research to fund the Foundation in the first place and had been willing to set in motion the costly and ponderous wheels needed to create the social study cover, it had been purely on a, 'Run it up the flagpole and see who salutes', sort of basis. Indeed, this was just one of a number of seemingly wacky projects they underwrote during those desperate, pull-one-over on the Communists years, when the atmosphere between East and West was frosty to freezing point.

However, quite a lot of testing sessions at the Foundation had been cine filmed and delivered to an anonymous office in Piccadilly, creating something of a stir. The film provided the Men from whichever Ministry, with irrefutable evidence of what did actually exist, if only they could get their hands on some of it. Running through their minds during their visit, as they looked at the wreck that was Peter and the slightly less wrecked Glory, were the unlimited uses to which such talents could be applied – espionage, international and industrial, warfare defensive and aggressive – the list was endless. They also knew the Americans were doing very similar testing across the Atlantic, were desperate to score first and at Newcombe, could suddenly see in the distance something that might be success.

They got very excited in a mutedly undercover sort of way, and exchanged a lot of expressionless looks, although each knew exactly what the others were thinking – as indeed did Glory. The Doctor, who'd spent a good many years fighting for recognition, determined to prove the worth of his project, suddenly found it proven. He was now, however, under intense pressure to deliver.

If in the first few days following the Atkins incident, Mrs Millsop, Glory and the rest of the staff were extremely distressed by what had happened to Peter, Doctor Dreck was distraught, one might almost say demented with grief. What infernal bloody bad luck, what a stinking blow from fate's unfeeling fist, to have stumbled across a talent such as Peter's only to have it snatched away. It might of course have been pointed out, that when it came to luck, Peter's wasn't exactly running high either. Also worth mentioning, might have been the fact, that had the Doctor not been dishing out L/24 pills like Smarties, such a catastrophe might never have occurred in the first place. But his complete inability to see things from anything other than his own viewpoint, was indicative of the not so sane way his mind was working and of the increasingly erratic paths it might follow in the future. It was, as Glory said, enough to send a shiver and a half down your spine.

Of course nobody gave up on Peter right away and for several weeks different neurological experts from various parts of the country came to consult and confer. Peter was given brain scans, 24-hour intensive nursing care and ministered to by a rotating team of physiotherapists. It reminded her, said Glory, of Christopher Robin having wheezles and sneezles – you know, when all sorts of physicians on lots of conditions came hurrying round at a run. But lip after lip was pursed, head after head shaken, they could find no brain activity whatsoever – poor kid, the prognosis was bleak. Dr Dreck thanked them for their professional opinion, shaking his head mournfully too, although he'd far rather have banged it violently against the nearest wall in frustration. L/24 was never mentioned to or by anyone, which only goes to show, said Ruth, you can get away with murder if you do it right. A massive stroke was the verdict, unusual but certainly not unknown in one so young and it was, undoubtedly, only the heroic attempts to save him that had ensured he survived at all.

The awful thing, Mrs Millsop told Glory afterwards, was that when his mother was told, and it fell to Mrs Millsop to do the telling, she took it remarkably calmly,

"'Orrible, really," Mrs Millsop had recounted, forgetting careful diction and professional restraint in her distress. "Done up like a bleeding dog's dinner she was when she arrived, drove down from London with some chap in a big car, all sobbing and shaking and crocodile tears and didn't stay in the room with the boy more than a minute. Mind you, she soon perked up and put her hanky away when Miss Merry started talking about insurance pay-outs." Mrs Millsop had sniffed in disdain, in all honesty she hadn't liked the little blighter either, but you had to feel sorry didn't you?

Peter's incapacity, together with the surge of interest from the Men with the Money, was not good news for Glory – as far as the Doctor was concerned she was, for the moment, the only game in town. Still shaken from how close she'd come to disaster, nevertheless determined against all Ruth and Rachael's strenuous objections, to stay on a bit longer at the Foundation, Glory knew she couldn't possibly warn everyone. But perhaps she'd become as obsessed in her way as the Doctor had in his. She also had a plan.

The Peacocks dismissed it out of hand, said it was the most ridiculous thing they'd ever heard and far too risky, but she was determined and they were genuinely worried about her state of mind. After discussing it at length, they felt perhaps if she accomplished what she wanted, they stood a better chance of persuading her to leave and the sooner that happened the easier they'd all sleep at night. What the three of them however had overlooked in all this major decision-making was that when it came to the crunch, Dreck might not be so happy to wave bye bye to Glory, in all senses of the word!

What she had in mind to do, before she shook the dust of the Foundation from her heels – and even she had the grace to admit, it was a bit of a hare-brained long shot – was to substitute something harmless for the large supply of L/24 the Doctor was preparing to dole out to whichever talented person next had the misfortune to cross his path. It was of course, only a short-term measure, but perhaps consistent failure of the drug would convince him to give up, or better still convince the money men to turn off the tap.

The Peacocks, still with grave reservations, contacted their research scientist friend and, calling in all sorts of favours, asked could he duplicate the appearance of the sample pills Glory had originally smuggled out. Could he produce something that looked identical but contained nothing harmful. Friend scientist was less than thrilled, but squared his conscience with the fact it wasn't the other way round – substituting dodgy for harmless. In due course he reported back with an air-tight container full of duplicates which were, even under the most anxious and intense scrutiny, pretty much indistinguishable from the real thing. These were duly passed to Glory on one of their tea outings.

As might have been expected, as soon as Mrs Millsop took her gimlet eye off the ball, the Doctor was in like Flynn, subjecting Glory to an ever more intensive programme. He was again convinced that improving her skills was merely a matter of time, patience and training. He'd also resolved if that didn't work pretty damn quick, he might just try a more positive move. There was a procedure he'd read about in the New England Medical Journal. Pioneered at Baltmore's Johns Hopkins, it was an experimental and high risk method of dealing with tumours and involved stimulating areas of the brain during surgery. What intrigued him was that some patients, post-operatively, had developed vastly enhanced memory and mathematical skills. The Doctor had immediately seen interesting applications – if some abilities could be thus stimulated, why not others? The fact that to do this he'd have to open up Glory's head and perform a life-threatening, relatively untried operation – added to which, he wasn't even a brain surgeon – didn't seem to bother him unduly. It certainly gave Glory a turn though when she saw what he was thinking.

CHAPTER THIRTY-FIVE

To speed Glory's progress in the ability stakes, Miss Merry was delegated to spend extra time working with her. Thrust ever more frequently into that chilly presence, at the same time as trying to ignore the Doctor, who'd developed an unpleasant habit of mentally drawing incision lines on her skull, was, Glory found, something of a strain.

The Merry mind was a complex one, convoluted and folded in on itself. It was unusual and somewhat alarming that often one part of the mind didn't seem to be all that aware of, or indeed much bothered by what was going on in other parts. There was though, one section interminably occupied, one might almost say pre-occupied, with the doings of the Doctor. What was he thinking, what was he saying? What was someone else saying to him? What might he be needing? What was he going to do next? This background cadence was such a constant, that the woman herself was hardly aware of it and it certainly didn't stop her performing her job in a ferociously efficient manner.

It troubled Miss Merry somewhat that there was a large area of human communication that for some reason, she simply didn't get. It had always been thus, even as a child, a sense of humour was ostensibly absent. She was, quite literally, humourless and that was no laughing matter. This lack had governed her childhood, making of her, if not a complete outcast then a fringe member of every group she'd ever been with, including her parents and two siblings. They were a normal enough family, older sister, younger brother. Father a civil servant both by profession and nature, mother involved in any voluntary organisation that didn't involve something depressing. They had a quiet, not unhappy home life and were in truth no great comedians themselves, nevertheless they were able to appreciate a joke with a smile if not a belly laugh and equipped to do their share of joshing at a friendly gathering.

For the young Miss M however, the total inability to grasp anything other than the literal, coloured if not corrupted her development, certainly nurtured her deep suspicion of others. She was aware, always, of an undercurrent to most conversations to which other people responded automatically, whilst she simply didn't know how. It was choice that directed her toward a scientific career, chance that assigned her to assist the Doctor when he first came to work in England. And only because he inspired devotion in her hitherto unmolested heart, had she become involved in this telepathy business, a branch of research which couldn't have been further from ideal for someone of her temperament. For her to be working with yet another hidden current into which she stood no chance of tapping, was more than ironic, it was adding insult to injury, rubbing salt in the wound and twisting the knife. In truth, she nursed a deep repugnance for the entire concept, sublimating this almost completely in order to do her damndest to help the Doctor achieve his aims.

She was more than highly suspicious of Glory and her ilk, cherishing a conviction, and she wasn't wrong was she, that there was far more to them than met the eye. She reasoned, if Glory was able to spot psi abilities from afar, she must be able to hear far more than she let on and the thought of that made her skin crawl. She was horrified at the thought of someone rifling through her mind, where there were areas into which even she didn't go. She'd constructed for herself, quite cleverly, considering she was working in the dark, a rudimentary shielding of a chanted nursery rhyme which although not effective with someone like Glory, would have thrown off other milder talents.

But if Miss Merry's faith in her own suspicion was strong, the doctor's in the accuracy of his tests was stronger and he pointed out frequently, if Glory was able to do more than she admitted, it would certainly have come to light long before now. As far from intuitive as anyone could be, but not a stupid woman by a long chalk, Miss Merry remained unconvinced and her antipathy grew, in direct proportion to the hours they spent together.

"And it was around about then," Glory aimed a nod in my direction, "That you came on the scene and that really put the cat among the pigeons!

CHAPTER THIRTY-SIX

"There was something about you that got Miss Merry's whiskers twitching right from the start. It didn't help that my timing was out that day. I knew what you were before you even got off the coach, but there were another couple of kids I wanted to check out. With you, there wasn't need for checking, you stuck out like a handful of sore thumbs. But by the time I got back to you, you were already wading through those tests like a bull in a china shop and scoring stupidly high marks." I was moved to register a protest in my own defence,

"How was I to know?"

"By the time I shut you up, word had already gone out and Dreck and Merry couldn't believe their luck. But then, when you were taken in to see them I'd blocked you off and they were completely thrown." She giggled, "It was rather funny really, Dr D was busy trying to send you all sorts of messages and images to which you normally couldn't have helped respond, but he was hitting a brick wall. It had never happened before. In most cases those who were warned, were alerted well before the tests and were careful how they scored and those who didn't want to be careful, responded in all the right ways once they were with the Doctor. He knew something was up, but couldn't work out what and he didn't have to be telepathic to see you were as baffled as he was. Then, when they hauled you off to the booths, you muddled things even more." I sat forward, indignant,

"I didn't."

"I'm telling you, you did."

"Girls," Ruth frowned, on peace-making alert even when not strictly necessary, I presumed she must have a lot of practise. Glory shook her head,

"You were so obviously scared to death in there and then you kept muttering, no matter how many times I told you not to talk – frankly you were a pain in the arse." I was silent, thinking back, actually she wasn't wrong.

"And then, when I was finally able to get you on your own, it took ages to get the necessary info across – all you did was ask questions.

"Well excuse me for being interested."

"Did you know Miss M had her ear against the door, the whole time?" I hadn't, and it gave me pause for thought and a chill.

"She didn't hear much, just the occasional mutter and squeak, but enough to keep her suspicious."

"That's when she took me upstairs and shot those awful baby pictures at me?"

"Uh huh, you managed OK, but not well enough to put her off the scent."

"And then the dice?"

"I'd forgotten about that – talk about cocky. My God, Stella, I don't know what you thought you were doing."

"Red herrings?"

"Well they certainly looked pretty damn fishy to Miss Merry. Couldn't you just sit still and look stupid – that would have been the clever thing to do."

"Glory." Ruth reproved.

"Sorry," Glory sighed and sat back, "I was so aggravated, I could have bashed your brains in with my stick." I grinned back,

"Not your favourite person then?"

"You'd better believe it. By the time I was called in to check out the room, Miss Merry was as hopping mad as I've ever seen her, grinding her teeth so hard you could actually hear. She suspected, no, more than suspected, was certain you were behind what was going on, wanted it desperately to be you. It was killing her that she just couldn't find a way of proving it and time was running out. She thought you were something special. I swore blind you weren't. I think though there was more to it than that, it was a personality thing, you simply got right up her nose – with me it was always my clothes, her reaction to them was like a bull spotting a red rag. With you I think it was your stupid sense of humour, you never know when to keep quiet do you?"

I was silent, again she wasn't wrong. I was well aware my mouth often worked ahead of and sometimes completely independently of my brain, with results which might keep me endlessly amused but had led to trouble in the past. I could see very clearly now, just how dangerously close I'd sailed to the wind at the Foundation. I had more to be grateful to Glory for than I'd fully appreciated. I put out my hand without thought and squeezed hers. Miss Peacock sniffed,

"Next time, think before you put yourself and others in danger." Trust her to enhance the moment.

"What happened after I left?" I asked, Glory frowned,

"It was as if a rather dangerous line had been crossed, she was more deeply suspicious than ever and determined to trip me up. I decided I needed to get the pill-swap done, sooner rather than later, and get the hell out of there while I still could. It suddenly became very clear to me I couldn't carry on the way I had been. I was tired and pretty drained – being on guard the whole time was exhausting – and the more like that I felt, the more likely I was to make a slip. Problem with the pill thing was I obviously had to do it alone and of course that meant working blind.

In fact, I'd spent a great deal of time memorising the geography of the Doctor's office every time I went in there with someone, and I thought I could find my way around comfortably enough. There was a large cupboard he used as a drugs cabinet and this seemed to be where the drug, in pill format was stored. It was obviously kept locked and as far as I knew there were only two keys, Miss Merry's and the Doctor's, kept on them at all times. I spent a lot of time practising with Ed, long distance.

"Ed?"

"For the lock. You either have a knack for that sort of thing, or you don't. I don't! So I took lessons. I was going to have to take my chances as regards timing and Ed couldn't wait around indefinitely and do it for me. Anyway, as it so happened, a couple of weeks after you'd been there, Dreck was entertaining a French scientist who was writing a paper on his own work with children and wanted to confer. I knew they were going out for dinner and taking Merry.

I waited till around 10.00. Late enough for there not to be lots of people around, not too late for it to look odd if I was spotted. It took me a good few dicey minutes to open the cabinet. Ed says it's a question of simply slipping your mind inside it and using that as the key." I looked across at Ed in astonishment, I couldn't imagine him saying that much at any one time.

"But obviously my mind's not as key shaped as his." Glory flashed him a smile, "It took me far longer than I could afford – I could've cried with relief when I finally heard that click.

There were twelve bottles whose shape I immediately recognised. I had the substitutes with me and had taken the precaution of wearing one

187

of the lab coats, which have huge pockets. I took the pill bottles over to the desk, two at a time, emptied them into one of my pockets and re-filled them with the substitutes from the other.

I was terrified of spilling any pills on the floor – I wouldn't have had a hope in hell of finding them again, so I had to go slowly. Eventually, I screwed the final cap back on, wiped all the bottles thoroughly in case there were powdery traces and blew like crazy on the desk to get rid of anything on there. And then the door opened and someone clicked the light switch." Glory stopped and reached for her cup, I didn't think I could bear to wait for another leisurely swallow.

"*Who?*" I hissed.

"Mrs Millsop, and she had as much of a fright as I did, nearly shot out of her skin. Her heart was going nineteen to the dozen, mind you mine was doing a few extra beats to the bar too. But you had to hand it to her when it came to reaction time. She didn't have to be Sherlock Holmes to know I was doing something I shouldn't, but she liked me and she knew something I didn't; Dr Doolittle and Miss Bloody Merry, who were supposed to have been out for the whole evening, had finished early and were, at that moment on their way to the office to go over the day's reports. She valued and needed her job, but she didn't stop to think, just acted purely instinctively.

She grabbed me by both arms, threw me behind the examination screen and whilst it was still rocking on its wheels and I was struggling to keep my balance, they were through the door. They were both thoroughly peeved. The French scientist had had way too much to drink and had turned contentious, holding forth on flaws he'd spotted in some of the Newcombe testing methods. And then, in the taxi back to his hotel, he'd put his hand on Miss Merry's knee, proving not only that he was very drunk but also, in matters of judgement, an idiot. Dr Dreck was offended by the opinions of a colleague with whom he'd hoped to have a fruitful collaboration and Miss Merry was mortified that the Doctor had pretended not to see the hand on her knee. Not what you'd call a good night out.

Thankfully, they didn't hang around, although it seemed like hours. I daren't move and knew if they looked down, they could clearly see my feet below the screen. By the time they left, I don't know which of us was in a worse state, me or Mrs Millsop. And I still had to re-lock the cabinet. Mrs Millsop stood and watched me grimly and didn't turn a hair when she too heard the click – I suppose she'd seen enough over the last few months not to be surprised at anything. Still without a single word being exchanged, she hurried me back to my room and if she noted my bulging pockets she didn't say anything, she really didn't want to know what I'd been doing."

Glory sat back. Miss Peacock, looked at her watch, informed us we needed to get moving shortly and got on briskly with the rest of the story.

CHAPTER THIRTY-SEVEN

Having once achieved what she'd made up her mind to do in relation to the L/24 supply, Glory knew the end was in sight. She'd set herself a target, shot a bulls-eye, survived a near miss and now conceded gratefully, if not graciously, time was up. Operation 'Glory Out', immediately swept into action. Miss Peacock phoned the Doctor to say she and her sister would, if it were possible, appreciate just a very few moments of his valuable time and sure enough, the following day brought the two to Oxford, one thin and darkly dressed the other plumply disconcerting in polka-dot pink.

They were, they said, grateful beyond words, not only for the medical care lavished on Glory, but for the opportunities she'd been given to assist the Doctor in a small way with his amazing work and to learn so much. However, they felt the time had arrived – and here the voice of Miss Peacock the elder faltered with an excess of emotion – when it was safe to hope Glory's disturbed times were behind her. This was, of course, entirely due to the wonderful work of the good Doctor, his excellent methods and his professional team. They felt, they said, exchanging a fondly moist glance, she should now resume her place at home with them and – most exciting of all – they'd obtained for her, a place at teacher training college, which would enable her not only to improve her Braille, but qualify her to teach others. An excellent career path, did not the Doctor agree?

The Doctor did not agree. The Doctor wasn't happy at all. He was seeing psi ability slip through his fingers like sand. He'd known he couldn't hang on to Glory forever and was lucky the arrangement had lasted so long, but he didn't want to lose her now. The Misses Peacock, heads cocked fetchingly to one side in feminine deference to the opinions of the great man were however, frustratingly steely in their determination not to be talked out of their plans. After all, she was coming up for twenty years old now and foundations for the future had to be laid, didn't they dear, enquired one Miss Peacock of the other.

And no matter what objections the Doctor raised – Glory's continued depression, reliance on familiar surroundings, valuable work in which she was participating, experience she was gaining – one or other of the sisters was ready with an answer almost before he'd finished. And as his agitation grew, his peculiarly opaque mind became more readable and they saw all too clearly, this was a train that was, perhaps not immediately but definitely in the foreseeable future, coming right off the rails. Of course, if the Doctor had been in any way aware of even a fraction of the combined psi abilities of the two wittery women smiling brightly at him, he'd probably, and who'd have blamed him, blown a gasket there and then. After twenty minutes of polite and intractable discussion, the Misses Peacock gathered their bags and rose to their feet, fluttery yet unyielding. They would, they said, be taking Glory with them right away, giving her just enough time to pack and say her goodbyes.

Ruth, Rachael and Glory all fully admitted afterwards, they'd got it wrong. Misread the signals. Perhaps they were lulled by the thought that they were so close to closing a chapter. Perhaps there was a false sense of security because the three of them were physically nearer to each other than they'd been for some time – Glory packing her suitcase, the Peacock sisters flicking through magazines in the consulting room reception area. Whatever the reason, they'd gravely underestimated the determination of the Doctor and he had calmed himself down by that stage. So, when he knocked politely on Glory's door to say his farewells, she really didn't have any idea as he walked towards her, hand outstretched, what was in it.

She felt the needle slide cold into her wrist and thought she sent something out to the Peacocks, but was unconscious in almost the same breath. In the waiting room they both felt her for an instant and then nothing. Five minutes later Miss Merry came to find them, her face grim – not that you could have told the difference – could they come quickly, poor Glory had suffered some sort of attack, Doctor and matron were with her now.

Following Miss Merry's smooth progress up two flights of stairs, along a corridor and into the clinic area of the building where they'd never been, but knew so well from Glory's descriptions, the two women didn't waste time blaming themselves, that could come later. Whether it was a measure of the Doctor's immense conceit, his increasingly slippery grip on reality or his conviction he was dealing with a couple of old fools that had prompted this somewhat transparent move, things weren't looking good.

Glory was deeply unconscious; they probed, but could find nothing. Some kind of a fit the Doctor suggested, her wrist between his thumb and forefinger – more a fit up thought the sisters grimly. They reviewed their options which didn't take long, there weren't many. They were quite capable of course, at that point in time and without any undue effort, of knocking out the Doctor, Miss Merry, Mrs Millsop and whoever else happened to be around and taking Glory. However, the decimation of a clinic full of people might require a fair old bit of explaining and keeping a low profile was a tried and tested policy of theirs. It had stood them in good stead in the past and they saw no reason to change things now.

They were in reluctant agreement, they should bide their time, watch and wait. They read Mrs Millsop's deep concern – she was aware the doctor hadn't wanted Glory to leave but couldn't believe he'd be so addle-pated as to pull a stunt like this. They saw that Miss Merry was still in two minds, if not more, about the situation. They also observed that the Doctor, having made his move was, like others of his slightly dodgy mind-set, so convinced of his own brilliance that he couldn't believe anybody would suspect anything. He did though, feel it might be advisable to bring forward his plans for the operation on Glory, which he'd temporarily put on the back burner – get it out of the way, sooner rather than later.

Sombre-faced he motioned the sisters gently away from the side of the bed. The situation was of course, he murmured, serious. He wasn't going to insult their intelligence and suggest otherwise. He didn't like to speculate, but it had looked when she first collapsed, like a grand mal seizure however, if that were the case, he would certainly have expected her to come round by now. It was impossible now to say how long it might be before she returned to full consciousness. But better safe than sorry – round the clock nursing, full range of tests, scans, no stone left unturned. Other possible causes? Well, difficult to hazard a guess at this stage, possibility of a local trauma sustained during the Atkins incident, undetected at the time, subdural haematoma, fatal pressure. Worst case scenario? Well he didn't want to worry them, but he wouldn't be doing his job if he wasn't giving some serious thought to emergency surgery.

The sisters twittered and sobbed, holding on to each other and the Doctor for reassurance, at the same time making a cold assessment of the time they had left. Ruth was convinced he'd go for it tonight, Rachael thought he might wait until morning. Both of them, and these were not women easily shocked at anything human nature threw up, were deeply alarmed at the strength and hunger of Dreck's determination to get his hands on Glory's brain. He was literally licking his mental chops at the chance of finding what made it tick and, perhaps, making it tick a whole lot louder in the future. It would also be awfully exciting, he thought if he could at the same time as stimulating her psi abilities, tone down, if not eradicate some of her more annoyingly individual personality traits. If he played his cauterisation tools right, he saw no reason why that shouldn't be achieved. As he patted and nodded, soothed and sympathised, he was running a pleasing and rapidly unfolding scenario in his head – marathon operation, heroic effort, mopped brow. And the Peacocks, listening, knew they'd underestimated him once and couldn't afford to make the same mistake twice.

The Doctor felt there was little the sisters could do for Glory that night. He also expressed concern, in view of her somewhat unusual sensitivities, that the agitation of her guardians might reach her and worsen her condition. He thought the best possible thing they could do, would be to head to a nearby hotel for a good night's sleep. This proposed course of action was greeted with further hysteria by the sisters who swore they wouldn't dream of moving so much as one step away from Glory's sickbed. A compromise was eventually reached in the form of a room for the night at the clinic and they were despatched, meanwhile, on the sturdy arm of Mrs Millsop to the small staff canteen. Despite both sisters dismissing, out of hand, any possibility they might force a crumb between their quivering lips they were, in fact able to put away, if not exactly enjoy, cheese omelette and chips followed by strong coffee and a slice of apple cake – these were after all, people who'd known what it was to go hungry. They were also aware they'd need all the energy and resources they could muster for the coming activities.

Miss Merry, gliding into their small but perfectly adequate clinic room later that evening, to ensure they had everything they needed and to give an update on Glory's condition – sadly no change – brought them each a mild sleeping pill, compliments of the Doctor. The mild sleeping pills, they clearly read, were in reality strong enough to knock out a couple of good-sized cart horses and put them in la la land for at least twelve solid hours. Miss Merry didn't seem altogether clear in her mind as to quite how the Doctor planned to explain that one away, maybe he hadn't given it a lot of thought himself – maybe explanations were beginning to bother him less and less.

The sisters were pathetically grateful for the care and consideration they were receiving telling Miss Merry and each other, several times over, how fortunate it was that if this terrible thing had to happen to Glory, it had happened whilst she was still under the care of the Doctor. And what an exceptional man he was, to even in the midst of this crisis, give thought to their welfare. They were so very thankful for the pills because neither of them had imagined they were going to get one single wink, whereas this way, they'd be out like lights till the morning, by which stage perhaps the dear Doctor would have better news.

By the time Miss Merry popped back an hour later, both women were spark out, snoring in gentle harmony. Miss Merry nodded, satisfied and left, closing the door quietly behind her.

CHAPTER THIRTY-EIGHT

I couldn't believe that at this point there would be a halt in the story, but Miss Peacock was suddenly getting busy, issuing us all with dark scarves and gloves. Ed had already donned a black knitted hat which, it has to be said, did him no favours, throwing into startling relief his pale complexion, sadly battered nose and stopping just short of his rather large ears. Still, if the aim of the game was to scare the pants of any opposition, they were on to a winner there. She was also handing round a black, viscous slightly gritty substance in a small tin.

"Camouflage?" I asked, half in horror half in amusement, wondering whether I'd also be required to balance some leaf-bedecked branches on my head. Miss Peacock gave me the look reserved by the impatient for the idiotic.

"Hardly, this is for the dogs."

"Dogs?"

"They may have dogs patrolling and they dislike this smell, keeps them away long enough to let you deal with them. Spread some on your arms and neck." I glanced around and Ruth nodded encouragingly her neck and wrist, already smeared. I smiled politely and complied. I felt the lunatics were taking over the asylum and I was along for the ride. I could smell though why dogs didn't like it, I didn't like it much either.

"Ready?" Miss Peacock eyed the troops and the troops, Glory, Ruth, Ed, Hamlet – who'd already demonstrated his displeasure at how we were all smelling – and me, all nodded back in a business-like way. And one of us – no names, no pack drill but in mitigation, I think a small note of hysteria might have crept in – snapped her a salute. She ignored me and we headed out to the van. We automatically sat in the same formation as before and as we drove through the darkness, they finished for me the final chapters of Glory's Great Escape.

Ruth and Rachael had snored on gently until Miss Merry had gone. They'd gradually felt Glory coming round over the last half hour and even as Miss Merry's coldly convoluted thought patterns were fading into the middle distance, the sisters were up and padding quietly in her wake.

Since her prompt action, which had undoubtedly saved the day at the time of the hoo ha with Peter, Mrs Millsop had, in the Doctors opinion, got a bit above herself. Nothing he could actually put his finger on, nothing on which he could take her to task, just an old fashioned look here, a frown there, a general air of potential insubordination. He'd decided therefore, in order to avoid any unnecessarily detailed explanations and justifications, it might be better for all concerned if Matron wasn't actively involved in the evening's planned emergency op. Accordingly, he'd instructed Miss Merry to slip another of those oh-so-useful sleeping pills into the strong black coffee Mrs Millsop was wont to knock back whenever she came off duty. In her stead, he planned to utilise the two agency nurses on duty that night, neither of whom had worked at the clinic previously and, the Doctor made a mental note, wouldn't be asked to work there again. Not, he reassured himself, that he was doing anything in any way untoward, just that sometimes people were ultra-critical of forward-thinkers whose lot it was to advance the cause of medical knowledge. After all, he reasoned, what would the future of heart transplant surgery have been, had Christian Barnard, so recently hailed a hero, heeded the nay-sayers?

It was Miss Merry's task to ensure Glory was up and kicking for her op. She needed to be conscious in order to react to the different brain stimuli. In fact, Glory had been awake for a little while and was being brought up to date on recent and pending events by the cavalry, which was even now, trotting briskly down the corridor, handbags tucked firmly under arms.

Leaning over Glory, to wake her, Miss Merry simply didn't straighten up again, just collapsed heavily across the bed with a small exhalation of surprise. Ruth was pleased. She hadn't taken anybody out in quite a while and of course, it was something you always had to do carefully. Too little pressure and it didn't work, too much and it worked too well, possibly permanently and whilst Miss M wouldn't have been Ruth's number one choice for best friend, she didn't want the wretched woman on her conscience.

196

The Doctor meanwhile, stern faced, green-capped, was scrubbing. It was a while since he'd performed surgery but as he flexed his thin, somewhat elongated fingers under the hot water, he didn't think they'd lost any of their dexterity. He'd always been quietly proud of his hands, inherited from his mother. She'd been rather elongated altogether; a tall, anxious, wraith of a thing – nerves, he was always told, Mother's nerves aren't good. Certainly she had a tendency to jump and emit little shrieks of shock at almost everything, which of course didn't do a great deal for the nerves of those around her either. The young Karl had found that neither sidling into a room softly nor stomping loudly to make sure his mother was aware of his pending arrival, ever did anything to alleviate her start of surprise and severe palpitations whenever she saw him. She always said, one pale elegant hand pressed trembling to her narrow chest, that her heart would be the death of her one day. And indeed it was, although not until her late eighties.

The Doctor didn't have a great deal of feeling for his late mother, her memory unfailingly evoking a certain jumpiness, but he was grateful for the fingers. He always felt that had he pursued surgery as his speciality, he'd quickly have risen through the ranks – still surgery's loss was paediatrics' gain. Hands pleasantly tingling, held upwards and away to avoid contamination, he looked round irritably for the nurse who should be waiting to glove and gown him, a process he particularly enjoyed. He fancied, he had about him, a look of Richard Chamberlain and never more so than when the rubber gloves slapped down tight over his wrists and the green of the gown threw the strong line of his jaw into bold relief. Swearing softly now, he strode to the swing doors opening into the clinic's small operating theatre. He was incensed to see, that although the operating tray prepared and covered, was in place beside the adjustable, dentist-style chair – the patient had to be upright – and packs of sterile sheeting were ready for draping; of the patient herself there was no sign, nor a nurse to be seen.

This was because both nurses were sitting cross legged on the floor of the sluice room. They were extremely relaxed. The elder of the two, Edna-May Banks had returned to nursing now her kids were older and was peeved to find, that in all the years she'd spent at home, bemoaning an unfulfilled career, she'd somehow managed to overlook what bloody hard work it was. She wondered how she could possibly have forgotten there was always some bossy busy-knickers telling you what to do – medication here Nurse Banks, pressure and pre-meds there Nurse Banks, do a handstand and wiggle your ears Nurse Banks. Also faded in her mind, though of course she hadn't had the varicose veins pre-kids, was the inordinate amount of time spent rushing around in squeaky-soled shoes on linoleum floors, from which the vibrations went right up the back of your calves, making head and legs ache.

Younger of the two nurses was Phillippa Betts. Phillippa Higginson as was. As was, of just three weeks ago in fact, confirmed by the shiny gold ring on her left hand, marker of her new status and state of happiness. And she was happy, ever so. Big white wedding, no expense spared to the barely concealed envy of her older sister – bridesmaid yet again with still no sign of any action of her own – and a pile of deliciously wrapped and bowed presents. Not to mention, a maisonette, spanking new from top to bottom. Fully fitted formica kitchen, small, but everything in it, full-length orange dralon curtains in the lounge and best of all, pale cream shag pile carpet. There was Tom too, of course. Mind you, in the two weeks since they'd got back from Spain he was always wanting to get busy. You'd think, wouldn't you, she'd said to her Mum, one married woman to another, enough was enough and sometimes when you got in from work all you actually wanted was a cup of tea and a Maryland Cookie.

Phillipa turned back to Edna-May. They were doing a cat's cradle with a length of suture thread. They'd several times got it to the stage of its third transformation, but that's where they lost it and they were having trouble keeping hoots of laughter under control. Miss Peacock had suggested to each of them, a thought planted deep in their minds, that whilst they were fully entitled to sit down for a bit – and where better than the sluice room – it might be advisable if they kept the noise down. She'd suggested the cat's cradle as a start and then intimated they might enjoy taking out the tight rolls of bandages kept in the supply cupboard, and seeing just how high they could build them, before the pile collapsed. Phillipa and Edna May, were valiantly stifling the giggles but the tangle they made on their next cat's cradle attempt quite undid them and they were now rolling around the floor, scarlet faced and snorting.

The Doctor was nonplussed to say the least. At first he thought they'd been taken ill, but on further examination they seemed to be laughing. The sight of him in the open door, slack-jawed with hands still held absently out in front of him, was probably amusing. It certainly finished off Phillipa and Edna-May who, in extremis, quite forgot about keeping the sound down.

The Doctor backed hurriedly away. He needed Miss Merry and he needed her now. Whatever was at the bottom of this aberrant behaviour she'd deal with it in her normal competent way, he really couldn't be expected to have to cope, not when he was about to operate. This thought pulled him back to the matter in hand. Where in hell's name was the patient? Thoroughly incensed and aware he'd have to re-scrub, he let the sluice room door swing to and strode back across the operating theatre, thumping the empty chair hard as he passed and heading along the corridor to Glory's room.

Miss Merry may have been thin as a rake, but to Glory lying underneath, the woman felt more like a lawn mower. She was also dribbling unpleasantly on Glory's hand. Glory lifted her gently, surprised at how much of a mental effort it cost, she must have been pretty deeply unconscious to still feel so woozy, God knows what he'd injected her with. She sent the limp Miss Merry sailing unsteadily across the room to land, as softly as possible, in a corner, tucked neatly next to and partially supported by a drip-stand.

She'd pushed back the bedclothes, a far more gargantuan task than it should have been and was struggling to get out of bed as Ruth and Rachael arrived. Nobody wasted time talking. They'd brought underwear, slacks and a warm jumper and simply slipped these on under and over her nightgown, but their timing was out. They all three became aware at the same instant, of the Doctor heading purposefully towards them. He was keeping himself calm by chanting a meditation mantra, but it wasn't helping.

They exchanged a few quick thoughts. They'd hoped to get out with as little fuss as possible and no confrontation. There was the window of course but Ruth vetoed that. Did she look, she inquired, like she was built for slipping through windows? The only other door led to the bathroom so, with Glory supported between them, that's where they headed. There wasn't a great deal of room in there, but they hoped they wouldn't be stopping long.

CHAPTER THIRTY-NINE

The first thing to meet the Doctor's eye, when he flung open the door was Glory's empty bed. The second was the estimable Miss Merry propped, incommunicado, next to the drip-stand. His mind skittered, sought for and failed to find any kind of logical explanation. On top of the nurses' behaviour it was really all too much.

He automatically bent to feel for a pulse, relieved to feel it strong and regular. He had no personal feelings for her but she was an extremely capable and reliable assistant. He regarded her sagging form with distaste and all three women in the adjoining bathroom, little as they liked the lady, were not sorry she was unconscious. A noise from the corridor outside made him straighten. Silently he moved across the room. He was most uncomfortable with the way things were going, not in their usual ordered fashion at all. And, until he had a better grasp of the situation, he had no intention of being caught unawares by any more unpleasant surprises.

Doors to patients' rooms are hinged to open completely flat against the wall, allowing free entrance and exit for beds. It's never a good idea to stand behind one. This was something the Doctor should have considered. When the door to Glory's room burst open, it did so with some considerable force and cracked him soundly on the nose. Reeling from the blow, blood flowing freely through his fingers and seeing a lot of stars, he stumbled forward, to be confronted by an extremely unhappy Mrs Millsop.

As the Doctor had discerned, much as she liked and indeed needed her job, over the last weeks Mrs Millsop, an excellent and ethical nurse, had become subject to increasing concerns about what was going on. She didn't know all the ins and outs, she did know though that when she'd come across Glory Isaacs doing something fishy with the drugs cabinet, she hadn't had to think twice where her sympathies lay.

She was a down to earth sort of a woman and didn't hold with a lot of airy fairy, arty farty theories, but things had been getting uncomfortably tense recently – take that incident with Peter and Glory – maybe mass hysteria, maybe not. In any event she was twitchy and when she'd taken a few gulps of eagerly anticipated coffee and detected an odd, bitter grittiness, she'd laughed at herself but had thrown it down the sink nevertheless and made fresh. Then, she'd found herself unable to keep her eyes open and had nodded off, jerking awake in annoyance because it was a crucial episode of the Forsyte Saga, highlight of the week, and she never ever fell asleep in front of the telly, however tired she might be.

When it kept happening, she was forced to concede, ridiculous as it seemed, that she'd been right, her coffee'd been interfered with, no other explanation. There must, she concluded, be some dodgy goings-on tonight that they wanted going-on behind her back. She was so angry she could spit nails. She, it was, who administered medication to others. The thought she'd been given some sort of a drug herself, violated and offended her on a deeply personal level. She suddenly didn't give a toss what was transpiring with Fleur, Irenée or any other member of the flipping Forsyte family. She switched off the television, splashed cold water on her face and headed down the war-path, to have it out with whichever so-and-so she came across first, whether it be Miss bloody Merry-go-round or the damn Doctor.

As luck would have it, it was the damn Doctor and she uttered a strangled scream when he staggered gorily out from behind the door, just as angry as she was. The sedative, albeit a fraction of the intended dose, was still kicking in and she was doing a fair old bit of staggering on her own account and could only focus by closing one eye. To the impartial observer it would all have looked a little odd; the tall thin doctor and the rather more substantial matron, both seeing stars, both trying to maintain their balance and, any port in a storm, eventually clutching each other in an effort to stay upright.

To Miss Merry, drifting gently upwards through the mists of the unconsciousness to which Ruth had consigned her, it appeared at baffled first glance as if they were dancing. She shut her eyes again briefly, while she digested this. She recalled that the evening's programme had included a brain operation but was pretty certain there'd been no dancing scheduled. She opened her eyes again cautiously, maybe she'd imagined it but no, there they were, swaying and executing a sort of syncopated two-step. As if this in itself weren't problematic enough, she couldn't imagine what she herself was doing sitting on the floor and started to get up, pulling herself hand over hand up the drip stand. This worked to a certain point, whilst she was pulling it towards her and it was anchored firmly against her feet but once she was upright, the equipment did exactly what it was designed to do – roll easily on its little wheels to wherever it was pushed. Miss Merry, still not very steady and therefore holding on tightly, found her only means of support, heading briskly away. She landed painfully back on her knees.

In the small bathroom, Ruth and Rachael, with Glory seated on the toilet seat between them, were having a silent but heated debate as to the best next step. Rachael was for knocking them all out and be done, Ruth favoured a diversion.

By now, Matron had given up the ghost for the evening and in a last moment of sense and self-preservation had taken the two necessary steps to the bed and collapsed thereon, absent-mindedly pulling the Doctor down with her. All of a tangle, they looked as if they were auditioning for the next Carry On film and the Doctor, struggling to extricate himself from the situation, found a supine Mrs Millsop wasn't to be taken lightly. Miss Merry meanwhile had finally regained her feet and although still a mite coltish, was doing her best to help him get out from under. They were both coldly livid, the loss of dignity anathema to each of them.

They had no idea exactly what was going on, nor how it had been engineered. It was a fair assumption though that Glory Isaacs was involved and they each, for their own reasons, itched to get their hands back on her and get her under the knife. They both had the same thought at the same instant. The door at the front of the building was rarely locked until after midnight – that's where she'd be headed, although she wouldn't be getting far, not with the amount of valium pumped into her. With a last, desperate, mutual heave they rolled the unfortunate Mrs Millsop onto her side, not batting an eyelid between them as she slowly rolled off the bed and hit the floor with a bruising thump.

They didn't waste time. The Doctor swiftly dampened his handkerchief at the sink and removed the worst of the blood from around his nose, gingerly fingering the swelling, he didn't think it was broken. Miss Merry, her back modestly turned, quickly straightened her clothing. Then without a backward glance at the unconscious woman on the floor, they headed off to retrieve Glory – two minds with a single thought.

Having effectively planted that single thought, the Misses Peacock deemed it prudent to get weaving. It wouldn't be long before the happy couple reached the front of the building and started to think for themselves. They hauled Glory up and stopping only to ensure Mrs Millsop was lying on her side in the recovery position, had a clear airway and was in no danger of anything other than a splitting headache, made their way to a side door of the clinic which was locked, but only briefly. Without Ed's finesse to hand, they simply blasted it open and as they hurried through, heard faint shrieks of laughter still issuing from the sluice room – at least the evening hadn't been a wash-out for everyone.

CHAPTER FORTY

"And then?" In the darkness of the van's interior I strained to make out their faces.

"We went home." said Miss Peacock, "But you can see why we're persona non grata at Newcombe, even though that was over five years ago."

"Didn't they come after you?"

"How could they? We were perfectly within our rights to take Glory."

"How did you explain everything?"

"Phoned the next day. Said my sister and I had been too nervous to take the pills, had consequently slept only briefly then gone to sit with Glory. She'd woken and was so distressed we simply decided to take her home there and then. Of course it was dreadfully impolite of us to do anything without notifying him but … middle of the night … terribly upset … did what seemed best."

"And he swallowed that?"

"Stuck in his throat but what could he say, we were her legal guardians."

"But the nurses … Miss Merry?"

"He thought they'd been drinking, I didn't mention them and neither did he. As for Miss Merry, he assumed Glory must have hit her."

"The door you forced?"

"Panic, we wanted to get home quickly, panicked when we couldn't get out. Appalling behaviour… so rude … don't know what came over us. Profound apologies and a cheque in the post."

"Mrs Millsop?"

"The sack, probably not a bad thing, she'd not have lasted there much longer, she's much happier where she is now."

"Now? You're still in touch?"

"You could say. Now I want to talk about tonight."

"No, hang on. You can't just leave it there. I want to know what's been going on at the Foundation since then – has he found others, before Sam I mean?"

Glory, who'd been leaving the talking to the others, filled a silence that went on a little longer than it should have.

"Some. It's not always easy to keep an eye on things, certainly nobody like Sam. But the focus has changed a bit."

"You mentioned that before. How?"

"We really don't have time to go into all that now." Miss Peacock was brisk, "All you have to do tonight is nip in, get Sam and nip out." Put like that it sounded a doddle, though I had my doubts.

"You'll go in at the back of the clinic. Glory will talk you through, so you'll know exactly where you're headed. Ed will unlock all doors as you reach them. The tricky bit will be when you reach Sam. Timing's crucial, we need him as un-sedated as possible, so you're going in just before his next medication, he's got to come willingly."

"And if he doesn't want to?"

"Persuade him."

"How?"

"Oh for goodness sake – rely on your instincts." Miss P's confidence in my instincts were stronger than mine. Ruth leaned forward from her seat behind us,

"You know, we wouldn't be asking you to do this if you weren't our best bet."

"How dangerous is he?" I asked the question but didn't need to catch their concern to know the answer – they couldn't really say. They suspected though and they were all, even Miss Peacock, a darn sight more nervous than they let on. Hamlet, in the back of the van whined quietly, I was tempted to join him.

Why didn't I say, there and then I wanted out? Perhaps the revelations of the last forty-eight hours had totally skewed any vestige of common sense I may have had left. Despite the fact they'd just spun me the most unbelievable story since Goldilocks had the problem with the bears, I was setting out, on their say so, to rescue a child I didn't know from Adam, who'd already killed once. Was I crazy? Given the choice again would I follow the same path? Actually, I didn't think there was a choice.

CHAPTER FORTY-ONE

Ed had doused the headlights. There was a full moon, but with a lot of obscuring cloud, it wasn't doing anything useful in the way of illumination. As we bumped to a stop and he killed the engine too there was only the metallic ticking of its cooling. Quietly we got out, Hamlet unnervingly gravitating to my side, as if he knew we were the only two mugs going in. I tentatively reached into his head, as warm and dog-smelling as ever. In the chill of the night it was oddly comforting.

"Make a lead." Ruth murmured and showed me what she meant, a sort of mental chain of interwoven links between my mind and his – typically she'd visualised a shocking shade of pink, still Hamlet seemed happy enough, perhaps he had no colour sense either.

"Take this." Miss Peacock handed me a heavy black rubber torch. "You shouldn't need to use it with Glory guiding, but just in case."

"Hey." Glory poked me in the back, "You're shielding too well now, stupid, let me in." I relaxed and lemon sherbet fizzed in, beyond her I could feel the others, familiar now.

Ed had driven the van onto a grass verge in the concealing shadow of a large oak and as we moved beyond its shelter, there was only the sound of our soft breathing and the occasional skitter of a startled nocturnal creature in the grass. It had rained during the day and although it wasn't cold, I could feel damp through the soles of my shoes. A dauntingly high brick wall surrounded the back of the building and its grounds, with curled barbed wire running uninvitingly along the top. Where we were standing, there was a large bush of some kind, planted closed to the wall. The trunk of the oak and the bush formed a two-sided small area of shelter, where the others would stay while Hamlet and I did our stuff.

"Go now." Ruth murmured in my mind, "We'll help you over, be with you all the way." And because there didn't seem to be any point in hanging about and I was getting more apprehensive by the second, I took a deep breath, felt them lend me their effort and rose. Slowly at first, all the balance-maintaining instincts coming back to me and then I was up and over the wall, taking care as I went, not to get feet caught in the razor-sharp wire. After all, we didn't want situation normal, all fouled up, before I even started.

It wasn't until I arrived on the grass on the far side of the wall, that I belatedly recalled my travelling companion. I needn't have worried, a second later he came sailing across, ten stone of dignified, if slightly puzzled dog. He landed gently next to me, waited for a moment to check he wasn't going anywhere else, uttered a small wumph of relief and shook himself thoroughly. I tugged experimentally on our shocking pink lead and he responded instantly, butting my side with his head.

We were standing, Hamlet and I, next to an unevenly paved pathway, running around the entire outer border of the broad lawns which spread out into the dark, either side of me. To the right was a central path, hedged on either side. It looked as if it followed a winding route, leading up to the modern extension at the back of the building, where the clinic was housed. It was very dark but,

"Don't use the torch," hissed Glory in my head.

"Can't see." I grumbled.

"Don't need to, just start walking." The distance was deceptive, the building further away than it seemed. Sight blunted, other senses were sharpened, filling my nose with the sweetly rotten scent of wet vegetation and my ears with the rustling of the hedges either side of me as they groaned and rattled against a brisk breeze. As cloud ebbed and flowed around and across the April moon, shadows and shapes kept starting out at me. I was making Hamlet twitchy too, he was pressing his massive self close to me, uttering soft little whines and making it hard to keep my balance, let alone my nerve. We were hardly the most intrepid pair.

"Concentrate." Glory again, "Follow the path." But I stopped. Heart thumping. There was some very loud, very frenzied barking, getting closer by the minute. From the darkness ahead of us, moving fast, charged two extremely large dogs. Hamlet and I froze as one.

"Stand still, they won't hurt you." I was tempted to remind Miss Peacock that people commenting from behind six foot brick walls, could afford to be optimistic. One dog was a full-grown German Shepherd, the other, dear God, a Doberman. They'd both skidded to a stop in front of us, stiff-legged, hackles raised, heads down and there was a lot of deep-throated rumbling going on. Two sets of muzzles were curled back over two truly impressive sets of teeth. My faith in Miss Peacock's smeared on dog-deterrent was being sorely tried and Hamlet, who was pressed so close he was almost on my other side, was shaking so hard I could feel us both vibrating – or maybe that was just me.

"For Pete's sake, girl, what're you waiting for? Oh I'll do it." Miss Peacock rapped out a command and the Hounds of the Baskervilles immediately stopped growling and looked sheepish. They both sat down abruptly and the Doberman put his head to one side in a winsome manner. Hamlet relaxed a fraction and uttered what might have been the beginnings of a growl, I gave him a nudge both physical and mental – this was no time for bravado, I wasn't sure we were out of the woods yet.

"You're fine." Glory was impatient, "Rachael's got them, look they're a couple of pussycats." I eyed them warily, where I came from, pussycats didn't stand quite so tall and certainly didn't bark so loud. I took a tentative step forward. Both dogs got to their feet. I stopped. They sat down again.

"Go *on*." Glory and Miss Peacock, in impatient unison. I shifted a nervous foot, the dogs rose. I moved forward and they fell into step behind me. I had to exercise all my self-control – and there wasn't much left at that stage – to avoid breaking into a trot followed by a shrieking hell for leather run.

"Listen to me," old peppermint-Pru in my head, sharply, "Pull yourself together, they won't hurt you, I won't let them, although you're perfectly capable of holding them back yourself. Anyway they've accepted you as leader of the pack, now get on with it."

I didn't have a lot of option, I could hardly stand there all night, so we set off again, all four of us in cosily close formation, the newest members of the party panting at my heels like a couple of asthmatic steam engines. Every now and then, one of them would give a little woof, as if to remind me they were still there – like I could forget. Hamlet, in the meantime, had developed a distinct, my-best-friend's-the-leader-of-the-pack swagger and even felt emboldened enough to move a couple of inches away from me. I felt like Barbara Woodhouse on location.

"When you get to the end, turn right" Glory instructed, "Good, now a little way along that wall you'll find there's a door. Yes, there." The upper half of the door was glass paneled and opaqued by thin wire mesh and as I approached, I heard the click of the lock being opened, good old Ed. When I tentatively turned the handle, it opened easily and no alarm went off. Laurel and Hardy at my heels whuffed uneasily.

"They're not allowed inside," Miss Peacock informed me. Them and me both, I reflected and wondered if the sentence was less for breaking and entering if, technically, you hadn't done your own lock-picking.

"Get *on* with it." Glory or Miss P again, wasn't sure which, they were starting to sound the same.

I shut the door quietly on my pedigree chums who both bore identical wounded expressions – no sooner do you find a pack leader than she ups and offs – and Hamlet and I found ourselves in a green-linoleumed, cream-walled corridor with closed, half-glassed, numbered doors at regular intervals to the left and right of us.

"Left." directed Glory and I swerved obediently. Everything was as quiet as it should be at that time of night, although I could hear low voices from one room as I passed and there was the constant underlying thrumming of the fluorescent, overhead lighting.

"This corridor turns to the right and then there's a flight of stairs, take those and then … " she stopped as a tall, thickset man came round the corner, "Uh oh!"

He had on a blue uniform shirt and was wearing his trousers slung well below a solid paunch. In his left hand was a walkie-talkie which was crackling slightly. He stopped when he saw me,

"Hallo there," he said, "Where would you be heading this time of night young lady and where the heck did your friend come from?" For a moment I thought he meant Glory, but of course it was Hamlet he was looking at, in some alarm. He was assuming, as I was too young to be staff, I must be one of the patients. If he read guilt in my non-response he only had a short time to think about it because Ruth was already doing her stuff. His expression drifted from inquisitorial to dreamy, his eyes glazed over and she angled him considerably towards a convenient wall, down which he slid gently. Which was all fine and dandy, except there was now an unconscious six foot, sixteen stone security guard, propped up in the corridor. I thought there was a fair chance that might raise the next eyebrow that happened along.

"Well, move him then!" Miss Peacock rapped.

"Me and who else's army?"

"That room, behind you, open the door, we haven't got all night." I felt power from them surge through me and the guard rose a couple of inches from the floor. Still in semi-sitting position, head lolling, he drifted gently into the mercifully empty room, the door closed softly on him and Glory resumed calmly,

"Round the corner, up two flights of stairs, through the swing doors and then you're in the clinic area." I moved off, the sooner I got in, the sooner I could get out and frankly, that really wouldn't be soon enough.

CHAPTER FORTY-TWO

Once through the swing doors, marked *'Strictly No Admittance To Unauthorised Personnel'* there was a distinct change of atmosphere. There was a sign with an arrowed direction to the Clinical Unit to my right and directly ahead of me a door with waspishly black on yellow signs. I wasn't sure what they all meant but the general tone wasn't welcoming. There was a *HAZCHEM* and a *BIOHAZ* and a *STAFF MUST AT ALL TIMES FOLLOW STRICT BARRIER NURSING PROCEDURES*. I could feel Glory perusing them through me and sensed her surprise and concern shared with the others, they hadn't expected this. There was a keypad on the wall and, within a few seconds, a series of internal clicks and churnings somewhere in the middle of the door which, I sensed, was a lot thicker than it looked. The red light above it now glowed green. I had to pull hard, but once the door started moving, it continued smoothly, propelled by its own weight. I hesitated for a long moment, every instinct screaming don't go in. I went in.

Softer lighting here, the self-absorbed hum of air-conditioning, smell of disinfectant under-laid with something else, something not very pleasant. Hamlet pressed closer again and whined softly.

"Well, don't just stand there like a lemon." Glory, urgent, "Don't know this bit, all new, after my time, but you need to keep going to the end of the corridor and then follow it round – hurry." I felt the consensus of the others, they all agreed, that was where they could feel him, Sam, I could too.

I pulled the door to behind me and turned and hurried. Moving down the corridor, the scent I'd noticed earlier became stronger. Together with something else, not seen, not heard but insistently there and causing an unpleasant tightening in the pit of my stomach.

They were holding something back – Glory, Rachael, Ruth, I could feel them, doing the mental equivalent of standing close, forming a screen. I wasn't impressed – I was the one in the thick of things, what the hell gave them the right to decide what I should or shouldn't see or know. It had something to do with what I thought might be animal laboratories, behind the doors on my right. I walked, sneakers squeaking against lino, along the low-ceilinged corridor, neon-stripped with that infinitesimal flicker which impinges, just at the edge of your vision, vaguely disorientating. But as I hurried forward I could feel that other disquieting pressure gradually easing.

Rounding the corner, a shorter stretch of corridor led to another solid door with a massive circular handle. Opposite that door, the corridor widened into a bay where a nurse's station held three screens in a monitoring console, alongside a couple of phones. A thin woman, uniformed in white tunic and trousers, emerged from a room to the left of the console. She was concentrating on and gingerly hoisting from hand to hand a polystyrene cup holding something hot. She saw me the second I saw her and, unlike the guard, knew instantly I shouldn't be there. She reached for the phone. I thought to stop her, but Ruth was there first. The nurse crumpled neatly where she stood, coffee cup flying, Ruth-assisted, from her hand and landing safely on the floor a few paces away,

"Far too hot." tutted Ruth, as a small, steaming river snaked its way across the floor. To the right of the reinforced door was another keypad on which Ed was already working. He gave me a mental nod and the circular handle turned at my touch.

"Go on, he's no different from you, you know," Miss Peacock was brisk, "Just younger and a lot more frightened." Reassured a little, cross that she'd know it, I moved inside, with some effort pulling the door nearly closed behind me and looked around. I was in a white tiled area, at the end of which was a blankly curtained window shutting off the room beyond. In front of the glass was a desk with a monitor screen, similar to the one at the nurse's station. There were a couple of wall-mounted drug cabinets and a sink with long-handled taps along one wall and along the other, a row of all-in-one suits hanging lifelessly. Nearby, on glass shelves were several sets of white masks to cover nose and mouth – I don't know how the suits and masks affected the kid in the next room, but they gave me the willies and that was with nobody in them. I could feel the irritation of the others too,

"Stupid, stupid, stupid," Miss Peacock was acerbically to the point. "What he's got they can't catch and if he wants to do damage, space-suits aren't going to protect anyone."

Adjacent to the shrouded window was the door into the next room. I drew a hitched breath and went in. The room was sparse. Plain pale walls, neutral lino floor and a range of medical equipment by the bed, drip stand, oxygen and another glass-screened monitor with wires dangling. Intermittent moonlight shone through the bars on the window, casting striped shadow on the floor. If the décor left a bit to be desired, they hadn't gone overboard on fixtures and fittings either. A hard wooden chair was drawn up to a small round white formica table, both anchored to the floor by short stretches of thick iron links. There was a sink in one corner of the room and a door leading off, bathroom and toilet I presumed. The child in the bed was small, his body hardly mounding the covers.

He was lying awkwardly. Both thin wrists were encircled with dark leather straps threaded through short metal chains which were anchored to corners of the iron bedstead. The chains weren't really long enough, pulling his arms uncomfortably, so he was lying half on his back, half on his side. Moving closer I could see the sore, scaley patches where the flesh of his wrists had chafed, bled, scabbed and chafed again. I could feel something rising in me, supplanting the fear. I absently registered it as ice-cold anger. The others were silent for once.

The child was sleeping, I didn't think deeply. He was an ordinary looking little boy, snub nosed, breathing softly through his open mouth, one front tooth missing. Dark hair that looked as if it hadn't seen shampoo in a while was damply matted on a high forehead and, as the moon moved briefly out from obscuring cloud and shafted light into the room, it showed where tears had dried on his cheeks and run down into his ears. His nose could have done with a good wipe as well. He opened his eyes and looked at me.

I reacted instinctively and if his strength was fuelled by fear and anger, I suppose mine was too. In that instant, as he woke, he used his mind to strike out as he had so often before at his tormentors. But he knew instantly, as he cut deep into me that I was something different. That scared him even more. The force of the onslaught was such that my knees buckled instantly, joints cracking in protest as they folded and hit the ground with a smack. As I went down, I banged my cheek against the iron frame of the bed and bit my tongue hard.

He flooded my head, shrieking, exultant, terrified. The savage instincts of a small boy, honed by his experiences so far and untamed by any mitigating kindnesses. Up till now, when he'd lashed out, he knew he'd been effective but never to this glorious extent. Behind me, the chair rose to the length of its short chain and met the table in mid-air and triumphant clash. The drip stand flew sideways and the monitor crashed back against the wall, showering me with spitefully sharp glass shards. It was too late to shield, he was everywhere. I lashed back in self-defence, pulling no punches and his head rocked to the left and hit the side-rail of the bed with a dull crack. When he hit out again, it was with the aim of hurting me anywhere and everywhere he could. I didn't want to match his violence, was scared of what I could do, but this was no time for finesse. I lashed out hard again and as his face crumpled in pain, I understood he expected no different. This was what life was all about – hurt and be hurt more. I knew then what I had to do if I had any hope of getting to him. I stopped.

Unprotected, the full force of him bulleted into me, I've never known, before or since, pain quite like it. He lashed out with all the fear, hate, anger and bile of an abused six year old. Like any child he'd learned from experience and he hurt me in the many ways he'd been hurt. I think I may have blacked out for a bit. I was only dimly aware, after a time, maybe minutes, maybe far longer that the storm was abating. Curled as I was on my side on the hard floor, I noted it was pretty dusty under the bed, someone certainly wasn't up to par with the housekeeping.

I spat some of the blood out of my mouth which felt bruised and swollen, come to think of it, so did the rest of me and my head – well the less said about my head the better. I didn't think I could, or indeed ever would want to move again. I lay there for a while longer, not thinking about anything in particular.

As some more time passed, reality slowly started to make its wary way back in. And after a couple of feebly false starts, I reached out just a bit further and grabbed hold of one of the bed legs. I used that to haul myself along the floor and then, very slowly and carefully, propped myself in a semi sitting position against the side of the bed frame. I didn't feel it was wise to go any further at that point because the room was spinning so rapidly. I shut my eyes and the room stood still while I whirled, which wasn't an improvement by anybody's standards. Someone was making hoarse little gasping sounds that were getting on my wick, I discovered it was me so I shut up. I rested there and concentrated on not throwing up. After a bit, and not easily, I turned my head, my eyelids felt bruised and swollen so I opened them one at a time. I was gazing, from a few inches away, into an unblinking, hostile, brown almost black stare.

He'd withdrawn as far across the bed as the leather strap on the side nearest to me would let him. There was a fresh smear of blood where it was biting into the flesh. He was still in that uncomfortable, half on his back half on his side position. His legs were pulled almost to his chest, every muscle rigidly poised, ready for an escape he couldn't make. His lips were back from his teeth in a snarl and his breathing made an ugly rasping noise in his throat. He and I could kill each other, right there, right then without either of us moving a muscle. I knew how easy it could be. Did he?

I cleared my throat gently and in a ladylike way, spat a little blood into the sleeve of my jumper. His eyes didn't waver.

"Nice welcome." I said, "What happened to hello, how are you?" He didn't react, probably appreciated my humour about as much as Miss Peacock. I soldiered on, talking softly, murmuring, as much to myself as to him, but letting him read me. His eyes flickered as he registered not only that he could, which was nothing unusual, but that I was fully aware and letting him do it.

I didn't want to make any sudden moves, in fact, didn't think I could, but we didn't have all night.

"Sam," I said, "I'm going to take the straps off your wrists in a moment, OK?" He flinched, eyes widening and I saw very clearly and with fury what they'd threatened him with. He could of course, have easily broken the straps or indeed the chains, at any time but when you're six, even if you do have some pretty special abilities, the threat of something unmentionably terrible hiding under the bed, leashed by the straps, released with their breaking is a pretty effective deterrent. For an instant I glimpsed in his head the monster he knew was there, and it scared the life out of me too.

I could feel him nibbling at the edges of my mind trying to find out more. He couldn't work out what I was. He knew now that although he could hurt me badly, I could do the same to him but I hadn't, I'd stopped. He was desperate to know more, scared to move any further forward in my head in case he provoked my violent response again. I let him see and feel exactly what I was doing – I didn't want to risk touching the leather for fear of hurting his sore wrists even more, so I concentrated on the metal chain links. It took a few moments and his fear kept distracting me.

Where the hell, I wondered, were the others, always butting in when not wanted and now, when I could really do with a little help from my friends, neither hide nor hair. For a few moments after the final link on the second chain gave way, he didn't move, could feel the release of the pressure on his arms but stayed in exactly the same position, I didn't want to rush him but time wasn't on our side.

"Try moving your arms a bit." I suggested. He shifted very slightly, never taking his eyes off me, grimacing a little as stiff muscles and strained joints adjusted to the unaccustomed movement. "See?" I said gently, "No monster."

And then he started to scream, shrill, hysterical shafts of sound drilling into my mind, hurting my head. His eyes were bulging with horror, lips twisting in panic as he tried to scramble backwards up the bed and through the wall behind to get away. For just a moment, so complete was his terror and his conviction, I bought into it and there were nearly two of us trying to get through the wall, before I pulled myself together.

Hamlet, who'd only just now mustered enough courage to move forward a little from the corner, where he'd been cowering, like the yellow-belly he was, looked bewildered at the reaction he'd provoked. But somewhere in there, was more intelligence than I'd given him credit for. He immediately stopped where he was, stretched his two front legs full out in front of him and sank down, folding his back legs neatly underneath, making himself smaller, less fearful. He knew he was scaring this small person, who was already more than scared enough and he was trying to make things better.

"Sam, it's a dog, a dog, he's only a dog." I was sobbing with shock too, desperate to reassure him, panic stricken this might spiral him into violence again, terrified someone would hear the screaming. "Look it's a dog, not the monster, a dog, I brought him, he came in with me, you just didn't see him at first." Hamlet, anxious to corroborate gave a soft little woof and put his head right down on his paws to make himself even less of a threat. Sam's screams were dying slowly but he was still shaking and as far from happy as it was possible for a small boy to be. I saw his point, I hadn't been a fan of Hamlet's from the get go either. Hamlet wisely stayed very still and waited, eyeing the boy mournfully as his tension began to drain away a little and he sniffed hard and wiped his nose on his pyjama sleeve – where were Ed and a hanky when you needed them?

Sam eased himself fractionally down the bed, I could see the white, now reddening mark on his cheek where he'd ground it against the bedhead in his desperate need to get away. I felt him reaching out, tentatively, feeling for the dog, checking the evidence of his eyes against the weight of his fears. Hamlet rose very slowly and gently to his full height, waited politely to see if that produced any adverse reaction and when it didn't, moving delicately for such a large creature, paced carefully round to the other side of the bed, his massive head level with the child's. They contemplated each other solemnly for a moment and Sam, reaching into the mind of the animal found, as perhaps had happened rarely in his short life, nothing there to fear. He tentatively reached out a small, leather-braceleted hand and the dog shuffled forward a little to allow his head to be softly stroked. O.K. Good. Excellent. I heaved a sigh of relief that came out a sob. But this was no time to get complacent we had to get our skates on.

CHAPTER FORTY-THREE

"Sam?" I touched him gently on the arm and as he turned away from Hamlet I was vastly relieved to see he'd lost some of his rigidity, although he was still an awfully long way from relaxed.

"Sam, I've come to take you away."

"Where?" he had a hoarse little voice, deep for a child and a soft, chocolate, buttery sort of a scent. This was the first time he'd spoken and straight away he had me stumped. I looked at him helplessly. Now I came to think of it, I didn't actually know. I thought back over all the conversations of the last few days and drew a blank. I know they'd talked an awful lot about getting Sam out, but where we were actually getting him out to, rather escaped me for the moment. I could feel a giggle working its way up from my stomach and swallowed it sternly. I had a feeling that once I started laughing, I might not stop. And of course, this wasn't a child you could fob off.

"Don't know actually," I admitted, "But let's face it," I indicated the room with a movement of my head. It hadn't looked like anything out of House and Garden when I got there, but now it was a complete shambles, with what little furniture and equipment there was, scattered and much the worse for the battering it had received. "Can't be much worse than this, can it?" He gave a quick glance round too and I could clearly read, poor little bugger, as Grandma would have said, he actually thought it could, had indeed experienced far worse. He looked at me and into me, across the vast chasm of our life-experiences to date. There was only ten years between us, but a lifetime of differences. He weighed up the pros and cons, came to a considered decision and nodded once, he'd come with me.

"Right then," I said, "Let's get this show on the road." I was, I realized, still sitting on the floor, Sam and Hamlet both looked at me expectantly and even I could see we weren't going to get far unless I made a move. I clambered laboriously to my feet, at least things were consistent – everything hurt – and extended a hand across the bed to Sam. After a moment's hesitation, he took it and scrambled off to stand next to me. I looked around, I couldn't see anywhere there might be clothes kept for him, he read the thought and shook his head. He was wearing a pair of Ladybird pyjamas. I couldn't take him out like that, he'd catch his death.

I pulled him after me to the outer room. The all-in-ones of which there were about half a dozen, looked to be pretty uniform in size, still needs must and at least that would also give him some kind of foot covering. I yanked one down, yelping at the twinge that hit when I raised my arm. The suit was a silvery, slippery textured item, but the material was substantially thicker than it looked – it would do the trick. It undid with a series of overlapping fastenings at the side, collar and wrists. I bundled him into it as fast as I could and he submitted wordlessly to my ministrations. Needless to say, there was a darn sight more suit than Sam.

Necessity being the mother of, I nipped back into the other room and yanking one of the trailing electrodes and flex from the broken monitor, knotted it round his waist as a make-shift belt, draping and tucking the slack of the suit in and around it. On the spur of the moment I grabbed another of the suits for myself, it was the sort of thing Napoleon Solo, the Man from You Know Where was always doing – blending in. Maybe, anybody seeing us would assume we'd just come from the restricted area – which indeed we had! Sam giggled, just a very small breath of a giggle but I took that as a tremendous step forward.

"Right," I said again, more gung ho than I felt, "Orft we go." Sam pulled back, he wanted a mask too – well, in for a penny. I grabbed one for him and took one for myself. Maybe, I thought, as we looped elasticated bands over our ears, it would alleviate the unnaturalness of that smell permeating the corridor on the way out. We looked a right pair, although of what, was open to question. Cautiously heaving open the outer room door I peered out. I could see the nurse, still nose to lino, she hadn't budged and the coffee had cooled to a dull brown puddle on the floor. I reached behind me for Sam's hand and he and Hamlet sidled out after me. I could feel Sam's recoil at the sight of the nurse, he thought she was dead and that he'd done it, I reassured him she wasn't and he hadn't. I paused, listened, couldn't hear anything other than the pervasive hum of the air conditioning. With an effort I opened the heavy door at the end of what I now thought of as 'Sam's Corridor'. We slipped through and I pulled it closed behind us, twisting the heavy round locking device a few times. I wasn't sure whether that would secure it, but it might just give us a bit more time before Sam's absence was discovered.

We turned back the way I'd come, padded the short distance to the end of that corridor where I flattened myself against the wall and peered round. I really think I might have seen one too many spy films. Everything seemed quiet, I motioned to my two companions and they obediently fell in behind me. Our jog down that corridor, which in reality wasn't that long, seemed to take forever. We were both also being badly affected by whatever lay behind the closed doors we were passing. Something I couldn't identify, but recognised instinctively as unnatural, was knotting my stomach and making my flesh crawl, worse now than on the way in. Sam's clutch on my hand had increased to bone-cracking proportions and what little I could see of his face above, matched the white of the mask below. There were beads of sweat on his forehead and it wasn't really that hot. Hamlet, on the other side of Sam, was pressed close, shivering and whimpering quietly as he walked. I absently noted Sam had replaced the shocking pink lead with one of his own design, a sort of tasselled wild-west thing.

Although I tried to quicken our pace, the atmosphere felt thickened in some way, so it began to seem as if we were wading through water. Sam was slowing down, pulling against my hand, eyes wide and turned towards the closed doors, I could feel something happening to his mind – a sluggishness overtaking him. I tightened my hold but he pulled back and away more strongly, I was losing him. His hand, covered as was mine, in the integral, slickly slippery suit glove, was sliding away, I couldn't get a proper grip. I stopped, turned and grabbed him, yanking him up off the ground. I don't know whether he was taller or heavier than the average six year old, he weighed a ton.

Grunting with effort, I tried to hoist him up further. He'd gone completely limp, I thought he'd passed out, and I had him in an awkward grasp, holding him against me with my arms round his waist, his arms hanging loose and his legs dangling and banging against mine as I tried to walk. The smooth surface of his suit against the surface of mine didn't help either, I could feel him sliding downwards and just didn't have the wherewithal to haul him up again. My arms felt like they were fast departing their sockets and although we were still moving forward, I didn't know for how much longer. In desperation I pulled Hamlet closer, showed him what I intended to do and when he didn't seem to have any objection, half lowered, half dropped Sam across his back. His legs dangled either side of the big dog, while I kept my arm round his waist with his upper body leaning against me. It wasn't that easy to keep in step and no-one could have described our progress as smooth, but Hamlet was now bearing much of the weight and I was in no position to be picky.

As we moved away from the row of closed doors and nearer to the one, still thankfully ajar at the end of the corridor, Sam started to stir. He gave a small grunt of surprise as he registered his unusual mount, but seemed happy enough and continued to lean against me although he was now tightly grasping some of the excess material in my suit and was holding on, which made things a whole lot easier. I didn't ask him about what had just happened, nor what had caused it, I thought perhaps there might be some things best not to know at that point.

As we reached the door, I heaved Sam off, pulled it just wide enough for us to slip through and then swung on it with all my weight, pulling it closed behind us and we headed full pelt through the swing doors and down the two flights of stairs,

"Left here, then we're on the home run." I gasped and perhaps it was the euphoria of getting past that ghastly stretch of corridor that made us hurtle round the corner with no precautions, smack bang into a familiar figure who, with another woman was hurrying straight towards us. The shorter of the two women, white uniformed like our friend with the coffee, had been carrying a covered kidney bowl in one hand and a small tray of food in the other, both of which went flying. The taller of the two had an armful of paper files which, with the force of the crash were distributed, and probably not in alphabetical order, all over the floor.

CHAPTER FORTY-FOUR

She hadn't changed in the nearly five years since we'd last met, although I'd heard so much about her in the last couple of days, it seemed far less time than that. She was, as always, white-coated, tightly buttoned into a starched, stiff-collared shirt and totally in control of the situation. You had to admire that. It was the middle of the night, she'd been knocked flying by two silver-suited figures where there shouldn't have been any and she didn't bat an eyelid, although I knew straight away, our disguise wasn't going to carry the day.

She leaned forward and ripped my mask off, the elastic twanging painfully against my ear.

"Ouch." I said. Despite all the kids who'd passed through the Foundation, her memory was faultless, her recognition almost instantaneous and in a second she'd mentally reviewed her file on our brief and frustratingly unsatisfactory encounter.

"You." She hissed. I couldn't resist it, after all things couldn't get much worse,

"Yes, 'tis I." I said, and regretted I had no swash to buckle. I was scared witless, but she didn't need to know that. She registered I was older but no less annoying and didn't waste further time, I had Sam with me and that wouldn't do. Her companion, a gimlet-eyed, skinny item in her early fifties with down-turned mouth, tight mass of permed black curls and regulation trousers and tunic, was scrabbling on the floor, gathering the contents of the bowl – hypodermic, antiseptic swabs and ampoules. She was made clumsier by apprehensive upward glances at Sam.

"Give him his injection here." snapped Miss Merry, "Quickly." Sam backed behind me and Hamlet backed behind him, I appreciated their confidence, but couldn't help feel it was misplaced. The nurse was torn between her fear of Sam and her fear of Miss Merry, she'd had bad experience of both. She made a snap decision based on economics, in favour of the woman who held her P45 and began to fill the syringe from one of the vials. Sam, from behind me, shattered the thin glass in her hand

and she jumped and let out a small shriek, but didn't drop the nearly full hypo. She started to advance and Hamlet, Sam and I backed away, moving in such perfect unison, we looked like a pantomime horse without its costume on. I could feel Sam's fear mounting,

"Don't touch him," I warned, "He's very scared, he'll hurt you, I won't be able to stop him."

The nurse paused, she'd been dealing with Sam for a good few weeks now and she knew I wasn't kidding. I could see Miss Merry calculating the odds. The boy had to be sedated first, then she'd deal with me.

"Do it, Muldrew," she barked, "*Now*." The unfortunate Muldrew jumped, then moved forward quickly. She was thinking, just a wee bit closer, one more step and she'd stick the little sod before he had a chance to play any tricks. Holding the needle like a dart, she drew her arm back,

"Sam, no," I warned, but too late. With an expression of surprise, Muldrew neatly and professionally administered the injection, shooting the contents of the syringe in and pulling the needle out in one swift, smooth, professional movement. Text-book delivery, job well done. Still astonished at the turn events had taken, she staggered two paces backwards and toppled over.

If Miss Merry was fazed, it didn't show. She reached out one hand and grabbed my arm in a painful grip. With the other she grabbed Sam by the hair. Hamlet gave a practice growl but she cowed him with a glare. As I started to struggle, she let go my arm for a second reached into her lab-coat pocket and sprayed something directly into my eyes. My world turned agonising, my mind chaotic.

As we were hauled bodily back up the stairs – there was surprisingly wiry strength in those thin arms – my main concentration was on clearing my painfully streaming eyes and stinging nose and throat. But I knew we were heading back towards whatever lay behind those closed doors and felt sick with fear. There was something else very wrong, I couldn't get into her head. I could feel Sam trying too but there was something blocking the way. He and I, true allies at last, exchanged confused thoughts as we were frog-marched in exactly the direction we didn't want to go. As we passed through the door with its ominous warnings, I could feel the now-familiar, stomach-clenching nausea and I began to sweat and where the hell were my support team?

Reaching the first door, she opened it and shoved us roughly inside, flicking on the light as she entered. Sam stumbled, fell and hit his head hard on the floor as he went down. The harsh fluorescence threw into stark relief, utilitarian desk and chair, shrouded typewriter, phones, metal filing cabinet and Sam's paper-white face, the only colour a trickle of blood from his temple. One of the walls of the office was busily occupied with charts and graphs, another was mirrored, two-way I imagined. The atmosphere was ghastly and not just on a social level.

Sam had taken his mask off, I wished he hadn't, I could have done without knowing his lips were turning an unhealthy blue. I didn't feel too clever myself, battered and bruised and now light-headed and even more swollen-eyed from whatever she'd sprayed. Hamlet had settled meekly in a corner in response to an intractably pointed finger. Laughing Girl herself seemed totally unaffected by whatever it was we were sensing. There were a couple of chairs in front of the desk. I didn't wait to be invited, but sat down and Sam climbed to his feet and sat too. Merry was at the desk, dialling and drumming her fingers impatiently as she waited for someone to answer the phone at the other end. When they did she was crisp.

"I'm in the New Block, get over here now. Get John too." The person on the other end must have looked at their clock and remonstrated, but she wasn't having any. "I said *now*. We nearly lost the boy. You need to be here." She put the phone down decisively and it tinged in protest. "Well," she said slowly, looking from one to the other of us, "Isn't this nice?"

Whatever was jamming my senses and preventing me reading her was as uncomfortable, unnatural and unpleasant as a lash in the eye or a hair in the throat. I couldn't shake it, couldn't understand it. I could identify Sam quite easily and in the background, soft flashes from Hamlet but Merry might just as well have not been there. I shifted in my seat, desperately probing outward. She smiled, a thin rictus.

"Oh I knew I was right about you," she said, softly, "Knew it all along, and so did that Isaacs bitch." I didn't say anything. Usually only too happy to partake in a bit of carefree banter, I was feeling so bad I wasn't sure I could open my mouth without throwing up. Sam was unmoving, face colourless, mind turned inward. If he'd been learning to put his faith in me, it had been a short, fruitless lesson.

When the door opened to admit Dreck, I was unsurprised – this was after all, old home week.

"Who the hell's that, lying out there?" He demanded.

"Muldrew."

"What . . . ?"

"Not important." Miss Merry dismissed the unfortunate Muldrew with an impatient hand.

"What's going on? Who's she?" Sleep rumpled, the Doctor looked even less endearing than I remembered. When Miss Merry told him, I could see, he recalled me, but only vaguely. Obviously I hadn't made as much of an impact on him but then during my previous visit, I'd spent so much more quality time with her.

His mind was as difficult as ever to get into but it was definitely there, and in the moments after he entered, I was able to read him a little. There'd been a seismic shift in the balance of power between them, a change in the dynamic of their relationship, I wondered what had happened. She slipped open a drawer and handed him a small black object, I couldn't see what, it was hidden by first her hand then his. He slipped it swiftly behind one ear and immediately, there he was – gone! As blanked out as she was. The device must have nestled neatly behind his ear, because only a thin black wire hooked over the top was visible. It was unobtrusive, but I now saw she had one too. Some kind of jamming device, I couldn't imagine how it worked but I felt genuinely affronted – how rude.

"I told you, back then," She was slapped her hand down hard on a pile of files on the desk, in exasperation "You wouldn't listen. We let this one slip right through our fingers, you wouldn't listen to me – that bloody blind girl knew." The Doctor was eyeing me like a butterfly-collector sizing up a specimen and deciding where to stick the pin.

"Shut up and let me think." He said, "Can we keep her?"

"Not for long."

"Hang on a minute." I protested, "You can't just go kidnapping someone off the street." Miss Merry smiled, "Hardly off the street, you broke in, remember."

"There are people who know I'm here." Aiming for defiant, I just about reached defensive.

"Bully for you," she snapped. "When they come looking, we'll just have to see what they can find. Meanwhile you're exactly what we need, couldn't have timed it better, especially as your little friend here's been so uncooperative." She looked over at Sam, unnaturally still and silent. In the presence of Merry and Dreck, he seemed to have shrivelled both outwardly and in. He was deathly afraid and the loathing and fear he felt for the two in the room, combined with the horror of whatever lay beyond, was piling on the pain for both of us. Things weren't going well. They got worse.

"Karl, the lights." She said,

"What now? We're doing it now?

"You brought John didn't you? We might never get a chance like this again. It's fallen right into our laps." He nodded and moved swiftly behind me to the switch. The lights in the office went off and as they did, lights in the room next door went on, mirror transformed to window. Miss Merry pressed a button on an intercom on the desk.

"Now, John." she said and her eyes were on me, waiting. The room beyond the glass echoed the one we were in but was unfurnished, other than with a small table and chair anchored to the floor as Sam's had been. The door in the mirror room opened and a man I'd never seen before led in, by the hand, something I'd also never seen before.

I wanted to look away, knew I should but couldn't. Instead I leaned forward, drawn implacably, trying to rationalise what I was seeing. Sam's monster hadn't perhaps been so much a horror of the imagination after all.

She'd been a little girl once, similar age, I thought, to Sam. She wasn't really that any more. Her shaved skull was oddly misshapen, hugely swollen, the very large forehead bulging and scarred, the size of the head completely disproportionate to the rest of her body and far too heavy for her neck. The Doctor, it appeared, had in the intervening years, found the time and opportunity for the odd operation.

She was dressed in Winnie the Pooh patterned pyjamas, the brightness of the colour, the familiarity of the design, shocking against the yellow pallor of her hands and what I could see of her face. There seemed to be something wrong with her co-ordination and she shuffled and stumbled a couple of times as the man who, I noted absently, was also wearing one of the black ear-pieces, led her across the room to the chair and table. She sat. Miss Merry pressed another button on her intercom and I heard a buzzer sound faintly in the room next door. The child looked up.

She couldn't see us, but she knew we were there. She found me immediately, I was new. My body reacted faster than my brain, tried to shut down, black out, but not fast enough. My shielding was less than useless. The malevolent madness of her mind flooded mine in a bitter rush of sewage which reached into every part of me. I felt myself surge forward, retching as my body sought to void her presence. Her world was one of stimulus and reward, disobedience and pain, nothing left of any kind of free will. As we mingled, I could feel no real memory of anything before this terrible existence – who she'd been, where she'd come from, how long she'd been subjected to this. I took with me, imprinted on my closed eyelids, a bright blue gaze, devoid of innocence in a dreadful, swollen face as I leapt, with desperation, into unconsciousness. But not before I'd shared with her the agony of the electric probe. That was what they used to switch her off.

I probably wasn't out for long, certainly not long enough. I'd fallen off the chair and was on the floor again. Everything was still hurting. I kept my eyes shut, I really didn't feel like re-joining the party yet. I probed very gingerly outward. Sam was ominously without thought. He'd met her before and because he'd known what was coming, had withdrawn deep down inside himself and was seeing no callers. Reluctantly, but I had to know, I probed further. I could feel the child in the next room but she was restrained for the moment, held back obediently by the pain of the probe, conditioned not to let her mind roam until the buzzer allowed it.

"Excellent." Miss Merry was quietly satisfied. The Doctor was pacing up and down as animated as I'd ever seen him,

"What a reaction eh? What a reaction!" He was muttering. "When she comes round, I'm inclined to get the others in too, see how she deals with all of them, not just Megan on her own. Your thoughts?"

"Agreed." Miss Merry nodded. Dreck walked over and looked down at me, he gave me a small shove with the toe of his shoe. I didn't react.

"She's exceptionally receptive isn't she, doesn't seem to be able to shut off in the same way as the boy though. Goddamnit, can't believe we had her here before and didn't know." He shook his head, "You were right, you were bloody right."

"Water under the bridge," but she was pleased.

I opened my eyes a mere crack, he was peering over at Sam,

"Don't like him un-medicated, too risky, even when we're blocked."

"He's out of it for the moment – he's done that before – with Megan."

"I need to profile these two together, see how they affect each other."

His tone rose with excitement, "God Almighty, what an opportunity, I want bloods and an EEG. Can't we keep her?"

"Not for long, there's family, I remember from her notes. We can't afford to have anything happen to her here."

"But she's in his league isn't she?"

"No question."

"You think she came on her own?"

"Can't be sure. Maybe she heard him in some way and decided to find out more – she was a cocky little cow when she was here before. But we can't risk it."

"How long've we got?" She looked at her watch, pursed her lips,

"1.30 now, at least until the morning I'd think. I'll set up the disposal people to pick her up then. As long as whatever accident she has is miles away, we shouldn't have a problem."

I wondered idly, if maybe this whole thing was simply a nightmare, a bad dream. It would certainly explain neatly how I, with my cosily cautious, North London upbringing – where the biggest risk might be sitting on a strange loo seat without first lining it with toilet paper – came to be lying, lacerated, on the office floor of a couple of scientific psychopaths, planning to put me out with the rubbish. And, more to the point – where were the people who'd got me into this crazy situation in the first place?

Then they were there. Suddenly, blessedly, in my head, all of them joined – I could feel the power of the *gestalt*. I could hear them soothing Sam too, although by that stage he was so traumatised he was probably beyond being shocked. I'd thought I was all out of energy but suddenly I was filled with all-consuming fury.

"Where *were* you?" I shrieked silently,

"We held back." Miss Peacock was distracted.

"Oh you held back? *You held back?* Well that's all right then." Glory was tense too,

"We didn't want to alarm Sam."

"Well you bloody well alarmed me!"

"You're coping. Now, let them see you're coming round." Miss Peacock again. I wanted to splutter and shriek. I wanted to drum my heels against the floor, throw something and thump someone – several people actually. I did none of that. I obediently moaned a little and then I moved my head slowly and painfully from side to side as if my neck hurt, not a lot of acting required, it felt as if it had been completely dislocated.

"She's coming out of it." No pulling the wool over Miss Merry's eyes.

"Start to get up now. Slowly." Instructed Miss Peacock. I struggled onto all fours with my head hanging down, did a bit more moaning and groaning then slowly sat back on my heels, looking around as if dazed. Merry and Dreck were watching with detached interest and he swiftly jotted down a note on a pad he was holding. I gritted my teeth, I knew where I'd like to ram that pad and the pen as well.

I heaved myself up, holding on to the chair and sat in it again, breathing heavily. I glanced across at Sam. His eyes were wide and disbelieving, his world had suddenly got a whole lot more crowded. His thumb had crept into his mouth for comfort, but he was proving to be quite the little trouper. And other than a swift, helplessly inquiring thought to which I don't think he even expected an answer, he didn't waste my time or energy. I could feel Ruth hovering anxiously over him.

"Rub your head as if it hurts, we need more time." Miss Peacock said.

"Stand up." Said Miss Merry.

"Stay where you are." Said Miss Peacock. I stifled a laugh, which came out as a snort. It had been a trying evening and there was really rather too much direction going on. Miss Merry couldn't see the joke and for once she was probably right.

"I said, *stand up*," She rapped, "We haven't got all night." She grabbed my arm, her fingers fitting neatly into the previous set of bruises she'd made, last time she grabbed me.

"Something's jamming us, what?" Miss Peacock was calm but her urgency was showing.

"A thing – they're both wearing black things behind their ear, like a hearing aid."

"Get them off. We'll help. Now." Ordered Miss Peacock,

"Now." Snapped Miss Merry. I was feeling decidedly hen-pecked but as I rose, hands at my side, I lifted the black hook from over her ear. She felt it moving but reached for it too late. I flung it into the far corner, at the same instant flashing to Sam what I needed him to do. Maybe it was expecting a lot of a six year old, but these were desperate times. Sam was up to it, though perhaps not as delicate as he could have been because the Doctor gave a little shriek. I don't think Sam was bothered.

I briefly felt the cold impact of Miss Merry's mind, acridly dry, bright with anger and then Ruth was doing her stuff and she started to go down, falling forwards. I automatically put out my arms to catch and lower her gently to the floor, somehow in the midst of everything, it seemed important to hold on to certain standards of courtesy. The Doctor's mind, crystal clear, evidence of his extreme agitation, flared briefly, before his eyes too rolled ceiling-ward and with a boneless thud he joined his colleague.

Sudden movement stirred at the edge of my vision and even as I turned, I knew what I was going to see through the glass. She, Megan must have, couldn't help but have felt the strength of the *gestalt*. She'd heard the instruction and obeyed. The man called John had lost more though than his little black jamming device. He lay in the corner of the room, eyes wide, blood oozing from where his ear had been, the electric probe, harmless now, by his outstretched hand. He was dead. And Megan knew, in that moment, she was free from both the buzzer and the probe.

We could all feel her mind ranging, seeking, sucking at ours, it wasn't a pleasant sensation and oh God, beyond her, in the other rooms there were others. All just as ragingly insane, all aware familiar restrictions were gone. They howled their horror, their history, their fear and their hate. The unholy chorus rose, fell and rose again, lacerating and assaulting our minds like fingernails raking a blackboard, overriding rational thought, creating only an overwhelming desire to escape, to get away. I could feel the others desperately trying to restore calm, gain control. They were strong, stronger because of the joining, but what had been created artificially, was stronger still and I knew they were on a hiding to nothing.

Sam was rigid on his chair, hands clasped neatly in his lap, the unconscious bodies of Dr Dreck and Miss Merry sprawled not far from his feet. His colourless face was turned toward the glass, behind which, Megan lurched and drooled and capered. He knew what he had to do, didn't want to do it but, untroubled by complicated adult ethics, knew it was essential for his own preservation and only fair to Megan and the other children.

"Sam, no." I screamed and heard the cry echoed by the others, but it was already too late. We felt the power build inexorably in him, drawing on the strength of all of us. First he took Megan – a pressure at just the right point, a small decisive twist in precisely the right place and, as her mind briefly flared, was there gratitude there for something that of all of us only Sam had the courage to do? Then swift and sure, no hesitation, he dealt with the others, there were four of them and I caught him as he collapsed.

CHAPTER FORTY-FIVE

I thought he was dead too. I fumbled for his wrist, trying clumsily to reach in through the fastenings on the suit to find a pulse,

"Not there," Miss Peacock's urgency pulled at my fingers, "His neck, there … no, no, higher … not your thumb, first two fingers." For an awfully long moment I could detect nothing then, a slow beat.

"I've got it, he's OK." I felt weak with relief, or maybe I just felt weak.

"You have to get him out of there quickly. *Move.*" I wasn't sure I had the strength to do that. Half crouched on the floor, the little boy in my arms was a dead weight and I was weary to the bone and beyond. I shut my sore eyes. Something cold was nudging my face, Hamlet's nose. I pushed him away but he came back.

"If you don't get that boy out," Peacock said, "He'll probably die."

"I can't."

"Rubbish." They were separate again, I could feel them individually now. Ruth's concern, Glory's frustration. I struggled to my feet and rested him on the edge of the desk.

"Fireman's lift?" Ruth suggested. "Quicker than using Hamlet." I felt them help me prop him over my shoulder, head and arms dangling behind me. We were both still slippery-suit clad, so I had to anchor his legs tightly. It would be a poor show if, after all this, I dropped him and broke his neck.

I turned to move out of the office which now, with people lying all over the place, looked a lot more untidy than when we'd arrived. On impulse I bent, holding tight to Sam and picked up one of the little black ear pieces. After a couple of attempts to find a pocket anywhere in the stupid suit I gave up, slipped it down inside the neck and hoped it wouldn't end up anywhere too uncomfortable.

"Filing cabinet." Miss P again.

"Right, I'll just slip that in too, shall I?"

"Facetiousness," she reprimanded me – it hadn't taken her long to get back in her stride after recent events, "Is never constructive. It's locked so what's inside's probably important. Get rid of it." I sighed. All I wanted was the child off my shoulder, the silver suit off my back, the whole episode out of my head and a good strong cup of tea.

"Quicker you do as she says, the quicker that's likely to happen." Glory at her most priggish.

"All *right*," I concentrated, reaching and easing past the metal to the papers inside, feeling Glory working with me, helping find just the right level. Warm, then hot, then smouldering, not quite strong enough to flame, but flickering just below. Holding it there wasn't easy, but very quickly we felt the papers within begin to blacken at the edges, then curl and in a gratifyingly short space of time, disintegrate, the metal file dividers buckling and sagging with the heat. Case histories, progress notes, whatever was in there – I didn't want to think too closely of the stories some of those files could have told – would be of no earthly use to anyone now. I put a cautious hand near the side of the cabinet, then rested it on the surface, warm but not hot. No danger of it flaring up and doing damage when we'd gone, in fact from the outside it looked fine – but oh, there'd be a gnashing of teeth and tearing of hair when next it was opened. I turned again to make my way out of the office, poised for a Peacock counter-instruction but thankfully, for once, she had nothing to add. The room next door was still illuminated brightly, I didn't look, I had more than enough nightmares to be getting on with.

Hamlet by my side, Sam over my shoulder, we retraced our steps. This time there was nothing emanating from behind closed doors, it had become just another corridor. I couldn't find it in my heart to believe Sam had done wrong, although recalling my own agonising over a situation when I too had taken what seemed to be the only option, I wondered how he'd view it in years to come.

Through the security door, down the stairs, past a still supine Nurse Muldrew – if the sedative had that effect on an adult, you had to wonder what it would have done to the much smaller Sam. We turned the corner and then there was just the long stretch to the side door where I'd entered. Sam was a dead weight, even with help and my arm muscles were shaking, locked rigid round his knees. The door didn't seem to be getting any closer and whilst Muldrew looked out for the count, I'd no idea how long before the Dr and Miss Merry re-surfaced. When they did, they really wouldn't be best pleased and I'd stupidly left one of the jamming devices in the office, so the first I'd probably know, would be when they grabbed me from behind. I seemed to have been plodding forever. I didn't see, or even sense the figure in front of me until I ran full tilt into him.

Typically, he wasted no time in idle chit-chat but in one smooth move, swung Sam off my shoulder and on to his, which being far broader and not half so slippery, was an all-round improvement. I hoped though that Sam wouldn't wake up just yet, he'd had enough shocks for one day. Ed put out his other hand to me and I grabbed it like a lifeline. It was only when I did, that I realised he was even more scared than I. He flashed me an impassive look and I smiled and gave his huge hand a squeeze. If I was disappointed that our knight in shining armour was, in reality, as jumpy as a cat on a hot tin roof, I was doubly touched by his courage in coming to get us anyway.

As we slipped out the side door there was a rush of eager panting. As security dogs, it had to be said, Laurel and Hardy weren't really much cop. Ed's hand tensed hard round mine, nearly breaking four fingers. Apart from Hamlet, who he regarded more as a person, Ed was terrified by dogs. In fact, I saw clearly, big-as-a-house, stone-faced Ed, was terrified by most things. He'd encountered these two already and his progress across the lawn, canine accompanied as I'd been, had unnerved him more than he could possibly describe.

"They won't hurt us." I said firmly, sounding more like Miss P than I cared to and hoping I was right.

It seemed darker outside than before, with the moon fully cloud obscured by now. It had also turned colder and there was a mist of fine drizzle overlaying our hair and chilling our faces. We could have done with the torch, provided so sensibly, so long ago but I didn't seem to have it with me anymore, must have put it down somewhere when my mind was preoccupied by other things. Our party – Ed had me firmly by the hand, although it was debatable who was reassuring who, Sam over his shoulder, Hamlet by his side and Laurel and Hardy weaving enthusiastic circles – made speedy if unsteady progress along the path. We were hampered by the uneven paving and fear of falling and as the wind rose, the hedges lining the way moaned and lashed and cracked around us. We'd crossed about half the width of the lawn when things started to go downhill again. Sam began to stir, there were assorted aggressive shouts from behind and someone pulled a switch that flood-lit the entire grounds.

Now we had absolutely no problem seeing where we were going, nor that there were people in hot pursuit. Ed demonstrated a sudden and admirable turn of speed, holding a wriggling Sam with one arm and hauling me, not the world's greatest sprinter, along with the other. Miss Peacock was on the case, swifter than Sherlock. I felt her rap out a command to the two dogs. They immediately stopped having a whale of a time with new friends and recalled they were there to do a job. If, due to the machinations of Miss P, this also meant a swift switch in allegiance, that was fine by them. Back to full-throated barking and snarling, Alsatian and Doberman turned as one and raced like things possessed, back the way we'd come. We could hear shouts of pursuit change to chorus of consternation, as it began to be appreciated, that for reasons unknown, the dogs had turned rogue.

The winding path, biliously bathed in yellowish illumination from the spotlights, was a sea of moving shadow from wind-hassled hedges.

"The lights, put out the lights." Glory, urgently bossy. I wasn't sure who she was instructing but as I was preoccupied enough keeping up with Ed and breathing at the same time, I assumed it wasn't me. I felt them searching, Glory frantic because she couldn't find anyone to see through; Ruth and Rachael calm but just as worried. Adept as they were with people and indeed animals, they didn't have anywhere near the same ability with anything else, it was Ed who shone at the mechanical stuff.

"Ed, the lights, we can't do them." Miss Peacock was as anxious as I'd heard her. Ed panting heavily, slowed as we rounded a curve in the path and the wall suddenly loomed ahead of us, impossibly tall, barbed wire trimmed. I felt his concentration as he visualised the light source, the bulbs within their glass and metal casing, their construction, contour, composition. I understood that only completely accurate assessment would allow him to find the weakest spot, and felt his surprisingly delicate manipulation of the awareness he'd accumulated. There was a small crack and a pop in our heads – we were too far away to hear the real thing – and I never thought darkness would be so welcome. Ed gave a small grunt and relaxed a little, but we really weren't out of the woods yet.

We could hear people spreading out to cover different areas of the grounds and the barking of the dogs, presumably now brought to heel. Sam's numbness at finding himself on the shoulder of a six and a half foot giant he'd never met before, was wearing off, and I could feel his mind casting around frantically, trying to identify all the different personalities, inside his head and out. He was very powerful and exercising no restraint whatsoever, I felt the others flinch too as his fear and volume rose apace. He almost completely drowned out everything else and made me want to cradle my head in my hands. It was like having two transistor radios turned to full volume and jammed against each ear. I was vaguely aware of Glory, Ruth and Rachael striving to get through to him. Ed had lowered him to the ground but still had, what I hoped, was a firm grip on the arm of the now violently struggling child. I could see the flashes of powerful torches getting nearer.

I looked around swiftly for Hamlet, he was just behind me. Dropping to my knees, I reached out and grabbed his collar and at the same time grabbed Sam from Ed's diminishing hold. The child's eyes were wide, straining desperately to see in the dark and he was wriggling, struggling and kicking to get free. I pulled him in close to me, pinning him tight against my body with one arm. With the other I hauled Hamlet in too, so the three of us were nose to nose but by then, Sam had launched himself so irretrievably onto a rising tide of hysteria, he'd lost sight of any way back. As reaction and shock set in, he was no longer capable of thinking coherently and if the power of what was building in his head was making me light-headed and nauseous, it was doing far worse to him. He was a ticking bomb that could kill us all.

I wrapped a handful of his suit material round my hand, yanked him back hard and snatched him in again, the force nearly knocking me off my knees. His head jerked back then forward, his forehead cracking against mine. His eyes were frighteningly unfocussed, deep black pools and for a further moment the lights were on but no-one was home, then slowly he began to focus on my sweaty, filthy, desperate face so close to his,

"Let it go, Sam, let it go, you have to let it go," I don't know whether I spoke or thought or both but I reached him. Hamlet's instincts, brilliant beast, didn't fail us either. He moved his head a fraction forward so he could gently lick the boy's cheek and the spiralling, lethal crescendo in Sam's head started to lose a fraction of its terrible destructive force. He stopped trying to tear away from my restraining arm and leaned heavily into me, eyes unwavering on mine. His mouth was slightly open and I could feel with the warmth of each small breath panted out against my face, the danger diminishing. As his whole body began to shake, I tightened my arms bone-crackingly round boy and dog. And if some of the shakes were mine and our faces were slippery with sweat and none of us smelt too good – well, who the hell cared?

"When you're ready?" If there was just a hint of a tremor beneath the normal acid Peacock tone, this was no time to comment, shouts were getting closer, we had to move fast. I was still on my knees, so we were on a level, Sam and I.

"We have to get over the wall. Sam, can you fly with me?" His eyes widened and I understood instantly he could, he'd done it before but the pain of the resulting punishment from a hysterical social worker, who'd had to get him down from the roof, had remained an effective grounding agent ever since.

"It's OK Sam my man, it's all right to do it now, it'll be fine. I promise." I heaved myself to my feet, using his shoulder as a convenient crutch. He was still trembling, but far less violently and had an arm wound tightly round Hamlet's neck and if Hamlet's head was thus at an acutely uncomfortable angle he was patiently forbearing. I understood though, that one was going nowhere without the other.

CHAPTER FORTY-SIX

I could feel the strength of the three women on the other side of the wall pouring into me, filling me up, temporarily flooding my tired, aching, energy depleted muscles. Sam, Hamlet and I gently let go of the ground and rose. And if I was a bit rusty and couldn't do, quite as easily, what I'd been able to, not that many years ago, Sam was well able to compensate. Hand tight in hand, both of us hanging for dear life on to Hamlet we shot up and up and over the barbed wire, coming down, none too gracefully, at the foot of the large tree from whence I'd started.

"Ed, what about Ed?"

"He's heavier." Miss Peacock, didn't waste time, she reached an imperative hand for Sam's and he unhesitatingly gave it to her. Obviously he was giving up on an old set of rules that no longer seemed relevant, in light of recent experience and was simply going with the flow, putting trust where instinct told him. He was still holding tight to my left hand with his right and Glory moved quickly closer, reaching out for me, her borrowed vision working poorly in the dark.

I grabbed her elbow, pulling her nearer and Ruth crowded in on her other side. As we closed ranks, I felt the familiar jolt and then an unfamiliar one that was Sam's reaction as the impact of the joining hit him. He didn't even try to pull away and then he was right there with us, equal and unafraid, his unmistakeable chocolate, buttery strength blending with those others I now knew so well. The power surged and swelled in and from us, perhaps we all swayed with it. If we did, there was only Hamlet to see, trapped patiently, in the urgency of the moment, in the midst of our swift circle.

Ed was no piece of thistle-down and exhausted as he was, couldn't offer anything much in the way of assistance. For what seemed like ages it didn't seem as if we'd be able to shift him so much as an inch, let alone up and over the wall. In fact I'm not sure we'd have managed it at all without Sam – rescued turned rescuer. Clasped and concentrating, we felt with relief the lightening of Ed, as the ground finally released him. Sadly our landing skills weren't as refined as they might have been and I think, in the general rush of things, we probably sent him a bit too high and misjudged slightly where we brought him down. He descended through the outer branches of the tree, bouncing from one branch to another with a high degree of drama and a series of muffled yelps. He hit the ground hard and awkwardly, feet first. As we ran over, he was holding his left leg squirming in agony.

"His leg." Ruth, stating the obvious, was crouched next to him, trying to ascertain the damage.

"There's two bones, coming down from his knee, it's the inside one's broke." The hoarse little voice made us start, it was indeed only the second time I'd heard it and I'd been with him for quite a while now. It was hoarser than earlier – but it had, after all, been a screamy sort of a night – it was totally authoritative nevertheless.

"Sure?" Ruth tentatively pressed her fingers along the lower leg, Ed groaned.

"It's broke and sticking out where it shouldn't. You won't be able to feel though, because his leg's …" Sam paused thoughtfully, not wanting to offend any new friends, "… sort of big. It's got sharp bits now where it's broke. That's why it hurts so much." he added helpfully.

"Well we haven't time to stand discussing it," Miss Peacock recalled our slightly stunned attention. "He needs a hospital doesn't he?"

It was a willing, if slightly motley crew that participated in the tricky undertaking of heaving Ed onto his feet. Ruth and Rachael positioned themselves as crutches either side of him with his arms over their shoulders for balance, whilst Glory and I took his weight, so he was floating along just above the ground like a poorly designed hovercraft. As we headed the short distance back to the van, every movement jogged the injured leg and when Ruth stumbled slightly over a tree root and jerked him, he lost consciousness completely for a moment.

"Is he hurt anywhere else?" Ruth worried. We all looked at Sam, who shook his head decisively.

I wondered if we might be considered certifiable, listening solemnly, as we were, to the diagnosis of a six year old but was reassured, as much by what he said, as by what we'd all glimpsed briefly in his head whilst he considered the question. Revolving gently in there was a kind of three dimensional, transparent image of Ed and his innards which, in its depth and complexity could not have been simply a product of the imagination. Sam was turning out to be all kinds of Strange. A thought occurred to me,

"Sam, can you fix it?" in the dark I could just make out the paler shade of his face as he shook his head, he didn't speak but we all caught the absolute certainty of the thought,

"Not yet."

"Not yet? What does that mean – not yet?" Glory was pragmatic,

"I think he means one day he'll be able to, when he's older, just not yet."

"Well what about the rest of us, can't we do it somehow?"

"If we could, don't you imagine we would?" Miss Peacock's tone was mild but only because she was out of breath, although she still managed to get in a final word, "To harm is so easy, to heal, a different thing altogether."

Sounds of pursuit could still be heard behind us, as could the furious barking of the dogs, although there was about that a certain apologetic element of making up for earlier shortcomings. It sounded like they were covering every inch of the grounds but it wouldn't take them long to widen the search. It might perhaps have been better, Miss Peacock remarked dryly as, with the hand that wasn't securing Ed's arm around her neck, she began to pat the various pockets of his dark leather bomber jacket,

"Ed, keys?" for me to have stuck to the original plan which was pop in, pick up Sam and disappear, as opposed to turning the whole place on its head.

"Things snowballed," I complained, "And then there were those ear pieces?"

"Some sort of high frequency transmitter, very effective. You kept them?"

"One."

"Both would have been sensible."

"Rachael," hissed Ruth, "Discuss later please and what do you plan to do with the car keys, you can't drive."

"Neither can you."

"I know that."

"Boris gave me lessons."

"*Gott in Himmel*, Rachael, fifteen years ago and you were so abysmal, he refused to do it again."

"I was not that bad."

"I beg to differ, on top of which it's illegal. No license."

"Ruth," Miss Peacock wasn't to be outdone in the hissing stakes, "Have you a screw loose – after what we've done here tonight, don't you think that might be the least of the charges?"

Sam, with a child's resilience, didn't seem unduly perturbed by our temporary driver's novice status for which I was more than grateful. Sam, perturbed was not an easy option. We'd eased Ed, as carefully as we could, onto the seats behind the driver but there was sweat standing out on his forehead and although he only moaned out loud once or twice, his lower lip was caught hard by his teeth and we could all feel his pain. Glory and I slipped into the seats behind to hold him steady, although you didn't have to be a physics professor to calculate that the mass of Ed, thrown forward at any velocity, wasn't going to be impeded by any opposing force exerted by us. The injured leg was stretched carefully along the seat next to him, with Sam, perched at the end by his foot, craning round to make sure Hamlet wasn't left behind. Ruth insisted on sitting in the front next to her sister, although what she thought she could contribute I had no idea.

"Right." said Miss Peacock, "Ed, just remind me, where does this key go?"

Ed was not a natural talker. I don't think I ever heard him string more than a few sentences together and short ones at that. So, whereas another person might have talked Miss P through – after all, he had as much of a stake in getting there in one piece as the rest of us – he simply rested his head on the back of the seat and waited for direct questions. For her part, she obviously felt too many might indicate she'd forgotten more than she wanted us to know. Our initial somewhat jerky progress – Miss Peacock and the clutch were not a natural combination – was a little tense. By the time though that we emerged from the shadows of hedgerows lining the unlit narrow lanes leading from the back of Newcombe and turned on to the main road, some of the fifteen year old instruction seemed to be trickling back. The route back was mercifully straight and, it being around 2.00 a.m. pretty quiet, which meant she didn't have to bother too much with the brakes which, she obviously felt were a bit of an unnecessary distraction.

Nobody seemed inclined to talk, or indeed communicate much in any other way. Rachael and Ruth discussed briefly and quietly whether we should drive straight to the nearest A&E, but decided in view of the range of our unorthodox activities, the safest plan was to head back to the cottage and call an ambulance from there. Glory had retreated deep within herself and Sam had fallen fast asleep, his dirt be-streaked little face tucked awkwardly into one shoulder. I was more tired and shocked, emotionally and physically than I'd have thought possible and yearned desperately to be able to draw a veil over and a line beneath tonight's activities. I could feel small involuntary spasms tensing the muscles of my arms and legs and however much I tried, couldn't seem to get my jaw unclenched. Despite that, my eyelids kept drooping, but there were images I really didn't want to see again and I kept jerking awake. It had started to rain in earnest now, water tattooing on the roof and swishing under the tyres. I was drifting off again when Ruth spoke softly in the front seat.

"Rachael."

"I am *not* going too fast."

"You are dear and there's a car. Behind." Miss Peacock clicked her tongue irritably.

"It's a road, it happens."

"Following us."

"I don't feel anything."

"I'm not usually wrong."

"No, you're not." Miss Peacock glanced briefly at her sister, "How do they know the van's us?"

"They don't. Yet. But we're coming from the right direction. I wonder …" Miss Peacock put her foot down and the van bucked, jerked and shot forward, gear box growling in protest. Ruth continued mildly,

"… if slowing down might have allayed suspicion."

If the heightened tension sharpened fear, it also honed senses. In a car which, after an initial dropping back because of our turn of speed, was now having no trouble keeping up with us, were three men. I probed, didn't recognise any of them but Ruth was right, it was us they were after and with some precise and unfriendly intentions. Miss Merry's descriptions of both Sam and me were unsettlingly accurate, as were her instructions on how we were to be handled when they caught us – she'd obviously woken from her nap in a very snippy mood.

Of the three men in the car, two were employed by the private firm in charge of security at the Foundation. Before setting out, they'd endured a tersely swift but bitterly severe tongue lashing on the effectiveness of their service, the reliability of their guard dogs and the unlikelihood of their contract being renewed at Newcombe, or indeed anywhere else in the foreseeable future.

Accompanying them was a third man who, boasting a build to rival Ed's, was a nurse, a long-standing friend, I immediately understood of Megan's friend, John. As he held us solely responsible for John's unfortunate and abrupt demise, he wasn't full of the milk of human kindness either. All three of them, up to a certain point that evening, had been jogging evenly along life's crazy paving, minding their own business, anticipating nothing more strenuous than the next tea break and a Chocolate Digestive. Now, in the space of a very short time, they'd found their necks, not to mention their livelihoods on the line. They were a pretty motivated car-full.

"Rachael?" If Ruth was concerned by her sister, hunched over the wheel, like a demented Stirling Moss she didn't let it show. "Rachael," she repeated calmly, "We're not losing them. We daren't lead them back to the cottage and Ed can't take much more of this rattling around. We have to stop and deal."

"You think?"

"No option."

"Main road's not good. I'll turn off"

"Right and Rachael – a little more braking? Couldn't hurt."

We skidded to a juddering stop, a little way into an industrial estate of low rise, unlit units. Sam woke with a whimper and in the sudden ticking stillness, my jaw finally unclenched itself and my teeth began to chatter. The pursuing car swerved round the corner at speed, saw us and stopped too. Nobody got out and then there was a sudden silence, the interwoven thoughts, fears and motivations of the three men, obliterated totally.

"Jamming devices." Glory complained. "How rude!"

"No Sam," If Miss Peacock's voice and thought were soft, the warning behind them was unmistakable. He glared at her and we all felt the dangerous build of energy escalating within him again. Sam, having got this far, simply wasn't prepared to be taken back. For a moment as their minds and eyes locked, it was as if there were only the two of them in the van.

"There's always another way, Sam." She was calm, as if the atmosphere wasn't crackling with something barely leashed. He shut his eyes, shut her out. She went straight in after him and her rapped command, with complete authority and the certainty of obedience made us all jump. But it did the trick, the power spiral slowed reluctantly. He opened his eyes and looked at her and into her and she nodded briefly and definitely in confirmation.

"No, you're not on your own any more. Trust me enough to leave it to us. Ruth?" Her sister grimaced, the three men were out of the car now, conferring and cautious. They'd obviously been told enough about us to be wary, I wondered exactly how much of the truth they knew.

Ruth shook her head,

"Can't get inside. Damned ear-things." she said, "Ed dear, I know you're feeling dreadful, but could you possibly …?" Ed said nothing but I could feel him reaching past me, probing with that surprisingly delicate touch. Silent seconds passed. The three men, having consulted, split up, one security man heading for the back of our van, his colleague together with John's friend, walking slowly to flank the driver and passenger doors. They each carried an obviously weighty, black cosh, although, I couldn't help thinking, Dreck and Merry would surely be less than thrilled if we were delivered back with our brains bashed in. But perhaps coshes were only a precaution, they also had in their hands, small aerosol cans, similar to that used earlier on me. Sam's quick thought confirmed,

"They use different ones. Some just hurt your eyes, some make you fall down."

There was a sudden crash as Ruth's window crazed then shattered inwards, she screamed softly, shielding herself from the glass. Cold wet air blasted in, along with a burst from an aerosol. Miss Peacock yanked her sister away, both from the spray and the grasping black-clad arm that shot through the window. Glory cursed and Sam slipped to the floor, hands over his head, huddling between the seats, making himself as small as possible. I wanted to reassure him, but really didn't know how this was going to play out. Hamlet was barking wildly, shaking the van as he threw himself around in the back, fiercely or in fright was debatable. Only Ed was still and then there was a muted explosion. It rocked our vehicle, first to one side then the other, cotton-wooled our ears and reverberated deep inside our chests, as night turned to crimson day.

I could see only one man, from where I was sitting, the nurse who'd moved round to the driver's door. His expression was a degree or two beyond dumbfounded. Various pieces of their car began to rain down on the roof of the van and from the amount of flinching and ducking, onto him too. What was left of their transport was now cheerfully blazing.

"Goodness Ed," murmured Ruth, brushing glass from her hair, "I only meant get rid of their ear pieces. Still, this might be a good moment …? " Miss Peacock nodded, started the van, spun a gravel-raising, several point turn, gave a wide berth to the burning vehicle and drew up briefly alongside the three men, gathered together now in a defensive small circle.

"We're leaving," she announced. "My advice? You should too. Fuel tank." As we drew away, they were starting to run.

"You see Sam," said Miss Peacock, "There are always options." The second explosion didn't come until we were back on the main road.

CHAPTER FORTY-SEVEN

I wasn't there when the ambulance arrived to take Ed, accompanied by Ruth, to hospital. I think the story was he'd fallen from a ladder although the reason they concocted, for him being up one in the middle of the night, now eludes me. But by the time they came to take him away, Sam and I had been dispatched summarily upstairs to get some sleep for what little remained of the night. Perversely though, once I'd had a regrettably cursory wash-down and collapsed into the bed beneath the warmth of the duvet, my mind wouldn't stop whirling like a souped-up carousel.

I must have fallen asleep eventually, because I surfaced from a heated nightmare to a figure, small and silent, watching me. I shot up with a smothered shriek and he jumped convulsively.

"*Sam*? What is it?" I recalled, guiltily, I hadn't really addressed more than a sentence or two to him during the course of our whole, ludicrously activity-packed evening. There'd been no introductions, no social niceties. In this strange world we were all a part of, things were very different, but there was no doubting, this was one bewildered small individual. I held out my hand to him and after a brief hesitation he took it and I noted we hadn't got around to removing the leather straps. As he clambered into the bed next to me, I realised he wasn't unaccompanied, but drew the line at Hamlet. Hygiene and my mother aside, there simply wasn't room. Hamlet settled resignedly as close to the bed as he could get, Sam put ice cold feet on mine, stuck a thumb in his mouth and went instantly to sleep and the oddity and reality of him there, beside me, dismissed many of the nightmare images chasing round and round in my head.

When I woke, I was on my own again and sun was pouring through the curtains, creating shifting patterns on the wall. I was too lazy for a while to move, but picked up the fact that Ed and Ruth had been back a while. I knew also that Ed, who'd indeed sustained a compound fracture of the tibia, was ensconced on the sofa and that Sam and Hamlet were having a late breakfast. I was vaguely aware of the Misses Peacock and Glory, somewhere around the cottage but could sense no undue panic from anyone, so turned over and went back to sleep for a while.

My conscience eventually woke me. I had to phone home, goodness only knew what my parents were thinking. I eyed my battered face in the mirror, how on earth was I going to explain the enormous bruise on my cheek, result of my brief but intense encounter with Sam's bed frame? There were, additionally, a wealth of other painful areas, indeed every joint ached, although I couldn't imagine how I'd managed to upset all of them. I really didn't think this physical stuff was quite me.

I dressed and made my way stiffly downstairs. Ed, massive on the sofa with his plastered leg on a footstool, acknowledged my entrance with his customary little head duck. I started to reiterate how grateful I was for his timely appearance in our hour of need but, aware of the sentiment before I opened my mouth, he was already starting to redden and didn't want to hear. In the few seconds before he started a Nat King Cole selection, I understood just how hard he'd tried to be brave for Sam and me, how badly he thought he'd failed. I was filled with frustration too. How could he not see, if you weren't hugely afraid you didn't have to call on equally large resources of courage.

"Leave it." Glory was curled in an armchair, "You'll only upset him more."

"But ..."

"Leave it, I said, what makes you think you can do what the three of us can't?" I subsided, she was probably right.

"*Probably*?" Always liked the last word did Glory. She'd celebrated the discarding of yesterday's dark outfit with an electric blue kaftan and her gold hooped earrings glinted in the sun. I wondered idly what Ruth's choice of the day would be, together she and Glory certainly made a fashion statement, I just wasn't sure what it said.

Sam, seated quietly on the floor Hamlet by his side, was leaning against Ed's footstool. They had a record-player and a radio on the coffee table in front of them and Ed had completely disembowelled both, mixing the resulting innards. He was now showing Sam some re-assembling. The blood-stained brown leather was finally gone from Sam's wrist. He looked up at me, taking in the spreading multi-hued bruise on my cheek and, disconcertingly, assessing all the other ones over the rest of me. He knew exactly which ones were attributable to him and felt bad about it. I winked at him it seemed the right thing to do. We were, after all, battle-bloodied buddies. I don't think a wink was something he'd ever seen before, but he instantly picked up on the brief movement and everything behind it. He winked solemnly, and with great concentration back.

Ruth and Rachael weren't immediately in evidence, so I ambled into the kitchen, suddenly ravenous and got the kettle and toaster going. Last night seemed a world away yet appallingly close. But nonetheless, here I was busy with the most mundane of tasks, physically battered and bruised, granted, but otherwise not as troubled as I felt I should be. Odd how the unbelievable became so swiftly the accepted. As I bit into toast I was listening absently to Sam, mightily relieved to hear him totally occupied in what they were doing. If he had lingering nightmares or guilt about Megan and the others, it wasn't showing.

"He has a child's clear-sighted logic." Ruth had come through the door leading up from the basement behind me. She was tastefully adorned in a blindingly bright, lemon sweater with what may or may not have been a green parrot on the front.

"Because of what he is, he knows, with absolute certainty, better than any of us perhaps, that Megan and the others, poor little souls ..." For just a second her anger, white hot, shone through, "... were so irretrievably damaged, there was only one thing that could be done to help them and he did it. Children are very pragmatic, could teach us adults a thing or two."

We both looked over at Sam, just as Ed raised his hand to point out a particular component flying back into the half assembled radio. We saw Sam automatically flinch then relax again. Ruth's mouth tightened,

"They have," she said grimly, "A great deal to answer for, our friends down the road."

"So, now what? Who do we go to?" I was attacking a second jam-loaded slice.

"Go to?" Miss Peacock, looking as fresh as a grey and white daisy, had appeared too.

"The police?"

"Ah yes, the police ..." she murmured, "And you'd share with them that you broke into a respected medical centre, rendered unconscious several members of staff, destroyed valuable records and kidnapped a small boy?" She paused thoughtfully, "Oh and silly me, I nearly forgot – while you were at it, five patients and a nurse were murdered." I put my toast down, it had suddenly lost appeal.

"But you know what happened, and why."

"And how would you put that in a statement, without explanation about things you may not want broadcast?" Miss Peacock raised an eyebrow.

"But we've got to do something."

"We've done something."

"But he's just one, there'll be others?"

"I know that. We do what we can." I glared at her,

"But …"

"We can't take the law into our own hands."

"We just did."

"We took a risk. We've done it before, we'll do it again. But we are what we are and must act with a certain degree of caution." She moved to the kettle, shook to check the level of water and re-filled, as always her movements economic and sure. "We can't right all wrongs, you know. We'd be a little inundated." I ignored the sarcasm and looked at Ruth, who nodded agreement,

"She's right. Only so far we can go. We've done some pretty unorthodox things in our time, come up against some exceptionally nasty characters. We usually though manage to handle things more smoothly, less violently, we'd no idea last night would turn quite so dramatic."

"But Dreck and Merry." I protested. "They won't take this lying down."

"They haven't a lot of choice. Their research hardly bears close scrutiny." Miss Peacock reached for a plate and began to dismember a grapefruit.

"But it's Government funded," I protested,

"Government funded doesn't mean public approved."

"But what's going on there's illegal, surely? And what about the disposal people Merry talked about? Surely that's incriminating enough?"

"Your word against theirs."

"But *you* know … " She raised that eyebrow again,

"We're hardly going to come forward as witnesses."

"But they know who I am, she recognised me. That means they know my address, everything."

"Dealt with."

"Dealt with?"

"The Doctor and Miss Merry are," she looked at her watch, "Round about now each receiving a hand-delivered letter from a well-known firm of solicitors."

"Saying?"

"That although most records were destroyed last night, enough have been retained to show exactly how far out of hand their experimental work has gone. A substantial number of photographs, together with tape-recorded material is currently held by the solicitor. Should Dreck or Merry or anyone acting on their behalf, attempt to approach you or any member of your family, now or at any time in the future, this material will immediately be distributed to all leading national newspapers, the police and, of course, relevant government departments. Prosecution would be inevitable and on a variety of charges."

"But you don't *have* any evidence."

"They don't know that."

"That's blackmail."

"And your point is?" she waited politely. I turned abruptly away. I don't know what I'd thought would happen to Merry and Dreck but I wanted to see them damaged, the way they'd damaged others.

"I'm sorry dear, there's only so much we can do." Ruth, as aware as I that tears of angry frustration were just around the corner, kept her tone even. I swallowed hard I felt ridiculously young, naïve and hard done by.

"Well, what about Sam?"

"Arrangements already in place." she reassured me.

"To live here with you?"

"He needs far more than we can give him. He needs to learn to mix, to cope with what he is."

"But you *can't* just abandon him, he's had too much of that."

"I assure you, we are not abandoning him." Ruth was mild but I'd hit the steel behind the softness. I made hasty amends,

"I didn't mean that, it's just I'm worried?"

"Not your responsibility." Miss Peacock was dismissive. She'd carried her coffee and grapefruit to the sofa opposite Ed. "You'll be going back home now anyway. We're grateful for all you've done, we couldn't have managed last night without you." She made it sound like I'd run down to the shops for half a pound of butter! I swallowed hard again I really didn't want them to know what I was feeling, wasn't even sure myself. Miss Peacock as ever had a view.

"You're mixed up at the moment, angry and hurt because you think we're shutting you out. Perhaps we are. Get used to it. It's for your own good."

"I don't understand, I can't just *go back*, after everything that's happened."

"Well you can't stay here, and in a few months you'll hardly remember it all."

"Oh, so now we tell the future too?" I was hurting, I wanted to hurt back. I should have known better, she ignored the remark, took a sip of her coffee replaced the cup neatly in the saucer.

"You have family, a strong supportive background, you can't and wouldn't want to abandon that."

"No, but ..."

"There are no buts, we're different, all of us here," she inclined her head to include the others in the room, "No families, no ties, different circumstances altogether. You're certainly one of us, but that's only part of what you are and you can't live comfortably with a foot in both worlds. When you're older you can make your own choices. My guess? You'll opt for as normal as possible." She took another genteel sip.

Ruth made to move towards me, I turned my back. I was aware of behaving like a sulky child and knew what had been said made sense, Miss Peacock had read me like a book. If they'd said stay, I'd have been horrified, there was never any question in my mind about that. But in the time I'd been with them I wondered if I hadn't been more truly myself than ever before.

"Oh please!" Glory, silent till now, "You're your own person. Wherever you are, whoever you're with, whatever you're doing and that's all there is to it." No-one quite like Glory to puncture your balloon. I gathered around me what shreds of dignity I had left.

"I'll phone home then, shall I?"

"We're staying down here for a bit, but we'll put you on the 5.00 o'clock into London." Miss Peacock had it all sorted, she must have hit the phone early. "There's a taxi coming at 4.30, get you to the station in plenty of time." It was as if having utilised my services, they couldn't wait to get rid of me and if I heard Ruth's quick protest, I ignored it. When you're feeling hard done by, you really don't want anybody interfering. I called home under the unsmiling eye of Queen Victoria but the phone at the other end rang on, unanswered. I'd try again later. If I couldn't get hold of them I'd simply take the tube back from the station. I knew, whenever and however I arrived, they'd be delighted.

The rest of the day was really rather quiet – nobody tried to kill anybody else in the basement, no one pushed anyone else out the window. There were things I wanted to ask, to find out before I left but somehow, nothing had the same quality of urgency as before. I can't even, after that one intense conversation in the morning, recall anything memorable anybody said all day.

Sam seemed to have settled in without a ripple. I hoped, when they took him to wherever they had planned, it wouldn't be too hard for him and wondered vaguely whether the learning to cope would be amongst normal people or with other Stranges? When the taxi driver rang the bell at precisely 4.30, I'd been ready with my bag packed for an hour and it was almost a relief.

I knew it wouldn't be a demonstrative farewell, you only need demonstrate feelings to people who wouldn't otherwise know. Sam was sitting next to Glory on the sofa. He'd found a medical textbook on one of the over-packed shelves. He couldn't read it but he was nodding sagely over some of the detailed anatomical drawings, delighted to find people drawn the way he'd always seen them. He still wasn't really talking, but Glory was quietly answering those unspoken questions she could and together they were looking up and finding answers to those she couldn't. I bent and gave her a quick, awkward, from-the-side hug, inhaling the familiar sherbet-lemonness of her. She wasn't a natural hugger, appreciated the gesture, just didn't know how to soften into it, but she allowed me a very swift glimpse of what she thought of me. I was surprised and pleased,

"Don't let it go to your head," she warned crisply.

I knelt on the floor in front of Sam.

"I'm going now, Sam my man. You'll be all right?" it was meant to be a statement, it came out a question. He didn't want to drag his eyes away from the book which was filling his whole mind with excitement and possibilities. Perhaps, wherever it was he was going, I didn't need to worry – with the discovery of that book, he'd already come home. I rose to my feet and he looked up. Someone, Ruth I supposed, had given him a good scrub, which was a huge improvement, but it was still an expressionless little face. And then he slowly closed one eye in complicity and thanks and that was more than enough.

I could feel Ed, cringing with embarrassment before I even got near him so I altered my course to pat Hamlet enthusiastically on the head, good old Hamlet I couldn't have done without him. I contented myself with a brisk little thumbs-up to Ed. I could feel his profound relief, a thumbs-up was about as up close and personal as Ed wanted.

The Peacock sisters escorted me out to the taxi.

"Will we stay in touch?" It was important for me to know and I meant the question to sound brisk and businesslike, certainly not as whiney as it came out. Ruth didn't seem to mind, she put a hand on each of my shoulders – she wasn't much taller than me – then wrapped her arms tight round me for a moment, pulling me into the rich, purple-deep lavender Ruthness of her. I put my arms round her too and squeezed back hard. When we drew apart, she nodded,

"You did well my dear. Thank you for your help." My eyes filled in response to her's, she was already fumbling for and not finding a tissue.

"Oh for goodness sake Ruth." Miss Peacock produced a paper hanky from one grey sleeve and thrust it at her sister. She bent and picked up my case and placed it in the open boot of the car, decisively slamming it shut. I saw the driver waiting patiently in the front seat, flinch at how decisively.

"In you get," she opened the passenger door for me. I climbed in and wound down the window.

"I almost forgot," Ruth was thrusting a brown carrier bag at me, "From Ed – to keep you going on the train. Now, have you got cash on you? If you need to get a taxi the other end?" Neither of them had answered my question, the driver switched on the engine.

"I don't want to lose touch with you all. It's important." Miss P was as briskly oblique as usual.

"You'll always have to make choices." We looked at each other, peppermint crisp and – I paused, what was I, I'd never thought,

"Milky," she supplied, "Here." She handed me another, smaller package and very briefly she smiled at me as she straightened, that astonishing smile of warmth and charm, lighting her face momentarily with depths of humour and affection. She tapped sharply, twice on the roof of the cab with the flat of her hand and stepped back next to her sister. I waved until we turned out of the drive. Ruth waved back, Miss Peacock nodded once.

CHAPTER FORTY-EIGHT

Ed had supplied enough food to get me across Europe, let alone back to London, even including a small thermos of hot sweet tea. I appreciated the warmth of the drink as much as the warmth of the gesture. Inside Miss Peacock's neat package, when I unwrapped it, was a small, brown leather strap. I'd last seen it braceleting Sam's sore wrist. Dark brown leather on the outside, there were blood stains turned paler brown on the inside. It was still fastened at the buckle but cut jaggedly through the middle of the leather. The sheet of paper round the strap held three words in Miss Peacock's distinctively strong hand – *Job well done!*

I looked at the broken strap in my lap for a long time. Then I re-wrapped it carefully in the note and put it at the bottom of my bag. I'd arrived at a crossroads and as Miss Peacock had pointed out, had choices to make. She was right when she said it wasn't easy to live comfortably with a foot in two camps. I'd had a taste of both and despite the deep-rooted conviction that getting Sam out was the best thing I'd ever done, I was pretty certain how I felt. I wasn't cut out for heroics. I didn't want an involvement in the sort of life or death, seat-of-the-pants situation from which I'd just emerged. I certainly didn't want to be doing battle with people who, in furtherance of ambition and obsession, could justify what they'd done to Megan and the others. Through some quirk of nature, I'd been born the way I was. I hadn't chosen to be different and although there were some undoubted benefits I thought, on the whole, the time had come for me to give Normal my best shot.

I arrived home to bustle and sadness. There'd been nobody there when I phoned earlier because they'd all been at the hospital. Grandma had died that morning, whilst I was sound asleep in Oxford and all the busy rites of a death in the family had moved into full and unstoppable swing. Whilst memories of the next couple of days are not as clear in my mind as those of the preceding adrenaline-fuelled ones, mixed with the solemn ritual of service, burial, tears and remembering, were images of more violent, unexpected and untimely ends. As I mourned the death of a feisty old lady who'd been so much a part of my life for all of my life, I also took the opportunity to mourn other briefer, infinitely more tragic existences.

I was acutely aware, back in familiar surroundings, of the privacy of which I was assured. Nobody could stroll in and out of my mind whenever they chose and I didn't have to work hard at guarding my thoughts. I was pretty certain I viewed this as a bonus and if my feelings were at times ambivalent, and if I thought fleetingly of the ease of communication I'd known with the others, I'd sense enough to realise that to regain any sort of equanimity, I had to accept the choices that had been made for me and by me. I was back in my world, I owed it to myself, my family and indeed my ex co-conspirators to deal with that. I was also wont to remind myself that whilst communication had certainly been a doddle, life with the Peacocks hadn't exactly been a laugh a minute.

Because of the timing of my homecoming, questions about my days away had initially been far more cursory than expected and certainly not answered as completely as they could have been. Even the bruising on my face had been only briefly exclaimed over and explained away by collision with a carelessly-open cupboard door. By the time there was a chance to go into things more fully, I had prepared a censored and sanitised version of events that wasn't going to alarm anybody unduly.

Also, and rather oddly I didn't waste any time worrying about official repercussions from my Oxford activities. If Miss Peacock had said they were dealt with, dealt with they were. And if my parents intuited there was more to the story than I was mentioning, perhaps they didn't really want to know details and were just more than happy I was back. I understood very clearly that they'd thought the temptation of being with others like myself would lure me away long-term. But when my mother asked, seemingly casually one day, whether I was staying in touch with Glory and the others I realised I didn't have even have their phone number, Peacock wasn't an uncommon name, I certainly couldn't have found the Oxford cottage on my own and I didn't know their exact London address – so the answer, even had I wanted it to be different, was no.

I returned to school after the Easter holidays; to my new slightly politer friendship with Faith, which only relaxed to a more natural state when we were together with Rochelle and Elaine. Faith had spent two weeks away with her mother and Shirley in Bournemouth where they'd been on earlier holidays. Her mother had said she didn't think she could cope with a new area right now. They'd stayed in a hotel this time, something they'd never have dreamt of doing before. Her dad had always preferred self-catering, said that way you knew what you were eating and that it'd come out of a clean pan, onto a clean plate.

And as it so happened, the hotel was all very clean and well-kept and the food was delish. But of course, she said, none of them really enjoyed it, it was terribly hard being three not four. We all hugged her and I read clearly, before I remembered I was going to try not to do that so much, that they'd eaten fish and chips whenever they wanted and Mrs Brackman had bought herself a swanky turquoise swimsuit which they'd all gone to choose, holding on to each other and rocking with laughter, when she mistakenly tried it on back to front. And she'd gone into the sea with them for the first time in their lives, laughing and splashing like a kid. And although they kept telling each other how sad they all were, deep in the depths of Faith's mind, buried where even she couldn't see it, was an indisputable fact. Whilst previous holidays had been a minefield, this was altogether a more relaxed affair than any of them could remember.

Rochelle had supervised, dried tears, found lost suitcases and comforted two new little step-sisters – who both threw up during the course of the evening – at her mother's third wedding. Before which, Rochelle reported, a complete wobbly had been thrown. On the point of entering the Register Office, Rochelle's mother had refused to go a step further until she was assured she was doing the right thing. Rochelle's mildly pointing out there was still time to change her mind had, unfortunately, launched her mother in an entirely different direction and she'd become hysterical and accused Rochelle of never really liking Ian and of being determined to spoil the big day. It wasn't really her mother's fault Rochelle said, she'd had a great deal of stress over the last few years but there was, she confessed, a fleeting temptation to find the nearest blunt object and utilise it to hit repeatedly, the head under the little pink marabou feather trimmed hat with the half-veiling. We couldn't help but laugh and Rochelle laughed with us, so much so that, still shrieking, we had to play the familiar hunt the inhaler.

Elaine and her parents had spent two sedate weeks in the South of France, their first time ever on foreign shores, a trip that had been over a year in the meticulous planning. Although, Elaine said they'd departed in such a flap that they'd got all the way down the road in the taxi before they realised her father wasn't with them. He'd gone back into the house for the fourth time, checking he hadn't inadvertently switched anything on during his three earlier checks. And, if we recalled, Elaine recounted wryly, the agonies of indecision her mother went through trying to make a choice in an English restaurant where she understood everything on the menu, picture France, where she didn't!

I listened and laughed and empathised and read between the lines of the trials and tribulations of my friends and somehow didn't think it appropriate, in answer to their questions as to what I'd got up to, to go into mine. So I told them instead about Grandma and they all apologised for not knowing, said they'd go round and see my mother, Rochelle gave me a long sympathetic hug and we moved on to safer ground.

CHAPTER FORTY-NINE

Friendships; unbreakable, immutable, bound to last forever, don't. The security of the quartet, Elaine, Rochelle Faith and myself, rock-solid through school years began to shift, realigning almost imperceptibly as we moved in new directions. Faith and Elaine were university bound and preoccupied with choosing 'A' level subjects whilst Rochelle, caving under a weight of emotional blackmail, gave up a coveted nursing college place to work in her newest step-father's handbag business. For lack of any other heartfelt direction, I accepted a place on a secretarial course at a local technical college – shorthand and typing, said my parents, will always see you right.

Although I reached my late teens at the end of the swinging sixties, what was going on in Carnaby Street, never really bothered to take the tube out to Hendon. True, at college, the halls and rec. rooms were filled with enough suspiciously sweet-scented smoke to make ambling between lectures quite a relaxing experience and our Social Sciences tutor was invariably so stoned, he regularly passed out toward the end of a lesson. But in our house, pot was still something in which you cooked soup, heavy drinking was anything more than two cups of tea and the sexual revolution was as far removed as the Russian one.

My social life over those next few years certainly wasn't what you'd describe as comfortable. I don't think anyone ever disputes the awfulness of self-doubt, dances and dating but if you recall how heart-stoppingly uncertain it was, wondering what someone you fancied thought of you, imagine how uncomfortable it was to actually know! I was desperately short-sighted and far too vain much of the time to wear the glasses I needed. But hopes that myopia lent a romantically dreamy gaze were definitively squashed when I overheard myself thought of as the short, squinty one. Then there was the figure-hugging tweed skirt, purchased with my first ever, Saturday morning job wages. If brevity and tightness produced what I felt to be an enticing wiggle, the thought, loud and clear as I walked past a resting builder,

"Look at the bum on that!" was not what I'd hoped for. Mind you, having a wheelbarrow full of half-mixed cement, up-end itself swiftly and inexplicably over his legs and feet wasn't quite what he expected either, so neither of us had a very good day. And yes, I was ashamed afterwards.

A course of driving lessons were my 18th birthday present from my parents. Mr Goldie, my driving instructor used to pat the dashboard of his trusty Triumph Herald and declaim it's never good enough to read the road, you must also read the minds of the other drivers – although he probably never had a pupil who could choose to take him so literally. I generally enjoyed my lessons, although appreciated that possibly the same didn't apply to the long-suffering Mr G. Despite nerves of steel he was still given to the odd squeak of panic in extenuating circumstances although, quite frankly, I always thought there was a lot that could be done to improve the signage for one way streets.

At the time I was taking lessons with him, Mr Goldie was a man not untroubled by challenges in his home life. I was often aware, as we drove our accustomed side-roads route round Hendon, chivvied by home-bound commuters, infuriated at being kept from their tea, that he was concerned – and not just with my driving. With his daughter recently married and his son backpacking in Nepal, Mr Goldie had been very worried his wife might be struck with empty nest syndrome. This however had proved not to be the case and Mrs Goldie – hitherto a pillar of the local W.I. with more jam under her belt than Robinsons – had slipped off, rather smoothly, the shackles of hitherto established domesticity.

She'd taken to cooking a lot of foreign, highly spiced meals and just last Friday, after a particularly stressful day, when a six-times driving test failure had made it to seven, Mr Goldie, trudging wearily up his garden path with thoughts of slippers and pipe was surprised to have the front door whipped open by the lady of the house. She had two glasses of wine in one hand, a rose between her teeth and an outfit that left far less to the imagination than might have been wise.

Mr Goldie was in somewhat of a turmoil over these unnerving turn of events. After all, he reasoned, last Friday, he could easily have been the

Man from The Pru and that would have done no-one's nerves any good. He appreciated the Change did funny things to a woman of her age but really couldn't say whether he'd be relieved or regretful when this phase passed. I did know that he'd have died a million deaths if he had even the vaguest notion that I too now, had a vision in my head of Mrs G and the rose, which somehow I couldn't quite shake off either.

Of course, I suppose what everyone craves in their life – me and Mrs Goldie no exception – is a spot of romance. But for my part, hormone-charged commentaries surging through the minds of my male contemporaries, to whom each new set of breasts was a revelation, each pair of mini-skirted legs a thrill and every slow dance an un-missable opportunity to press throbbing areas of anatomy against an unwary hip, came as a bit of a shock. There were also occasions when I could have well done without knowing that the youth, in whose sweaty grasp I was currently clasped, had screwed his courage to the sticking point to ask the girl standing next to me for a dance, lost his nerve at the last minute and grabbed the nearest thing to hand – me.

I was constantly striving to improve the blocking of general stuff coming in as well as limiting my lamentable tendency to reach out and read. It was so much more vital, now I knew exactly what I wanted and what I didn't, so I worked on it painstakingly in a way I'd never needed to when I was younger. After a while, inhibition of both incoming and outgoing, became ever tighter and having once clambered painfully aboard that wagon, I did my level best not to fall off too often. As a consequence, life became easier, certainly far less mortifying. I'd made my decision as to which side of the fence I wanted to be, Normal was the name of the game. And if, as time passed, my part in Faith's family misfortunes became something I didn't care to take out and look at too often and my time with Glory and the Peacock Girls became ever more bizarrely surreal, then that was no bad thing either.

CHAPTER FIFTY

I left Technical College after a couple of enjoyable and not too studious years, armed with an impressive array of office skills and landed myself a pleasant position with an office bureau, just off Berkeley Square. The company provided ad hoc secretarial and typing services for businessmen who chose not to employ their own staff or who simply wanted a base and a good office address in town.

Jointly owned and run by tweed and twin-setted Mrs Hillyer-Bowden and The Colonel, there was little doubt where in reality lay the seat of power – and a not insubstantial seat at that. Although Mrs H-B ostensibly deferred to her spouse on all decisions, it was clear he, despite impressive military moustache, bearing and monocle would have been pushed to say boo to the mildest of geese. The Colonel and Mrs Hillyer-Bowden shared a small, overheated office at the front of the building from which she stentoriously issued instruction in his name, despite the fact he was given to disappearing for much of the day,

"Club." He'd mutter "Seeing a chap … damn nuisance. Back in a jiff."

"Ladies," Mrs H-B would bellow as the door closed behind him, "The Colonel says, he'd rather hear the sound of typing than talking!"

In addition to the Hillyer-Bowden's office, there was a Board Room and four desked and telephoned rooms, let by the half day. The plushly armchaired reception area and busy switchboard was manned, with laxity and a cut-glass accent, by the Hon. Antonia Beresford, who made up in elegance what she lacked in efficiency. She invariably got messages muddled and was always double-booking offices, but tackled, would look down her nose like the slightly offended thoroughbred she was, leaving just enough of a languorous pause for you to realise the sheer unimportance of the matter you'd just raised.

We three secretaries or Temporary Personal Assistants as Mrs H-B preferred us to call ourselves, worked cheek by jowl, crammed into a decidedly un-plush, rear-office area that accommodated three desks, the telex, the hand-cranked Gestetner duplicating machine and two filing cabinets. So squashed in were we, that we used to joke we had to hit carriage return in unison to avoid clashing arms. The quantities of differently headed stationery, stacked below each desk didn't help much in the leg-room department either.

Lauretta Sears had been with the business since its inception – ten years earlier. Mid forties and single, she was sweet natured and angularly awkward, weighed down at ear, neck and wrist with quantities of chunky jewellery – her 'little weakness' she called it, returning frequently from lunch breaks with a sandwich, a guilty look and something new, shiny and more than she could afford. Her misty brown gaze was framed by meticulously applied false eyelashes and magnified by oversized glasses. Her pride and joy, was her thick mane of tumbling red curls, restrained during the week by black velvet Alice bands and clips, released to profusion only for special occasions such as our sedate, annual staff dinner treat at the nearby Mayfair Hotel. Lauretta was one of those people totally out of sync with the weather, chilly days invariably caught her without a cardigan; temperatures soared if she wore one and she only ever brought her umbrella when it didn't rain. She was, she swore, meteorologically jinxed and was always either fanning herself in front of the open window or shivering over our two-bar electric fire.

Possessed of a particularly flawless, creamy complexion, Lauretta kept her own concoction of Nivea and rosewater in her desk drawer for frequent application, to counteract the effects of West-End traffic. She went to bed, she told us with a chiffon scarf tied over her face and had trained herself only to sleep on her back to avoid pressure and creasing. She commuted daily into London from Kent. There, with the patience of several saints, she shared a bungalow with Mother, a woman unfaltering in her resolve that her daughter should miss out on no aspect of her ever downward-spiralling state of health.

My other colleague, Rajitha Sathasivam, was just a couple of years older than me. Hair so jet black it shone, Twiggy-thin and immaculate – you never knew, she maintained, who you might come across in the course of any day, nor how important they might turn out to be and first impressions count. Her extravagances were a never-ending succession of Bond Street expensive, heels and matching handbags and she teamed these with black or navy, tight-skirted, beautifully cut suits made skilfully at home for her by her father who used to be a tailor. Despite the elegant shoes, she was chronically flat-footed, with feet turned outward in endearingly ungainly fashion. When she remembered, she devoted intense concentration to keeping them on track, giving herself a curiously stilted gait.

Rajitha was formidably intelligent, ferociously efficient – leading to daily clashes with the Hon. Antonia – drivingly ambitious and cuttingly articulate. Over sandwiches and coffee on the summer grass of Berkeley Square, or steamy baked potatoes in the local Spud-U-Like on dull already-darkening winter days, we interminably discussed our futures. Raj was outspokenly appalled at my aim to meet the right man, marry and produce children. I was equally astounded that she was saving to start her own employment agency, working evenings as a theatre usherette, to supplement funds and that, moreover, she saw the opening of her first establishment as just the beginning. She was part of a close-knit family, but had come down to London from Leeds and was living in a small bed-sit near Charing Cross, because she wanted the opportunities the bigger city could offer. Her room was, she said, not brilliant but cheap and cheerful and walking distance to both her jobs.

Despite, or perhaps because of, our disparate backgrounds we all got on well, laughed a lot and worked comfortably together. And no day's work was ever the same, with the variety of different personalities who, in search of secretarial services and shepherded haphazardly by the Hon Antonia, hired the offices, some on a regular basis, others just needing assistance with a one-off project. I had a salary sufficient to cover lunchtime fashion forays and work varied enough to keep me busy during the day, undemanding enough not to have to give it a second thought, when I joined the masses disappearing down the tube each night. Life was undramatic and evenly paced and I was troubled only by the same issues affecting other young women of my age. I really felt I'd finally got the balance right. Maintaining necessary shielding had, like any exercised skill, become second nature and to all intents and purposes I was Miss Average. That's not to say, of course, there wasn't the odd occasion when a situation called for just a little more on the action front and with what I now considered to be my far greater control, I saw no reason to hold back if it suited me not to.

Travelling the Northern Line in the rush hour was never fun – it hadn't earned its misery title for nothing. Cramming in daily, cheek to armpit, with sweaty strangers was stressful enough without added unpleasantness, such as the middle-aged chap, epitome of respectability – Homburg, Burberry, FT folded pinkly beneath one arm who certainly, one evening, picked the wrong girl to rub up the wrong way.

He'd probably done it a hundred times before, his practiced smirk and shrug of apology when I turned and glared, had obviously worked in the past. Not with me it didn't. As I placed my large handbag pointedly and strategically between us, I reached into his head, just enough to confirm I hadn't been mistaken. Goodness me but it was murky in there. This was a man with brain firmly in his trousers. So I gave him an itch he couldn't scratch, at least not in respectable circles. That wiped the smirk off his face smartish. I watched cheerfully as he shifted desperately from one foot to the other, his discomfort growing by the minute. He got out at the next station, it wasn't his stop, he didn't seem to care. Last I saw of him, he was hurrying up the platform in an interestingly jerky way as he tried to deal with a burning private issue in a public place, without getting arrested for it.

Equally satisfying was the opportunity of being public spirited with no risk of getting into a fight. Drawing up at the traffic lights once, I held my breath as a battered red Morris Marina hurtled up behind me, screeching to a halt less than a hoot away. The windscreen was labelled over driver and passenger side respectively, *Stu* and *Stu's Chick* – clearly a chap who believed in keeping his options open. As we idled at the lights, their passenger window wound down and I watched in my mirror as a Wimpy box complete with half-eaten burger, chips and a polystyrene cup full of coffee were chucked out of the car. I didn't even stop to think, why would I? Burger and box shot back through the car window before Stu's Chick had even begun to wind it up again, followed closely by the cup, coffee and all. As I pulled away, it was apparent from a certain amount of shrieking and a rapid evacuation of the car behind, that not only had the reappearance of the rubbish created a certain amount of surprise, but that those polystyrene cups keep coffee piping hot, far longer than you'd think.

CHAPTER FIFTY-ONE

Lauretta was assaulted, brutally beaten, stabbed and left for dead, not far from her local station, one unseasonably sunny, mid-October Thursday evening.

We didn't hear about it until around 11.00 o'clock on the Friday morning, when a neighbour who'd been called in to minister to Mother, thought to phone Mrs Hillyer-Bowden. Ashen-faced in the doorway of our office, the Colonel pacing back and forth behind her, she told us Lauretta was in Ashford General, currently undergoing an operation to relieve pressure on the brain from a severely fractured skull. It wasn't certain at this point whether she'd live.

You probably remember reading about it – Autumn of 1971 it was – it got a huge amount of coverage because it was the Lollipop Man. Commencing three years earlier, the series of murders had rocked a nation, already believing itself beyond shock after the horrors of the Moors. Striking as he did, at the heart of Kent and the south coast, choosing his commuter victims at random, the killer redefined the travelling habits of thousands. Fathers collected daughters, husbands escorted wives, car pools were organised and in some areas, train-companion groups flourished – women travelling alone, meeting up with others to head in and out of town.

It was the papers of course, certainly not the police, who gave him the Lollipop label. And whilst a sober-faced Shaw Taylor on Police Five, broadcasting appeals for information was as un-sensational and non-specific as he could be – there was no denying the macabre incongruity of the killer's calling card. The garishly coloured lollipop thrust into and left in the mouth of each victim, stuck as painfully in the mind of the public, as did the other details of his appallingly violent and random attacks.

When, a week later we knew Lauretta was going to live, Rajitha and I travelled, knock-kneed with trepidation to Kent to see her. Our day off and fares were courtesy of the Colonel,

"Least we can do. Best for you girlies to go. Won't be up to seeing me and the lady boss." He'd hurrumphed awkwardly and pressed an additional ten pound note into Raj's hand.

"Eventualities – taxi from the station, that sort of thing. And fruit, flowers – whatever you think, maybe chocolates? Some of those magazines she's always got her nose in? Leave it to you."

Lauretta was in a side room, away from the rest of the ward, with a sturdy policeman seated to the left of her door. He stood slowly, feet planted squarely apart as we hurried towards him, shepherded by an overworked Irish Staff Nurse, name-tagged Bridie Brogan. She was brusquely to the point as we trotted breathlessly alongside.

"You've not to let her see you're shocked now."

"How is she?" Rajitha's calm tone belied her white knuckled grip on a smart clutch bag that perfectly complemented black patent shoes. I didn't look nearly as smart but matched her in apprehension. I was also extra-fiercely mentally cordoned. Hospitals were a minefield of emotion and beyond my barriers there would be, I was uncomfortably aware, vibrations of disturbing intensity.

"Out of I.C. not out the woods – not by a long chalk. Now, not too long and no nonsense mind. I want no weeping and wailing – we've enough problems with that mother of hers. Well, what are you waiting for? In you go." And she opened the door, put a firm hand on each of our backs and pushed.

In the dimly lit room a policewoman, trousered legs neatly crossed, was sitting by the window catching what daylight was seeping below the drawn floral curtain onto the pages of a newspaper. She nodded at us, kept her voice low,

"WPC Lynton. Best get your coats off – like a hothouse in here." She indicated a corner of the room where a chair already held her thick uniform overcoat and jacket. I slipped out of my coat, adding it to the pile but could already feel sweat prickling my armpits.

"Chairs by the bed, see? Make yourselves comfortable. She's dropped off again I think, but she doesn't sleep long. Friends are you? Family?"

"Work with her." I cleared my throat, summoning a bit of saliva to a suddenly parched mouth as we turned to the bed. I could hear Rajitha's light, rapid breathing behind me, when I glanced back, her face was unreadable. We moved quietly but Lauretta heard us. The covers convulsed as she surged up wide and white-eyed. She saw us coming towards her and started to whimper, then shockingly, to shriek.

"Ah, for goodness sakes, don't just stand there gawping like a pair of eejits the two of you, take her hand, let her see who you are." Sister Brogan hurtled back in, reaching the bed in a couple of swift strides.

"There darlin', you're all right, you're all right. We'll have no more of this racket if you please, Dr'll have my guts for garters. Now, will you look, sweetheart," she reached a hand behind her and pulled me ungently forward, "See who it is come to visit." Under the professionally soothing hands and tone, the ghastly shrieks were subsiding into sobs and dying. The woman, breathless in the bed, and I stared at each other. I wouldn't have recognised her and I don't honestly think, out of context and without her glasses on she knew who I was until Raj moved up beside me. Bridie was still bustling,

"Sit down now, sit down, can't chat standing can you?" We were pushed, shocked and unresisting into two chairs at one side of the bed and Lauretta, re-eased down now on to the pillows, turned her face slowly towards us.

The whole of the left side of her head was encased in thick, cream colored bandage, stained yellow in places with some kind of ointment. The crepe, extending low over her left eye, gave her a clownish appearance, compounded by wisps of thinning red hair, flaming garishly against the cream material. I realised, abruptly, that the normal luxuriance of curls of which she was so proud, must be a hairpiece. Somehow – and ridiculously – this seemed a greater violation of her privacy than anything else.

Twin drip tubes snaked into the back of her left hand which she kept twitching, as if to dislodge the discomfort. Another tube emerged from below the blankets and dripped into a urine bag, inadequately concealed beneath the bed-frame. I hoped Lauretta, so ladylike at all times, didn't know we could see that. Surrounding her right eye, panda-like was a deep, bluely black bruise. It leaked down to her cheekbone where it was turning sour green. A crescent-moon, stitch-puckered, partially scabbed cut, curved from below her other cheekbone to disappear under her chin. Her lips were cut and swollen and her eyes, denuded of their customary lavish lashes were watery, red-rimmed and deeply bewildered.

"Won't let me have a mirror." she murmured, "Look a fright I expect?" We both shook our heads in pointless denial and each received a painfully sharp prod in the back from an admonitory nursing finger,

"Cat got your tongues?" Rajitha obediently leaned forward across me and carefully took Lauretta's hand, the knuckles scraped and scabby the carefully filed almond oval nails, undressed without their usual red Revlon.

"Don't be silly, you look fine, Laur." she said, "Just fine. How're you feeling?"

"Feeling? Oh, well, thank you." Lauretta smiled politely with her newly shaped mouth, "Well," she repeated, "Bit shaky still at times of course. So sweet of you both to come."

"Couldn't miss the chance of a day off, could we?" Rajitha said, "And Colonel and Mrs H-B send you all their very best and we've brought you chocolates, Suchards you like those – from them too."

"Kind. Lots of people've sent flowers." Lauretta gestured with the dripless arm in the direction of a serried rank of vases.

"Shame," she said, " You've just this minute missed Mother, she's here every single day. Taxi there and back … won't hear of not coming, bless her. Have to get out soon, she's not managing well on her own." She licked dry lips that trembled,

"I want to go home, they won't say when I can." a tear slid out of one eye and traced the path of the bruise. She sniffed hard, "Sorry girls, all the way to see me and here I am wet and woolly. How's things at the office? What about all those letters I'd taken for Professor Kenyon, did you find them?" I leaned forward, shoulder to shoulder with Raj, so Lauretta could see us both easily. I took her hand from Raj's,

"Done and dusted. No problem, I found your notebook and your shorthand's always so easy to read. He said they were fine, says get well soon." My voice sounded far too jolly.

"Does he know … what happened? Another tear leaked and dribbled. "Does everybody know?" she moved her head restlessly from one side to another, voice rising, "I didn't want everyone to know, I really didn't, they didn't need to know." I looked helplessly across at the policewoman, who moved to the other side of the bed.

"Now then Lauretta," she said firmly, "We've been through this haven't we, no point in upsetting ourselves all over again. You know it was in the papers, we talked about that. But we have to catch the so and so, don't we?"

"I can't tell you any more. I'm sorry, so sorry, don't remember, I've said, haven't I? Want to, just can't. I'm sorry." With each sorry she was turning her head back and forth on the pillow in escalating upset, small bubbles of spittle gathering at the corners of her lips, nose running. Her raw distress was breaching my barriers. I belatedly realised, tried to pull away but could do too little, too late. With a rush, all the more devastating for its suddenness, I was suddenly open to her, flooded.

My head rocked back with the shock and I knew, to my shame and without a shadow of doubt, I'd have run if my hand hadn't been wrapped tight in hers, a grip so frantic I couldn't loosen it. Slamming into me was her pain, disbelief, grief, shame and overwhelmingly vivid images. She couldn't sleep, couldn't rest un-drugged, the recollections were continuous and, all the more terrifying, out of chronological order. No beginning, no end, no time frame. Shock had reduced memory to a never-ending parade, a grim merry-go-round of sight, sensation, smell and pain, all the more surreal because she was unable to sort them into any sort of coherent order. But I could.

I let out a breath I hadn't known I was holding, hauled another one in through a constricted throat. Like a ripped picture book, images were scattered every which way. I didn't want to look, but of its own accord my mind sought to make sense out of what it was seeing. Order out of disorder, placing things in sequence and context, however dreadful. I knew instinctively that for Lauretta, order might be the only path back from endless re-living.

"Out the way now, quickly." Nurse Brogan had a hypodermic. Lauretta saw it and began to sob louder.

"No, no. No injection. Please, not again." she didn't want to be put under. Awake was haunted enough, unconsciousness worse – no control. They thought they were helping but they were only intensifying and prolonging her nightmare.

"Wait – please wait, just a moment," I said "She'll calm down, I promise." I turned back to Lauretta, leaned over her, obscuring view of nurse and needle.

"He hurt me." she said softly to me and something in her voice had changed, hysteria giving space to acknowledgment. The policewoman, alert at her other side, leaned forward too.

"Lauretta, have you remembered something? What can you tell me?"

"He hurt me."

"I know my love. That's why we need you to tell us as much as you can. Can you tell me what he looked like?"

"The time. He asked me the time." Lauretta was staring at but not seeing me. In her mind, and mine, was the terrible tale told by the scattered pages. Together, we found the one she was looking for, the beginning. She winced but didn't turn away. Her eyes widened, but not at anything in the room.

"How could I have forgotten, how silly? When I got off the train – he was there, he asked me the time. That was him. I didn't know, I didn't know." WPC Linton perched precariously now on the other side of the bed had notebook and pen.

"You saw him clearly? Are you sure this was the same man who later attacked you?" Lauretta shut her eyes for an instant, re-opened them on certainty.

"Yes. He smelt. Same smell." She paused as we were both swept by an over-sweet after-shave, then mintiness – toothpaste, masking cigarette smoke. "Yes, I smelt him, on the platform … he came very close and then … later. She swallowed convulsively. "Later I … I'd forgotten but I did, I recognised the smell."

"How old? Was he tall? Short?"

"I think maybe 35 – 40?" Together we searched, I turned over images she'd deliberately hidden away, fed the pictures back to her. She flinched but didn't stop.

"Yes, late thirties, fair skinned, very smooth skin, no stubble, smooth." She shuddered, "Hair, sandy coloured I think, long, brushed very neatly back, I noticed that, he didn't look scruffy."

"Tall? How tall?

"Don't know, can't … no, wait … when he stopped me, asked the time, I didn't have to look up much, so not that tall I suppose. Thin, though, very thin, but later… so strong. I didn't realize…"

"Take your time, you're doing so well Lauretta, what else can you tell me. Everything, any little thing helps."

We're walking briskly through the shortcut – takes you from the side of the station to the main road, past the wooded area running round the back of the railway. Saves going through the busy forecourt where all the buses stop and local kids congregate, cuts a good five minutes off the walk home and we've to get Mother's prescription before the chemist shuts, should just do it. Oh and mustn't forget, Aspirin, used the last yesterday. No harm going this way at this time, broad daylight, lots of people around. Feet hurt, lovely shoes but oh now, they so need coming off. Thank goodness train on time for once. Lamb chops for supper with mash. Potatoes peeled before we left this morning, in cold water ready for boiling, meat seasoned on a plate in the fridge, most of the fat cut off because Mother hates fatty. Enough rhubarb crumble left for afters, with ice-cream, or maybe custard – use up yesterday's milk.

The sudden yank on our hair that jerks our head back is both agonising and entirely, shockingly unexpected. In that moment, our rational mind struggles to make sense – an overhanging branch? The hairpiece always so securely pinned and anchored has been ripped right away from our head. We twist round and see the almost comically astonished reflection of our own expression on the face of the man close behind, the man holding a mass of red curls in one still-upraised hand.

He's angry, why's he so angry? Our hairpiece has thrown him, he's surprised and we know, with absolute and complete certainty this is not someone who cares to be surprised. He's disconcerted for the barest second. Why're we frozen like a light-dazzled rabbit? There's an instant when we could run, but we don't. What's happening is so completely unlikely that common sense insists we've got it all wrong, there's been some kind of a mistake. He draws back a fist and punches, the blow connecting at the very moment we realize that sometimes, terrible things do happen to ordinary people. Our head jerks back with the force of this reality. Glasses fly off and hit the ground, someone'll tread on them and they're only a couple of months new. He slides an iron arm round our waist – to anyone coming up behind, we seem like a suddenly reunited couple – and slips swiftly sideways – from the path into the trees.

We should shout, we should scream – isn't that what they always say, make a noise, make as much noise as you can? – but our mouth is full of blood. Feet dragging, we've moved so far into the trees now, we can't assess the way back to the path. We've lost a shoe – they were expensive, kitten-heeled suede, last year's Russell & Bromley sale. Mother always said they'd spoil, wearing them to work, though this probably wasn't what she had in mind. We take a breath, swallow blood that makes us gag. Another blow, to the side of the head this time. The world spins and starts to darken. He's got a knife, like the carpet layer used, a Stanley knife? He reaches for the neck of our shirt and as the short blade slips so easily through the fabric, it bloodies a line down our chest too. We're so bewildered and appallingly, paralysingly, fear-full and we hurt so very much. I ripped my hand from Lauretta's grasp, my mind from hers.

Half kneeling, half crouching and clutching cold porcelain, the stink of disinfectant and vomit made my eyes water. I voided the contents of my stomach and carried on heaving, I needed to get rid of what I'd seen and felt and the more uncomfortable and the longer it went on, the less chance I had to think. A cool hand was suddenly firm on my forehead, I tried to shake it off, this was one of those times you really want to be alone. She went, but only temporarily. A moment later she was back, reaching over me to flush the soiled toilet and place a wet handkerchief on my head.

After a few more moments I had to accept nothing more was going to come out, however much I might want it to. I staggered to my feet and sat on the toilet. Rajitha handed me a handful of paper towels to wipe my mouth and leant back against the door, arms folded.

"What's going on?" she said

"Going on?" my voice hurt coming out.

"I am not," she said firmly, "An idiot. Don't bullshit me."

"Can we go somewhere else?" She wrinkled an elegant nose.

"Absolutely, If you're sure you've finished, there's a canteen, next floor up. I promised we wouldn't be long though, just as soon as you felt better – this is the first time Lauretta's told them anything. That policewoman was over the moon, dashing off to phone her boss. She wants us back a.s.a.p." I shook my head,

"Can't."

"Certainly can." She leaned down and grabbed my elbow – in spite of her waif-like build, I'd often seen her haul full sized electric typewriters from office to office – and pulled me to my feet. She took the dampened hanky from my forehead and tried to shift some of the mascara accumulated underneath my eyes. She gave my face a further swift wipe-over for good measure, tucked an errant piece of my shirt back into my skirt.

"There, you'll do. Look I know it's all pretty dreadful but we owe it to her." I shook my head again,

"Raj, I'm telling you I can't go back."

"And I'm telling you, you can." She plucked a piece of paper towel from her black jacket, disposed of it down the toilet.

"Now, you're going to promise not to throw up again, I'm going to buy you a coffee and a biscuit and you're going to tell me what exactly happened in there."

CHAPTER FIFTY-TWO

So I did. For the first time, I told everything to someone who didn't already know. And considering my stomach ached as if kicked by a particularly feisty mule, the attempted reinstatement of my shielding was giving me the mother and father of all headaches and I couldn't stop shivering, I thought I managed to précis it all rather neatly. When I finally wound down she was silent for a long moment. Then she said,

"OK."

"OK? What's that mean, OK?"

"It means OK. If that's what you're telling me, I believe you. You can't possibly have made it all up on the spot and I was in there, remember? Something weird was going on and this is as good an explanation as any."

I was flabbergasted, I'd lived, all my life with the risk of letting my secret slip. Now, it had emerged, with more of a whimper than a bang and certainly with a less than cataclysmic reaction. I didn't know whether to be relieved or insulted.

"Show me." She said.

"Show you what?"

"Move something." I slid her coffee cup to the opposite side of the table. She reached out, retrieved it and nodded.

"I'm impressed."

"No," I said sharply, "*I'm* impressed. Can't believe you're taking this in your stride." She shrugged,

"Why shouldn't I? More things in heaven and earth etc. How are you feeling? You don't look good."

"Thanks! Head's splitting." I said. And that was only the half of it I was icy cold, bone-deep. Around us hustled the bustle and clatter of a busy cafeteria with its mixed aromas of coffee, tinned tomato soup and fried food.

"Can you read my mind now?" she asked, she didn't look particularly worried. I shook my head impatiently,

"Told you, I try not to do that. Specially not here, hospitals are terrible places for me. What happened with Lauretta was an accident, I'm keeping buttoned up till we're away."

"We're not going anywhere."

"You don't expect me to go back? Not after what I've told you?"

"You don't have a choice."

"I bloody do." I was gripping the edge of the table and shivering so hard, it was vibrating the surface of my coffee – I'd only managed half a cup. I tried and failed to loosen my grip. "I thought you understood. I can't risk that again. I was with her Raj, I was with her. I was seeing and feeling everything, everything that happened to her."

"I know, you said."

"No. You *don't* know. You haven't the faintest. What he put her through, what it felt like …" I stopped I could feel just-consumed coffee churning and rising. I tried again to relax my hands. I wasn't sure whether the tightness of my grip on the table was intensifying the shakes or whether I was gripping so hard to try and halt them.

"Look," I tried again in explanation, "I'm truly, desperately sorry for Lauretta, what happened to her was too awful for words, I feel terrible, but Raj, it happened to her, I can't … won't have it happen to me too. The memories, those horrible, dreadful memories – they're her's not mine."

"Can you describe him – the man?"

"Yes."

"You know what he looks like?"

"Said so, haven't I? I saw him."

"Then you've no option."

"What're you talking about?" My voice rose and a couple at the next table looked over at us, I lowered my tone, leaning forward,

"Lauretta – she saw him, she can tell them, give them a description."

"But she couldn't before."

"Because all the stuff in her head was jumbled up by what he did to her, she was in shock I suppose – couldn't think properly, that's all."

"And?"

"And what?" I snapped

"You helped her put it in order – that's what you said."

"So now she can carry on."

"You can't know that." She drank some coffee, met my hostile glare.

"I wonder," she mused, "How you'll feel when you pick up a paper

275

and see a picture of the next woman he kills? He's killed before. Lauretta's here, purely by chance because he was interrupted. He'll kill again. When that happens, mightn't you think things would have been different – if they'd caught him?"

"Rajitha, why don't you just mind your own bloody business and stay out of mine?" She smiled equably at me.

"Fine." She was rifling through her bag, taking out a notebook.

"What's that for?"

"A note, the policewoman, what's her name? I'll say we're sorry, we couldn't stay."

"You think I'm weak, right?"

"Look, I haven't the faintest idea why you can do what you say you can. But my God, girl, you've got the chance to make a difference – how many of us can say that?" She raised a holding hand as I started to interrupt, "O.K. so I can't get inside Lauretta's head, can't really know, but I can imagine some of what he did to her, can see what it's doing to you but so what?

"*So what?*"

"Well, there's no doubt you'll have to wade through some pretty crappy stuff. But at least you'll know."

"*What*? What'll I know?" I was shouting again and half-rose. The couple leaving the next table looked back, not hostile, sympathetic, they thought I'd just had bad news. Perhaps I had.

"You'll know," Raj remained seated, looking up at me. "It's not really happening. Like watching a film – you'll know it's not really happening. If you can help Lauretta sort her head out, help her help the police, then isn't it worth a bit of second-hand suffering?"

"Don't you realise the risk, if people know what I can do?"

"Oh, don't be so dramatic. Far's I can see there's only risk when people are specifically on the look-out for someone like you. In there," she jerked her head "They're just pleased Lauretta's remembering, they think it's because she's reassured by us being there. The truth wouldn't occur to them in a million years."

"You don't know that and talk's cheap." I was bitter, she could have absolutely no idea how ill I was feeling, nor how terrified. Apart from which, a life-time of dire warnings doesn't go into your boots. She shrugged,

"You're right. None of my business." I nodded, but still needed to justify myself.

"Look, try and understand, I never asked for this. I don't want it. I just want to be as normal as the next person." Raj snorted,

"But you're not are you?"

"No but …"

"And you can't change what you are."

"No."

"No." she repeated, "But look, if you want to use what you've got to give litterbugs a fright, teach dirty old men on the tube a lesson, that's up to you. Just one question. How did it feel when you got that kid out?"

I opened my mouth to answer but didn't get the chance,

"You just finished telling me, it felt great. You made a real difference to someone, right?"

She rose, brushed invisible crumbs off her uncreased skirt and reached behind the chair for her jacket.

"I'll go get our coats. I'll leave the note for the police and another for Lauretta. Meet me in the main entrance hall, if we get a taxi quickly, we should get the 3.55."

"And that's it?" I asked. She shrugged.

"I just don't want to get involved." I said miserably. She shrugged again as she turned away.

"You already are."

At the next table an elderly man and a girl of about ten unloaded two cups of tea, propping the empty tray carefully against the table leg. They were both crying. There'd been a death, his daughter, her mother. I thought about the decisions I'd made, things I wanted to do, things I didn't. I thought about a small, blood-stained, leather strap wrapped in yellowing tissue paper at the bottom of my drawer.

"Raj, wait," I said, "I'll go back."